BY DAN CHAON

ILLWILL

ILLWILL

A NOVEL

DAN CHAON

BALLANTINE BOOKS

NEW YORK

Ill Will is a work of fiction. Names, characters, places, and incidents are the product of the author's imagination or are used fictitiously. Any resemblance to any persons, living or dead, events, or locales is entirely coincidental.

Published in the United States by Ballantine Books, an imprint of Random House, a division of Penguin Random House LLC, New York.

BALLANTINE and the HOUSE colophon are registered trademarks of Penguin Random House LLC.

An earlier version of Chapter 2 was originally published as "What Happened to Us?" in *Ploughshares*, Spring 2014 and *Pushcart Prize XL: Best of the Small Presses 2016*, edited by Bill Henderson.

LIBRARY OF CONGRESS CATALOGING-IN-PUBLICATION DATA
Names: Chaon, Dan, author.
Title: Ill will : a novel / Dan Chaon.
Description: New York : Ballantine Books, [2017]
Identifiers: LCCN 2016034066 (print) | LCCN 2016039804 (ebook) |
ISBN 9780345476043 (hardback) | ISBN 9781101885345 (ebook)
Subjects: | BISAC: FICTION / Literary. | FICTION /
Psychological. | FICTION / Crime. | GSAFD: Suspense fiction.
Classification: LCC PS3553.H277 I45 2017 (print) | LCC PS3553.H277
(ebook) | DDC 813/.54—dc23
LC record available at https://lccn.loc.gov/2016034066

Printed in the United States of America on acid-free paper

randomhousebooks.com

246897531

FIRST EDITION

TITLE-PAGE IMAGE: iStock/aleroy4

Book design by Simon M. Sullivan

For Paul

We often meet our destiny on the road we take to avoid it.

—Jean de La Fontaine

PART ONE

November 2011–April 2012

SOMETIME IN THE first days of November the body of the young man who had disappeared sank to the bottom of the river. Face-down, bumping lightly against the muddy bed below the flowing water, the body was probably carried for several miles—frowning with gentle surprise, arms held a little away from his sides, legs stiff. The underwater plants ran their fronds along the feathered head-dress the boy was wearing, across the boy's forehead and war-paint stripes and lips, down across the fringed buckskin shirt and wolf-tooth necklace, across loincloth and deerskin leggings, tracing the feet in their moccasins. The fish and other scavengers were mostly asleep during this period. The body bumped against rocks and branches, scraped along gravel, but it was mostly preserved. In April, when the two freshman college girls saw the boy's face under the thin layer of ice among the reeds and cattails at the edge of the old skating pond, they at first imagined the corpse was a discarded man-nequin or a plastic Halloween mask. They were collecting pond-water specimens for their biology course, and both of them were feeling scientific rather than superstitious, and one of the girls reached down and touched the face's cheek with the eraser tip of her pencil.

During this same period of months, November through April, Dustin Tillman had been drifting along his own trajectory. He was forty-one years old, married with two teenage sons, a psychologist with a small practice and formerly, he sometimes told people, some occasional forays into forensics. His life, he thought, was a collection of the usual stuff: driving to and from work, listening to the radio, checking and answering his steadily accumulating email, shopping at the supermarket, and watching select highly regarded shows on television and reading a few books that had been well reviewed and helping the boys with their homework, details that were—he was increasingly aware—units of measurement by which he was parceling out his life.

When his cousin Kate called him, later that week after the body was found, he was already feeling a lot of vague anxiety. He was having a hard time about his upcoming birthday, which, he realized, seemed like a very bourgeois and mundane thing to worry about. He had recently quit smoking, so there was that, too. Without nicotine, his brain seemed murky with circling, unfocused dread, and the world itself appeared somehow more unfriendly—emanating, he couldn't help but think, a soft glow of ill will.

2

A FEW DAYS after the body was discovered, Dustin picked up the phone and it was his cousin Kate calling from Los Angeles.

"Listen," she said. "I have some very weird news."

Dustin said: "Kate?" They spoke regularly enough, once every few months or so, but it was usually on birthdays or holidays or around the edges of holidays.

"It's about Russell," she said.

"Russell, my brother Russell?" He was sitting at the desk in his office, his "study," as he liked to call it, on the third floor of the house, and he stopped typing on the computer and glanced over at his ashtray, which was now full of little sugar-free hard candies, loz-

4

enges wrapped in cellophane. "Don't tell me," Dustin said. "He's escaped."

"Just listen," Kate said.

Dustin hadn't spoken to Russell, his adopted older brother, since Russell had been sent to prison. He had not written to him or even kept tabs on him, really, and the thoughts that he had of him were of the most cursory sort. For example, he'd see a movie or a TV show that took place in a prison and he'd think: *I wonder what Russell is doing right now?*

He had a general idea of what prison would be like. This included things like homosexual rape and "shanks" carved out of toothbrushes or spoons. Sometimes he would picture men in the prison library, studying legal books, or in cafeterias, eating the terrible casseroles, or lying moodily, fully dressed, on metal bunk beds, glaring at the ceiling.

Various images of this sort had come to Dustin over the years.

But mostly he'd imagine Russell as he had been when they were growing up together—Russell, six years his elder, who had shot him once with a BB gun in the back while he was running away, Russell, listening to death-metal music and carving a pentagram into his forearm with the sharp end of a drafting compass, Russell, who had used improvised kung fu moves to destroy a magnificent snowman that Dustin had built, Russell, who was delighted by Dustin's fear of the dark and would wait until Dustin was comfortably alone in a room and then sneak by and turn off the light and pull the door closed and Dustin, trapped in darkness, would let out a scream.

ON THE NIGHT that their parents were going to be murdered, Dustin Tillman and his cousins Kate and Wave were sitting at the kitchen table in the camper, which was parked for the moment in the driveway of Dustin's family's house in western Nebraska. It was the beginning of June, 1983.

Their two families were planning to leave the next morning to go on vacation together.

They would travel through Wyoming and up to Yellowstone, and they would stay at various campgrounds along the way.

But that night, the camper was like their own little private apartment that they were living in. The three of them were playing cards. A transistor radio emitted songs from a distant Denver rock-and-roll station. A heavy beetle-bodied June bug beat its wings and ticked thickly against the light fixture on the ceiling.

The girls were only seventeen, but they were splitting a light beer, which they had taken from the refrigerator in the camper. They had poured it—half and half—into two glass tumblers. The night was warm, and the girls were wearing their bikini tops and cutoff shorts. They had used a curling iron to make flips in their shoulder-length blond hair, but the flips had grown a little limp.   They were twins, not identical but almost. Dustin was thirteen, and he sat there, his cards fanned out, and the girls said:

"Dust-Tin! It's your turn!"

And Kate reached down and without thinking scratched a bug bite on her bare ankle and Dustin was looking surreptitiously, the way her fingernail made a white mark on the reddish tanned skin,   the fingernail which had some polish on it that was flaking off.

IN RETROSPECT, DUSTIN couldn't remember much that was significant about that particular morning when they discovered the body. The day was clear and cold and sunny, and he woke up and felt fairly happy—*happy* in that bland, daily way that doesn't even recognize itself as happiness, waking into a day that shouldn't expect anything more than a series of rote actions: showering and pouring coffee into a cup and dressing and turning a key in the ignition and driving down streets that are so familiar that you don't even recall making certain turns and stops; though the mind must have consciously carried out the procedure of braking at the corner and rolling the steering wheel beneath your palms and making a left onto the highway, there is no memory at all of these actions.

You were not even present, were you?

In retrospect: another day, late in the morning, early in the century. Another long Midwestern interstate corridor in Ohio. This particular road connected a whole series of fertile little towns to the cities, though lately what was once farmland was being developed, and rows of identical houses rose out of the muddy fields instead of crops. The backyards of these new communities were punctuated with aboveground pools and swing sets, and many featured little manmade ponds, which at this moment in spring looked like parking lots made of water instead of asphalt. Once they were landscaped, maybe they would look more appealing.

There was a lot of roadkill these days, as well. The highways now cut the countryside into narrow parcels, and the displaced woodland animals were often caught moving from one section to the next—raccoons, opossums, deer, foxes, their bodies tossed onto the berm in the positions of restless sleepers, mouths open, eyes closed, almost peaceful-looking.

People, too, seemed to meet their end more frequently on the roads, and Dustin had noticed the way that mourners seemed more and more to erect small roadside shrines to those who perished in accidents, crosses fashioned out of picket wood, often surrounded by a pile of brightly colored objects: usually plastic flowers—pink roses, yellow daffodils, white lilies—but sometimes green Christmas wreaths or plastic holly or ribbons; very frequently clusters of stuffed animals, bunnies and teddy bears and duckies; and sometimes items of clothing such as shirts or baseball caps, which gave the crosses a certain scarecrow-like quality. There was probably a good essay in this, Dustin thought.

Coming up to the exit, he saw the flashing of the police cars gathered together, their blue and red lights dappling in the mild spring rain. Some orange road cones had been set out, and a policeman in a reflector-striped raincoat stood there waving the cars past with a plastic Day-Glo baton.

Dustin slowed and turned down the radio and steered into the detour around the roadblock that the policeman indicated with an elegant sweep of his wand. There was a clutch of cops gathered at the edge of the bridge, grim and damp from drizzle and drinking coffee out of Styrofoam cups, and Dustin observed them with interest. He enjoyed watching police-procedural dramas on television, and he had loved it, back in the day, when he would sometimes be called to testify as a court-approved expert. Remembering this gave him a wistful twinge.

He guessed that whatever was going on must be fairly serious.

THERE WAS A famous photo of Dustin and Kate and Wave—the picture that had been in the newspapers, which had been nominated for the Pulitzer; it didn't win but it was recognizable. A remarkable and memorable crime photo.

Here were the children—the beautiful blond twins, and the skinny freckled boy between them—and the police are leading them, hurrying them from the house. In the photo, Wave is weeping openly, her mouth contorted, screaming maybe, and Kate is looking off to the side, fearfully, as if someone is going to attack her, and Dustin is staring straight ahead and you can see that there is blood on the front of his shirt, a Jackson Pollock of blood, and he is stricken, glazed with camera-flash light, stumbling away from the crime scene, and there behind the children and the police is the body of Dustin's mom, Colleen—you can see her corpse, perfectly framed in the background, her limbs thrown out in a posture that is clearly one of death, violent death, and a broad stain of blood beneath her.

& the imprint of her blood on Dustin's T-shirt where he had held her, his mom, for a moment when he found her body on the front stoop beneath the porch light.

The other bodies—not in the photograph—are Dustin's father, Dave, who is in the living room with a gunshot wound to his chest, and his aunt Vicki, who is dead beneath the kitchen table, where she tried to hide from the gunman, and his uncle Lucky by the sink, the corpse slumped against the bottom cabinets, his head thrown back, arms open as if falling backward. Shot in the mouth.

These bodies weren't the kind that you could show in the newspaper, but the picture of the three children was just enough to convey a vivid sense of massacre—

By the time Dustin reached his office, the news of the discovery had already begun to circulate. Most people assumed—correctly, as it would later turn out—that the body was that of Peter Allingham, a college sophomore and lacrosse player who had gone missing in the wee hours of November 1, after an evening of barhopping and Halloween parties, dressed in a cartoonish, racially insensitive Native American costume: feathers, buckskin, et cetera. Seen by large numbers of people and then gone—very improbably vanishing, people said, on his way to the bathroom at the Daily Tavern, and he never came back to join his friends.

Aqil Ozorowski was sitting in the waiting room of Dustin's office, wearing earbud headphones and gazing at his smartphone, texting vigorously. His dark, shaggy hair hung down like blinders on either side of his eyes, and Dustin stood there in the doorway with his briefcase, waiting to be noticed. He felt a bit nonplussed. They didn't have an appointment, but Aqil had the habit of simply appearing.

He was an odd case. He had ostensibly come to Dustin for smoking cessation hypnotherapy, but his susceptibility to hypnosis was very low. Instead, their sessions had devolved into loose, vaguely intimate discussions, with no clear goal in mind. They'd talk about some conspiracy theory that Aqil had read about on the Internet, or they'd talk about Aqil's insomnia or about his resentful feelings toward the pop star Kanye West—but after the first few appointments they had all but ceased to mention smoking. "I just don't think I'm ready yet," Aqil said. "But I do think you're helping me, Doctor. You're a good listener."

Actually, Dustin wasn't sure that was true. In fact, he had learned very little about Aqil in the months that they'd been meeting. Aqil was about thirty years old, Dustin guessed, and based on his name Dustin thought he might be biracial, but he wasn't sure. Aqil had dark, deer-like brown eyes, and his long straight hair was either black or a dark auburn, depending on the light. His complexion could indicate any number of races. He gave no indication of his family background, even when Dustin asked direct questions. "Honestly," Aqil said, "I'm not really interested in that stuff. These shrinks always want you to tell stories about your childhood and your past, like that's supposed to explain something. I don't really do that."

The one thing that Dustin *did* know was that Aqil had been a policeman and that he was now on medical leave from the Cleveland Police Department, though that situation, too, had never been clearly explained.   Some kind of psychological difficulty, Dustin assumed. PTSD?

Paranoia? There were no medical records that Dustin had been able to access, and even when he'd undertaken a surreptitious Google search it had yielded few results. Aqil was listed as a graduate of the Cleveland Police Academy. There was a grainy photo of him on his high school football team, where he'd been a running back. He had a defunct LinkedIn page. Whatever he'd done to get himself on psychological leave from the police department, it hadn't made the news.

Still, there was apparently something he needed. He glanced up at last and gave Dustin a grin. He politely pulled the plastic cowrie shell of earbud from his ear, as if Dustin's waiting room were his own private space and he was surprised to be interrupted.

"Hey," he said.

"Hey," Dustin said. "I didn't realize we had an . . ." and Aqil blinked a couple of times.

"Did you hear the news about the dead kid?" Aqil said. Dustin turned on the light and set his briefcase on a chair and Aqil stood up and stretched.

". . . appointment?" Dustin said.

"Do you want to hear my theory?" Aqil said.

"IT's ABOUT RUSSELL," Kate said.

"Russell, my brother Russell?" he said, and she said, *just listen!* and she began to read to him from a news article:

. . . now nearly twenty-nine years after his arrest, independent DNA tests by three different laboratories, she read.

DNA tests on genetic evidence confirm what Tillman has long contended—that he is not the person who killed his mother, father, aunt, and uncle that June night in

"What newspaper is this?" Dustin said. "This is unbelievable."

Tillman will be the latest person to be exonerated by DNA, according to officials at the Innocence Project, a nonprofit legal clinic that investigates wrongful convictions. The test results show what Russell has said from the day he was arrested that he is innocent said Vanessa Zuckerbrot an attorney for Innocence Project

"I don't understand why we weren't contacted about this," Dustin said. "When was the last time anybody talked to him?"

All these years I knew I wasn't the one, said Tillman in an interview, I believe there is a higher power greater than me and that's been helping me all these years, keeping me together

WHEN HE MET his wife he was a sophomore in college and six years had passed since the whole thing, the murders, trial, et cetera.

There were whole days when he would only think a little about those events, when the thoughts would graze lightly across the surface of his consciousness and then sink into the waters—he found himself visualizing his memories this way, imagined certain images drifting down into dark green ponds and sending up a few gurgling bubbles as they vanished. He was so spacey during those years, barely tethered to earth, he thought later—

His wife was a student assistant in his American history Revolution to Constitutional Convention class, and as he was leaving class she walked along beside him for a moment and very lightly touched him on the arm.

"What are you taking?" she said. "Ativan?"

". . . Huh?" he said. And they looked at one another and he guessed that something in his face made her raise her eyebrows appraisingly.

"Oh my," she said. "I think you better have a seat over here for a minute, don't you?" "Well," he said. "I'm a—" but she took him by the elbow and steered him toward a bench, which sat below a Sargent-like painting of an ancient turn-of-the-century trustee.

"Sit," she said. "I used to have a problem with BZDs, so I know a little about what you're going through." She eyed him thoughtfully. "Don't worry," she said, "I'm not like a narc or a religious nut or something, it's just that you look familiar."

9

AQIL TOOK OUT a map and unfolded it carefully on Dustin's desk. "Listen," he said. "This isn't just another weird rabbit hole I'm going down. This one is real. And you, Dr. Tillman—I think you are going to get this, more than anybody else I could tell. This is right up your alley."

Dustin shifted uncertainly. "Why do you say that? Up my alley in what way?"

13

"Just give me a minute," Aqil said. "Let me, you know, lay it out for you."

He placed the map on the desk between himself and Dustin, and Dustin looked down at the little red stickers that had been pasted along the edges of the interstate corridors and the waterways in a kind of curving pattern, possibly a pattern—he thought of the way that light pollution, seen from outer space, revealed the outlines of the Eastern Seaboard and the Great Lakes.

"Look," Aqil said. "So each of these dots? Each of these dots represents an apparent accidental death, *apparent*," he said, and he pointed to the northern corner of the state. "Here: JONATHON FRISBIE," he said. "Twenty-one years old, student at Ohio Northern University, went missing 1/1/01. Found 1/2/01, Maumee River; cause of death, drowning. Blood alcohol level was 0.23.

"VINCENT ISOLATO, nineteen, student at Ohio Northern University, reported missing 2/20/02, found 4/20/02, Maumee River, cause of death, drowning; MATT POTTS, twenty-one, student at Kettering U. Missing, 3/30/03, East Lansing, Michigan, found 4/02/03, Red Cedar River; cause of death, drowning."

"I can see where this is going," Dustin said. "But."

"Just wait, wait," Aqil said.

10

HE WAS IN his study when Kate called and he saw her name come up on the caller ID and he felt aware of the old feeling of attraction, not even such a big taboo to be drawn to your cousin when you were a thirteen-year-old boy but he had been embarrassed nevertheless, had never admitted it, though of course the girls knew, surely.

They had been a certain kind of teenage girl, *working class*, Dustin thinks now, though of course back then they would have never used that term—*trailer trashy*, maybe people might have said, *slutty*; at the very least it was clear that these girls were experienced.   Shrewd, practical.

Tube tops, short shorts, heavy makeup. Not virginal.

And later, years later, there was this moment when he had been visiting Kate at her place in L.A. and she had seemed so amused—this was when he was speaking at USC at a conference—and Kate had said, *so tell me about being a therapist. What's that like?* She had never been to college—she had worked as a hairdresser her whole life—had no interest in that kind of thing and he was aware that her only concepts of "therapists" were from TV or movies or whatever, the tweedy dithering absentminded snob, and she was smiling at him her eyes turned slyly sidelong and she said, *what do you talk about with them, have any of them been really, like, dangerously crazy? I just can't imagine . . .*

And now here he was, a forty-one-year-old man in his "study," how pretentious, at his desk, at his computer, checking his email and going over his "notes" and he picked up the phone and he wanted to be in the mode that was the person he would have been if

11

"JESSE HAMBLIN," Aqil said, "twenty-one, student at Michigan State, missing 4/4/04.

"Never found.

"CLINTON COMBE, nineteen, student at Brownmeyer College, missing 5/5/05. Found 5/16/05, Olentangy River. Cause of death: drowning. Blood alcohol level: 0.34.

"ZACHARY OROZCO, eighteen, freshman at Ohio University,

missing 6/6/06; that sends up some flags, right? Found 6/8/06, Hocking River, cause of death: drowning. Blood alcohol level 0.34.

"JEFF WAMSLEY, twenty-one, Ohio Northern University, missing 7/7/07, found 7/24/07, Maumee River. This is interesting— his father says to reporters that, and I quote, *rumors circulating that there might be some kind of mad drowner in our midst.*

"Now look at this one. JOSHUA McGIBONEY. A microbiology major, from University of Dayton. Went missing . . . you guessed it, Doctor, I can see . . . 8/8/08, after leaving a rugby party, his body found three days later facedown in Wolf Creek. Blood alcohol level: 0.40. It's hard to imagine how he could get so drunk and walk away—

"It's interesting, right? It makes you curious, doesn't it, Doctor?

"LUKE GORRINGE, Delta College student from Bay City Michigan, reported—note: reported—missing 9/11/09, East Lansing, Michigan. Found 10/15/09, Red Cedar River.

"VINCE NORBY, another student from Brownmeyer College— went missing 10/10/10.

"Found 2/11/11. Olentangy River."

"How many are there?" Dustin said. He looked at the folder that Aqil was holding, a sheaf of paper, and Aqil gave him a wry smile.

"How many? Including Peter Allingham, do you mean?"

12

THIS WAS THE day that Kate called to tell him about Russell, about the DNA evidence, Russell to be released from prison, a few days after Peter Allingham's body was recovered from the pond near campus. There was no real connection to be made between the two events except that later they adhered in Dustin's mind.

"So I'm just a little confused about the time line of all of this," he said to Kate. "The dates. At what point did this group—Innocence Project, right?—at what point did they begin to work on Russell's case?   And I don't understand why they didn't contact us. Why they weren't required by law to contact us since we are the victims' families and we were the ones who testified."

"Listen," Kate said, "I'm as freaked as you are, honey. Believe me."

"But it doesn't make any sense," Dustin said. "Surely this whole thing has been under way for a long time, and the fact that we aren't hearing about it until he is practically out the front gates of the"

"I *know*," Kate said. "I'm in, like, shock. I don't even know what to think. It's like one blood test and suddenly your whole life is—"

13

. . . KIND OF UPSETTING, he thought. Extremely, extremely upsetting.

A chilly April afternoon but he was outdoors wearing only that wool herringbone sports jacket that looked so much like a psychologist would wear that it was a little embarrassing, actually, and he glanced over his shoulder.

He was standing in the backyard along the side of the house holding an unlit cigarette when he heard the boys coming up the driveway, home from school; it was later in the day than he realized, and he bent down on his haunches and buried the cigarette in the dirt of a newly planted wisteria bush—

"Hey," Dustin said as the boys appeared. Aaron and Dennis and their friend Rabbit, that loping, clumsy yet vaguely predatory gait that teenage boys develop, and they looked at him.

"Hey, Dad," Dennis said laconically. "What are you burying?"

"Nothing," Dustin said. "Just checking this, um . . ." He gestured.

"Plant?" Dennis said.

"Bush?" Aaron said.

They had decided that it was hilarious to finish Dustin's sentences, because he had long had the habit of drifting off into ellipses, groping through increasingly long silences for the right word and not finding it. Distracted, always distracted, maybe even to the point of something wrong with his brain.

"—Wist," he said. "Wisteria," he said, and the boys exchanged glances; grins.

14

RUSSELL AND DUSTIN—RUSTY and Dusty, that's what their parents sometimes called them, as if they were a matching set.

Though of course they hadn't chosen Russell's name. Russell was a foster boy when he came to them, son of a drug-addict mother, father unknown. He'd been living with a different foster family for several years, but then there had been a house fire, and he was orphaned again.

Dustin's father had been deeply moved by this tragedy.

Russell was fourteen when they adopted him, and Dustin was eight, and Dustin can remember that day. There had been a party, and after the party had dispersed he had seen Rusty standing in the backyard, staring out toward the horizon. Western Nebraska, bordering on Colorado: the fields, lined with telephone poles; the grasshopper oil wells, gently nodding their sleepy heads. At the edge of the horizon, a ridge of low hills rose up from the flatland. Along the tops of the hills were gnarled volcanic cliffs and boulders, pocked and jagged. In the summer, when the sun was right, the shadows of the cliffs and rocks could be said to resemble faces, or the figures of animals.

Dustin sat on the back steps and looked out along with Rusty. After a time, Rusty turned.

His face was solemn, maybe brotherly.

"What are you staring at?" Rusty said, and Dustin shrugged.

"Come over here," Rusty said, and when Dustin did, Rusty didn't say anything for a while.

He considered Dustin's face. "You want to know something?"

"What?" And Dustin breathed as Rusty's eyes held him.

"My actual mom died," he said. "They say that she hung herself, but I think they probably killed her."

"Who?" Dustin said. "Who killed her?"

But Rusty only shrugged. Then, abruptly, he gestured at the sky. He pointed. "You see that?" he said. "That's the evening star."

He put his palms firmly over Dustin's ears and tilted Dustin's head, swiveling it like it was a telescope. "You see it now? It's right . . . there!"

And he drew a line with his finger, from Dustin's nose to the sky.

Dustin nodded. He closed his eyes. He could feel the cool, clay-like dampness of his brother's palms against his head. The sound of the hands was like the inside of a shell.

"I see it," Dustin said softly.

HIS WIFE'S MAIDEN name had been Jill Bell, which she loathed. She said that it always made people think that she was going to be a nicer person than she was, it always made the teachers think that she would be a placid, goody-goody little girl, the name, she said, of a fairy or a milkmaid or a flower that people sang about in the nineteenth century—"When Springtime Jill Bells Are A-Bloomin'," she said, and she even had a tune for it, which resembled something Stephen Foster might have composed.

In any case, she liked Jill Tillman better: There was something a little snappier about it, more acerbic, which suited her. She got on the phone—to talk to one of the boys' teachers, or a construction contractor whose work wasn't quite up to par, or some bureaucratic functionary—and she had found a perfect, crisp snap to the words. "This is Jill Tillman," she would say, and a perfectly pleasant chill would spread across the syllables. "May I speak to your supervisor, please?"

It was the kind of voice that had gotten them through the first years of their marriage, when he had been a PhD candidate and she was in law school and they had the boys one after the other. It should have been a disaster but she was a person who liked to put things in order, to make lists and schedules, to discover neat little shortcuts and inventions.

She knew about Dustin's past, of course, but was not interested at all in the psychology of it, in dwelling on it, in dredging things up and examining them.

This was one of the things he loved most about her.

DUSTIN WALKED DOWN the hallway to the bedroom where his wife was stretched out on top of the covers in her jeans and bare feet, reading a book. It was about ten o'clock at night.

He stood there in the doorway looking at her and she continued to read peaceably. She had an odd habit. She would take the corner of a page between her thumb and forefinger and begin to turn the page over before she had read it all the way, craning her head a little to catch the last couple of lines. He didn't understand why she didn't just finish the page before she flipped it.

They had been married twenty years and they had never once talked seriously about getting divorced, although there were long periods of silence in their marriage where they were living more or less like roommates. Companionably aloof.

"It's hard for me to concentrate when you're staring at me," she said now, glancing up as he came in and lay down on the bed beside her.

"What are you reading?" he said.

She showed him the book cover: **Despair**, *by Vladimir Nabokov.*

"Oh," he said. "That sounds fun."

"It's actually hilarious," she said.

He rested his chin on her shoulder, glanced at the top of page 73:

> *shine, sea waves. A nice cosy life. Can't understand why you should criticize*

He pressed his face down into the soft shirtsleeve crease of her arm, right above her breast. Breathed in, smelled, and her chest rose slowly and she rested her hand on the back of his head.

"I have something weird to tell you," he said.

He closed his eyes. Her fingers ran lightly across his hair.

"I have something I need to tell you, too," she said.

"You go first," he said.

He felt her draw in a long breath and hold it.

"No, you go first," she said, and there was a thin line of tension in her voice, almost like she was gritting her teeth. Was she mad at him? Had he done something inconsiderate?

"How was your doctor's appointment?" he said, and when she didn't speak he lifted his head to look at her face.

17

From: Aqil Ozorowski (Ozorowskiag@yahoo.com)
Sent: Fri April 8 2012 1:26 AM
To: DrDTillman@outlook.com
RE: Crazy

Dear Dr. Tillman,

I hope I didn't come on too strong today as if I was trying to push things down your throat or so forth. I know I have had my moments of seeming "off the wall," but I think we've got a good enough relationship that you can tell when I am going down the rabbit hole and when I am being real.

This is *the real deal.*

First of all, let's just put aside the weird coincidence with the dates. It's just too much, right? It makes me sound like one of the conspiracy guys with the tinfoil hats! So put it aside.

Instead, just think for a minute about the facts that tie all these deaths together. What sets up a flag for me is all the stuff that's missing. The evidence investigators didn't find. Right? The only obvious connection is the extreme amount of alcohol consumption by each victim, and since the corpse is always recovered in a local waterway the cause of death is always *assumed* to be drowning, with death *assumed* to occur on the night the victim went missing.

So we cops look at this and we say, simple. An accidental drowning. "Death by Misadventure" is what we put on the report. Case closed. It's sad, but no further investigation is needed. Binge drinking is an epidemic on these college campuses, and when you have that amount of drunkenness somebody's going to die, right? It's just the odds.

But then look at the actual circumstances. The blood alcohol level in many of these cases is crazy. So they would have to be consuming very quickly. Most of the time they are in a crowd, at a party or a bar, and then suddenly nobody has seen them for a while. They've gone off somewhere. I won't use the word "vanished."

Now, as drunk as they supposedly are, somehow they negotiate their way to a riverbank without a single witness seeing them.

Then "happen" to fall into the water. "Help!" they yell. "Help! Help me!" Nobody hears them. Unheard and unseen.

Are any of these kids troubled, accident-prone alcoholics? Not really. Most of them are A and B students, a lot of them athletes in good physical health, lots of friends and good stable family relationships. Not to say that kids like that don't also die. But you might expect some flags with deaths like these. Not a single one of these was ever listed as a suicide. There's no evidence of that.

And why is it that most often their bodies aren't found immediately? Instead, it's days, weeks, months later, downstream of the "accident." There are never any signs of FOUL PLAY but there are also no signs of AN ACCIDENT. Whatever happened to these kids happened without witness or evidence. Every time.

Which is one of the things that makes me think that maybe there's something purposeful about these deaths. Almost like they've been arranged.

Am I crazy? Everything I say to my court-appointed shrink, he comes back at me with "delusions of reference." He's looking at me for signs of mania, paranoia, some diagnosis he can pin on me.

And maybe you think the same thing. But I trust you more, Doctor. I could tell right away when I met you that you were a kindred spirit.

Will you be my second set of ears and eyes on this thing? I'll give you all the files I have; I'll lay it all out for you. Then, if you don't agree, explain it to me. Tell me there's something I'm exaggerating. Something I'm "projecting" too much into. If you say that I am delusional, I will believe you.

I do remember your little saying, Doctor. "Sometimes a dead bird is just a dead bird." That story you tell. But these are not birds, Doc. They are dead young men. I just want somebody to think about it with me.

Help me.

I am, most humbly, your patient,

Aqil Ozorowski

18

"IT'S ABOUT THE size of a grapefruit," Jill told him. "Dr. Watanabe could literally press down on my stomach and feel it. I can't believe it. I've been walking around for . . . years?

"Probably years. And I didn't notice anything."

"So maybe it's nothing," he said. They were sitting cross-legged on the bed, facing each other, holding hands, and it must have looked, he thought, like they were children, like they were reciting a rhyme together. "Before we panic," he said, "let's look at the most optimistic side.

"These things can be completely benign."

In his mind, the tumor was really a grapefruit. It was yellow and had a thick, pocked skin, and it was full of pink quarter-moon chambers.

"I love you," he said.

"I know," she said.

They both lifted their heads and listened. From down the hall, they could hear the music of their sons' video-game console. The two boys side by side on Aaron's twin bed, their thumbs and forefingers twitching over their controllers, their eyes fixed and aglow.

"Will you go make them go to sleep?" Jill said.

"Yeah," he said.

He lifted his hands from her grasp. Their palms had grown sticky.

"I don't want to tell them anything until I'm ready," she said. "Okay?"

It occurred to him that he had not told her about Kate's call, about Rusty. And then for some reason he thought again about the dead boy in his Halloween costume, under the ice.

It makes you curious, doesn't it, Doctor?

"Okay," he said.

19

Sometimes a dead bird is just a dead bird.

Jill told him that, back when they were first dating. They had been walking together along the main street of town, holding hands—it was the first time they had held hands, and when their fingers clasped she had looked at him and raised her eyebrows and grinned

And then a robin fell on the sidewalk in front of them.

Apparently it fell out of the sky. Possibly a bird of prey had accidentally dropped it, they decided later. But at the moment they were both astonished. They stood staring at the limp body, and their handhold fell away.

"Fuck," Jill said. And then, without another word, she grabbed his hand up again and held it tightly.

"Listen," she said fiercely. "It's *nothing*. Sometimes a dead bird is just a dead bird."

Which he had always remembered. It was one of those little private phrases that married people take up and repeat to one another; it had become a mantra for him, though Jill had no idea that it was also an anecdote that he sometimes told his patients—one of those humorous but poignant personal stories that you introduce to help build trust, et cetera.

"Sometimes a dead bird is just a dead bird," he would say. "When Jill told me that, I felt something kind of . . . unlock inside me."

And he'd look at the patient. Thoughtful. Puzzled for a moment.

"I realized," he'd say. "I realized that *I had the choice*. I could give this moment a meaning, or I could choose to ignore it. It just depended on the kind of story I wanted to tell myself."

He could feel himself smiling earnestly, as if he'd never thought of this before.

"We are always telling a story *to* ourselves, about ourselves," he'd say.   Sometimes he would make a gesture that was almost like a touch, though he actually rarely made skin-to-skin contact.

"But we can control those stories," he'd say. "I believe that! Events in our life have meaning because we choose to give it to them."

PART TWO

Summer 1978

Rusty Bickers went walking through the fields at dusk, Rusty Bickers with a sadness and nobility that only Dustin could see. He'd dream of Rusty Bickers at the kitchen table, eating Cap'n Crunch cereal before bedtime, his head low, lost in thought; Rusty Bickers, silent but awake, beneath the blankets on his cot, his hands moving in slow circles over his own body, whispering, *Shh . . . shhh . . . hush now;* Rusty Bickers standing in the morning doorway of the kitchen, watching Dustin's family eating breakfast, his shaggy hair hanging lank about his face, his long arms dangling from slumped shoulders, his eyes like those of someone who had been marched a long way to a place where they were going to shoot him.

Dustin heard his mother's bright voice ring out: "It's about time you got up, Rusty!"

Dustin was eight years old, and Rusty was fourteen, an orphan, a foster boy. All that summer, Rusty slept on a folding bed in Dustin's room, so Dustin knew him better than anybody.

Rusty was beginning to grow a man's body. His legs were long and coltish, his feet too big; hair was growing under his arms and around his groin. He had his own tapes, which he listened to through enormous, spaceman headphones. He had a souvenir ashtray from the Grand Canyon. He had some books, and photographs of his dead family, and newspaper clippings. Rusty sometimes wet the bed, and it was a terrible secret that only Dustin and Dustin's mom knew about. Dustin's mom said that he should never, ever, tell.

Sometimes, late at night, when Rusty thought that Dustin was asleep, he would slip into Dustin's bed because he had peed in his own. He curled his long body against Dustin's smaller one, and

Dustin stayed still. Rusty put his arm around Dustin as if Dustin were a stuffed animal. Dustin could feel Rusty quivering—he was crying, and his tears fell sharply onto Dustin's bare back. Rusty's arm tightened, pulling Dustin closer.

Rusty's last foster family—the mother, father, and two younger brothers—had died in a fire. Some people—Dustin's older cousins, Kate and Wave, for example—some of them whispered that they heard that Rusty had started the fire himself. Anyway, he was weird, they said. *Psycho.* They stayed away from him.

Before Rusty had come to live with them, Dustin's father was in a bad accident. He had been working as an electrician on a construction site when a roof collapsed. Dustin's father and his father's best friend, Billy Merritt, had fallen through three floors. Billy Merritt had died instantly. Dustin's father had broken both legs, and his right arm had been severed. His fall had been softened because he landed on Billy Merritt.

Now Dustin's father had a prosthetic arm that he was learning to use. The prosthesis looked like two hooks, which his father could clamp together. For example, Dustin's father was learning how to grasp a fork and lift it to his lips. Eventually he would be able to turn the pages of a book, or pick up a pin.

There had been a settlement for his father's injury, a large sum of money. The very first thing Dustin's father did was to go and speak with the people at County Social Services. He wanted to take in a foster boy, he said. This had been one of his dreams, something he'd always wanted to do. When he was a teenager, Dustin's father had been sent away to a home for delinquent boys. After a while, Dustin's father had run away from that place and joined the Army. But he still vividly remembered that awful time of his life.

Dustin's father loved Rusty Bickers. Rusty's story was so sad that perhaps it made Dustin's father feel better. He felt that he could help Rusty somehow. He wanted to provide an atmosphere of Love and Happiness.

There was so much money! Dustin had no idea *how* much, but it seemed bottomless. His father bought a new car, and a pool table, and a huge stereo system; his mother got her teeth fixed; they began to plan an addition to the house, with a family room and a bedroom for Rusty.

When they went to town, to the big store at the mall, Dustin and Rusty were allowed to pick out a toy—anything they wanted. While their father looked at tools and electronic devices, Rusty followed Dustin through the rows of toys: the pink and glittery aisle of girls; the mysterious and bookish aisle of games and puzzles; the aisle of action figures and toy weapons and Matchbox cars; the aisle of baby stuff—rattles and soft-edged educational devices that looked like dashboards, things that spoke or giggled when you pulled a string. Rusty stopped for a long time in the aisle of sports stuff, the aisle of BB guns and real bows and arrows. He touched the sharp razory tips of the arrows with his thumb.

"Nobody knows what they want, not really," Rusty Bickers said, sometimes, when they were in bed at night. Dustin didn't know whether Rusty had made this up or whether he was quoting some movie or song. He said this when he was talking about the future. He was thinking about becoming a drummer in a rock band, but he worried that it might be pointless, living out in western Nebraska. He thought that maybe he should live in New York or L.A., but he was worried that if he was in such places, the black kids would be always trying to beat him up.

"They hate white people," Rusty told Dustin. "All they want to do is fight you."

Rusty had met black people. He had lived with some black boys in a group home, and he'd had a black teacher.

Dustin hadn't yet seen a black person, though he wanted to. There was a cartoon on TV called *Fat Albert and the Cosby Kids*, about a group of black children who lived in a junkyard. This was Dustin's favorite show, and he longed to make friends with a black child.

"You can't *make friends* with them," Rusty said. "All they want to do is kick your ass." Dustin disapproved of this, but he didn't say anything. They weren't allowed to say *ass*.

But Rusty didn't even seem to notice. He was thinking of where he would like to go, if he could go somewhere. He closed his eyes and leaned back, playing drums on the air above his head.

It was a summer of parties. They were happy times, Dustin thought. Friday. Saturday. People would begin to wander in around six or so, bringing coolers full of icy beer and pop, talking loudly—Dustin's uncle and aunt and cousins, his father's old friends from work and their wives and kids, his mother's high school friends—thirty, forty people sometimes. They would barbecue, and there would be corn on the cob, bowls of potato chips and honey-roasted peanuts, slices of cheese and salami, pickled eggs and jalapeños. Music of Waylon Jennings, Willie Nelson, Crystal Gayle. Some people dancing.

Their house was about a mile outside of town. The kids would play outdoors, in the backyard and the large stubble field behind the house. Dusk seemed to last for hours, and when it was finally dark they would sit under the porch light, catching thickly buzzing June bugs and moths, or even an occasional toad who hopped into the circle of light, tempted by the halo of insects that floated around the bare orange lightbulb next to the front door.

Rusty hardly ever joined in their games. Instead, he would stake out some corner of the yard, or even a chair inside the house, sitting, quietly observing.

Who knew what the adults were doing? They played cards and gossiped. There were bursts of laughter, Aunt Vicki's high, fun-house cackle rising above the general mumble; they sang along with the songs. After he got drunk, Dustin's father would go around touching the ladies on the back of the neck with his hook, surprising them, making them scream. Sometimes he would take off his arm and dance with it. Sometimes he would cry about Billy Merritt.

The night grew late. Empty beer cans filled the trash cans and lined the countertops. The younger children fell asleep in rows on the beds. If he was still awake, Dustin would sometimes gaze out the window, out to where the last remaining adults stood in a circle in the backyard, whispering and giggling, passing a small cigarette from hand to hand. Dustin was eight and wasn't supposed to know what was going on.

But Rusty told him. At first, Dustin didn't want to believe him. Dustin had mostly heard frightening things about drugs—that wicked people sometimes put LSD in Halloween candy, to make the children go crazy; that if you took angel dust, you would try to kill the first person you saw; that dope pushers sometimes came around playgrounds and tried to give children pills, and that, if this happened, you should run away and tell an adult as soon as possible.

Rusty had smoked pot; he had also accidentally taken LSD, which someone had given to him in a chocolate bar.

Dustin wasn't sure he believed this, either. The depth of Rusty's experience, of his depravity, seemed almost impossible.

Later, when Dustin's parents were out, Dustin and Rusty went through their dresser drawers. They found copies of pornographic magazines in Dustin's father's T-shirt drawer, at the very bottom; in his mother's bra and panty drawer, they found a small baggie full of what Rusty said was marijuana.

Rusty took a little for himself, and Dustin nearly started crying.

"Don't tell," Rusty said to him. "You're not going to tell, are you? You know your mom and dad could get in trouble with the police if they ever got caught."

"I won't tell," Dustin whispered.

Dustin's father seemed like a regular father, except for his arm. Sometimes, on Saturdays after breakfast, Dustin and his father and Rusty would drive up into the hills with Dustin's father's 10-gauge rifles. Dustin's father lined up beer cans and mayonnaise jars and such along a fence, and they would shoot at them. Dustin's father could not hold the gun well enough to aim it himself, but he showed Dustin and Rusty how.

The first time Rusty took the gun, his hands were shaking. "Have you ever handled a gun before, son?" Dustin's father said, and Rusty slowly shook his head.

Dustin's father showed Rusty where to hold his hands, how the butt of the gun fit against his shoulder. "Okay, okay," Dustin's father said. He stooped behind Rusty, his chin right next to Rusty's ear. "Can you see through the crosshairs? Right where the lines meet?"

Dustin watched as his father and Rusty took careful aim, both their bodies poised together. When the mayonnaise jar burst apart, Dustin leapt up. "You hit it!" he cried, and Rusty turned to him, eyes wide, his mouth slightly open in quiet wonder.

Dustin's mother was waiting with lunch when they got home. She made hamburgers and corn on the cob.

She seemed to Dustin like a typical mother. She was slightly overweight, and bustled, and was cheerful most of the time. When Rusty first came, she would sometimes give him hugs, but he would always become rigid and uncomfortable. After a time, she stopped hugging him. Instead, she would simply rest her hand on his shoulder, or on his arm. Rusty wouldn't look at her when she did this, but he didn't move away, either.

Dustin thought of what he was learning about plants at school. They drank in sunlight as their food; they breathed, though you couldn't see it. He thought of this as he watched Rusty sit there, with Dustin's mother's hand on his shoulder. Her hand briefly massaged his neck before she took it away, and Dustin could see the way Rusty's impassive expression shuddered, the way his eyes grew very still and far away.

Dustin saw Rusty standing at the edge of the backyard, the silhouette of Rusty, so motionless he might have been a fence post. Dustin observed silently as Rusty seemed to stare out into the distance. Miles away, the red taillights of semitrucks were moving along the interstate, and Dustin was suddenly aware that there were people inside them, that they were traveling to distant places and they would never know that he and Rusty were watching them. It made him feel a strange, tingling kind of ache.

"What are you staring at?" Rusty said at last, and it was startling; it was like being woken from a dream. Rusty didn't turn to look at Dustin. His voice came out of his shadow. "What do you want?" he said.

"Nothing," Dustin said.

"Come over here," Rusty said, and Dustin stepped forward uncertainly. He felt suddenly shy. He was afraid of being tricked. Often, his older cousins, Kate and Wave, would fool him by talking softly in that way.

But Rusty didn't even glance down when Dustin crept up beside him. He just kept peering out toward the interstate. "God!" he said. "You're so stupid, you know that, Dustin?"

"I'm not stupid," Dustin said, and Rusty turned his face to him at last. Grinned.

"Ha-ha," he said. "You're like Little Red Riding Hood skipping through the forest." He tilted his head, considering Dustin's face. "Do you know what would happen if a kid like you got sent to a foster home?"

"No." And Dustin breathed as Rusty's eyes held him without blinking.

"They do really nasty things to the little kids. And if you try to scream, they put your own dirty underwear into your mouth, to gag you." He stared at Dustin ruefully, as if he was imagining it.

Then he pointed up toward the sky. "You see that?" he said. "There's the Big Dipper." Rusty stood behind Dustin and put his hands over Dustin's ears, his fingertips pressing firmly into Dustin's scalp. He tilted Dustin's head back.

"You see it?" Rusty murmured, and Dustin nodded. He let himself lean back into the grip of Rusty's hands, imagining that his head was a globe that Rusty was holding, that he was floating in space and he could see galaxies. But he kept his eyes closed.

"Yeah," he said. "I see it."

Sometimes, they all seemed so happy. Here they were, watching TV in the evening, his mother sitting on his father's lap in the big easy chair, laughing at some secret joke, his mother blushing. Here they were, camping at the lake, roasting marshmallows on sharpened sapling sticks over a campfire; Dustin climbing on their father's shoulders out in the lake and standing up, his feet flat on either side of his father's neck, wobbling, balancing, raising his hands into a diver's pose.

Jumping into the water as if his father were a diving board.

At night, Dustin and Rusty would wade along the edge of the shore with a flashlight, catching crawdads. Rusty wasn't afraid of their pincers. He would grin hard, letting them hang dangling like jewelry clamped to the lobes of his ears.

Dustin didn't know what the feeling was that filled him up in such moments. It was something about the way the flashlight's beam made a glossy bowl of light beneath the water, the way, under the beam, everything was clear and distinct—the bits of floating algae and minute water animals, the polished stones and sleepy minnows flashing silver and metallic blue, the crawdads, sidling backward with their claws lifted warily. It was the sound of his parents' voices as they sat around the campfire, the echoing waver as their father began to sing. Rusty was a silhouette against the slick blue-black stretch of lake, and Dustin could see that the sky wasn't like a ceiling. It was like water, too, deep water, depth upon depth, vast beyond measure. And this was something Dustin found beautiful. And he loved his young mother and father, and his aunt and uncle, laughing in the distance, and his girl cousins in their tent, already dreaming, and Rusty himself, standing there silently in the dark. He was filled with a kind of awed contentment, which he thought must be happiness.

Later, deep in his sleeping bag in the tent, Dustin could hear his parents talking. Their voices were low but he found that if he listened hard he could understand.

"I don't know," his mother said. "How long does it take to get over something like that?"

"He's all right," Dustin's father said. "He's a good kid. He just needs to be left alone. I don't think he wants to talk about it."

"Oh," his mother said, and breathed heavily. "I can't even imagine, you know? What if I lost all of you like that? I don't see how I could go on. I'd kill myself, Dave. I really would."

"No, you wouldn't," Dustin's father said. "Don't say stuff like that."

And then they were silent. Dustin looked over to where Rusty was lying and saw that Rusty was awake, too. The tent walls glimmered with firelight, and the glow flickered against Rusty's open eyes. Rusty's jaw moved as he listened.

Dustin woke in the night; he could feel something pressing against him, and when he opened his eyes the tent's thin walls were almost phosphorescent with moonlight. Rusty's sleeping bag was rolled close to his, and he could feel Rusty's body moving. Inside their sleeping bags, they were like strange, unearthly creatures— thick caterpillars, cocoons. Rusty was rocking against him and whispering, though the words blurred together in a steady rhythm, rising and falling until Dustin could almost make out the words, like something lost in the winds: "Waiting . . . I've . . . when are you . . . Oh I am waiting for . . . and you never . . ." and the rocking quickened and he thought Rusty was crying. But Dustin didn't dare open his eyes. He kept himself very still, breathing slowly like a sleeper would. Rusty was making a sound, a high thread of tuneless humming, which, after a moment, Dustin realized was the word *Mom*, stretched impossibly thin, unraveling and unraveling. And Dustin knew that this was something he could never speak of, to anyone.

Yet even then, even in this still and spooky moment, there was a kind of happiness: something wondrous in Rusty's whispered words, in the urgent pressing of Rusty's body, a secret almost glimpsed. What was it? What was it?

He couldn't ask Rusty, who was more silent and sullen than ever in the week after they returned from their camping trip. He would disappear for hours sometimes, trailing a heavy silence behind him, and if Dustin did encounter him—lying faceup in a ditch thick with tall pigweed and sunflowers, or hunkered down by the lumber pile behind the garage—Rusty would give him a look so baleful that Dustin knew he shouldn't approach.

When Rusty had first come to live with them, Dustin had said, "Am I supposed to call Rusty my brother?"

They were sitting at the supper table, and both his father and mother stopped short and looked up. "Well," Dustin's father said cautiously, "I know we'd sure like it if Rusty thought of us as his family. But I think it's up to Rusty what you call him."

Dustin had felt bad at the way that Rusty had shrunk when they all looked at him. Rusty froze, and his face seemed to pass through a whole series of uncertain expressions. Then he smiled. "Sure, Dustin," he said. "Let's be brothers." And he showed Dustin a special high-five, where you pressed your thumbs together after slapping palms. You pressed your thumb against the other person's, and each of you fluttered your four fingers. It made the shape of a bird, probably an eagle or a falcon.

Of course, that didn't really make them brothers. Dustin knew that Rusty had probably only said something nice to please Dustin's parents, just as he called them "Dad" and "Mom" to make them happy. But that was okay. *Something* had happened. Something strange and unexplainable passed through the pads of their thumbs when they slid against one another.

Dustin remembered that handshake again as he watched Rusty. Rusty was slouching thoughtfully near an abandoned house not far from where they lived. Dustin had tracked him that far, but he kept his distance. He watched through a pair of his father's binoculars as Rusty picked up an old beer bottle and broke it on a stone, throwing back his arm with a pitcher's flourish. The windows in the old house were already broken out, but Rusty hit at the empty frames with a stick for a while. He lifted his head and looked around suspiciously. He didn't see Dustin, who was hidden in a patch of high weeds, and after a time, feeling somewhat content, Rusty settled onto his haunches and began to smoke some of the marijuana he'd taken from Dustin's parents' dresser.

Dustin observed: the way his eyes closed as he drew smoke into his mouth, and the way he held it in his lungs, then exhaled in a long breath. Rusty let the handmade cigarette hang loosely from his lips, as if he were a movie detective. Then he inhaled again.

Rusty seemed more relaxed when he finally came back to the house, around dinnertime. He even deigned to play a game of rummy with Dustin, which he almost never did. They sat side by side on the living room floor, and when Dustin said, "Gin!" and laid down all his cards, Rusty wasn't even mad. Rusty gave him the old high-five. The eagle or falcon flying. He grinned at Dustin kindly. "Rock on," Rusty said.

But that night, as he and Dustin lay in bed, all Rusty wanted to talk about was leaving. New York. Los Angeles. Nashville. Learning how to play electric guitar. He was thinking of writing a letter to the rock band Black Sabbath and asking if he could work for them.

"I'll take you with me," Rusty said. "When we go. Black Sabbath are very cool. I could tell them you were my little brother. And we were, like, homeless or something. They'd probably teach us to play instruments. So, you know, when they got older, we would take over. We'd be, like, Black Sabbath, Part Two."

"What would I be?" Dustin asked. He wanted to see himself in this new world clearly, to imagine it whole, as Rusty had.

"Probably the drummer," Rusty said. "You like drums, don't you?"

"Yes," Dustin said. He waited, wanting to hear more about himself as a drummer, but Rusty merely folded his hands behind his head.

"We'd probably have to kill them, you know," Rusty said.

"Who?" Dustin asked. "Black Sabbath?"

"No, asshole," Rusty said irritably. "Dave and Colleen. Your parents. I mean, we could get the gun while they were sleeping and it wouldn't even hurt them. It would just be like they were asleep. We could take your dad's car, you know. I could drive."

Dustin thought of his father's new Jeep Wrangler, in the driveway, still shiny. He pictured sitting in the passenger seat, with Rusty behind the wheel. He didn't say anything for a minute. He didn't know whether Rusty was joking or not, and he was both scared and exhilarated.

He watched as Rusty drew his bare foot out from beneath the covers and picked at a knobby toe. "You could kill them while they were sleeping. It wouldn't hurt them. It wouldn't matter."

He paused dreamily, looking at Dustin's face. "And then if you lit the house on fire, no one would ever know what happened. All the evidence would be burned up."

He said this steadily, but his eyes seemed to darken as he spoke, and Dustin felt his neck prickle. He watched as Rusty's mouth hardened, trying to tighten over a quiver of his lips, a waver in his expression. He said, "They'd think we died, too. They wouldn't come looking for us, because," he whispered, *"they wouldn't know we were still alive."*

Rusty stared at him, his face lit silver in the moonlight, and Dustin could feel a kind of dull, motionless panic rising inside him, as in a dream. A part of him wanted to shout out for his mother, but he didn't. Instead, he slid his legs slowly onto the tile of the floor. "I have to go to the bathroom," he said, and stood uncertainly. For a minute he thought he would start to run.

But the minute Dustin stood up, Rusty moved quickly, catching him by the arm. The sweet, coppery smell of feet hung on his bare skin as he pulled Dustin against him.

"Shh!" Rusty's fingers gripped, pinching Dustin's arms. "Don't scream!" Rusty whispered urgently. They stood there in a kind of hug, and Rusty pressed his mouth close to Dustin's ear, so that Dustin could feel Rusty's lips brush against the soft lobe. Rusty didn't let Dustin go, but his grip loosened. "Shh," he said. "Don't cry, Dustin. Don't be scared." He had begun to rock back and forth a bit, still holding Dustin, still shushing. "We're brothers, aren't we? And brothers love each other. Nothing bad's going to happen to you, 'cause I'm your brother, man, I won't let it. Don't be scared."

And Dustin looked up at Rusty's face. He didn't know whether Rusty was telling the truth or not, but he nodded anyway. Rusty's eyes held him as they rocked together, and Dustin swallowed tears and phlegm, closing his mouth tightly. It was true. They did love each other.

For the next few days, or maybe weeks, Rusty paid attention to Dustin. There were times when Dustin thought of that night that Rusty had talked of killing, of lighting fires, and there were even times when he felt that it would happen, sooner or later. But when he woke from a bad dream, Rusty was always awake, sitting on the edge of the bed, saying, "It's okay, don't be afraid," passing his hand slowly across Dustin's face, his fingers tracing Dustin's eyelids until they shut. During the day, Dustin and Rusty would take walks, strolling silently out into the bare stubble fields. An occasional jackrabbit would spring up from a patch of weeds and bolt away, leaving little puffs of dust behind its large, fleeing feet. They turned over rocks and found sow bugs, centipedes, metallic-shelled beetles. Sometimes, Rusty found fossils, and he and Dustin took them home and examined them under a magnifying glass.

After a while, Dustin's worries passed away; he stopped thinking he should tell his parents about what Rusty had said that night. Rusty himself never spoke of it again. Sometimes, as they looked at the fossils—imprints of fish bones and ferns and clamshells—Rusty would lean over Dustin, letting his face brush Dustin's hair. It was said that there had once been a great sea covering the land where they now lived. That was where the fossils came from.

There were times, during that last month of summer, when it seemed that he and Rusty were the only ones alive. The rest of Dustin's family seemed to be in a kind of trance, sleepwalkers that he and Rusty moved among. Dustin imagined them jolting awake, suddenly, blinking. *Where are we?* they would say. *What happened to us?*

But the trance didn't break. Instead, Dustin's parents often seemed like statues in a faraway garden, people under a curse, frozen. Across the stubble field, in the old abandoned house, Dustin and Rusty gathered wood together and made a little bonfire in the center of what must have been the living room. They pretended it was after a nuclear holocaust, and they were the only two people alive. The smoke rose up in a sinewy column and crawled along the ceiling toward the broken windows. Dustin and Rusty took vegetables from the garden and put them in a coffee can with water and made a delicious soup, boiled over their fire. Later, they put one of Dustin's cousin's Barbies in the can with a G.I. Joe. They watched as the dolls' plastic limbs melted together, drooping and dripping. Removed from the heat, the two were fused together in a single charred mass.

Kissing: on the floor of the old house, shirtless, Rusty on top of him, their hands clasped, Rusty's sticky skin against his own, their mouths open. When Dustin closed his eyes, it felt as if a small, eager animal were probing the inside of his mouth. It felt funny; he liked it.

It didn't mean he was a fag, Rusty said, and Dustin had nodded. There were children at Dustin's school who were called fags. They were too skinny, or too fat; they were weak, or sissies, or wore glasses.

"You can't tell anybody," Rusty said. "Ever." He traced his finger along Dustin's lips, and then down, along Dustin's neck, his chest, his belly button.

"I know," said Dustin, and let his tongue move over Rusty's chest. *They wouldn't know we were still alive*, Dustin thought, and he closed his eyes. For a moment, it was true: His family was dead, and he and Rusty were on their way together somewhere, and it was all right. He wasn't scared anymore. His lips brushed against Rusty's nipple and he liked the strange, nubby way it felt. He pressed his tongue against it and was surprised by the way Rusty's body jolted.

Rusty rolled off him, pushing away, and Dustin's eyes opened. He watched as Rusty knelt in the corner of the old house, unzipping his jeans.

"What are you doing?" Dustin said, and Rusty hunched over himself fiercely.

"I'm jerking off, you moron," Rusty said hoarsely. "What, do you want me to fuck you?"

Dustin took a step closer, trying to see what Rusty was doing to his penis, but Rusty gritted his teeth and glared, so he kept his distance.

"Would it hurt?" Dustin said, and Rusty hunched even further, the muscles of his back tightening.

43

"Yes," Rusty hissed. "It would hurt." And he was silent for a moment. "Get the fuck away from me, Dustin. Get lost, I mean it!"

And Dustin had slowly backed away, uncertainly. He stood in the high weeds at the door of the house, waiting. There was the summer buzz of cicadas; grasshoppers jumped from the high sunflowers and pigweed into his hair, and he shook them off.

"Rusty?" he called. "Rusty?" After a time, he went cautiously back into the house, but Rusty wasn't there. Though Dustin looked everywhere, Rusty didn't appear until suppertime.

And then suddenly it was over. A week later, they returned to school. They didn't go back to the old house together, and, though they would wait together for the bus in the morning, Rusty was distant. Whatever had happened between them was gone. *Why?* Dustin thought. *What did I do?* But Rusty wouldn't say anything. When Dustin tried to talk to Rusty at night, Rusty would pretend to be asleep. Once, when he tried to get in bed next to Rusty, Rusty had kicked him, hard—hard enough to send him across the room with a clatter that brought his mother running.

"Dustin fell out of bed," Rusty said solemnly, and Dustin just sat there on the floor, crying, while his mother stared at them.

"What's going on here?" she said, and Rusty shrugged.

"Nothing," Rusty said, and Dustin crawled back into his own bed, silently. "Nothing," Dustin said.

Afterward, Dustin lay there for a long time, silent, his eyes open in the darkness. He could hear Rusty breathing. He could hear the distant yodels of coyotes in the hills, and nothing circled in his mind. *Nothing,* Rusty said. *Nothing,* Dustin said. Nothing: It settled into him.

I would have done it, he thought. He would have chosen Rusty over them.

Maybe he wouldn't have killed his parents himself, but he knew he'd have let Rusty do it. He would've stood watching the house burn down, and then he'd turn and get into the passenger seat of the Jeep, and he and Rusty would have driven off to California to meet Black Sabbath. They would have seen the Grand Canyon; they would have seen the saguaro cactuses and the desert and then the Pacific Ocean. He would've been sorry—he would've cried for his parents, he would miss them terribly—but he had accepted the new life that was being offered to him.

And he saw now that it wasn't real. That it had never been real. He could feel that other life shrinking and losing its possibility, and he knew that it was something that he should never, ever, think of again.

PART THREE

Fall 2013

1

My MOM HAD been dead almost a year, and my dad was losing his mind. He would hang out with this guy named Aqil Ozorowski, who I guess was once his patient? They would meet up at a bar down the road called Parnell's, and they'd talk through their paranoid conversations, pints of beer and shots of Jameson whiskey, and then my dad would walk home through the suburban greenery of Cleveland Heights, carrying a six-pack of beers that he bought from CVS and a pack of Marlboro cigarettes, and the streets were utterly empty, and the trees were dripping from a thunderstorm, and he'd be stumbling along in the dark and his feet would splash in puddles on the sidewalk and the old houses would stare at him, their windows lightless, and he was a widower, forty-something years old, sad and wobbly and flushed and intoxicated with a plastic bag swinging from his hand. One time he saw a deer; one time he thought he saw a bear walking down Briarwood.

"It's not completely improbable," he told me. "There are between seventy and ninety wild black bears in the state of Ohio."

Was that true? How crazy was he? Maybe a lot, I didn't know for sure.

I was eighteen and supposedly starting college and living home alone with him. My brother, Dennis, was out of the picture: a sophomore at Cornell, very very very busy. Not interested in what was happening with his crazy dad and loser brother at home.

I remember waking up and hearing my dad come in and I saw his silhouette in my door tilting back and forth a little, and he had for some reason decided that he needed to wake me up to inform me about a serial killer.   Some person murdering college boys, he said. Drowning them.

How 1990s, I thought.

He was investigating it, he said. Possibly writing a book about it.

And I was like, "Cool." And then I rolled over and faced the wall.

2

"I'VE HEARD ABOUT that," my friend Rabbit said the next day. "It's like an urban legend among college kids. Supposedly there's this serial killer who kidnaps drunken bros and then tortures them and dumps them in a river so it looks like a drowning. They call the guy Jack Daniels, which I think is hilarious. Or else some people think it might be some kind of cult initiation ritual."

He had his hypodermic kit out and was cooking some heroin on a spoon with his lighter. He grinned at me. "How'd your dad get into *that*? He's really losing his shit, isn't he?"

Rabbit liked the needle. He preferred it to snorting or smoking, but when he heard his mom open the door to the basement, when he heard her slow heavy steps begin to clump down the stairs, I watched the way he sprang quickly to tuck the syringe under the cushion of the couch.

He put the little baggie of heroin in his pocket and the spoon into a coffee cup. He left the bong where it was, on the coffee table in front of us.

"Bruce?" she called. Which was Rabbit's actual first name. "Sweetheart? I need your help."

Rabbit looked at me sidelong. One of the first personal things he explained about himself was that no one, *no one*, called him Bruce. Whenever that name was spoken, he'd give me a warning glance.

"What do you want?" he said now, looking hard into my eyes. "Ma, I'm busy."

"I can't reach the cupboard above the refrigerator. With my leg like it is, I don't want to try to climb up on a chair."

"Ma," he said. "What do you need so bad at one in the morning? Why don't you just go to sleep?"

"Ummm," I murmured. I made some kind of weird gesture thing with my hand. "Rabb," I said. "I could help her, if . . ."

But Rabbit froze me with a glare.

"Go to sleep, Ma," Rabbit said, which made no difference. Like in a horror movie, his mom kept plunking down the stairs and then her body came into view. She was somewhere in her forties. Not really bad-looking for her age. Barefoot. Sweatpants. A T-shirt that was cut off at the midriff.

"Okay, I'll admit it," she said. "It's vodka. I put a bottle of vodka in that cabinet and I need it. God damn it, Rabbit, I'm in pain."

And actually, she probably was in pain. Rabbit's mom had cancer. Ovarian cancer.

Cancer of the see you in tee, Rabbit said, because he took pleasure in making me wince with how filthy he could be. It's the one main game that guys play together after they turn about thirteen or so: Who can be most offensive, who can be most callous, who can care the least?

How fuckin' fucked up is that? Rabbit said, and his mouth twitched, very rabbit-like.

And yet: Even more fucked up—unspeakable—was that my own mom died of the same kind of cancer. To me, this was the kind of coincidence that could make you suddenly think that some Higher Power or whatever was watching you. And not in a friendly way.

This wasn't something I could say to Rabbit, of course. Rabbit knew how my mom died, obviously, but he had studiously *unknown* it, and it was not something that would ever appear in our conversations.

3

When I found out my mom was going to die, I cried for about five minutes. Ten minutes, tops.

But it was the kind of crying that you never forget.   Let's call it *weeping*. You don't know the difference until you experience it—the way that your body suddenly turns into a, like, organism; all your molecules are steaming out of your skin and you are being pumped full of a hotter, heavier matter. Up to that point, you thought that emotions were part of the brain, but then you realize that in truth they are part of the body, that they are processes of your muscles and lungs and bones.

My mom was in a hospice, and at the time I didn't know what that actually meant. My dad took me out onto this hospice patio, which had a wooden boardwalk lined by trellises, like you were supposed to be walking through a grape arbor or something.

"I'm not sure your mom is going to make it," he said. And then cleared his throat.   "I mean, I'm pretty sure. That she's not."

And now, ten months later, he was concerned that I hadn't cried enough. Tearlessness: It's a symptom.

I'd been to a colleague of my dad's who prescribed Zoloft. Which, by the way, I was selling. And I'd been to another colleague of my dad's who thought I might need lithium. Which nobody was interested in buying.

4

I WAS SUPPOSED to be going to college.   I hadn't gone in for the whole apply-to-a-bunch-of-expensive-schools-and-wait-with-bated-breath-to-see-if-you-get-into-the-Ivy-League! thing that my brother had turned into such a huge drama. Instead, I was going to live at home and take classes downtown at Cleveland State, and I'd gone so far as to register for an English and a math and a political science, though as it turned out school had started two weeks ago and I had somehow not attended any of the classes yet.

My dad didn't know this, of course. He doled out money for "books" and "expenses" without even blinking an eye—I guess he'd gotten some money from my mom's insurance—and honestly the majority of our conversations involved him opening his wallet and handing me some cash. Sometimes he would pop up and attempt an amateurish performance of a dad—he would go off on some digression about how constellations aren't real, or how kale is really good for you, or how he wished we would have gone camping more when I was little. Did I want to go camping? Or he would lay some wisdom on me, *Sufi wisdom*, he said, which seemed completely random and impenetrable. Then he'd roam off, trailing his wisps of positivity through the house. Mostly we avoided each other successfully.

Sometimes, I'd see him standing in the backyard smoking a cigarette; I'd smell it wafting up through my window, and I'd watch from above as tendrils of smoke curled out of his mouth and nose, as he looked around nervously, and it was kind of sad, in a way, that he didn't know I was gazing down at him. Kind of hoping that he would glance up and see me, that it would be one of those *moments* from a corny movie. Eye to eye: Epiphany! Connection! Cue up a gentle alternative-rock song. Still, for a second, I couldn't help but wish for it. *Look up here, Dad!*

Instead, I found a cluster of stubbed cigarette butts in a potted plant. It looked like a diorama of a crime scene, the bent cigarettes curled up like bodies that had been executed.

It was September, and leaves were still green on the trees. The big old elms outside spread canopies that were twice as high as our three-story house, and I loved the darkness they cast at night. I loved the corridors of side streets as you walked along, the smell of cut grass, the four-way stoplight blinking wetly red, the smell of a skunk that would linger for a block or so, the chirr and zuzz of insects and the barking of toads, and the moths glowing gold in the high, hard streetlights.

And then I emerged out onto Lee Road, which is a business street, and a while or so back they put up surveillance cameras because of loitering teens, and then a little later they made a curfew law for the street—because of, they claimed, teenaged "flash mobs"—so that until this year it was actually illegal for me to be walking here, and I instinctually put the hood of my sweatshirt up and slid on into the all-night CVS for some chips and Skittles and a large energy drink.

Outside, I leaned against the wall that faced the parking lot and dined. It was 3:23 in the morning, and I didn't know what I was waiting for. I put a lozenge of Skittle into my mouth and then drank some of the NRG tea. Looked over at the shadows beyond the dumpsters at the edge of the fence.

Better hope you don't see any bears on the way home, I thought.

5

MY UNCLE RUSTY called late at night. And usually when he called I was extremely high.

Picture me spread-eagle in my underwear on my bed. I'd been without language for maybe two hours, staring at the textures on the ceiling, which are possibly rotting leaves, or centipedes marching single file, or Chthulus. Imagine that my phone would begin to vibrate from somewhere underneath my body and it sent a slow tentacle of awareness through me and at last I put my phone to my ear and my eyes were still on that fucking insanely alive ceiling.

And Rusty said, "Hey there, man."

His voice was kind of scratchy and deep, and it made me think of stoners and heavy-metal music from the 1980s. The intonation and inflection, and so forth. First time I heard him it occurred to me that there are certain ways of speaking, maybe even certain ways of moving your tongue and your voice box, that only a particular generation of humans learns how to do. I sometimes thought that my uncle had a way of talking that was preserved in amber from 1983, and even from the first time he spoke to me I thought it was amazing.

"Hey," I said. After a pause that seemed really overly long. I was imagining him with a beard. Maybe wearing a paisley bandanna. Shitty orthodontia, but not in a bad way.

"Man," he said. "Are you on dope again?"

"Kind of," I said. "I'm 'shrooming."

He was silent for a moment. Then he said: "I'm sorry to hear that." He said, "I thought you said you were going to—"

"I am," I said. "I am, I am, I am."

6

RABBIT'S MOM AND I smoked a little weed together, and then I drove her to the chemotherapy. "The infusion room" was what she called it.

This was about nine in the morning and Rabbit was still sound asleep, and Terri told me what a good person I was. "You're such a sweetie," she said. "Why don't you have a girlfriend?"

But that was not really a question, because she kept talking. She told me about the other women in the infusion room. She had nothing in common with them, she said.

There was an old widowed white lady with one of those perms that made her hair look like dandelion fluff, and she was super proud that it hadn't fallen out yet.

There was a "spiritual" one, a hippie in a big bright colored scarf over her bald head, who brought plants and little statues of the Hindu god Ganesh. *The remover of obstacles*, this woman explained to Terri.

There was one who was so thin, probably less than ninety pounds, a kind of aloof or meek black woman; the only thing Terri knew about her was that she loved the television show *Law & Order*. This woman always had the TV tuned to *Law & Order*, and kept the volume loud, and watched avidly with her skeleton eyes.

And so I pulled up in front of the Kaiser Permanente building and I hadn't said a word— Terri was talking the whole time—and I said, "Should I wait for you?"

And she put her hand on my knee and gave me one of those looks that was impossible to read. One part of my brain said that her expression was very sad, the way my mom would have looked if she had been willing to tell me that she was going to die.

And another part of my brain said that Terri was kind of weirdly, creepily, flirting with me.

And then another part of my brain said, *Wait, what if she just wants to be your friend? What if it doesn't matter that she's Rabbit's mother, that she's dying, that she has spent twenty-five years more than you on earth? What if it's just, like, you got stoned together an hour ago. You did her a favor. The two of you are pals, that's all.*

"Go on," she said.   "I don't know how long I'm going to be."

"Well," I said. "I could hang out. If you need me to."

"Aaron," she said. "You don't owe me anything. You know that, right?"

"I know," I said, and she smiled.

The smile was in this way that I hoped I'd never see again, because it wasn't a smile—it was a black hole, a magnetic field. A rush like you are in a spaceship passing, video-game style, through stars and stars and stars.

7

I STARTED TALKING to my uncle Rusty about six months ago.

This was after he was released from prison, after most of the stuff that my dad had testified at the trial was proved to have been a lie.

Also, about half a year after my mom died.   He kept his distance for a while. *I didn't want to intrude*, Rusty said. *I mean, yeah, it's a lot to deal with. I wanted to give you all some space.*

Not that it mattered. No one would talk to him: Not my father. Not my aunt Kate.

He had no one in the world. They just put him out at the prison gates, and the government didn't make reparations for what they'd done to him. They didn't even give an apology.

Basically, he got so screwed, there are no words for it. His trial had happened back during the 1980s, when the idea of "Satanic Ritual Abuse" got very popular. That's how he put it: "The idea of Satanic Ritual Abuse got very popular," he said, and it made me think of a crowd of eager fans rushing toward a stage, as if Satanic Ritual Abuse were a rock band.

I'd never heard of that term before—"Satanic Ritual Abuse." It sounded so corny that I kind of chuckled until he explained it to me, and then I started doing some Internet searches.

According to the World Wide Web, Satanic Ritual Abuse was basically an urban legend (*a moral panic*, according to Wikipedia), which the people of the 1980s started to believe was real.

Seems like a lot of people accepted it as truth—that there were hidden Satanic cults all over the country, secretly doing human sacrifices and torturing children and calling up Satan in graveyards. There was actually a news special on television—*Exposing Satan's Underground*—which you can watch on YouTube. You will not believe their hair. You will not believe how simple-minded they all are. Looking back from the future, it's kind of embarrassing how superstitious and gullible they were back then. The famous reporter named Geraldo Rivera says, "Estimates are that there are over one million Satanists in this country. The majority of them are linked in a highly organized, very secretive network. From small towns to large cities, they have attracted FBI attention to their Satanic ritual child abuse, child pornography, and grisly Satanic murders. The odds are that this is happening in your town!"

And you think, okay, that was a knee-slapper, but then you go on to read about how the whole country was mesmerized by this bullshit. So there were local police departments starting their own "cult task forces," and there were arrests and witch trials where preschoolers testified that they had seen their teachers disemboweling infants and drinking their blood, kids claiming that they'd been forced to have orgies while hooded figures watched. Psychiatrists were swamped with people who had "recovered memories" of past Satanic abuse that they'd repressed.

You travel through a K-hole of link after link after link, and the stories grow more absurd and impossible as they go along. You read that Father James LeBar, appointed chief exorcist for the archdiocese of New York by Cardinal O'Connor, spoke of an international conference of Satanists that he claimed took place in Mexico, in which the Satanists discussed plans for world domination. It was said that there was a global network of the ultra-rich, who made use of flunkies from local police departments, who had minions who were school superintendents and CIA agents and congressmen, and that women and children were ritually sacrificed, or forced into sexual slavery, and there was bathing in the blood of infants, and children were boiled alive in front of a host of Satanists, and their organs were lavishly eaten.

It seems like people must have truly believed this shit, because, as it happened, "SRA"—as the cognoscenti call it—had been a big component in Uncle Rusty's trial. They brought in the fact that Rusty loved death-metal music, and that he had drawn pentagrams on his school notebooks, and basically they made the trial about Satanicness rather than the fact that they had no real evidence.

My dad testified that he had seen Rusty sacrificing baby rabbits to Satan. Which, my uncle Rusty admits, was true. He really did kill baby rabbits. With a brick. In the middle of a pentagram that he had drawn on the floor of an old abandoned house. At the time, he thought this was hilarious. He loved trying to freak my dad out.

"It's probably not forgivable, when you do shit like that," my uncle Rusty said. And then he was silent for a long time, so that I checked my phone to make sure that we hadn't been disconnected. I cleared my throat.

"I was, like, fourteen or fifteen," Uncle Rusty said. "And your dad was about eight, I guess. And he would follow me around like a puppy dog, and I just wanted to scare him, maybe, to make him go away." And he let out a stream that was like a long, soft exhalation of breath, but emotional.   "Shit," he said. "I fucked up so bad when I was your age. I was seriously an awful person."

"Well," I said.

He knew he had a lot of amends to make, because he was abusive to my dad. And if my dad wouldn't talk to him, maybe he could pass on the amends through trying to help me? "I want to be an uncle to you," he said. "Like, a real uncle. Someone you can trust and count on."   And then he told me: "I'm not going to judge you.

Because I've been in all the dark places, and I've tried every drug there is, and I know what it's like, bro. My mom died, too."

8

WHEN YOU ARE eighteen, it is hard to look at your father.   Whatever the situation.

For example, you might wake up to his terrible coughing.   It goes on and on while he is in the shower, that rich, loamy, phlegmy sound until he gags and you hear him throw up.   And you know that he has been smoking like a chimney since your mom died, it's probably two or three packs of Marlboro Reds every day, and you think: *if he dies*

And then he'll come into your room and stand in the doorway as you fold a pillow across your head like the *typical disaffected teenager* and he's bitching that you forgot to take the garbage out last night like you promised you would. *Did you get the oil changed in your mom's car*, he wants to know; he still refers to it as "your mom's car" even though you've been driving it for almost a year.

Your Mom's Car.   Think about that. Try to wrap your mind around the supernatural and spiritual implications that the name bears down toward you. *Your Mom's Car*, holding its hands out straight, fingers curled, a zombie reaching for your neck.

And yet you'll still feel this weird pinch of tenderness toward him. It was his dream to have sons who adored him, to be the fabled Good Dad, to be sweet and kind and wise, to be your buddy in your time of need, and you feel a twinge of compassion but combined with the urge to flee, to put as much distance between the two of you as possible.

You will soon be on your way to someplace like Austin or Boulder or Seattle. Portland, Oregon, possibly? Humboldt County, California?

You'll come in and he'll be on the couch, watching TV in his underwear. He'll have an old knitted afghan across his shoulders like a shawl, smoking a cigarette openly now, drinking from a tumbler of his whiskey. Watching that one comedy series about loser hipster girls trying to make it in New York City, but his face won't have an expression until you tap on the doorframe and he'll lift his head and his eyes trace nothing across you.

Hey, you say   *Hey, he replies*

You never really thought that much about what he did for a living. Which maybe made you a shitty person, bad son, et cetera. He provided for you, but you had no idea how that happened. Food, shelter, spending money, taxes and electric bills, and all that. He worked as a psychologist, and he had what he called a "practice" and "clients" who came to speak to him about their troubles and sadnesses and addictions and so forth, but he never talked much about it because of privacy reasons, and honestly you'd never been interested enough in it to ask him.

Imagine him as a child of eight. That kind of gullible.

"At that age, they don't know the difference between reality," Uncle Rusty said. "It's so easy to fuck with them."

"Yeah," I said.   "Sure."

"Like—if you want to make them believe in God or the devil or ghosts or vampires. Whatever. It's easy to convince them."

"Yeah," I said.

"Back then—like, maybe 1981 or so—Ozzy Osbourne bit the head off a dove," Uncle Rusty said. "And then later he bit the head off a bat. I was just kind of copying him."

"I thought you said you killed the bunnies with a brick," I said.

"I did," Uncle Rusty said. "But it was the same basic idea."

The phone was quiet for so long that I took it away from my ear and looked at the screen. The call was still connected. "Uh," I said.

"Fuck!" he said. "It's hard to admit this stuff! But I promised I'd be straight with you, about everything that happened. I will never tell another lie; I will never try to screw with another person's head. That's what put me in prison, Aaron. And in a lot of ways, I deserved what I got."

I thought about this. "Well," I said.

I was the kind of person who got high at some girl's house on the night my mom died. While my mom was taking her last breath, the girl was giving me a blowjob. I had my phone turned off, even though I knew my dad was trying to find me. Calling and calling, my dad was.

"She wants to see you, buddy," my dad said in one voice message. "And you need to see her, too. You don't want to regret this."

"Well," I said now. "Well," I said to Uncle Rusty.

And I wondered what I deserved.

9

WE WERE SITTING in Rabbit's basement and he was showing me this website called Silk Road. You had to access it through an anonymous hidden server, and it was basically like Amazon.com for anything illegal you wanted. Drugs. Guns. Uranium. Human organs. He was scrolling through photographs of different kinds of heroin that was apparently for sale. He was looking for a certain Thai White #4 that he'd heard about.

"I don't get it," I said. "You'd think it would be super traceable or whatever. If you give them your credit card."

"You have to pay in Bitcoin," Rabbit said. "Which is getting expensive."

"It doesn't sound legitimate to me," I said. I took a bong hit and held it, clenching my fist to the center of my chest. "What? Do they just, like, send a baggie of heroin to a P.O. box? It seems like the DEA or the FBI or whatever would have caught them."

"Ha-ha," said Rabbit. "That's the thing. 'Cause it's the Internet. It's not a real place. You can't catch them, because they don't exist."

"That's profound," I said.

I offered him the bong, which was a tower of blown glass, fluted at the top, a little bit like a miniature bassoon. But he shook his head. He took out his kit—the beautiful syringe he'd bought, so steampunk, like something that Sherlock Holmes would have used to shoot up with in the Victorian times. I watched him flex his hand.

"Have you ever heard about the Satanic Panic of the 1980s?" I said. "Dude, you have to watch this fuckin' video—this guy, this reporter, Gerardo Ravira. It's, like, so insane it's hilarious."

"Geraldo Rivera," Rabbit said, and tilted his head back, his eyes closed, and I watched as a distant spaceman smile opened on his face. "What's hilarious about it?"

"I don't know," I said. I hadn't told Rabbit about Uncle Rusty. I hadn't told anyone, and for a second I thought about what it might be like to talk about it. To say, *I've got this uncle. He went to prison for murders he didn't commit. My dad was one of the ones who testified against him.*

"I don't know," I said. "All this corny stuff. Back in the day they thought Satanists were around every corner. There were even, like, these kind of trials. Like witch trials, you know? And little kids had all this, just, like, wacked-out testimony about being in orgies and watching human sacrifices, and I guess people thought it was a big conspiracy of Satan worshippers all over the country. It was ridiculous."

Rabbit smiled quietly. "Really?" he said. He let his head loll back, and his Adam's apple moved in the center of his throat. "So you think that all these people who had experiences with Satanic rituals, they just made it all up? They hallucinated it or something?"

"Well," I said. "I don't think there's millions of cultists out there drinking baby blood and performing human sacrifices. That's just stupid."

"Ha-ha," Rabbit said. "I have to say, I think just the opposite. I think we can't even fathom the extent of the depravity and fuckedup-ness that's out there. Me? I hear a conspiracy theory, I'm more inclined to believe it than not. You know? I think there's more bad shit going down in the world than we are privy to, not less. Just look at the darknet, Sweetroll!"

"Ff," I said. He had been talking about the darknet for a while now—he'd downloaded this browser that let him go into anonymous sites, and he claimed to have seen all sorts of horrors.

There was a site supposedly full of photos of dead naked children, for people who were both pedophiles and necrophiliacs. There was a site that claimed it would sell you living human dolls, orphan girls from some Eastern European country, who had their arms and legs amputated, their eyes blinded, their voice box removed. There was a site that said it would allow you to direct your own snuff film. A victim was tied up in some kind of bondage on live video, and you got to choose the way they would be tortured. My guess was that most of it was fake.

But Rabbit only shrugged.   I watched as he scrolled through rows and rows of artistically arranged pictures of heroin.   Amber Mexican Tar.   Sweet powdered brown sugar.   Raw #1.

"So what are you on?" said Terri.

Rabbit's mom. Mrs. Berend. Terri Berend. Early October and she was in her kitchen, wearing one of Rabbit's skullies because all of her hair had fallen out, and she looked kind of badass as she put a bowl of oatmeal down in front of me.

"Are you boys shooting up?" she said. "I've noticed that I'm missing a lot of spoons."

She took a long, considering drag from her glass pipe and held it out to me before she exhaled a fat puff of white smoke. I took the pipe gingerly and breathed a little hit. It was deadly pot, this stuff they called AK-47.

"It's not like I'm ignorant," she said. "I used to do horse with Bruce's dad. I was, like, a fucking motorcycle chick. I'm not blind, Aaron."

I didn't say anything. Her eyes were sunken so deep into her skull that it was crazy; you could actually see the edges of the bone around the sockets.   I took a bite of the oatmeal and she slid a little sugar bowl across the table toward me.

"Thanks," I said.

She considered me ruefully.

"There aren't any happy heroin stories," she said. "You know that, right?"

I kept my eyes down. Her skull goggles beamed into me as I stirred sugar into my oatmeal.

If you compared her emaciated face to my mom's emaciated face, her skeleton-ness to my mom's skeleton-ness, you would calculate that she probably had one or two months left.

"We're not, like . . . *junkies*," you hear yourself mumble. "It's not like . . ."

I WAS SITTING in *your mom's car* in the parking lot of the Kaiser Permanente building and smoking a joint when I saw a bunch of crows
over in the corner near the fence. Maybe ten or twenty of them.

They were landing and fluttering and then they were clustering
and pecking at something. Some garbage, a scatter of fast-food,
roadkill maybe. A hair extension?

And here suddenly: What do you call that feeling when you're
certain that the world is doomed? It's one of those feelings that's
physical, like low blood sugar or too much caffeine, a message from
the lizard brain. But for a moment you *know* that it's not just you.
Not just Cleveland. It's everything. We, the creatures of earth, are
really and truly fucked. "We're the last generation," Rabbit said,
even though I pointed out that a lot of people our age already have
kids themselves, so, worst-case scenario, we're really the *second to
last.*

"Okay, fucker," said Rabbit thoughtfully. "The penultimate generation, then. If you want to be a nit-prick about it."

Back in the day, Rabbit was one of the smartest kids in school.
Straight A, college track, trying-to-learn-calculus-on-his-own-in-
eighth-grade sort of dude. Then he began to see through too many
things. He cogitated all the hope out of his life, which of course is
the danger.

And then I opened my eyes. I felt the hot cherry of my cigarette
against my fingernails and I looked down and the cigarette was
nothing but a cylinder of ash and the minute I glanced at it it collapsed and fell off. It landed on the knee of my jeans. *Paphf.* Like an
eyelash or an asteroid.

And then *chunk* the car door opened and Terri got in and I glanced
at the clock on the dashboard and somehow three hours had passed.

UNCLE RUSTY LEFT the Tecumseh State Correctional Institution in Tecumseh, Nebraska, on May 4, 2012. He was given $5.30, and he had a duffel bag full of his possessions—some clothes, a few books, a few photographs. He was forty-eight years old.

He was amazed by the smell of the world. He had been breathing refiltered air for almost thirty years. Even just seeing motion—a car rushing by—was so startling!

He walked along the side of highways, down gravel roads, passing through little farm towns, sleeping in ditches and abandoned sheds. He didn't dare to hitchhike. Fifty-two miles to Lincoln.

In Lincoln, his lawyer sent him some money by Western Union— just out of the goodness of her heart; Vanessa Zuckerbrot, she was the best—and he took a bus to Chicago.

He got a job washing dishes at a restaurant, and he slept on the streets until he'd earned enough to get himself a little apartment. His lawyer helped him with the deposit.

He tried calling my dad a few times but my dad wouldn't answer.

He didn't know that my mom was dying.   He didn't have that much information about us—only what he'd been able to glean in a Google search on the Internet. And, amazingly, he had seen the Internet for the first time only recently, and of course he didn't really know how to work it.

And then Vanessa Zuckerbrot called him again and put him in touch with some people.

He started going to meetings with other *exonerees*—other non-guilty guys who had been released from prison, and that was helpful. He started to think a lot about social justice.

He told me all this in our first conversation but he did not tell me that my dad was the testimony. I didn't know that until later.

Rabbit and I were in the basement and I was listening to him geek out about the techniques for shooting up. He liked to find veins, and he'd been reading up on which ones were good and bad, and now he was complaining about how in the movies people shoot between their toes.

"Bullshit," Rabbit said. "There are just medium and small veins there, so it takes a lot of knowledge of your feet. Plus the sites fuck up fairly quickly."

Rabbit was into the great saphenous vein of his calf. I watched him roll up his pant leg and swab with a little alcohol pad and we both observed as he pulled back on the plunger until blood seeped into the barrel.

Watching cartoons on his laptop. His mom upstairs, asleep and dying. Sitting on a couch on an old Oriental rug with the coffee table and the TV and the Xbox and Rabbit's kit spread out before us, washer and dryer and baskets of unclean clothes in one corner, looming freezer in the other, full of leftovers no one would ever eat.

I didn't feel exactly paranoid. Mostly, I felt peaceful, with a little veil of sadness over it. "I know a dude who apparently puts his drugs up his ass," Rabbit said. "I guess that works as well as snorting."

"Who's that?"

"This dude. Xzavious Reinbolt."

"That's not a real name," I said.

"Word," said Rabbit. "Sometimes he goes by Amy."

I considered this. I could hear Rabbit's fish tank bubbling. "Is he, like, trans or something?" I said.

"Not that I know of," Rabbit said. "He just likes putting junk in his butt and telling people his name is Amy."

"Huh," I said.

"Actually," Rabbit said, "I think it's kind of badass."

And then Rabbit and I stared for a while at this gray thing on the wall while we were listening to old Wu Tang. The thing was kind of floating or drifting, like a shadow but with three dimensions.

. . . . . .

C
o
b
w
e
b
.

14

"HE'S GOING TO be fucked," Terri told me.

We were sitting on the couch and Rabbit wasn't home for some reason. We were watching an infomercial about how anyone can make a million dollars.

"He has no idea how much money it takes to run a household," Terri said. "And I could never afford life insurance. We're living on my disability payments as it is."

She took a long draw off her pipe and passed it to me. I thought about saying, *Terri, you're not going to die*, but then I realized that would be insulting, probably. So I just snagged her lighter from the coffee table and lit up.

"He'll be fine," I said. "He can get a job. He's not stupid."

"No one will help him," she said. "His dickhead dad is in prison. My brother married a Mormon and moved to Utah. My parents are dead. His father's parents are both evil alcoholics; he hasn't seen them since he was three. God! Aaron, you are the only one I can count on."

She started to cry a little and I sat there beside her on the couch. What are you supposed to do when a cool lady who is turning into a skeleton starts weeping next to you? I reached out and put my hand over hers. And she gripped me very hard.

"It doesn't surprise me that he's a junkie," she said. "But it makes me sad. He had me fooled for a while, you know? He *loved* school when he was a kid. *Loved* it. And he was so smart! *Bright!*—that was what his kindergarten teacher told me, and she gave me this look, this suspicious look, like how could a poor white-trash hag like me have a bright child? And I didn't believe it, either, until I saw it with my own eyes. He seemed like he *wanted* to do homework; he just loved learning, you know? In a way that never existed for me."

She laughed, lifting my hand in her tiny claw and pressing it to her heart.   There was no boob there anymore, just skin and ribs, but she had the strength to push my hand hard against her nipple, which still existed.

"By the time he was in high school," she said, "I was starting to feel like he was going to be fine. National Honor Society. Math Club. Computer Club. Friends like you, sweetie, with nice parents and big houses. I let my guard down. Maybe he could be somebody special, I thought."

She kept my hand against her chest, and I wanted to pull away but it would've required a certain kind of breaking from her grasp, which would seem rude and violent, and so I let her roll the ham of my palm against her breast like someone who is kneading bread.

"But his father's genes were too strong," she said. "As it turns out. Just about the time the testosterone kicked in, suddenly all his dad's reckless, stupid assholery? It took him over completely. He didn't even *know* his dad. But he transformed into him—almost overnight."

She pushed my hand against her and made a circling movement. I could feel the hard nub of nipple beneath my palm and I didn't say anything. With my free hand I picked up a lit cigarette from the ashtray and took a shaky drag.

"Jesus Christ, Aaron, please kiss me," she said, and it was a kind of irritable, scolding whisper.   "Give me a break," she said. "I'm never going to be kissed again before I die."

I started crying, I couldn't help it. Stupid tears ran out of my eyelids, but I did it. I put my mouth on her mouth, and it tasted of metal, and it was dry, and her hands clutched the side of my head and pulled me into her and I felt her tongue press against my teeth. *I love you*, I wanted to tell her, but all we were doing was mashing, middle school spin-the-bottle type making out, clumsy and embarrassed, licking each other's teeth.

And then I glanced up and Rabbit was standing in the doorway, watching us.

15

"I'M THINKING ABOUT leaving somewhere," I told Uncle Rusty. "There's a lot of bad influences in Cleveland, I'm starting to think. It's a shithole, you know? I think if I'd been born in a nicer place I wouldn't be such a fuckup."

"Yeah," Uncle Rusty said.   And then he was quiet like he was remembering a shithole of his own. A whole series of them.

"You know," he said at last, "there's something to be said about putting some distance between yourself and your problems."

I loved his deep, 1980s rocker baritone. It was hard to believe that he wasn't stoned. "I don't have any money, though," I said.

"Mm," Uncle Rusty said. And then we were silent. "I don't have no money, either, buddy," he said. "Or you know I'd give you some."

"I'm just trying to think," I said. "I don't know. Maybe there's a way to convince my dad that I need to move to a different state and get my own apartment or whatever. I keep thinking that if I told him the right thing, he might be convinced."

"Yeah?" Uncle Rusty said.

"I don't know," I said. I opened my baggie of H and smelled its weird odor—like a box of Band-Aids, or vitamins, or something. I thought about snorting some but I wanted to conserve. My dad was generous and oblivious, but even *he* was going to start wondering eventually, with all the money I was hitting him up for.

"Could I come live with you?" I said.

"Nah," he said. "Your dad wouldn't like that at all."

It had been a week since the kiss—since Rabbit had seen me kissing his mom, since I'd left in a hurry and pulled out of their driveway in a blind rush. I hadn't spoken to Rabbit and I was almost out of heroin, and it worried me that I put those two things in the same sentence. But I felt anxious about both things equally. When I texted him, Rabbit didn't answer. I couldn't call his house phone, because his mom might pick up.

Uncle Rusty and I were both still silent. There was a weird piece of light on the ceiling.   It kept quivering. It was, like, gelatinous.   I had no idea where it was coming from.

16

MY DAD REMINDED me that picking out a Christmas tree used to be my favorite thing when I was a kid, and he pointed out that I wasn't doing anything except sitting on the couch playing Skyrim on Xbox, *how many hours of that game have you played,* he said, *this won't even take an hour,* he said, and it was clear that he wasn't going to stop blocking my view of the screen until I spoke.

"Why don't we wait until Dennis gets home," I said.

"Dennis won't be through with his finals until the twenty-second," said Dad. "I want to have a tree up before then."

And so I rose reluctantly—I had been parceling out my heroin, trying to make it last, relying more on weed and fentanyl, which for some reason made it harder to hold my ground in an argument.   Besides which, I'd been considering how things might play out when he finally realized I dropped out of school.   "Okay," I said. "Let's go."

The tree place was a garden center just down past the high school, where we saw kids out running on the field in the falling snow—who knew what they could be thinking on a Saturday morning—and my dad recalled when Rabbit and I went out for lacrosse in ninth grade, too bad we didn't stick with it, he wished I got more exercise, and then we pulled into the garden center, where "Carol of the Bells" was blaring out of tinny speakers that had been mounted on poles. It was like the kind of music you'd play if Santa was a serial killer.

"I was thinking about Scotch pine this year," my dad said. "I really like the smell."   And I checked my phone, no one had texted me in a couple of days, kind of creepy how far out of touch I'd gotten, and he turned to look at me. "You okay?" he said, and I shrugged and we walked into a row of evergreens with their branches bound in twine and they reminded me a little of corpses.

"I heard that Rabbit's mom passed," he said, after a moment. And this was the sort of shit he liked to pull—he'd take you somewhere, like a grape arbor in a hospice, then spring some dreadful news upon you. I heard him say it and it fluttered hard in my chest for a few seconds before it settled, perching heavily inside me.

"Fuck," I whispered, and he tilted his head and eyed me—attentive now in that Psychologist way that I'd always hated.

"Have you talked to Rabbit at all?" Dad said. He'd found a trio of tightly trussed Scotch pines, and he considered them, stroking his beardlet. "I know you guys used to be close."

"Nah," I said.

I hoped that I wasn't shaking, but I felt like I might be. I didn't make eye contact when he looked at me again.

"I imagine it would be tough," he said. "Being around someone who was going through the same thing you went through. I can understand how you'd want to protect yourself from—"

"We just don't have that much in common anymore," I said. "Don't turn it into something."

"Okay," he said. Then he shut up for a while. "Carol of the Bells" finally ended, and "Santa Claus Is Coming to Town" started. *He sees you when you're sleeping*, Mariah Carey sang. *He knows when you're awake*. My dad took out a tape measure and started autopsying one of the victims.

"If you wanted to go to the funeral," he said, "you should just take the day off from school. You've been working very hard, and you can stand to miss one class. Just email your professors."

I watched as he stood the chosen tree up and turned it around slowly.   He cleared his throat.   "It might be good for Rabbit to talk to someone who's been in his," he said. "Um."

"Shoes," I said.

"It might be good for you, too," he said. "I know you're not a big believer in counseling, but what about talking to someone your own age? He's probably going to need someone, I imagine. It was just him and his mom, wasn't it? Does he have close relatives?"

"I don't know," I said. I could see the surface of my coat vibrating, or at least I imagined it was. That was how fast my skin was shaking.

"I don't know," I said. "I don't know, I don't know."

17

IN *your mom's car* in the parking lot of the church I smoked up the
nub of a blunt in Terri's honor. Not sure I could go through with it.
Get out, walk across to the front steps, open the door. I thought of
that old nursery-rhyme game my mom taught me when I was little,
the way she would knit her fingers together: *Here's the church, here's
the steeple, open the door and see all the people.*   And then you opened
your palms with the fingers still intertwined. Weird that this would
come to me now, and I sat there for a while behind the steering
wheel, folding my hands like I was praying, then turning them over,
open the door, wiggling my fingers   *see all the people.*

I was in the suit that I wore to my mom's memorial, a bit too small
for me now, and I had a tie, even, though the knot was fucked, I
couldn't figure it out and finally just wrapped it around my neck as
best I could, and I had on these shoes my dad bought me, so shiny
and polished that they seemed gaudy and pimpish, even though they
were black. Was this the way Terri would want me to dress, I wondered? And then I figured that since she was dead she probably had
better things to worry about than my ugly shoes.

I never would have guessed she'd want to have a funeral in a
church. *Seventh-day Adventist.*

It was one of the fringe ones, I thought, like Jehovah's Witnesses
or Christian Science, but I didn't know for sure what the differences
were with all of the various religions.

Maybe it was her family's religion when she was a kid? A part of
her life she never talked about? We never spoke of God, and I was
glad of that. My family didn't go to church when I was growing up,
and I was never interested, either. It all seemed so judgmental.

So I took another couple of pulls on the blunt and then I got out
and walked toward the church. TEMPLE OF PRAISE, it said over the
door.   It wasn't even a real church—just a cheaply built one-

story building, ranch-house style with brick, and it might as well have been a motel or a cheap suburban bank, except it had a little white steeple on its roof. TEMPLE OF PRAISE, SEVENTH DAY.

I was anticipating what Rabbit would do when he saw me. If he freaked out and punched me or started calling me names, it would be bad. If he ignored me—that would be worse maybe. I hesitated at the door before I opened it.

But nothing. Inside it was like you'd expect. Some pews lined up facing an altar and some stained-glass windows. Pretty empty. Maybe a dozen people up at the front. I glided into the very back pew, hunched down, turned invisible.

There was the casket. All the way at the front, just below the preacher's podium, and I watched as a lady walked up to it and peered down, her arms folded, like she was at a buffet in a Chinese restaurant where all the choices were horrific and she shuddered but kept looking. Terri's sister? She looked a little like Terri when she turned up the aisle and took her seat next to a big long-haired dude in a bandanna and white dress shirt. I couldn't see Rabbit anywhere, and so I started running my eyes along the backs of people's heads, row by row.

Rabbit was the kind of guy you notice—six foot four, two hundred fifty pounds, *hulking*, you would think if you didn't know him; he could be imposing if he needed to.   The back of his neck was like a block, with three distinct folds of fat in it like bread dough. Head the shape of a pear.

But there was no one here by that description.

I passed my eyes over the backs of their heads again, counting. Thirteen people. Rabbit not among them. Could he be late? Maybe his alarm didn't go off? Eleven was early in the morning for Rabbit, and I almost laughed. It was almost like one of those things that Rabbit and I would joke about: Sleeping through your own mom's funeral? How fucked would that be?

76

I WAS IDLING OUTSIDE of Rabbit's house with my brother, Dennis, sitting in *our mom's car*, listening to whatever new indie-rock shit he had on his iPod.   He was telling me about all his new Cornell friends, kids from Manhattan, San Francisco, Austin.

"Sounds really white," I said, and he gave me a silent once-over.   After a year and a half at college, he didn't even seem like the same person.

Meanwhile, his old best friend from high school was missing. It had been five days now since Terri's funeral, and Rabbit was nowhere to be seen. There was a light on in his house, in one of the back rooms, and the porch light shined down on the snowy unshoveled front steps and the petrified footprints the postman left as he trudged up bitterly to fill the mailbox.

"You really think he's in there?" Dennis said. "Maybe he, like, flipped out and went somewhere. Like, you know, his mom dies and he goes into a, like, fugue state or something."

I looked at him. Had he ever known Rabbit to go anywhere?   Had Rabbit ever left the state of Ohio? Had Rabbit been outside of Cleveland? Maybe, but doubtful.

"Well," Dennis said.   "Why doesn't he answer the door, then?"

I stared at the big front window. The blinds drawn. I shrugged. "We had a falling-out," I said after a while, and Dennis let this sink in.

He took up the one-hitter pipe from the dashboard and drew a long hit of weed.

"Well," he said. "We could just go around to the back and break in. It's not like he's going to call the police on us."

"Nah," I said, and our eyes met then in a way they used to when we were kids—when we were almost twins, "Irish twins," my dad called us, and we pretended we could read each other's minds.

"Oh," Dennis said finally.   "You don't want to go in because you think he

19

THINGS STARTED GETTING bad—the hallucinations and stuff—just a little bit before Christmas. I thought it would help if I made a list, but it just freaked me out more.

1. Feelings of being watched.
1a. In the bathroom, waiting to pee and hearing a voice out-side the bathroom door whispering but maybe it's your own breathing and then the sound of your piss hitting the water and the way the sound is musical in a kind of upper-key ice-breaking-apart cascade—when you are this high, ordinary body functions seem to take forever—and the whispering gets deeper and deeper from beyond the door, deeper and quieter, so maybe it's the sound of the radiator?
2. Legs aching and restless, unable to sleep, kicking at the covers, twitching. A heavy shape leans over me when I close my eyes. *Rabbit?!*
3. My dad and Dennis getting along swimmingly, laughing about stuff that doesn't make sense.   You have the ter-rible feeling that they are talking about you in some kind of code.
4. How am I going to get more heroin?
5. Actual orc—such as from Skyrim or *Lord of the Rings*—standing at the bus stop in full armor.

6. Flickering; time jumping. Objects flattening into two dimensions and pixelating.
7. My mom's voice coming from downstairs, the sound of her humming to herself.
8. Unable to form a pleasing visage.   Dad: "Why do you have that look?" Me: "What look?!" Feeling of panic.
9. Cold. Antarctica cold.   In the mirror, pallor.
10. You're *not* a heroin addict. It doesn't happen that fast. Maybe you're just a pussy. What's wrong with you? Maybe you're losing your mind? Maybe you should just snort up a little bit and calm down?

20

Voice message from Uncle Rusty, 10:00 a.m., December 25: "Hey, young dude. Thinking of you. Merry Christmas!"

Voice message from Uncle Rusty, 10:35 a.m., December 25: "We know the official story isn't true. That's all we know." Silence.
    "That's all we know." Silence.
    "Merry Christmas."

Voice message from Uncle Rusty, 10:51 a.m., December 25: "Dude, ignore that previous message. I get very emotional on the holidays and

"Never mind I don't want to bring you into this"

21

AT ELEVEN-THIRTY MY dad knocked on my door and asked if I wanted to come downstairs and open presents, and I couldn't think of a better gift than another hour's worth of sleep. But he kept standing in the doorway, and when I tried to drift off he came over and pulled the covers off me.

"I swear to God," he said. "Aaron David Tillman, I'm going to bring up some ice cubes if you're not out of bed in fifteen minutes."

So I unaffixed myself from the mattress and put on some sweats but I couldn't shake this feeling of shitty unfriendliness. There was the distribution of wrapped packages, the forced jollity, the desperation of a widower trying to make "family memories." I couldn't stand it. I was thinking like, *Oh, a book. Oh, a cheap video game. Oh, a sweater I will never wear. Thank you. May I go now?*

But I didn't say it. Even I myself was shocked by the riptide of sullenness that had me in its grip, and I did my best to mumble, *nice, cool, oh sweet*, as I pulled off the gay wrapping paper that he had pointlessly taped around some shit he bought at Target.

There's this spiral where you can't stop feeling horrible about your horrible self, and it makes you act more horrible. I was fighting it. My dad and his friend Aqil and Dennis were in the TV room, watching an anthology of Chris Farley skits from *Saturday Night Live*, all of them laughing, and there was a ham cooking in the oven, which we would be forced to feast on at some point, and I came in and stood there and pretended to watch and when something funny seemed to happen on the TV I tried to make an appropriate facial expression.

I focused on my phone. I listened to Rusty's messages, tried to call him (no answer), texted back and forth with a couple of random people, and no one mentioned that I was being a standoffish asshole, *because it's Christmas*, and we're all trying to be peaceful.

WHEN UNCLE RUSTY called again it was early afternoon and now my father and Aqil and Dennis and me were watching a DVD of *The Big Lebowski* that Aqil brought over, and for some reason the ham was showing no signs of being done.

"So," I said. "When are we going to eat?" and then before my dad could respond, my phone rang and I said, "I've got to take this," and I answered as I was walking upstairs to my room.

"Hey," I said. I closed the door, a bit surreptitious. Even after all these months, there was still a kind of illicit thrill of talking to him—the fact that my dad didn't know, the fact that Rusty never called Dennis, the fact that I was the only one, which made my heart feel strangely open.

"Are you having a good time?" Rusty said.

"No," I said. "Bored."

"What are you doing right now?" he said.

"Watching *The Big Lebowski*."

"Is that a TV show?"

"A movie," I said. "Coen brothers."

"Oh," he said. And there was this little gap of silence where I realized that he had been in prison for thirty years. He'd never heard of the Coen brothers. He'd never heard of most of the crap that took up prime real estate in my brain—music, movies, video games, memes, pop-culture factoids, all the *stuff* I'd larded my mind with, which wasn't even reality.

"So how about you?" I said. "What have you been doing?"

He sighed. "Working at a soup kitchen," he said. "Dishing up turkey and dressing from steam trays. It's a good shelter, they helped me out, so I want to . . . you know. Give back, right?"

"Yeah," I said. I settled onto my bed and held the phone to my ear, and I could see a framed photo of me and my mom from when

I was about ten and we were at Butterfly World in Florida and the two of us were posing together. "That's very cool," I said.

"I don't know," he said. And then through the phone I heard him light up a cigarette. "I was thinking about," he said, "like, your dad always liked Christmas so much?" Then he was silent for a long time. My mom stared at me, a butterfly in her hair.

"I think about him," he said. "He was always so full of, I don't know, *wonder*. Like that starry-eyed shit kids do in commercials, except for real. And that had to be pretty hard to pull off, given all the fucked-up shit that was going on all around him."

"Um," I said.

And I actually *did* know what he was talking about. That kind of hopeful excited look he'd get, which was so dopey that it activated the meanest part of you, the bully part that wanted to squash it. "Yeah," I said.

"Does he ever say anything about me?" Uncle Rusty said. "I mean, does he ever . . ." He hesitated, and there was a weird, weary sound in his voice.

". . . does he ever talk about what happened?"

"Um," I said, and I'm not really sure what he was asking me. Rusty and I have been over it about a hundred times. "I mean, like I told you, I didn't even know that . . ." I heard him clear his throat.

And then, just then, a text comes from Rabbit's phone.

23

Is this Sweetroll?

I read the text and it took me a second to calibrate.

"Sweetroll" was the nickname Rabbit gave me back in middle

school. I don't even remember its origin story—only that he and Dennis couldn't stop laughing when it first stuck. Something about me, my personality, was perfectly represented for them.

"What?" I'd said. "I don't get it." And this made them laugh even more.

"That's such a Sweetroll thing to say," Rabbit said. I knew he would never let go of it.

So now I sat looking at the little balloon on my phone and I said to Uncle Rusty: "I'll have to call you right back."

And then I stared at it some more and before I could type anything another text popped up.

> This is Rabbit's friend Amy he left his phone at my house and I don't know how to reach him so I'm calling his contact list.

> Are you his GF?

> Hey yea I am Rabs friend Aaron but not a chick tho

My heart was beating very fast. Because, I realized, yes, I maybe did think Rabbit was dead, or at least I was dead to him, and even this ghostly touch was more than I expected.

> Do you know where he is?

> No. Do you?

> When was the last time you talked to him?

IDK like a week ago?   Should we be worried?

He was mad depressed bc his mom died and some dude he thought was his friend betrayed him

Are you busy tonite? You know where House of Wills is, right? E. 55th S of Carnegie

24

VOICE MESSAGE FROM Uncle Rusty, 2:15 P.M., December 25:

"You know what? I just need to be happy. This is my second Christmas of freedom! Right? I don't want to hold on to things. I really don't."

My dad and Dennis and Aqil laughing, and I tried to smile, even though what was happening on the TV didn't seem remotely funny. My dad looked over at me *so full of wonder* and I glanced down at my phone.

I hadn't talked to Mike Mention in probably two months but I texted him:

> What's House of Wills

And then I had to wait awhile. I stared at the TV and my leg was twitching and I wondered how bad I looked. I didn't look like a junkie, I didn't think, but Aqil, I knew, was a former cop and maybe he could tell? But none of them were even looking at me until my phone made its text-arriving bloop, and I looked down immediately.

Ha-ha Crack house

Bloop!

Why? Are you going?

Bloop!

Supposed to be a great party

25

AFTERWARD, I STARTED having this weird hallucination. Things were moving in slightly slow motion, and they were fragmenting in an uncomfortable way. When someone spoke, it sounded like a clip, a sample. When I observed the images before me, it felt like I was taking snapshots with my eyes; the frame seemed to freeze for a moment.

And that horrible iPhone bloop sound seemed to have crept out of my device and into the real world.

"Are you asleep?" my dad said. (Bloop!) "You look really pale," he said. (Bloop!) "Are you feeling all right?" (Bloop!)

"Oh, I . . ." (Bloop!) "Yeah, I'm fine." (Bloop!)

And then suddenly I was sitting at the dining room table and my father was bringing the ham in on a platter and Aqil said, "There it is!" and my eyes freeze-framed.

Bloop!

Seriously, it was like my dad actually got paralyzed in the doorway for a moment, his mouth half open, his eyebrows raised the pink meat glistening with fat sweat jolly distorted like a bad illustration in a magazine a cicada flutter over my skin

26

Voice message from Uncle Rusty, 4:45 P.M., December 25:

"Maybe this is weird to say because you're his son, but . . . I don't know.

"If you found out the person who supposedly killed your family was innocent . . . Wouldn't you want to talk to them? Wouldn't you be curious? Like, if I didn't do it, who did?"

Voice message from Uncle Rusty, 4:48 P.M., December 25, 2013:

"I'm sorry, that was not cool of me to say."

Silence.

"I'm sorry. I'm kind of drunk. I shouldn't be. But this stuff can be hard, you know?" Silence.

"I thought I'd give him some time, but it's been over a year."

Dennis put his hand on my shoulder as I passed through the kitchen. "Bro," he said. "What the fuck are you tweaking on?"

THE NIGHT OF Christmas, 11:36 P.M., December 25, pull out of the shoveled driveway and you get a flutter in the stomach the way you do going downhill on a roller coaster, and then out onto the street, the homes of Scarborough Road, the dark snowy boughs against the streetlights, everything you look at has a melty quality. There's no way the tires are touching the ground.

And you're driving west into the Carnegie hospital corridor, the complex that looms around you on all sides, a massive parking lot and then a hotel full of sick people and then another hotel full of sick people and then a glass bridge that curves above you, you can see an old person being pushed in a wheelchair as you pass underneath, and this is probably near the place where Terri died.

Then there's the stretch of vacant lots and empty red-brick factories, the urban rot, and then turn left on East 55th, with the grand, abandoned, dilapidated churches on one side and, on the other, a grim public housing project called "Enterprise Village."

And then: *House of Wills.* It has been abandoned for a long time—an old funeral home, giant three-story Victorian house, and you park in the lot in the back, where there are a number of other cars—some occupied, still running, the exhaust chugging out in fluffy puffs of carbon dioxide. Some are pretty expensive-looking; there's even a Maserati convertible.

You open the door of *your mom's car.* A white girl is sitting in a Prius texting, her face fascinated, lit by the little screen.

THIS PART WAS the casket showroom. A long corridor, empty now, the walls covered in graffiti and tags and beer cans and crack pipes. But then on the ceiling was a huge, intricate crown molding that took the shape of curlicues and paisleys.   Like something out of the French palaces of Marie Antoinette, and you couldn't believe you were this crazy to be walking down such a hallway.   At the end of the corridor, people were moving through the darkness by candlelight, or maybe sitting beside little fires that they'd made from detritus.

A long strip of fucked-up carpet ran down the center of the corridor, an actual red carpet, like celebrities walked down at the Oscars, but this carpet would be for, like, the zombie Oscars, so rotten and full of unimaginable stains of food, weather, insects, bodily fluids, mold, that it made you feel filthy to put your shoes on it.

But you kept walking toward the darkened room. Exactly like the stupidest one in a horror movie, practicing your lines in your head. *Yo, hey, what up,* or maybe just a lift of the chin, and then *Hey, can you help me out with . . .* Or: *I'm looking for Amy, yo.*

And you entered the darkened cathedral-like space, which you guessed was one of the chapels where funerals were held.   You could dimly make out an altar at the front of the room, and around the nave there were little campfires going.   You glanced over and three teenaged white boys sat around a fire that was built inside an old stainless-steel mixing bowl, crouched on their haunches and their faces alit only by firelight, their eyes darkened.

And then someone said, not all that far away from you: "Hey— you're the friend of Rabbit's, right?"

29

"I RECOGNIZED YOU right away," the guy said. "I've got a little psychic ability, so they tell me." He had a kind of mellow, radio-friendly voice, this dude who was sitting in an old rotting wing chair in a crack house that used to be a funeral home. About twenty years old, muscled like a regular gym rat, and wearing a tight white T-shirt to show it off. He had long black hair and a goatee and gold ear gauges, his earlobes stretching around a three-quarter-inch hole. Very straight white teeth, which once upon a time his parents must have paid some serious money for.

"You're Aaron, right?" he said. "Hey, man, I'm Amy!"

And then something, I don't know what exactly, clicked in my brain. I remembered about that guy that Rabbit used to talk about— Xzavious Reinbolt. He stood and his hand extended and gripped mine in this odd, quick grapple, like some kind of secret handshake, and his palm was unpleasantly wet—almost, like, viscous, you could say, and when I drew back he laughed.

"Ha-ha," he said. "That's the trouble with being a vampire; my palms are gross, right?"

"Um," I said.   I was trying to remember why I thought it was a good idea to come here—like, what? Investigating Rabbit's disappearance?

No. I was here because I wanted to buy some heroin. Probably this had been in the back of my mind all along but it didn't bloom into full awareness until just this minute. I was like: *Oh.*

"Come over and sit with me!" Amy said. "I'm so glad you showed up. Everybody's really worried about Rabbit, right? Like, so much tragedy and shit. We've been doing some chants and burning incense and the whole deal, but he's vanished, right? It's very worrisome."

"Yeah," I said. And I felt a kind of clamminess as Amy draped his thick arm across my shoulder. He gave me his expensive grin.

"Rabbit is so great," he said. "I love that dude."

"Yeah," I said. "Me, too."

"I hope that you don't mind," Amy said. "I just drank a little from your aura. I can't really help it, because I'm a vampire."

"Oh," I said. What else do you say? "Well." And his arm seemed to grow tighter and heavier as it settled around my shoulders.

"The thing is," Amy said, "everybody's like so hung up on like fangs and blood and I don't even like want to go into that bullshit. Blood is just a metaphor, right? If I'm going to feed on you, I'm like dipping into your aura, I'm like draining a little of your life force into my own life force.

"See?" he said. "I just drank a little of your stuff. Did you feel it?"

I doubted very highly whether this guy even believed his own bullshit; it just seemed like a line, a performance, though at the same time his arm felt hot and heavy and my own body felt little—of a skinnier and frailer species—and, yes, I *did* cringe, and my voice was hoarse.

"Listen," I croaked. "I was hoping you might be able to hook me up."

"Of course, brother!" Amy said. And he still didn't take his arm off me. "But you didn't answer my question. I was like, do you feel me drinking your aura?"

It was the worst sensation. That arm, you can feel the prickle of forearm hair on your neck, you can feel the fingers casually blanching your biceps and a kind of vibration.

"Yeah," I said softly. "I feel it."

"Do you like it?" he asked, and I shrugged beneath his heavy arm.

"I don't know," I said. "Not really."

30

I WATCHED AS Xzavious/Amy took out his kit, and it scared me because I suddenly felt a great rush of friendliness toward him, not unlike a dog would feel toward a person opening a can of meat.

The heroin was beautiful. It could be #4, I thought, China White.

Not sure if it was really #4 or maybe just cut and fentanyl? #4 didn't have the vinegar smell, did it? Or any smell?

He had a really cool double snorter, stainless steel, which he offered to me the way a prince might offer a magical dagger to an adventurer.

"Don't worry," he said. "It's clean. I use alcohol wipes after every use, right?"

Of course, I couldn't have cared less. I inserted the snorter into my nostrils and bent over the CD jewel case he'd used to lay out the lines. "You're going to be so happy," Amy said.

And it hit so sweet. I pictured those old cartoons, when you get banged over the head and a bump rises like a hill and things whirl in a halo around your head: stars, chirping birds emitting wobbly eighth notes, waffles with butter, smiling suns wearing sunglasses.

Amy felt up my deltoid.   "It's special, right?" he said.

"Ah," I said, and then my mind disconnected from my body and joined the bluebirds and waffles in their airy circling. A French woman from the 1960s began singing "Do Re Me, Do Re Me." My dick tingled.

And when I lifted my head after the black-hole untime had begun to dissipate, I saw that he was holding something out to me.

"Rabbit's phone," he said. And we traded. I gave him back the silver snorter, and he put the thin little brick of electronics into my palm.

"I figure you'll probably see him before I do," Xzavious Reinbolt said.

31

A PERIOD OF lost time.

Snorting in your bedroom, sleeping, not even watching TV, not even listening to music.

Blank.

Blank.

Blank.

And then a text from Amy with an Internet link to a news item about Rabbit's death. Early January, maybe? One and a half paragraphs in a corner of *The Plain Dealer*.

Found under the Hope Bridge. Facedown, frozen in the ice. Only his legs sticking out.

Discovered by some people who were giving coats and blankets to the homeless.

Drowned.

PART FOUR

June 1983

THE GIRLS DID not want to go to Yellowstone. They were seventeen, it was the summer before their senior year in high school, and the last thing they wanted was to spend two weeks camping with their parents and their aunt and uncle and their younger cousin, Dustin. Kate, in particular, thought it was outrageous. Wave was more resigned.

Kate and Wave—that was what they called themselves. Katelynn and Waverna Tillman.

They were twins, and they lived in a little town on the edge of Nebraska not far from the Colorado border. Things might have turned out differently if they'd been born in a nicer place.

But this was all they had been offered. Wave woke up in the old camper trailer that was parked in the driveway outside her uncle Dave and aunt Colleen's house, and fat flies were vibrating against the windows near her head. In the bunk below, her sister let off a soft, protesting noise in her sleep, a kind of anxious animal whine that made Wave unnerved to hear it.

Wave was having a lot of uncomfortable thoughts lately.

They'd been doing bad things. Not *evil*, Wave thought. Not criminal. Just the sort of things that seemed "crazy" and "hilarious" and "punk" and then you woke up the next day feeling dirty and depressed.

Like, for example, giving a blowjob to the same guy on the same night.

Like, driving drunk and sideswiping a parked car and then just driving away. And laughing.

Like, riding on the hood of some guy's car and feeling him speed up, knowing that he was going to brake suddenly and you'd be thrown. Like this was a silly kid's game. Like nothing could ever hurt you.

Like, talking sexual things about Uncle Dave, how his ass looked in those tight cutoff jean shorts, and what would a beard feel like if he ate your pussy, and what would he be like as a lover, and could they seduce him if they wanted?

Like, playing cards with their thirteen-year-old cousin, Dustin, and doing these exaggeratedly sexy gestures. Kate opened her mouth and put her thumb on her tongue like she was licking a bit of sauce and she whispered "oooh," and then Wave scratched her calf with her bare toe, canting her shoulders and murmuring "mmm," and giving her ass a little squirm like scratching felt *really great*. And they were almost peeing themselves, watching poor Dustin silently freak.

And now Dustin was in a sleeping bag on the bunk where the kitchen table folded down into a bed, and Wave couldn't help but think *that was so fucked up*. Asleep, Dustin's face had too much child in it, and Wave turned away from him and opened the door to the camper. She sat down on the steps and took out a slender, girlish cigarette. It must have been about 7:00 A.M.

Sometimes the two of them pretended that Kate was the instigator. And Wave was the (slightly) nicer one. The conscience. Not true, really, except that Wave was the one who was more bothered on hungover mornings like these.

Using her big toe and her long toe as pincers, Wave picked up a rock from the gravel driveway and was semi-successful at tossing it, but it didn't land anywhere near where she was aiming. She ran her fingers through the tangles at the end of her ponytail, and she liked the sharp tug as the tiny knots stretched and resisted and broke apart. Took another drag of her cigarette.

When she was little, her parents told her that smoking was bad, a filthy habit; she should never smoke, they said, though *they* both did. But when she and Kate had taken it up a couple of years ago, Vicki and Lucky had not complained or scolded. It was almost like they were relieved—now they didn't have to feel judged anymore. The girls could walk up to their dad and ask to bum a cigarette and he would just hand them one without a word.

They were bad parents, Vicki and Lucky.   She'd known that, vaguely, for years now. They were not like parents on TV, or even the parents of classmates that she had seen, who were mostly normal, sweet, aging drudges.

For one thing, they partied a lot—Vicki and Lucky, Dave and Colleen. They got shit-faced drunk maybe four or five times a week, and she had recently begun to understand that such habits were not only unusual but kind of *sick*. Once she'd had a few of her own hangovers, she realized that normal people couldn't function if they got drunk nearly every night. She saw now that they were actual alcoholics.

And she had never really understood how creepy it was that Vicki and Colleen were sisters and Dave and Lucky were brothers. Wave remembered this girl in middle school; she'd thought they were friends.   "Wait," the girl said, wrinkling her nose.   "Doesn't that mean that you and Kate are sisters *and* cousins at the same time?"

"No!" Wave had said, greatly offended, and later, during lunch period, she and Kate had both walked past the girl and spit gum into her hair and then they wrote threatening notes and left them in the crack of her locker door.

But now she saw that the girl had actually been very perceptive. There *was* something perverted about it. It *was* gross and kind of incest-y.

And then there was the other thing. The thing that Rusty had told her about. He said that they were swingers. They all had sex together, the four of them. She realized now that he was bullshitting her, trying to be funny—but for a while she'd almost believed him.

She was thinking of this when Uncle Dave came out of the house. He was in his underwear—white briefs—and she gripped a rock between her toes as he trudged barefoot across the grass and planted himself in front of the lilac bush and took out his dick and peed.

From her vantage point she couldn't see his penis. But she was aware that it was there. He was close enough that she could hear the thick patter of water.

And then he looked over his shoulder and saw her sitting there, watching.

"God damn it!" he yelled. And tucked his cock back into his Jockeys in a flash.   "Wave! Shit! I'm sorry. I had to pee. You got your mother and your aunt in there, and they are occupying that bathroom like the fuckin' Soviet Army. I couldn't wait any longer."

Of the four adults, Wave thought, Uncle Dave was the most human. He was the one you would trust to tell you the truth, and probably the one who would save you if there was an emergency. He was a short man—five foot six inches, maybe?—but with a broad-shouldered, muscular body, hairy on the chest and stomach and even shoulders, with a thick beard and a ponytail, a grin that showed all his teeth. He had been in Vietnam, and then when he got back from the war he had lost the lower part of his right arm in a construction accident, and she supposed that gave him a good excuse for being honest.

He lifted his stump. He wasn't wearing his prosthetic hook, but maybe the ghost of his hand was making a gesture. He shrugged apologetically.

"Sorry you had to witness my biological functions," he said.

"No problem," Wave said.   She stubbed her cigarette against the side of the trailer. How old was he?   Late thirties? Wearing Jockey underpants like an eight-year-old—sheepish, but not overly perturbed. He scratched the back of his neck. He had decided to pretend that being caught in his skivvies was more or less normal.

"What're you doing up so early, Wave?" he called cheerfully. "I heard you kids up giggling and carrying on way past one in the morning! Thought you'd still be stuck to your pillow!"

She rolled her eyes. "Dunno," she said, and dug in her pack for another cigarette. "It's hard to sleep once the sun comes up."

"If you say so." Uncle Dave grinned.

And Wave watched as he turned and ambled back into the house.

"I'd probably fuck him," Kate had said once. "He has a hot ass." And Wave had made a grossed-out face.

But now, with Uncle Dave's back to her, Wave considered the ass. It *was* hot, actually.

Not that they would ever do anything. Not really.

At some point, not that long ago, Kate and Wave had discovered that it was fun to think really dirty thoughts and say the filthiest things that came into their heads. They took turns trying to shock each other.

And, yes, they were a little wild, but not in the kind of way that would screw up their future. They weren't going to get pregnant and marry some oaf who wanted to stay in St. Bonaventure his whole life. They weren't going to get arrested, or have a drug overdose, and they would graduate in the top ten percent of their class, enough to get them into a decent state college.

But their mother had a low opinion of them. There was the scrape on the side of the car that they had been driving drunk, for example. There was the discovery of condoms in their purses. Also that they didn't tell her that they'd stopped working at the movie theater after a week; they let her believe that they were working from seven to midnight when in fact they were partying.

For these crimes and others, they were sentenced to go to Yellowstone.

For a while, they tried to fight their way out of it.

"We're not going," Kate had screamed. "That's final." And their

99

mom, who Kate now called "Vicki," had folded her fat, wobbly arms and made a face that she thought was sarcasm.

"After these past months, you think I'd leave the two of you home alone for two weeks?"

"But we're not going," Kate said. "You can't make us."

There were going to be so many parties this summer. They were going to have the time of their lives. Rusty was one of the best drug dealers in town, and they had a personal connection to him. He could get pot, uppers, downers, cocaine, mescaline, even possibly angel dust.

Plus, if they had the house to themselves for two weeks, it would be like owning a nightclub. Everyone would come.

"You wouldn't sass your dad like that," Vicki was saying now. "Why don't you say that to him? Go tell him, *Can't make me*, and see how far that gets you."

Kate gave Vicki a killing look. But whenever Vicki tried to stare her down, Kate broke eye contact and made a bored face, which was a way she could stab Vicki repeatedly.

"I wouldn't leave you girls alone in this house for a million dollars," Vicki said.

"You can't make us," Kate said. "We'll hitchhike back home when you stop at a rest area."

"Try it," Vicki said. "I'll call the police and have you both registered as runaways."

Kate snorted. "I don't know why you don't ever trust us," she grumbled. "I'm so sick of being watched every minute with a fine-tooth comb."

And Vicki waved her hand and blew a dismissive plume of smoke from her cigarette and left the kitchen in a triumphant huff.

"I hope she gets cancer," said Kate under her breath, which shocked Wave a little, though she kept her face neutral.

Still, it was clear that they were not going to resist anymore. They had only two days before they left for Yellowstone.

Wave had been sitting outside the trailer for a little over an hour, drinking halfheartedly from a can of Tab soda, staring down the long dirt road that led toward the highway. *Why are we even here?* Kate kept asking. *Just to keep us prisoner?*

It was a weird arrangement. Kate and Wave and their family lived in town—in St. Bonaventure—while Rusty and Dustin and Uncle Dave and Aunt Colleen lived in an old farmhouse about ten miles out in the country.   It had been decided that they'd spend the weekend at Uncle Dave's house before they left.   Vicki and Lucky would occupy Dustin's bedroom, and Dustin, Wave, and Kate would stay in the camper. Rusty had his own room, which wasn't up for discussion.

"It's moronic," Kate said. "But I can tell you exactly the reason. It's so they can party more before we have to descend into camping. Lucky and Vicki just don't want to have to drive back to St. Bonaventure when they're juiced." She shrugged grimly. "It doesn't matter," she said. "The summer's ruined anyways. But Rusty said he's going to hang out with us on Saturday night, so . . . at least we'll have some decent pot to take with us."

Of course, Rusty wasn't going to Yellowstone. He had graduated from high school the year before, and now he worked as a truck driver for the 7Up bottling plant and couldn't get time off.

"That's the life of a working man!" Uncle Dave had said.   "You have to wait till you get your arm chopped off before you can take a vacation."

This was on the first morning of the sleepover, and they'd been in the kitchen eating breakfast.   They watched as Uncle Dave lifted his prosthetic hand and did a little hip wiggle that made Kate raise her eyebrows with exaggerated alarm.   It was an expression that Kate wanted Rusty to see, but Rusty didn't lift his head from the cereal he was rapidly spooning into his mouth. He made his distinctive laugh. "Fuh-huh-huh," he said, as if he'd started to say *Fuck!* and then it dissolved into sheepish, dumb-boy chuckles.

"Just stick your hand into something sharp," Uncle Dave said. "I'll bet you 7Up will give you a better settlement than Johnson Controls gave me."

"Fuh-huh-huh," Rusty said. He gave his mouth a quick wipe with the back of his knuckles and lifted his eyes for a brief moment, first to Wave, then to Kate. They both saw his sharp dog-brown eyes glint with hilarity.

"I'll take that under advisement, Dad," Rusty said, and slid his chair back from the table. That grin: sunny and yet vaguely malevolent.

Later, she would remember these moments so vividly. The days before the murders: The way the flies on the camper windowpane woke her up.   Uncle Dave peeing in the lilac bush.

The sound of Kate getting out of bed, the transistor radio turned on: David Bowie, "Let's Dance."

Those last two days, when she still called herself "Wave," when she still had ideas about possibly going to college, becoming a talent agent, possibly someday getting married, having children, even, after she was done with her wild times.

She would remember thinking those things, and later, at forty-seven, she'd cringe to think what her old self would think of her. How had she turned into a middle-aged hippie woman? She'd never even liked hippies, but here she was. She wore homemade smocks and mostly went barefoot, and her hair had been in a long braid down her back until she decided to cut it so short that people thought she was getting chemotherapy. She ground her own flour and raised goats and made cheese from their milk. She had never owned a cell phone or had an email address and had only glanced a few times at the Internet, when she stopped at the library on her weekly trips to town. Like most people she associated with, she was afraid of the government, and she imagined that they might be watching.

Still, it was not a terrible life. She had made a place for herself in the world, and though it might not have been what the teenaged Wave would have wanted or expected, she had done her best. If she could send a message back in time, that would be all she would say.

I did my best. Sorry.

Both Wave and Kate had fucked Rusty.   Kate did it first. Then Wave—twice. Then Kate again, three times.   It was not a big deal, they decided.   It was just something they were experimenting with, and it was especially fun to talk about it, to compare notes.

For example, he liked to have his long hair pulled. He would put his head down and tent his hair over their faces and say, "Yank my hair."   And then he'd say, "Harder. Harder!" Until they were afraid they'd come back with a handful of scalp!

For example, he was uncircumcised, which neither of them had ever seen. Wave thought it had a strange smell that she didn't like.   Kate said she thought it was interesting.   *Kinky*, she said.

Once, with Kate, Rusty had started crying, and he pushed his face against her stomach and rubbed his nose into her belly button, and she couldn't believe how warm the tears were when they hit her skin, *almost hot*, she said.   He had started to tell her about his mom, and then about the foster family he had when he was a kid and how they all died in a fire, but Kate told him that she didn't want to talk about anything depressing after she'd had sex.

"I do think he's evil, though," Kate said. "He gave me a hickey that won't go away. It's like a scar."

"That's not a hickey," Wave said impatiently.

And anyway it had all ended almost two months ago. They had, all three of them, decided that it would be better to go back to being cousins or whatever they were, and there wasn't any discussion about it, it just happened, and Kate and Wave both thought that this was the best way possible for it to be concluded. Though they also both agreed that he was really good in bed.

Still, they thought about it, a little.   Like that morning, they both sat in lawn chairs drinking Tab and listening to the radio, and Rusty had coaxed Dustin into playing Frisbee.   Rusty was a really good Frisbee player, and Dustin was an uncoordinated and easily frustrated thirteen-year-old, so it was not much of a game.

But it was fun to watch Rusty's legs—the calves were thick and you could see the sinews go taut when he jumped, and his bare feet had a weirdly knotty, prehensile quality, like an ape's feet, and that seemed weirdly hot.

And then Dustin missed catching the Frisbee and it hit him in the face and he got a nosebleed, and he was embarrassed and angry, and Rusty said, "I didn't do it on purpose!" and "I hope you're not going to run and tattle on me. Don't be a baby!"

So then they had to get out the first-aid kit and find a towel to stanch Dustin's nose and Rusty went off somewhere. Kate put ice in a dish towel and pressed it to Dustin's face. She gave Wave a significant look.

As twins, they used to have fantasies about having psychic powers. Could they read each other's minds?   Were they exquisitely empathetic toward one another's moods?   Would they know, even if separated by great distances, if the other had died?

So far, the evidence suggested: probably not. But Wave caught Kate's look as they bent over the wounded Dustin, and their eyes met, and Kate mouthed silently:

Rusty has mescaline

And Wave understood her perfectly.

Years later, when Wave was trying to make a living doing palmistry and tarot readings on the streets of Portland, she would occasionally have actual psychic glimmers. Just enough to make her feel like she wasn't a complete fraud.

She was eighteen when she moved to Portland, and the truth was she had been having some trouble distinguishing one reality from another.   Her old life rippled like a mirage in the distance.

Sometimes, she blamed this confusion on the trial.   Kate and Dustin had said things—had recounted things—that she didn't think were true.   The authorities had questioned the three of them for many hours over the course of several days. There was a social worker and two policemen, and when they told her what Kate and Dustin had claimed, she said, *no, of course not, that's ridiculous!*

And they seemed displeased. They wondered if maybe she had blocked it out.   "That's very common in traumatic situations," the social worker said. "The mind will create a buffer. But if you concentrate, you may discover some memories—maybe just fractured images—that you didn't know were there before."

"Waverna," said one of the policemen ruefully. He cleared his throat.   "Did you ever have sexual intercourse with Russell?"

"No!" Wave said, and she felt her face flush.   "How disgusting!"

Of course, it wasn't just the interrogations. It was the news reports, it was that photograph that was reprinted everywhere, it was the interview on TV that she had refused to be a part of.

After Rusty was sentenced, she remembered, they had lived with Grandma Brody for a while, but her mind must have created some sort of buffer, because to this day she couldn't recall how she'd managed to arrive in Portland. Hitchhiking was involved, she remembered, but she couldn't picture any of the people she rode with.

Then she was living on the streets. Sleeping sometimes in abandoned squatter houses, or in parks under bridges.

And then there were the times when she would set up her blanket along the streets where there were bars and some drunk would hold his palm out to her and she'd run her fingertips along the seams of his hand and a jolt would go through her.   Like you got when you hit your funnybone.

There was this one old guy she remembered. So awfully sad, she felt it. As soon as she touched him she saw that he would die before the year was out. She saw that he had no future, that nothing more would happen to him except drinking and loneliness, and that no one except her would feel him passing.

"What is it?" he'd mumbled blearily. He'd given her a ten-dollar bill, and he grinned because she was touching him so gently.

"Nothing," she said. She hesitated.

"I think you'll be lucky in love," she said. And she knew that he would give her more money if she kissed him.

And then she saw that the man looked exactly like Uncle Dave.   Uncle Dave, alive again, sixty-four years old.

Uncle Dave sat back in the lawn chair and spread his knees wide the way men did—*like they're ready for a blowjob*, was how Kate put it— and he gave his cigarette a couple of little flicks.   Wave sipped her Tab.

"I don't know," Uncle Dave was saying.   "My dad? Lived until sixty-four. And back then that wasn't considered a short life span."

Wave watched as he ground his bare toes into the grass ruminatively. "Sixty-four seems like enough, I guess," he said. "If you live it right."

She had been sitting in the sun outside of the camper, reading, and he'd ambled over and flopped down in the chair next to her. It was early afternoon, but he was already flushed and cheerful with alcohol. She could smell the beer emanating off him.

She wasn't sure what had prompted this musing on mortality, but she hadn't been paying close attention.

"How old are you?" Wave said after a moment, and he looked at her wistfully. "Thirty-six," he said. "Oof."

"I'll bet you'll change your mind when you get closer to sixty," Wave said.

"Ah, you're right." He smiled, and she watched as he thoughtfully crushed his beer can.

"I can read your cards for you if you want," Wave said. She had been interested in tarot cards for almost a year by that time, carrying them around with her wrapped in a scarf that had belonged to her grandmother. Uncle Dave's mother. She had gotten to the point where, when she turned a card over, a little movement could be felt in the back of her mind.

"Mf," said Uncle Dave. "You kids and your hoodoo shit. You know, when Rusty was in high school we had to go in and talk to a counselor about him drawing them pentagrams all over the place. He just about got kicked out of school. And I said to him, what's the point of it? You know it's not real."

"I know," she said agreeably.   "It's just for fun."

"It's always just for fun," Uncle Dave said. "Until it ends in tears." But he didn't say it with any degree of seriousness. He was so much nicer than her own dad.

Wave knew the basic facts of Uncle Dave's biography. She knew that he was her father's younger brother by three years; that they had grown up on a farm in Iowa; that he had always been the little one, the wiggly one, and while her dad was tall and rangy, Uncle Dave was compact and muscular as a gymnast. She knew that their father had died when they were young and that Uncle Dave had become a troublemaker as he got into high school. He had been sent to a juvenile-detention place because he had nearly killed another boy when they were fighting.

She knew that he had been to Vietnam, that he had been sent there when he was nineteen and he had fought in battles, and she knew that her aunt Colleen, who was her mother's younger sister, had begun to write him letters and they fell in love.

The pasts that adults carried with them had a kind of blurry, swimmy quality, Wave thought. Maybe this was because it was impossible to imagine so much time passing—as a teenager, you knew the difference between thirty-six and sixty-four intellectually, but at the same time you didn't really have any concept of how it might feel to live that long. And maybe it was because the past itself seemed so ridiculous, so stupid in its innocence. She had seen pictures of Colleen and Vicki in their embarrassing 1968 hair. You couldn't help but feel that they were idiots for wanting to look like that. You felt a little sorry for them: all the stuff that was going to happen, that they were ignorant of.

And so she watched as Uncle Dave rose and trudged toward the house, where her mom and Aunt Colleen were bickering. No one knew that all of them would be dead before the weekend was over.

Once, when she was in her late twenties, Wave got a postcard from Kate. *What happened to us?* it said. She imagined that this was supposed to make her feel guilty, that it was a call for reconciliation of some superficial sort, but maybe it was a legitimate question.

What happened to us?

It was a question that interested her. Most people seemed to believe that they were experts of their own life story. They had a set of memories that they strung like beads, and this necklace told a sensible tale. But she suspected that most of these stories would fall apart under strict examination—that, in fact, we were only peeping through a keyhole of our lives, and the majority of the truth, the reality of what happened to us, was hidden. Memories were no more solid than dreams.

Her friend Riordan had once tried to convince her that something was wrong with her. *"Losing time,"* he said, and held out his pipe. "That, to me, is a sign of a serious illness. You mean blackouts? Because . . ."

They were sitting under a bridge and there was a slow, chilly Portland drizzle falling. "Not at all," she said. "I don't think *anybody* really remembers the truth of what happened to them. They just remember the pieces that fit together logically."

What happened to us? She drew smoke, considering the question. Was it possible that we would never really know? What if we were not, actually, the curators of our own lives?

For example, she *thought* that she remembered that night, completely vividly. *That night:* the night before the murders. Their parents and their aunt and uncle were partying again, and Dustin was in the trailer, reading, sulking about his swollen nose, and suddenly Rusty and his friend Trent showed up in Trent's car. Kate and Wave were sitting in lawn chairs, smoking, and Rusty called out to them from the car.

"Hey, foxy ladies! You want to go to a party?" And they got into the backseat without bothering to tell anyone they were going.

But it wasn't a party, not exactly. Not what they expected. It was a trailer house, in the part of town that Wave considered shady, and the only other person there was a girl who couldn't have been more than twelve or thirteen, though she was wearing a halter top made of some kind of silver metallic material and smoked cigarettes as if she'd been doing it for some time. She said her name was Montgomery, and she took Wave's hand like they were girlhood friends.

"Come on," she said. "You can help me prepare the peyote buttons!"

Montgomery opened a plastic container and there were the buttons: round, fleshy dried chips that had once been a part of a cactus, wrinkled like disgruntled babies.

They had to break them apart very carefully, Montgomery said, to remove the seeds.

It appeared that this was women's work. Montgomery and Kate and Wave sat at the kitchen table, while Rusty and Trent looked through the record collection and argued about what songs to play.

Meanwhile, they put the peyote into a pot with some water to make a soup. They stirred it and Montgomery talked about her interest in becoming a veterinarian. "I want to help animals," Montgomery told them. "I feel like I was put on this earth to help God's creatures." They watched as she stirred the boiling peyote with a wooden spoon. "Okay," said Montgomery, and she lifted the spoon and blew on it a few times and then held it out toward Wave's mouth.

"Taste it," she said.

For a while, it didn't seem like it was going to hit. The bitterness touched all corners of their mouths and tongues, and it lasted, and the task was to keep it down. "I think I want to go home," Wave said. "I really just want to puke and go to bed."

But Montgomery put her small freckled hand gently on Wave's forearm. "Just wait a couple more minutes," Montgomery said. "Don't get uptight."

In the next room, Kate and Rusty and Trent were involved in a conversation about a book that Kate had read, which was supposedly a true account of a five-year-old girl who had been abused by a cult of devil worshippers, *tortured, imprisoned, and used most evilly as an instrument to raise Satan himself*, according to the book's back cover. *Michelle Remembers*, the book was called, and Kate was fascinated by it. *A troubled young woman begins to visit a gentle, compassionate psychiatrist, and finally the long-buried memory of a childhood agony comes screaming forth with terrifying clarity*. Kate liked to wonder if she herself might have repressed memories, too.

"That book is such bullshit," Rusty said. "That chick doesn't know anything about Satan."

"Like you're an expert," Kate said.   And despite the complaints she had made about Rusty giving her hickey scars, she was sitting very close to him, practically on his lap, Wave thought.

"I know enough," Rusty said. "I can smell lies when I see them."

"They couldn't publish it if it wasn't true," Kate said. And Wave watched as Kate did her thing of leaning her head against Rusty's arm as if by accident.   "There are laws," Kate said.

Meanwhile, Montgomery lit a cigarette and looked at Wave, considering. "Are you feeling okay?" Montgomery murmured.

"I don't know," Wave said. "You've done this before?"

"All the time," Montgomery said. "It's not unhealthy or anything. Peyote is a plant of the earth; it's all natural."

"Is that guy Trent your brother?" Wave said, and Montgomery scoffed.

"Not hardly," Montgomery said. "I'm running a Dungeons and Dragons game, and Trent and Rusty are players, and I'm the Dungeon Master. I don't hang out with them much otherwise."

Wave tried to take this information in. But abruptly she felt the first golden-brown glimmer of the peyote, and her brain began to flex. Suddenly, her peripheral vision came into view, much more sharply than her frontal vision.

"You want to see what a real Satanic ritual looks like?" Rusty said. "I can show you."

At this Montgomery looked at Wave and raised her eyebrows skeptically.

"He doesn't know anything about the dark arts," Montgomery said. "He's such an idiot."

In a lifetime, maybe there is only one true experience of bliss, and maybe this was Wave's. The peyote came forward in a surge and she heard herself say, "Oh!"—the way an actress would portray a sudden realization.   "Oh," she said, and then she wasn't altogether in her body.

She was aware that this trip to Yellowstone was going to be so awesome, that they would all grow closer and reveal beautiful human things about themselves, and they would never forget it. Kate would start acting more like the funny, goofy sister she once knew, and they'd have to have one big argument, but it would cure things; and Dustin would have a moment of surprising bravery and heroism; and from underneath Wave's mom's goody-goody exterior would emerge her true neurotic and controlling self, and Aunt Colleen would confront her, and Vicki would realize how awful she was and run out into the night, sobbing.

And there would be a moment when she and Uncle Dave were alone together and she'd gently touch the stump where his arm was amputated, the soft, smooth-scarred skin, the healed mound that seemed like the body part of something otherworldly, and he'd be moved by the tenderness of her fingers and lean down and kiss her, and then he'd pull away and so sadly tell her that this could never be, and she'd understand and nod gravely and a single tear would fall silently down her cheek.

And her dad was the one who'd die at the end, tragically. He'd be the actor that nobody really cared about but then when he died they'd feel bad that they didn't care.

She looked up and Trent had his arm around Montgomery, though he must've been over six feet and she could hardly be five, though she couldn't weigh much more than her clothes.

This idea made her start laughing silently to herself. She looked around the room. Where was Kate?   She wanted to tell Kate— *Montgomery couldn't weigh much more than her clothes.*

Kate and Rusty weren't in the room, and she thought—oh. Didn't they agree that they weren't going to do that any- more?   Kate was more and more keeping secrets from her, Wave thought, but then maybe it didn't matter. She went back to the dream of the Yellowstone trip. There would be the confrontation, and then the release, and they would hug and cry, and then closure.

The sensation that she will never forget: The way a car feels when it begins to go down a hill, the way you tilt along with it, and *down* is something your body feels. The descent will last for the rest of your life.

They *did* go out to the graveyard, just like Kate and Dustin later claimed. As Wave remembered it, they rode in Trent's old tank of a

Buick, a green GS 400. Trent and Rusty were in the front. Kate and Montgomery and Wave were in the back. Dustin was not with them—how could he possibly have been with them?—though later he testified under oath that he was.

The cemetery was notable in particular because of the number of trees. In this part of Nebraska, in the high rocky prairie, trees were an extravagance. They were planted in yards, frugally, but they were only immigrants.   Outside of town for miles upon miles were treeless hills and hard sod.

Still, this cemetery could be said to be an actual grove. Not quite a *woods*—yet enough to feel keenly what she had been missing for her whole life. Forests. Seas and Oceans.

Without trees I will never experience true oneness, she thought. Rusty handed her a Coors and she took it gravely. They walked among the headstones, and the trees bent their boughs over them, the shadows of leaves trembling in the wind.

He looked at her and winked.

Then he showed her the backpack he was carrying. He lifted up the flap. Inside was a cheap plastic baby doll, about the same size as an actual infant.

"Sacrifice," said Rusty confidentially.

The "Satanic ritual" was pretty sophomoric, as Wave remembered, because both Rusty and Trent were fairly well wasted at the time.   They had found a gravestone that Rusty claimed was his mother's, and they drew a pentagram in the dirt and placed candles at the five points and then finally the baby doll in the center of the pentagram.

Montgomery said, "They're not even doing it right."

"Mm," Wave said. She was watching the trees as they were moving and gesturing. The trees were able to manipulate their leaves and the shadows of their leaves to make shapes so they could communicate with her. She watched as Uncle Dave came out of the bushes in his underwear and started dancing. It appeared that he was only about a foot high, and he was really adorable. She smiled at him fondly.

Later, Kate would "recover" the memory that she had wakened from a kind of trance, and that she was naked and spread-eagled on a pentagram in a graveyard, and that she was clutching a bloody naked doll in her arms.   A crucifix had been put into her vagina. Later, Dustin "remembered" being sexually molested by Rusty and Trent and a group of hooded figures, who also beheaded baby rabbits and made him drink their blood.

Later, no one except Wave remembered that Montgomery had been there. Montgomery—or whatever her name might have been—was never questioned, was never called to testify, and Wave had no idea where she even lived.

Had she just imagined Montgomery? Was *she*—*Wave*—the one who didn't remember things correctly? Was it possible that she blacked out? Riordan didn't think so.

"Jesus," he said. "If there was a bunch of robed motherfuckers making me drink baby rabbit blood and putting a crucifix into my sister's twat, I really do think I'd remember. That's like . . . people really, like, accepted that as testimony?"

And then they grew quiet.

God! She remembers being so happy.

Even now, it seems that they were all having a good time. Rusty brought out his boom box and played Black Sabbath, and he and Kate danced around to "Sweet Leaf." And Wave sat there watching and laughing, and various figures moved inside the trees, the dancing Uncle Dave emerged, then some long-fingered shadows, and Rusty stumbled around trying to read from one of his Satanism books while Trent and Kate laid the doll on the pentagram and poured ketchup on it.

"*I conjure thee, O Guland, in the name of Satan, in the name of Beelzebub, in the name of Astaroth, and in the name of all other spirits, to make haste and appear before me. Come, then, in the name of Satan and in the names of all other demons. Come to me, I command thee,"* Rusty yelled, stumbling and shouting up toward the sky—but he kept losing his place and dropping the book and finally he got caught up in another song and started dancing again.

And then Kate joined him. "Please, O Guland, in the name of Satan, don't make us go to Yellowstone!" she said, and laughed wildly.

And then they were all dancing in a circle underneath a thing of trees and passing around a bottle of Jim Beam, and it was only for fun, they were just being crazy, it was just being young and alive and stupid. It didn't mean anything.

That's all that happened.   She's sure of it.

PART FIVE

2012

I WAS TRULY happy.   I will always believe that.

I was settled into a normal life.   Married. Children. Owned a home.

I believed I was good at what I did. I helped people deal with dysfunctional thought patterns, catastrophizing anxiety, panic cycles, obsessive–compulsive issues, addiction, body dysmorphia, unhelpful thinking styles of all types. Trying to make a small difference.

But I doubted that I could do anything for Aqil Ozorowski. There was a pathology there that was beyond what I

There was a *potential* pathology—disturbance?—that was beyond what I felt comfortable trying to diagnose. Paranoia? Obsession? He gave me these folders—*dossiers*, he called them—about the boys who died. In each there was a picture of the corpse, an autopsy report, and then occasionally a few printouts from their Facebook page and their obituaries, and Aqil's eyes were alight with excitement.

I cleared my throat.

"Okay," I said, "Yeah, sure, this is"

Let's say that I was happy, but there were personal issues pressing upon me.

My wife was seriously ill.

I'd recently heard some disturbing news regarding my

What to call him? My foster brother? My adoptive brother?

That he'd been released from prison.

And there were many things about that which I hadn't thought about, which hadn't crossed my mind, in many years.   Which I didn't care to revisit.

It was during this period that Aqil Ozorowski wanted to talk about a serial killer.

"Just listen to me," he said, and grinned in a way that showed both his top and bottom teeth. "Why not? Maybe it'll make you curious, right?" He had a quick, aggressively friendly demeanor, as though he'd gone through some sort of rigorous sales training at one point in his life and had learned to make eye contact and hold it. He had enormous dark brown eyes, like a fawn in cartoons.

"I was a good cop," Aqil said. "I was on my way, I was going to do homicide, I was going to be a detective. And then I got fucked over."

He had been placed on leave from the force, for reasons that he refused to discuss—psychological reasons, I assumed, though that wasn't confirmed, either. "Look," he said, and gave me his grin. "It's not what I'm hiring you to talk about. I've got to separate my realities, you know what I mean? I've got a court-appointed one of you guys and I have to talk to him once a week about my policing issues. So when I'm with you, I don't want to talk about my policing issues, right? I want to talk about my dossiers! Did you read them?"

"Well," I said.

I didn't know why he would approach me with this . . . information.

At first, he said he wanted smoking cessation therapy, which was one of my areas of specialization, and that seemed reasonable. Then he said he wanted help with relaxation techniques. He had insomnia, he said. Then he said he just needed someone to talk to. "Someone who isn't part of the system," he said.

"What do you mean by 'system'?" I said.

"You know," he said.

To be honest, most of the work that I had been doing recently was a bit colorless. I taught people breathing techniques and talked to them about the difference between helpful and unhelpful rumination; I had them fill out behavioral activation worksheets when they were too depressed to pay their bills; I tried to guide them through the various woes that we face, the shame and self-blame, the inexplicable sense of loss or dread, the ordinary sorrows for which there is no true cure.

But I didn't get many like Aqil Ozorowski—who was, for lack of a better word, *interesting.*   I have to admit that a part of me was grateful to him for bringing me this mystery—this "case," as he called it, as if we were going to be Sherlock Holmes and Dr. Watson together.

The deaths—the "killings"—had become a kind of urban legend. Aqil was not alone in imagining that there was some kind of pattern in these apparent accidents. There were websites devoted to various theories, and conspiracists had tried to christen the murderer with a nickname: "Jack the Dipper," "Jack the Drowner," or—popular among college students—"Jack Daniels," since apparently the killer would single out young college men who did shots of whiskey at a bar. There was even a hashtag on Twitter: #JackDanielsKiller.

"It seems silly, doesn't it?" Aqil said. "That's what's brilliant. You just can't take it seriously. A drunk frat boy can drown in a river and people are kind of a little amused. They say, 'There's a killer, all right! And his name is Darwin!' and everybody chuckles."

Investigations had been made, of course. The police had judged these cases "Death by Misadventure," or "Auto-assassination"—by which they meant that the victims had been so reckless that an ordinary, sensible person would expect to die as a result of their actions. He showed me a newspaper clipping:

"I think there's definitely a serial killer on these college campuses," said Police Chief Wilkinson. "And its name is 'Binge Drinking.'

These are students who drink alcohol very quickly, without a lot of forethought. The inebriates become separated from their cohorts. They encounter a river or waterway. And they drown. I am sorry to say that there is nothing to indicate anything other than a very tragic and preventable demise for these young men."

"It makes sense, right?" Aqil said. "He doesn't sound unreasonable, does he? And none of these deaths has ever—*ever*—been considered a criminal case."

"Well," I said. "It *does* seem like the logical explanation. Even with your thing with the dates. It seems to me that even if you have someone who drowned on October tenth, 2010, we could also probably find a similar sort of drowning on October eleventh, or October ninth. People can find patterns in all kinds of random events. It's called apophenia. It's the tendency we humans have to find meaning in disconnected information. For example, some people believe in what's called the 'twenty-three enigma.' That everything is related to the number twenty-three. It's a surprisingly involved belief."

"Ha-ha." Aqil grinned. "That's a movie, isn't it? With what's his name? Ace Ventura? But you're right. You're absolutely right. Just until you shift your oculus a little bit."

And I watched as he performed this "shift of vision," turning his chair away from me, toward the window. He looked down silently at the cars moving along Cedar Road.

"Imagine for one second if this was a bunch of drowned sorority girls," Aqil said. "People would be losing their minds over it. The thing that's interesting to me about this is that nobody thinks of white guys as vulnerable. We don't think of *ourselves* as vulnerable. And that makes it so easy, doesn't it?"

Ourselves.

It was a big breakthrough in some ways, because up until that moment I wasn't entirely sure what race Aqil identified himself as. He appeared to be a white person, but he was ambiguously complexioned, and it always felt too uncomfortable to ask him directly.

He refused to talk about his family.   "Estranged" was how he described it, which was an oddly formal term for Aqil—a word he would have mocked me for using.

Estranged.   Were his parents dead or alive? I didn't know. Did he have brothers or sisters? "Not that I'm aware of," he said.

I *did* know that he grew up in Cleveland. Once, I was driving down East 55th toward the interstate, and I passed by the place where he claimed to have grown up—a clutch of low-income-housing apartments. "Enterprise Village," he'd said. "How fucked up is that? Maybe they should call it 'Pull Yourself Up By Your Own Bootstraps' Village, right?"

I didn't say anything. It seemed as if the residents would be primarily African American, but it felt awkward to bring this up.

Once I had commented that he had an unusual name, and he'd given me a suspicious look. "Ozorowski?" he said. "It's a common Polack name. People think it sounds funny because it has 'Oz' in it, but I swear to God if you ever call me the Wizard of Oz, I will kill you."

"Well," I said. "I meant that . . . 'Aqil' is a name that I don't really see very often."

"Really?" he said. "There were, like, three Aqils in my high school. All different spellings, but still. I don't think it's that uncommon for people my age."

I nodded. I kept my face mildly quizzical. "So," I said at last. "Was there a story behind why your parents decided to call you . . ."

"Pff," he said. "Who knows?"

I'd heard about his former colleagues in detail. There were the ones who he knew were his enemies, and then there were the ones who he thought were his friends but who betrayed him. Karen, Spark, Davis, Constantine. I'd heard stories about them all; he'd painted scenes so well that I felt as if I could picture their faces: Karen, in the late-night McDonald's, confiding in Aqil about her abusive teenaged son; Spark—this pale red-haired kid, no more than twenty—playing basketball with the teens in a poverty-stricken precinct, using awkward slang, trying to get people together for a "community policing seminar." Davis, tackling the psychotic woman and tasing her, and then afterward weeping in the police car. Poor Constantine, with his weight-lifting addiction that never seemed to cure the high blood pressure and low blood sugar, and then the lymphoma diagnosis.

But when I'd ask him directly about the medical leave, he'd shake his head vaguely. "I don't really know," he'd say. Or: "I think I had been too outspoken on a couple of occasions." Or: "Some people thought there were irregularities in the way I interrogated suspects." Or: "I rubbed the wrong people the wrong way."

APRIL 2012

The Tao that we speak of isn't the true Tao.

I found myself thinking this over and over for about a week—or not even *thinking* it, exactly. It just kept repeating in my head.

It was a line from a poem by the ancient Chinese philosopher Lao-Tzu that I'd come across, and it had struck me. It seemed like something I could tell my patients. It could potentially apply to a lot of things, I thought.

I considered trying it out on Aqil. *Are we really talking about a serial killer,* I imagined saying, *or is the serial killer a stand-in for something larger and more abstract? There's a saying by the Chinese philosopher Lao-Tzu . . .*

No, I thought. Probably not.

I came home that evening and Jill was already asleep, and the boys weren't home. I made myself a bowl of cereal and sat watching a cooking program on TV, turning my worries over in my head. *Rusty.*

I still hadn't made any decisions about it—about what to do, when to tell Jill. And meanwhile she had not decided about how she wanted to tell the boys about her illness. She was going to start chemotherapy at the beginning of May, and Aaron and Dennis still knew nothing.

What should I do? I thought. And then: *The Tao that we speak of isn't the true Tao.* And then I leaned my head against the arm of the couch and closed my eyes for a moment, to try to reach a calm, logical state of mind.

I woke up and I was curled on the couch, and I hadn't even taken off my sports jacket or shoes. Very disorienting. It was almost ten o'clock at night.

When I came into the kitchen to make myself a sandwich, Dennis was at the table with his books spread out, studying. "Hey," I said, but he didn't look up. He continued reading.

It was hard, this new stage of things between us. We used to have a great rapport—we used to try to find the dumbest jokes to tell one another, we used to talk about what he was reading, we used to go to movies together a lot—but over the last few years of high school he'd become more and more distant. This is what happens, I told myself.

And so when he didn't answer, I quietly made a peanut butter sandwich, and then I leaned against the counter a respectful distance away and tried to chew without making noise.

You can never be a passive parent. That's what I often told my patients. *Passive Parent is an oxymoron, like Jumbo Shrimp. If you're passive, you're not parenting!*

I cleared my throat. "What are you reading?" I said at last, and he glanced up grimly. "Lies and propaganda," he said. He showed me the cover of the book: *AP U.S. History Study Guide.* And I smiled and nodded.

"The Tao that we speak of isn't the true Tao," I said. "The name that can be named is not the real name."

Dennis used to be very interested in philosophy. He actually read Camus's *The Stranger* when he was twelve, and he'd even tried to dip into a little Heidegger. We used to have good discussions. But now he said nothing, and so I took a bite of my sandwich and chewed thoughtfully for a time.

"It's a good quote, isn't it?" I said. "It's from a poem by the Chinese philosopher Lao-Tzu. From around the sixth century B.C.E. I was thinking that it would be a cool kind of mantra to give to my patients. Like a kind of thought puzzle to mull over."

"Hmm," Dennis said. He didn't look up from his reading. "I don't think you should use Chinese sayings," he said.

"Really?" I said. "Why? I think it's very beautiful. And thought-provoking! *The Non-Existent and Existent are identical in all but name. The identity of apparent opposites I call the profound, the great deep, the open door of bewilderment*," I recited.   "Don't you love that? *The open door of bewilderment!* How would you interpret it?"

I smiled and shrugged. His mom was sick and he didn't know it, and I wished I could hug him, but that wouldn't have been welcome. So I offered this little token. This little quote.

"Look," he said. "Dad. I wouldn't tell that to your patients. There's just some . . . cultural-appropriation stuff that I think you'd need to . . . frame more carefully. I mean, you're not a Taoist. You're not Chinese, so . . ."

"Right," I said. I smiled a bit more tightly, and I felt a little flush in my cheeks. I remembered how red in the face Kate would get when you'd contradict her. "Right," I said, because he thought I was a kind of racist, I guess. A sentimental Orientalist looking for fortune-cookie wisdom. He couldn't understand that I thought that the poem—the translation of the poem—was beautiful and profound. He couldn't—wouldn't—tell me what he thought of those words. How he understood them. *The name that can be named is not the real name:* That was the tragedy.

"Can I make you anything?" I said, after a while. "Can I make you a sandwich?"

"Yeah, sure," he said.

So I wiggled my fingers like a magician. "Poof!" I said. "You're a sandwich!" And that, at least, brought out a wan laugh.

MAY 2012

AFTER THE FIRST chemotherapy treatment, we waited for her hair to fall out. She had pretty hair, but not in a vain way. It was blond, naturally wavy, shoulder-length.

Two weeks passed and nothing happened. "Maybe it won't," I said. "It doesn't always."

She gave me a grim look. The snow had finally begun to melt, and the lilacs were out, and she had cut some blooms and I watched as she put them in a vase.

"Honey," she said. "I don't think being hopeful is a good idea. Let's not be the kind of people who are hopeful."

At work, I hypnotized Mrs. O'Sullivan. She was a secretary in the alumni office of Case Western, fifty years old, divorced, and she had constant pain that could not seem to be diagnosed. Pain in her fingers, in her feet, in the sides of her neck. The doctors had found nothing, and the word *psychosomatic* had been suggested.

"But I'm not making it up," she told me hoarsely. "Why would I make up something so awful? Why would I *invent* my own suffering?"

I told her to show me the places that her pain was emanating from, and then I told her to imagine an elevator that was taking her to a place of her choice. A beach, maybe. "Any place that you'd like to be right now, that you can picture vividly." We stood in the elevator and went down together. "There's a little bank of buttons," I said, "and each one lights up as we go. Here we are.

"Negative one. Negative two. Negative three . . ."

When we reached negative one hundred, I said, "I think we've reached our destination. Are we there?" And she smiled shyly.

She was in a good state of relaxation and suggestibility. I said, "Mrs. O'Sullivan, I want you to repeat after me."

"Yes," she said.

"I trust myself," I said, and she whispered it back to me.

There was a verse from the Bible, from the Book of Psalms, that I had discovered in a book of quotations, and I had been trying to adapt it into something more like a mantra.

"I will walk safely in my way," I said.

"I will walk safely in my way," she repeated, and smiled privately.

"And my foot will not stumble," I murmured.

"And my foot will not stumble," she said, and made a thoughtful frown.

"When I lie down I will not be afraid. Yes, I will lie down and my sleep will be sweet."

"When I lie down I will not be afraid. Yes, I will lie down and my sleep will be sweet."

"I trust myself, I trust the universe, I accept myself for who I am."

"I trust myself, I trust the universe, I accept myself for who I am."

"Let's say it again," I said.

There is a kind of peacefulness that settles over the face of a hypnotized person. There is a moment when you can see the child they once were, what they must have looked like when they were four or five. Some people have a phobia about being watched while they're sleeping. It's creepy, they think—they feel vulnerable, exposed. But there's also something beautiful about it.

I put the fingers of Mrs. O'Sullivan's hand in my palm, and I let them rest there until they were warmed by my skin, until our two skins seemed to be the same temperature. Then I lowered my head and breathed softly along the length of her pinkie.

"Do you feel a tingling in your right pinkie finger?" I said. My voice was so low as to be almost inaudible. But she heard it.

"Ah," she said, and I breathed across it again.

"Is that where the pain is in that finger?" I whispered. "Yes," she whispered back, and I exhaled breath again.

"You should begin to feel the pain lifting out now," I said. "Like vapor."

A tear slipped out of her eyelid and slid toward her ear. "I feel it," she whispered.

Later, when Aqil showed up, I was still thinking of the face of Mrs. O'Sullivan. The way her mouth twitched as the pain left her pinkie. The way the mask of her face played through a whole series of expressions, the way a person's face changes while they are dreaming.

Afterward, untranced, she told me that her pinkie didn't hurt anymore, and we made an appointment to work on the remaining nine fingers. The neck. The feet. We would need to meet weekly, I told her, for about six months or so, and as I was ushering her out, Aqil was sitting there in the waiting room. He stared at us with his big dark eyes.

"Wow," he said, after the door had closed and Mrs. O'Sullivan had disappeared down the hall. "She looked satisfied."

I cleared my throat. "Okay," I said. "What are we discussing today?"

It was the usual.

Aqil wanted to talk about his idea that the drowned boys had been drugged. Rohypnol can be more difficult to detect than similar drugs, he told me, because it is in low concentrations and is cleared quickly by the body.

He put his face in his hands. "These autopsies," he said. "These autopsies are so bad! Just lazy—it's depressing! Was the victim dead or alive before he went into the water? Is it possible he was drowned elsewhere and then placed at the site of discovery? There's no sense that they even thought of that. What if they were held for a time before they were placed in the water?"

"So," I said. "Wait. You're saying that there's evidence that the dead boys had ingested Rohypnol?"

"Not evidence, no," he said. "They didn't test for it. The autopsies failed in a lot of ways."

"Okay," I said. "But I'm struggling to understand why this would even occur to you. Why *should* they have tested for Rohypnol?"

"Well," he said. "Let's just look at the things that don't make sense here, right? First: All of our victims are at a bar with friends. They're not walking down a dark lonely road by themselves.

"But then, lo and behold, they get 'separated' from their buddies. I mean, really? You just wander away from the friends that you're having fun with? You just leave without telling anybody?"

I nodded. We walked through these steps nearly every time we went over his "case," and sometimes he repeated himself almost word for word. It was like a zoo animal circling in a cage, thinking that *this time* he was going to find an opening.

"Second, once you've stumbled away from the bar or the party, what's the first thing you do? You make a beeline for the nearest body of water you can drown in? Look at the blood alcohol level in some of these jokers. They couldn't walk across a room, let alone maneuver their way for blocks until they just happened to fall into a river. Really? Nobody sees them wobbling along? They don't pass out on the way? They're like lemmings with a purpose, you know? They're like hypnotized or possessed or sleepwalking with their arms out. *Got . . . to . . . find . . . river. . . .* How can you not think that is weird, Doctor?" he said. "How can you think that sounds in any way reasonable?"

"Well," I said.

And I paused, because for a moment I allowed myself to be a drunk boy, leaving a bar, leaving my friends behind. People ignored me as I brushed past them. I took a path downhill, because it was easier. Ahead of me was a flat surface. A parking lot?

We're more attracted to our doom than we think we are, I thought. But I didn't say that, and Aqil shook his open palms vehemently.

"I don't know how they do it," he said, "but I can't help but think that *if* there is foul play here, it's not just a thrill killing. These victims aren't just chosen opportunistically. There's a window of time, and they disappear, and then they're floating facedown. How do we get from A to B to C? Could it really be the exact same accident, over and over?

"But! What if you had a thing for a specific kind of athletic white male, aged eighteen to twenty-four, how would you get them? You'd have to stalk them and plan it out, right? And they'd probably put up a good struggle, so you'd want to prepare for that."

"Hmmm," I said. "That's actually a question I have. Because it seems to me that"

"Have you ever seen someone who has been roofied?" Aqil said. He leaned back in his chair and gave a long sigh. "They're incredibly pliant. You could tell them, 'Come with me to the river,' and they'd say, 'Yeah, that sounds great,' and you could put your arm around them and they'd stumble along beside you, chuckling all the way."

I frowned. "But—it doesn't seem that there was any evidence of sexual abuse, though. Or torture? That would be the typical serial killer. Some form of sexual violence."

Aqil lifted his eyebrow. "I didn't say sexual," he said. "Did I imply that?"

"I'm just," I said. "I'm not sure why . . . What's the motivation?"

"Ha-ha," he said. "You're a hypnotist? And you never wanted someone in your power?"

By the end of the month, the hair had begun to come out in her brush in clumps. I found a ball the size of a fist in the trash can, and I took it out and washed it and tried to make a braid with it.

"What are you doing that for?" she said, and I shrugged awkwardly.

"I don't know," I said. "It seems wasteful to throw it away. We could make a—"

"I don't want a wig," she said. "I'm not wearing a wig."

As the baldness became pronounced, the remaining straggles hung down in strands like moss, and she began to buy caps.   Turbans.

"God, I look stupid," she said. "Fuck. It's useless."

And she tightened the purple velvet genie bandore. She was on her way to work, but it would be the last case she would try.

MAY 2012

I TALKED TO a colleague who worked as a therapist for the Cleveland PD. "If he's been placed on leave due to psychiatric issues," she said, "it could be anything.   Maybe he suffers from PTSD. Maybe he's a psychotic. Maybe he's just a screwup, and this is the easiest way for them to get him out of their hair without getting the union involved."

"Would you," I said. "Actually, would you be able to look at his records and so forth?"

"No," she said coolly. "I don't think so."

And Aqil was no more forthcoming.

"Listen," I said. "I'd like to talk a little bit about your life up till now. I mean, it's clear that these deaths are very important to you, and I think it's valuable for you to work through these ideas. But do you ever think about *why* you've found yourself focused on these— these particular . . ."

"Because I think they're murders that nobody else is noticing. I don't like the idea of somebody getting away with murder. Do you?"

"No, but," I said. "There are root causes. For our obsessions. For example, what made you decide to become a policeman in the first place?"

"Really?" he said. "Really, Doctor? You think this is about my backstory?"

"The backstory is often more relevant than we think," I said.

"I don't think so," he said.

MAY 2012

"HE GOT OUT on May fourth," Kate said. Her voice was tight, and I could sense how upset she was. "But they won't tell me anything else. I have no idea where he's at right now. He could be in the next room, with an ax."

"Well," I said. "That doesn't seem," I said. "Doesn't seem likely."

"I don't know how you can be so calm," Kate said. "I mean, as far as we know, he could be standing outside *your* house. Have you looked out your window lately?"

"I'm in the car," I said. And actually I was. I had patched together my practice as part of a health-care consortium and did a lot of commuting, sharing offices in various suburbs around the city, rotating with other therapists. Currently I was on the interstate, driving to the office in Bay Village, a stretch of a certain kind of emptiness. There was a roadside memorial: the cross, the plastic flowers, a handmade sign with a weathered, enlarged photo of the deceased. R.I.P. DYLAN, it said. CHILL WITH US 4EVER!

I cleared my throat. "So," I said. "To be honest, there are some.   There are some issues with Jill's health." I activated my turn signal. The exit was a quarter of a mile away.

"You haven't told her," Kate said. "You didn't tell her that Rusty's been released."

"No, of course I," I said. I sped up to pass an elderly woman in a Volvo.

"And what's her advice? She's a lawyer."

"Well," I said.

God!" Kate said. "I can't believe you. Don't you think she has a right to know? There's a person out there who could be stalking her family."

"That seems melodramatic," I said. "I don't think that . . ."

"Really? Because I think that we are in a very dire situation. You and I. I even called Wave, which tells you how serious I think this is.   He's on the fucking loose, Dustin! He's been released from prison and we don't know where he is. Doesn't this concern you at all?"

I tried to picture myself telling Jill. Imagined the questions she would ask me, the alarmed, angry expression she'd have, sitting there in her turban with her thin hands trembling a little around a mug of tea. She would look at me as if it were all my fault. *God!* she would say. *Why now?*

To be honest, that was much more frightening to me than the idea of Rusty crouching in my bushes.

JUNE 2012

THE BOYS GOT out of school. It was Dennis's senior year, and we went to see him graduate in his cap and gown, and there were photographs with Jill posing in her spangled bandore and silk scarf, and Dennis smiling under his mortarboard, and Aaron looking sullen in a black beanie, and me, hatless but trying to be present. Trying not to float away. There were a lot of different thoughts vying for my attention.

Show up. Be present. Tell the truth. Don't be attached to results.

This is Sufi wisdom, I tell my patients. It was one of the mantras I especially liked to share, but when I imparted it to Aqil he seemed doubtful.

"I don't know what you mean by that," he said. "I *am* attached to results. I don't think I want to live a life without results."

"Well," I said. "There are *always* results. It's just that we shouldn't expect the results that we want. We have to be open to the possibility that things won't turn out in the way that we imagine they will." I cleared my throat. "We have theories about how things will turn out, and when we cling to those too tightly, it . . . closes off our experience of the world. Our ability to see things for what they are."

He considered, and I watched as he gazed out the window, scratching the tip of his nose. It was about three in the afternoon. Traffic down below was quiet.

"Seeing things for what they are," he said. "Seeing them for what they really fucking are. Wow. That's a project, isn't it?"

"Well," I said. "Yes. It's an idealized"

Aqil cocked his head.   And the

"Concept," I said. "A way of trying to live in the world."

"You look pale," Aqil said. "Are you eating enough?"

The boys had made themselves scarce. Sometimes days would pass and I wouldn't see them and there was a particular kind of absence in the house. A brief feeling of the uncanny, though of course it wasn't. Dennis was working as a delivery boy for a sub sandwich shop. Aaron was volunteering at a homeless shelter with his friend Rabbit. I sat at Jill's bedside as she vomited into a Tupperware bowl, and then she had a fit of coughing. Barking, phlegmy.

"Motherfucker," she said. "This shit is going to get into my lungs."

"No," I said. "No it's not. Let's not jump to conclusions."

I lay down on the bed and we curled up together.

I drove to work. I passed the sign that said CHILL WITH US 4EVER!

Who is *us*? I wondered.

JUNE 2012

"YOU'RE GOING TO be fine," Jill said.   "I really think so."

"What?" I said.

We were in bed, and she was stretched out with her head propped on the pillow, and I was kneeling at her feet. I was giving her a foot massage.

"I don't know," she said. "I just worry."

"That's confusing," I said. "I don't even know what we're discussing."

I was pushing my thumbs against the hams of damp pink foot soles, running slowly along the ridges of skin that were as complex as fingerprints, but she only frowned.

"You don't look great," she said. "You're taking your meds, right?"

"Of course," I said. "I'm just—obviously, I'm worried. But you know: I've gotten very good at self-care."

"Dustin," she said. "Promise me that you won't lose it. If I die. The boys need you!"

"Shut up," I said.

I closed my mouth over her big toe, tightened my lips around it, and I felt her body arch.

AQIL AND I had reached an impasse in our last session. I had been reading through the folders that he'd given me, and the more I looked at them the more I realized that he'd been stretching the truth—confabulating, a bit.

One of the cornerstones of his theory was that the drowned boys' deaths had some ritualistic significance, that the disappearances had occurred on dates that had some numerical pattern in them.   But the more I looked at Aqil's information, the more discrepancies I saw. While it was true that Jonathon Frisbie had gone missing in the early morning of New Year's Day, 2001 (1/1/01), and Peter Allingham had last been seen on November 1, 2011 (11/1/11), many of the other deaths didn't fit into Aqil's formula as neatly. Vincent Isolato, for example, was *reported missing* on 2/20/2002, a Wednesday, but was actually last seen on Saturday, February 16. Jesse Hamblin, who disappeared on 4/4/04, was not a drowning death but rather a missing person, since no body had ever been found. Zachary Orozco was not reported missing on 6/6/06, as Aqil claimed; he wasn't reported missing at all. His body was found on 6/8/06, and the autopsy suggested that his body had been in the water for several days. The date of disappearance, with its ominous significance, was more or less Aqil's invention.

In the end, I saw, only three of the deaths—the "murders," as Aqil called them—actually fit into the pattern he'd ascribed to them.

"I'm trying to understand," I said to him. "Why would you feel the need to alter the information you present so it fits your prescribed pattern more neatly? Why do you think you might have done that?"

"I didn't alter," Aqil said. "I conjectured."

"Ah," I said. He was staring at me hard, and his mouth had grown small. "I would say that this goes beyond conjecture." I cleared my throat. "It's a bit more like a kind of confabulation."

"I told you in the very beginning," he said. "I said, *don't pay attention to the dates*, didn't I? I told you, *that's just frosting*. All the other connections are way more important and significant."

"So why present the dates at all? If the way you're presenting them isn't accurate, doesn't that seem like . . . ?"

"I think I may have exaggerated a little, to some extent," Aqil said. "To pique your interest."

"And how would you differentiate 'exaggeration' from 'lying'?" I said. I spoke as gently as possible, but his face grew tighter, and his lowered eyebrows hooded his eyes as he stared at me.

"I didn't want to make it overly complicated," he said. "I wanted it to be clear and simple when I first presented it—"

"Because?"

"Look," he said. "I stand behind all of the dates that I gave you. Any discrepancies between what I told you and what the police reports say, I think there are good explanations for. Sometimes those reports are in error. They're sloppy, they make assumptions, they don't see the whole picture. I mean, we can sit down and go through every one of the ones where you think I've been dishonest, and I can show you how I came to my conclusion logically."

"Are you sure that you're not trying to *impose* a pattern on these deaths that isn't there?" I said. "Think of the constellations. We look up at the sky and think we see a flat surface with these bright dots called stars that we can connect. We put that cluster together and say it looks like a dipper, or a bear. We put another together, and it seems to be in the shape of a fish, or a scorpion. We forget to imagine the stars in three dimensions. They aren't clustered together—they're light-years, billions of miles apart. They only seem like they could line up from our one, limited perspective, here on the planet earth."

I looked at him earnestly. "We think about our own problems that way, too," I said. "We look at them in one dimension, and it seems that they are all connected. We think that there's some image we can make out if we connect the dots. But more than likely the dots are not connected. They're on separate geometric planes, light-years apart."

I had made this speech to patients with obsessive thinking patterns before, and I thought it was a good one. I thought the metaphors were nicely turned, and it wasn't accusatory, it wasn't saying that they were lying, or crazy. But Aqil's face had turned frankly hostile.

"Damn," he said. "You know, I really thought you were different."

JUNE 2012

I THOUGHT THAT Aqil and I might have a turning point. After he'd had a week to think things over, I thought, we could begin to reframe and refocus our sessions together. We could begin to look behind the curtain of this obsession he had and see what was driving it. *I'm not saying that you have to completely give up on your case*, I would tell him. *I don't disbelieve you*, I would say. Which was true. I thought there were some genuinely troubling aspects to these drowning deaths, and I found some of the connections he'd made convincing. *But!* I would say. *I don't think it would hurt to approach this with a clearer eye. And a greater self-knowledge.* I considered this last part. Did that sound condescending?

Of course, there was the possibility that, having been called out, he wouldn't come back at all. I may have been too forceful in challenging his belief system; it may have been too soon.

But I hoped not. I liked Aqil. I liked talking to him, and I thought his "investigation"—his mystery—was actually pretty fascinating.

139

So I was relieved when he showed up the next week at his regular time.   Smiling. Seemingly not upset, showing none of the signs of sullen anger and hurt that he'd displayed when we'd ended the last session. He settled comfortably into the sofa across from me and gave me a hopeful, determined look.

"Listen," he said. "I've been thinking a lot about what we talked about last time, and I think you're right. I need to be more up front with you."

"Good!" I said. "I look forward to that."

He nodded. "I want to show you something," he said. And he handed me a sheaf of papers that I at first assumed was another "dossier" of a dead college boy.

Then I glanced through it. It was about me.

I always assumed that I would not be an easy person to research on the Internet. I'd once done a Google search, and there were a lot of Dustin Tillmans in the United States. There was one in Weeping Water, Oklahoma; one in Minerva, Ohio; yet another in Milton, Florida; and another in Leander, Nevada—in all, easily more than a hundred of us. I'd never felt particularly visible.

So it was unnerving when Aqil showed me the information he'd gathered.

There was, of course, the famous photo of the crime scene from 1983 and articles about the murders. This surprised me—though it had been widely reported on at the time, I thought it was mostly forgotten, buried under the steady, unceasing accumulation of sensational American killings. How many of them are there every year, in every state?   Some of them rise to national attention for a few days and may linger in local newspapers for a bit longer. But as time passes they vanish.

How many people recall the most famous massacres of ten or twenty years ago, even when they were covered widely by journalists?   A select few become legendary, of course, but most sink silently beneath the constant waves.

But apparently there were little dark corners of the Internet where people hoarded all kinds of forgotten things, and Aqil had discovered the blog of a person who had obsessively collected stories about Satanic killings. There were crime-scene photos on this website that I had never seen.

"You probably don't want to look at that," Aqil said, when I turned over a photo of my father's body on the floor of the living room.

"What is this?" I said. I flipped the picture over quickly, and I felt sudden heat in my face.

There was a very loud, metallic tinnitus in my left ear. *"Fuck,"* I heard myself say.

On the next page was a printout from—a blog? The heading said: TILLMAN FAMILY. ST. BONAVENTURE, NEBRASKA, 1983.

This was the second time Russell Bickers had been implicated in a murder, the blogger had written. *His previous foster family had died in a house fire under unexplained circumstances, but the Tillmans innocently took him in, despite his history of violent and antisocial behavior. It seems clear that Bickers was part of a Satanic network long before he was adopted by the hapless Tillman family. Bickers's biological mother, a prostitute and drug addict, had been sentenced to prison when he was five, and there are tantalizing suggestions that she may have been connected to one or more of the covens that operated a child pornography ring in the Grand Island, Nebraska, area during the 1960s and '70s. It could well be imagined that Bickers began his life as a victim of the coven before graduating to become one of their valued servants—even as a child. The deaths (by fire) of Bickers's first foster family bear some hallmarks of ritualistic killing, which Bickers would come to perfect later when he slaughtered his adoptive mother, father, aunt, and uncle in 1983.*

I stopped reading, but by this time I could feel the edges of a full panic attack beginning to take shape: pounding heart, tightening chest, the high-pitched razory sound in my left ear, and I closed my eyes tightly because I was not going to have a panic attack in front of a client. *You will walk safely in your way and your foot will not stumble; when you lie down you will not be afraid; yes, you will lie down and your sleep will be sweet—*

"Doc?" Aqil said, and his voice was suddenly solicitous with concern. "Hey. Are you okay?"

I took in a long, slow breath, held it for a count of five, then exhaled steadily for a count of seven. I pressed my fists together under my sternum and did it again. When it appeared that the attack was beginning to pass, I opened my eyes and looked calmly at Aqil.

"Where did you get this?" I said, and my voice was possibly colder and more hostile than I intended.   "Who wrote this?"

"Hey," he said. He was taken aback and made an apologetic grope with his palms. "Doc, it's just some crazy man on the Internet. I'm not saying I believe it. It's just stuff that's out there."

"Aqil," I said. "This is not appropriate. I don't feel comfortable with—this is private information."

"Actually, it's not," he said. "It's on the Internet. Look, I'm really sorry if you're upset; I can see now that I approached this wrong. It wasn't my intention to piss you off. Really."

"Be that as it may," I said. "I feel very. I feel a   extremely invaded right now. I don't want to use the term *stalking*, but I find this very disturbing and troubling and we need to talk about professional boundaries. In any case, I think the session for today is finished."

"Whoa, whoa, whoa," Aqil said, and mimed a cringe, putting his hands on his forehead. "Wait—I screwed up. I did a bad thing. I realize that now! Please don't throw me out. Please."

And then he did the most uncomfortable thing I could have imagined.   He got down on his knees and clasped his hands as if praying.   "Please," he said. "Don't freak out on me, Doc. I'm sorry, okay? I'm really sorry."

"Please get up," I said. "Please take a seat, Aqil. We are in such an inappropriate place right now that"

"Just hear me out!" Aqil said. "Just—five minutes."

"Really," I said. "I need to take a break. I'm not feeling well."

"Doc," Aqil said. "I'm a cop. You don't think I'm going to do research on you before I talk to you? I'm sorry you feel disturbed, but I knew all this stuff before we even met. Honestly, this is the *reason* I came to you in the first place. Did you really think I wanted to stop smoking? I came to you because you know things. You know what's *real*."

I was keeping my fists pressed to my chest, and I saw that the knuckles were blanching. "I think that we may need to discontinue"

"Please," he said. "Don't do this. I'm really sorry." He made another pleading gesture. "It's just—I needed to be sure that you were the real thing before I got straight with you. I needed to know I could trust you. But you *are*, Dr. Tillman. You *are* the real thing.   And that's why I'm telling you now. You are maybe the one person who will understand this case. Because I do think a cult is involved. Satanic, whatever you want to call it. And I need your help."

"Look," I said. "Seriously." And as is often the case, I was of two minds.   On the one hand I was unnerved—that he would have "researched" me, that all along he knew more about my personal history than I knew of his, that he had been *playing* me, in a way, I thought; it gave me bad signals and, as a therapist, as a psychologist, was very concerning.

And this document—this blog, whatever it was, the fact that this information was public and being read by

And that photograph of my father—I hadn't seen him, hadn't looked at his image for . . . how long? Not since it happened?

It sent a trickle of nausea through me.

"Look," I said. "I think it's best for us to end this session now. I'm not going to charge you for the hour, but—we may need to reevaluate   the"

He reached out and clasped his hand over mine. "No," he whispered. "Dr. Tillman," he said, "Dustin, this is important. Please. Don't be scared."

And then, abruptly, he stood.

"I'll come back next week, okay?" he said.

And I said nothing.   I'd glanced down to the papers Aqil had given me, and a paragraph caught my attention.

Later, the blogger wrote, *the youngest surviving member of the Tillman family, Dustin Tillman, became a student of well-known psychologist Dr. Mary Beth Raskoph and wrote a dissertation on*

From: Aqil Ozorowski (Ozorowskiag@yahoo.com)
Sent: Fri June 29 2012 3:14 AM
To: DrDTillman@outlook.com
Subject: Apology

Dear Dr. Tillman,

I want to once again apologize for my behavior today. I saw how upset you were and I realized right away that what I had done was wrong and that I crossed the line. I am still struggling with understanding appropriate boundaries; it's been a problem for me my whole life but I am particularly sorry in this case, because I feel I may have damaged a relationship that I value as much as anything in existence. You are like a brother to me, Dustin.

I am writing to very humbly ask for your forgiveness. I would be happy to meet with you in any form that you choose to discuss this and hopefully resolve it so that we can continue to work together.

I can see now that it seemed as if I was invading your privacy and that it might even be construed as harassment or menace (i.e., "stalking"). This was in no way my intention. I don't know what I was thinking when I gave you that material without any explanation. The fact that the packet contained photos and descriptions of the tragedy you experienced while a child is unforgivable, and I cringe now to think of the pain I must have caused you to be presented with such a thing without warning.

The reason I wanted to discuss this matter with you was because I wanted to appeal to your expert opinion. I know that back in the 1990s you wrote your doctoral dissertation about cults and have also given testimony in court concerning witnesses who recovered repressed memories due to cult abuse.

I have been slowly formulating a theory that these drownings may be the work of a cult of some kind, but I really need you to help me walk through some of these ideas. I need your clearheaded intelligence and knowledge, someone who can guide me if I get off track, but also someone who is an expert on the subject. Someone who won't dismiss the possibility out of hand. I know that if I am distorting or confabulating, you will say so, but I also know that you are not prejudiced against the concept of cults. You have researched it, and you have your own personal experience, as well.

I realize that I have screwed up in the way that I approached this, and I only hope that you can find it in your heart to give me another chance.

Please, Doctor, don't abandon me.

Yours truly,
Aqil

JULY 2012

IF THE SITUATION were different, I might have gotten advice from Jill. "So I need to ask for your thoughts about a patient," I said.

"Oh, honey," she said, and winced. "No, I can't."

And I felt myself flinch inwardly. We were in bed watching TV, and it was a beautiful summer evening, not too hot, the windows open and the curtains moving in the kind of breeze that moths drift on, and I realized that she had been comfortable, that she had probably been dozing a little, and that before I spoke she might have been free, for a moment, of worry. I watched as she shifted her body awkwardly and gave me an apologetic look.

"Please," she said. "Please, let's not talk about your patients."

"No, of course not," I said. And it was that feeling of being stricken, beyond the point that the situation calls for. A feeling of awareness trickling into you and you think, *I'm such an idiot, I'm so selfish, I'm so inconsiderate*, a kind of deep embarrassment that you can feel in the blood rushing to your cheeks, and I said, "Do you want some ice cream?"

Dennis and Aaron and Rabbit were downstairs in the living room, playing some kind of video game. Even from the kitchen, I could tell from the sounds of women's screams that it was inappropriately violent and misogynist.

But I didn't say anything.   I took out a container of ice cream and scooped two balls of it into a bowl. I rinsed the scooper off under warm tap water and then put it in the dishwasher.

Stupid! I thought. *I'm so stupid!*

"Oh my God!" Rabbit cried from the next room. "Dude! Why would you do that?"

I took the ice cream up but she was already asleep, and so I stood there eating it myself, standing in the doorway of the bedroom while a police-procedural drama sent its voices through the room, the television lighting the bed with an aquarium glow. I watched as Jill slept, her face gaunt and frowning like a statue of a stern queen in the pale light.

A part of me knew exactly what Jill would have told me if she'd given me advice about Aqil Ozorowski. *Of course I shouldn't continue to work with him*, she would say. *Obviously.*

But a part of me was less sure than she would've been. A part of me was moved by Aqil's email; a part of me *had* spent a long time researching twentieth-century cults, and the idea of investigating a possible

was not unexciting.

Standing there in the doorway, gaping at the television, spooning ice cream into my mouth, I felt more than ever that I was not one person. I was the awkwardly shuffling, distracted dad that the boys may have vaguely noticed as he opened the freezer and rummaged; I was the kind of fussy, self-involved husband who pestered his dying wife with petty issues about his work life, until she had to beg him: *Please. I can't;* I was the kind of man who would sit by your bedside and feed you ice chips from a spoon; I was also the one who thought that the ending didn't have to be so grim, if only you tried harder. If only you'd be less pessimistic.

No doubt this must happen to everyone at a certain age: You look up for a moment and you're not sure which life is real. You've split yourself into so many honeycombed parts that they barely notice each other—all of them pacing, concurrently, parallel streams of thought, and each one thinks of its self as *me.*

Is it foolish to think that we selves are all connected? That we are all following the same thread—the tributaries that lead to the people we'll be in the future, and the trails we followed once in the past? I think of the boy who testified at Rusty's trial, or the young PhD student writing his feverish, barely acceptable dissertation on the now long-discredited idea of "Satanic Ritual Abuse"; I think of the night, years after the murders, it must have been my sophomore year in high school, living with Kate at Grandma Brody's house in Gillette, Wyoming, the night Kate came into my room and got into bed with me. I was fifteen and she was . . . ? Nineteen, I think. She was crying.

"What? What's wrong?" I said. And even then, there was not just one person asking that question.

"I'm scared," Kate said. She pressed her wet face against my collarbone, and I awkwardly put my arm around her, and I guess for a moment I was briefly connected to the person whose wife would say, years later, *Please. I can't.* "What if we made a mistake?"

"What do you mean?" my fifteen-year-old self asked. As if I didn't know. That was the last time we ever talked about it.

I watched her grow thinner.

It was hard for her to quit working, but there was the day that she had stumbled before she went into the courtroom, that she'd fallen to her knees and people gasped and came to her aid and even though she rose to her feet and went into the trial and won there were supervisors in the prosecutor's office who felt that she really needed to take time off.

She was ill, after all.

She needed some time away, they said, and she said "Are you firing me?" and her supervisor said *of course not,*   to be honest Jill a cancer victim is the most successful prosecutor we could have because they are so sympathetic, but you're at the point where you're falling down in the

And you're skeletal and kind of scary and obviously once you're a little healthier of course you will be welcomed back this has nothing to do with your performance

"He didn't actually say that I was skeletal and scary but that's what he meant," she said. "He was terrified of me."

I watched Aqil take another folder out of his backpack.

I have a theory, Aqil said. Of course, I need to be aware that this could be a series of coincidences.

Accidental drowning of young white men with very similar body types, very similar social profiles, and it's just a problem of binge drinking on college campuses.

Or maybe this could be the work of a serial killer. Someone who's stalking these kids, and there's all kinds of shit on the Internet about "Jack Daniels," who goes after these guys when they are drunk and overpowers them somehow and then takes them to the river and drowns them. Which doesn't seem very plausible to me.

But what if it's a group effort?

What if it's a team, a trained team?

Watch, I told myself. Pay attention. Be more aware of your environment.

I stood at the window of my office on the third floor of the house, thinking maybe Kate was right, that he'd show up on my doorstep.

What would he look like? I wondered. I tried to picture his face, and I couldn't conjure up anything.

He would be forty-eight years old. Long hair, short hair? Fat, thin? Shaved, beard?

I thought I had a clear picture from when he was a teenager, but even the images from the trial are blurry. I remember that he had a powder-blue suit, like a prom tux, I thought; and that his long hair was pulled back in a very severe ponytail, and his face had been shaved so hard that the skin on his cheeks was shiny and sore-looking.

But I couldn't put together an actual image of his face.

You feel like you're being watched. That physical sensation—scopaesthesia, it's called—the prickle on the back of your neck when you sense that someone you can't see is looking at you.

It is often described as an unpleasant feeling, an insect-y scuttling, centipede legs.

Turn around, you think. Then: *Don't turn around.* Which is worse?

In high school there was an urban legend about a killer hidden in the backseat, a killer beginning to rise up behind the driver, just out of his eyesight, an unseen hand reaching around to grab the driver's neck. That image always stuck with you and sometimes in the car there would be the tingle of scopaesthesia and you would have to quickly, almost a startle reflex, glance behind you because you felt the shape of something rising up. Once you even gasped and swerved the wheel for a moment.

"He was terrified of me," Jill said, and I nodded for a moment, thoughtfully.

"Well," I said. "Maybe it's not a bad idea. For you to take some time off work. Maybe he's not completely un-right."

"I *am* scary and skeletal," she said. "Do you think I don't get that? I feel it whenever I walk into a room!"

"No," I said. "Not at all."

"Oh my God," Jill said. "Don't tell me 'no.' If you could only see your face! You're so scared to look at me your eyes are rolled up in their sockets. Look, I *know* how awful I look. I should just run with it. I should just go to work tomorrow wearing a black robe and carrying a scythe."

Which—I couldn't help it—the image made me laugh. And she burst out laughing, too.

Aqil waited for me to nod, and when I did he nodded, too. *Right? he said. Right?*

This group would decide on a night they were going to take the target out.

They would follow him.

They would set up positions in various parts of the bar where the intended victim is drinking. And I think the victim would probably be drugged at some point. They would find a way to get him away from his friends, maybe he goes to the bathroom, or they lure him outside somehow, and probably he would then be forcibly placed in a vehicle—a van, I'm guessing—and taken to a location where some kind of ritual is performed.

At the end of the ritual, he's drowned.

His body is recovered days—or weeks—or months—after he disappears. There isn't much physical evidence that can be garnered from a body in this condition, and the police are inclined to see it as the sorry end to yet another drunken frat boy.

I would not recognize him, I thought. If he was behind me in line at the Quik-E-Mart, where I was buying an e-cigarette, just to try it; if he was in the car next to me on the interstate, merging together onto I-90, on my way to see Mrs. O'Sullivan in Bay Village; if he was walking his dog by my house, would some shape, some familiar movement, wake up in me?

I did an Internet search. There was, of course, the famous photo—and a few grainy mug shots and courtroom-steps pictures—but nothing of what he looks like now.

In the courtyard of the Cleveland Heights office, I surreptitiously smoked my e-cigarette. A man with large white hair, very big-headed, was loitering outside the front door. Another came in on a motorcycle and parked at the far end of the organic grocery and then walked very slowly along the asphalt. Was he staring at me?

I put my e-cigarette in my pocket and turned, headed back to the office. Where I sat in the waiting room, my eyes closed, listening to the waterfall sculpture that played soothing electronic music

There are the shadows of birds or airplanes that pass over in a blink. There is the fermata hum coming from somewhere, maybe fifty yards in the distance, there is the vague smell of batteries and lightning, there is the sound of a screaming baby one night and you go out on the back porch and you see the neighbor's cat has a baby rabbit in its mouth, and the scream is repulsively human. "Hey!" you yell at the cat, and it drops the rabbit and they both run off in different directions and you are left alone with the sudden feeling of being regarded with disapproval. As if you'd interrupted an important religious ritual.

You can feel across your back, across your face: There is a presence that doesn't like you.

That was one of the things I loved about our marriage. About Jill. How we could make each other laugh in the middle of an argument, in the midst of a serious talk.

And then, when we were done laughing, the mood was different.

"You're right," I said. "You don't look good. I don't think you should go to work anymore. I think you need to stay home and reserve your energy and"

"Don't use the word fight," she said. "Or stay positive, or whatever you were going to say. Promise me that you're not going to Life Coach me."

I put my hand on her wrist.

I held her in my gaze.

My guess is that they are held at some location and tortured for a period of days. Not tortured in a way that would leave obvious physical evidence, but in some kind of ritualistic way, maybe psychological mostly—and then later after the victim is dead they take the body to a local waterway and dump it.

Does that seem plausible to you, Doctor?   That there is an actual cult of some sort—Satanic or otherwise—and that they have carried out these attacks after a very methodical process?

If you look at the evidence, this just seems like the only logical way to understand what's been going on.

Basically, I think these kids are human sacrifices.

What would I do if Rusty walked into the room right now? What would I say to him? What would he even want from me?

And then I opened my eyes and Aqil was standing in the doorway.

"Doc?" he said.   Very concerned.

You walk into the Cleveland Heights office building at eight in the morning, up the brass and marble 1920s staircase and the narrow halls with the row of closed doors and only the door to your office is open and the waterfall sculpture is playing its music and you pause on the threshold.

"Hello?" you say. "Is someone there?"

And you can feel the frank hostility of the room that doesn't want to be entered.

You know, of course, that this is just an illusion. The mind is tricked by all kinds of stimuli and stress makes it worse.

But the room hates you. You can feel it.

THERE WAS THE first message on the answering machine.

Hey, man. It's Rusty. And I just want to try to reach out. I mean—I know there's a lot for us all to wrap our heads around. But let me talk to you one time. That's all. I . . .

I erased it before I listened to the whole thing.

This was the last thing that I needed. Jill was just starting another session of chemo, and I still hadn't told her that Rusty had been released from prison, the Innocence Project and all that. It would have upset her unnecessarily. *It would be cruel to tell her,* I thought.

I unplugged the landline phone from its jack. If anyone really wanted to get in touch with us, they would call us on the cell. I said to Jill, "I'm sick of all the telemarketing calls," and she looked at me blearily. Already, the mundane problems of the living were beginning to puzzle her.

"Fine, fine," she said.

"It's not that I disbelieve you," I said to Aqil Ozorowski. "I just feel like we're at a standstill. We've got a lot of speculation but very little evidence. And—from my perspective as a listener—there tends to be a lot of repetition and circling."

"I know," he said. "If I had anything solid I'd be talking to an FBI task force, ha-ha."

"In lieu of that," I said. "Let's say we're investigating. What would be the next step?"

"That's the thing," Aqil said. "Apart from rereading and looking for connections? I thought maybe you'd see some connections that I didn't."

"Well," I said. We were sitting in my office in Cleveland Heights, and I could hear the soft gurgle of the waterfall sculpture in the waiting room.

"What about . . ." Aqil said. "There's the possibility to talk to some witnesses. There's this kid I met on the Internet—friend of Peter Allingham—and I think he'd be willing to sit down, but what if *you* talked to him. I think you'd be better at it than I would."

"Hm," I said. I tried to parse it. We were already in questionable territory. I didn't feel as if we'd successfully reframed the "investigation," from a therapeutic standpoint, though he had become more cautious in his use of speculation. I thought we were making headway in looking at the "case" in a more logical and clear-eyed way. Still, it seemed that "interviewing" a "witness" might be ethically problematic. There were issues already with the way I was proceeding, *he shouldn't even be your patient*, I thought, *client*, I thought.

"Okay," I heard myself say. "I'm glad to talk to the witness. If you think it's a good idea."

This would make a good TV show, I thought. The therapist and his troubled patient, a former cop who is obsessive, post-traumatic, possibly delusional, but the therapist helps him to get steady enough to solve the crime. Or—to discover that in fact there is no crime, after all. In the end it's just as heroic to be a

"There might need to be some paperwork for him to sign," I said.

And there was the awareness that he was a cop, and we were connected, and I could call on him if I needed to. There was a feeling of being safe. Things were bearing down on me, and the answering-machine message from Rusty moved through the back of my mind.

"Listen," I said, "if I needed to buy a gun, what would you suggest?" Aqil tilted his head and lifted one eyebrow.

"For protection," I said.

THE YOUNG MAN's name was Ben Tramer. He was twenty-one years old, a junior at Kent State, so it was easy enough for him to come to my office in Kent.

He had been a friend of Peter Allingham, had been at the bar the night that Allingham disappeared, and now he sat uncomfortably in the armchair across from me, hands folded in his lap.

"So," I said. "Thank you for coming in, Ben. This is just a very informal"

"It's kind of weird that you guys are just getting around to this now," he said, and stared uncertainly at Aqil, who was standing at the window with his back to us. "It's been almost a year."

"But you've previously given a statement to the police, I assume."

Tramer raised an eyebrow the way one might when faced by an incompetent bureaucrat. "I never gave any statement," he said. "This is the first time anybody asked."

"Ah," I said. And his gaze drifted again. His eyes fell on a framed motivational poster: a picture of an arctic lake that was captioned EXCELLENCE.

> We are what we repeatedly do. Excellence, then, is not an act,
> but a habit.
> —ARISTOTLE

This made Ben Tramer frown.

"In any case," I said. "I wanted to get just a very informal picture of your recollections of that night. If you think back on that night, what's the first image that comes to you?"

"I don't know," Tramer said. "It's a long time ago, and I was pretty drunk. I mean, so was everybody. Pete was drunk. All our friends were drunk. Everybody in the bar was drunk. You know what's weird? When Pete first went missing, his mom went on Facebook and put up posters and everything—trying to find somebody who saw him leave the bar, trying to get a sense of when he left the bar, which way he might've gone, who was the last person to see him—and *nobody* came forward. *Nobody* remembered seeing him leave the bar. It's crazy."

"When was the last time *you* saw Peter?" I said.

"I don't know," he said. "There was a group of us. I mean, I remember him being there. And I remember him *not* being there. But in terms of the last time I saw him? His mom asked me that a bunch of times, and all I can say is that I draw a blank. I wish I had a better answer."

"Do you remember seeing anyone who seemed unusual or suspicious?" I said.

Another raised eyebrow. "Uh," he said. "It was Halloween? People were in costumes. There was some insane stuff. There was a girl wearing a thong? Which was just, like, a little strip of spandex that barely covered her ass crack? And then she had, like, a bikini top, and a werewolf mask. And there was this girl that had, like, a bondage halter? And she was carrying a teddy bear that had the exact same bondage halter?"

"Good," I said. "That's a good start." I cleared my throat. "I'm wondering—would you possibly be willing to try hypnosis? Just to get you in a more relaxed state—maybe there are some things that you might recall if"

"No," Ben Tramer said. He balked in a way that was so abrupt that it startled me. "Uh, no! Absolutely not. I don't believe in that shit."

"Excuse me?" I said, and Tramer made an agitated gesture.

"Are you guys cops?" he said. "Because, like, hypnotism? That's not even real! It's, like, Ouija board shit."

"No," I said. "That's actually not"

"Wait," Tramer said. "Are you guys really cops?"

"You know," I said afterward. "It's probably not a good idea to misrepresent ourselves. Isn't that," I said, "illegal? Impersonating a"

"Yeah," Aqil said. "There are some things we need to refine." He sank into the easy chair that Tramer had previously occupied and let out a long sigh.

"I have something for you," he said.

He reached into his pocket and pulled out a gun. Colt .380 Mustang XSP. "He's in Chicago," Aqil said.

And he was silent for so long that finally our eyes met. "What?" I said—but I knew who "he" was.

"Homeless, I think," Aqil said. "Working in a restaurant as a dishwasher. Doesn't seem like he's going anywhere."

I paused. Fingered the cylinder of the e-cigarette in my jacket pocket. "So," I said calmly. "How do you know this?"

"You know, a man gets released from prison after thirty years, it does make the news in a few places. Not *USA Today*, but it's on the Internet. Besides," he said, "I'm a cop; I have my sources. I know lots of databases."

"Actually," I said. I folded my hands in my lap. "Aqil, you're not a cop. You haven't been a cop for well over a year."

Aqil grinned. "Well, then," he said. "I still have a few cop powers lingering on. And I'm using them for your benefit, Dustin. I can tell you for a fact that he's in Chicago. I thought that might ease your mind."

There were a lot of things to consider in this statement, and I gave it some thought, until Aqil cleared his throat.

"I'm not trying to be inappropriate," he said. "I'm just trying to help. As a friend."

Of course, it was entirely inappropriate. That he had been researching my life, such as it was, on the Internet. That he had discovered things about me and then had discovered things about Rusty, and there was a—what? A breaking of the therapist/patient dynamic, a

We were silent. *As a friend,* I thought. There was a beat, and then another one, and he glanced out the window and I

I BROUGHT THE gun home with me in my briefcase and I tried to think of a place in my house where no one would ever look, and my first thought was behind the big row of diagnostic manuals on my shelf. If the boys had ever snooped in my little office—of course they must have—they would have long ago realized that there was nothing personal or titillating to find, nothing precious that I had hidden in it. Long ago, I thought, they would have lost interest, and so I put the gun behind the editions of the DSM-III-R and the DSM-IV, and it fit snugly behind them but the books didn't noticeably protrude.

And Jill was upstairs in bed watching a horrible reality show about rich housewives that somehow mesmerized her with the awful emptiness of the subjects and I said, "Can I get you anything, sweetie?"

"Hot tea, please," she said, even though it was ninety degrees outside and she was under the covers and had a cap on.

It would've been wrong to tell her about Rusty. It would have been cruel.

Downstairs, Aaron was getting himself a snack—for most of the summer, we hadn't been doing our traditional family dinners—and he observed as I put the kettle on.

"So what are you up to today?" I said, and he shrugged, sliding a layer of peanut butter onto a piece of bread in that slow, careful, focused way he had. His expression hooded.

"Could you do me a favor?" I said, and he shrugged again, so resentfully that if I were like my own dad was, I would've smacked him hard on the top of his head. I would have slapped him into the middle of next week, as my dad used to say.

"Can you please take some tea up to your mother?" I said. I imagined him coming into her room with the tray, and that they would sit for a while and talk, and that she would finally decide to confide in him. That she might decide to explain to him that she was probably dying.

It *did* disturb me that she hadn't told them much.

She had once been a fairly social and engaged person. She had a full circle of women friends, and they met in groups to go to movies or restaurants or talk about books—though she pulled the plug on those friendships pretty soon after she started chemo.

She'd also been deeply involved as a mother, much more intimately involved in their daily lives—the school days and teachers and homework and who their friends were, and who their friends' parents were—far more than I ever was. So it was surprising to see that she was beginning to abandon them, as well. Her illness had coincided with a certain drop in household temperature that comes with teenaged boys—the way they become secretive and aloof and embarrassed in an almost hostile way. And so maybe that closeness between Jill and the boys would've ended anyway, but it struck me as very abrupt and pronounced.

There were times when it felt more like a dream or hallucination.

The feeling that I would wake up at any minute and it would be the way it was six months ago. Jill would be well, our family would still be a warm place that I could settle into, everything would be normal again. If only I could wake up.

This was of course a very common sensation for people who are experiencing a difficult or traumatic life event. Not at all unusual.

There was a quote that I remembered. The German psychiatrist

Karl Jaspers talking about what he called "the primary delusionary experience":

> Patients feel uncanny and that there is something suspicious afoot. Everything gets a new meaning. The environment is somehow different—not to a gross degree—perception is unaltered in itself but there is some change which envelops everything with a subtle, pervasive and strangely uncertain light . . .

And the other thing about a dream, I thought: The way it collapses when you wake, the way it stops making logical sense and you can't hold it in your conscious mind anymore.

Because it doesn't exist in language. There are images, layered upon one another, which communicate each to each. There is a face that is four faces at once. You are you but not you.

In Freud this might be symbolic. In most current practice, it means nothing. It means a variety of synapses firing together.

I came into the television room with a cup of tea on a tray, and Aaron looked up at me. I wasn't sure how the tea had been made, or why it was on a tray. It was a fancy, embossed silver tray that I didn't recall seeing before.

"Will you please take this to your mom?" I said. "And sit and talk to her for a little bit, okay? She's lonely."

And Aaron looked at me silently: baleful but resigned.

And so then I made myself a smoothie and called Kate. "He's in Chicago," I said.

"What?" she said.

"He's in Chicago. He doesn't have an address yet, but he's working at a restaurant as a dishwasher. In other words, he's not stalking you."

Kate was silent. She had told me that she could see the Hollywood sign from her window, and I imagined that she was looking at it.

"How do you know this?" she said at last, and I looked down from my study window at a car idling in the driveway. Rabbit was in the passenger seat, and Aaron was opening a rear door, and the driver looked like he was not a high school student. Nineteen? Twenty? The car was full of smoke.

"I," I said.   And I watched the car make a display of backing down the driveway.   "I have a private detective who's keeping an eye on it for me," I said. "I'm consulting with him on a case right now, so he's doing me a favor."

"That's a relief," she said. "It's something, at least. I feel like I haven't been able to sleep for three months. How's Jill doing, by the way? Is she feeling better?"

"Yeah," I said.

And then it was abruptly 10:00 or 11:00 P.M. And I took out the dossier on Peter Allingham.

Okay, I was trying to picture him in that bar on Halloween night. Without question he's drunk, hanging out with his friends, talking and laughing. He leaves to go to the bathroom.

How could no one ever see him again? He's dressed in a costume. If he's stumbling down the street and makes his way finally to the river, is it plausible that *no one* saw him, despite all the posters and searching and social-media blitz that went on for months?   And that he could have been under the ice for so long?

Let's say they've been stalking the target for a while, in advance.

Less and less unconvincing.

DENNIS PACKED HIS things and drove off to college and it was a very bad day. Once his car was loaded, Jill slowly made her way down the stairs from the bedroom and stood on the porch. She lifted her hand and waved with a kind of grim blankness. She was like an elderly person in mid-stage dementia, and when she called, "Have fun!" in a rheumy, toneless voice, Dennis took a step back and put his hand on the hood of his car as if it were a talisman of protection.

Of course, they knew that their mother was undergoing chemotherapy, but we'd told them everything was going to be fine. They didn't know that it had spread by this time to her brain and her lungs—but really? Did it need to be spelled out to them?

Aaron came home late that day—he had begun his senior year in high school—and when he finally appeared, he sat on the couch in the TV room with a bowl of microwave macaroni and cheese. He didn't look up from his program when I stood there in the doorway.

"Your brother left for college today," I said. "I was—I felt surprised that you weren't here to say goodbye."

"I didn't realize it was supposed to be a, like, ritual," Aaron said. Still not looking up. "I texted him two hours ago."

And that was when it occurred to me that it was truly over. It was finished.

This little island that I'd built for myself, this family that had seemed so safe and stable, was dissipating beneath my feet.   I watched as Aaron forked noodles into his mouth, and they were yellow like warning signs on a construction site. I felt a gaze pressing on my back.

Besides Jill and her doctors and me, the only one who knew the extent of it was Aqil. He was sitting on the couch across from me in my Kent office when I told him about the metastasis into her right cerebellum, and he lowered his face into his palms.

"They're using the word 'palliative' now, but I don't think she understands."

"I'm so sorry," he said, and shuddered. And for a few seconds, it appeared that he was weeping into his hands.

Somehow, over the past months, we'd talked about my life more that we'd ever talked about his. Somehow, I'd managed to tell him about Jill's cancer, about Rusty's release from prison, all the things my children didn't know about.

There was a word for this, I thought. A syndrome, I just couldn't remember the name of it. When the therapist begins to rely on the patient for emotional support. When the therapist begins to confess secrets to the patient. When, somehow, you have bonded with them, they have almost become *your* therapist.

He put his hand out and touched the top of my head gingerly, giving my hair an uncertain stroke. "Shhh," he whispered. "Shhhhh."

SEPTEMBER 2012

THERE WAS A kind of comfort in thinking about the case. The "investigation," which I wasn't sure I should put in quotations anymore. Maybe there wasn't any killer, but the more I read about the Allingham drowning, the more compelling I found it. More than any of the others, it felt like a kind of locked-room mystery—and when I focused my attention on it, my mind seemed to solidify out of its haze.

I said we should reach out to Allingham's mother. "His widow," I said, and then I realized that was the wrong word: There wasn't even a term for a parent who had lost a child, not in English at least. "She was very outspoken after his disappearance," I said. "The statements she made to the media. She didn't think it was an accident, either."

We were sitting in my office in Cleveland Heights, and Aqil was pacing at the window, looking down at the cars passing on Cedar Road. His hands were folded behind his back. It was the kind of pose that a president might make in the late nineteenth century, and for a second I had a kind of—what? A picture rose up, liquid and woozy in my mind.

I remembered the look of a man with his hands behind his back. The—gib? *Gibben?* I thought.   Coming forward, something hidden behind his back, I guess. I saw a little flash as the image touched the front of my mind sharply for a moment, and I blinked.

And then Aqil was looking at me curiously. *What are you thinking?* I heard him say. "I don't know," I said.

OCTOBER 2012

"I DON'T BELIEVE in accidents," the woman said.   Mary. Mary Allingham, Peter's mother. "I don't believe that my son died for no reason.   I just don't think it's possible."

We were sitting there in my office in Bay Village, and she was on the sofa across from the desk, and Aqil was standing near the bookcase, staring at the bindings and rubbing the hairs on his chin as if the volumes on the shelf had completely absorbed him, and Mrs. Allingham sat across from me in the easy chair as if she were an ordinary patient. She was, I would guess, not quite fifty: thin; dark brown hair cut just below the ears; a dainty, pointy face; large, hollow eyes. And I assumed that she had not been getting therapy; if she had been prescribed antidepressants, she had not been taking them. She seemed addled with grief.

"I'm just grateful that you reached out to me," she said. "Because there's nobody else. My husband—" she said, and shook her head sadly. "We don't have a marriage anymore."

I cleared my throat. "Mrs. Allingham," I said. "You know, you've been thinking about this with the conscious mind for so long. And your conscious mind has done the best it could: We've got all this information that you've compiled, and you've presented it to us in a lot of detail."

"It's all I think about," she said. She was staring at the back of her own hand with the blank look of someone who's beginning to have a recollection.

"Mary?" I said, and she looked up—a dying person, I thought. Or no: already dead. "So you've been working your conscious mind very hard. Maybe it's time to try to talk to your unconscious," I said. "I wonder if you're willing to talk to me while you're under hypnosis? I   wonder if you"

And she gave me a surprisingly gentle, quizzical smile. "Sure," she said. "Why not?"

"Okay," I whispered. "Let's imagine you're in an elevator. And you're going to a place you need to go. . . . Maybe it's the last time you saw Peter. Maybe it's the last time you talked to him. Maybe it has nothing to do with Peter at all—it's just a memory that draws you in. There's another part of your brain that doesn't have language, it can only think in images, and I'd like you to let that part of the brain come forward.   Close your eyes.

"This is not a test, Mary. We just want to show up, be present in the moment, be truthful about what we see. We're not looking for results, we're just looking for what you *see*, whatever that might be.

"Are you ready?" I said. "Are we going down in the elevator together?"

"Yes," she said.

"Don't tell me where we're going," I said softly. "I want you to surprise me. But I'm going to push the button now, and we're going to go down, and down, down to the very bottom floor.

"I'm pressing the button now," I said, "and I want you to repeat after me. *I trust myself. I trust the universe. . . .*"

There is almost always a moment of dissociation when you are hypnotizing someone, when you stare hard at the stony, dreaming face and you hear your own voice vibrating in your skull and when they open their eyes you close your own.

"Where are we?" I said.

"I'm in the kitchen of my house," she said. "I'm reading a magazine. *People? People* magazine. The radio is on."

"What time of day or night does it seem to be?" I said.

"It's," she said.

"Where's the light coming from?" I said.

"Windows," she said. "It's afternoon. Peter is missing and I'm waiting for some kind of news and I don't know what else to do."

"Okay," I said. I kept my eyes closed. I imagined myself sitting there in the kitchen with her. We are at the table. NPR is playing, those soft, novocained voices, background music. She's reading about the young soldier who was disfigured in Iraq, now winning the hearts of millions of viewers on *Dancing with the Stars*.

"I'd like you to lift your head from your magazine and look around the room," I said. "There's something here that you might have forgotten. Something that's important."

"The telephone? The telephone is going to ring?"

"And . . . ?"

"It rings. And it's Peter. I don't understand why he would call me on the landline. Usually he *texts* me on my cell phone. That's the way everything is, these days.

"But I remember that I put down the magazine and I went to the phone and when I picked it up. It was Peter. I know it was his voice, even though he was whispering and there was a lot of static. And he said, 'Mommy.' He said: 'Mommy, help me.' And I heard it. I heard him say it and then the phone went dead.

"Afterward . . . I called the police afterward," she said. "I told them, 'He's out there, someone has him, someone is hurting him,' and I could tell by the sound of their voice that they didn't believe me.   And when we looked at the phone records. We looked and the only call that had come to my landline that afternoon was from one of those . . . telemarketing things. Robocallers, is that it? Registered to a company in Houston. And then I didn't believe it myself anymore. I must've dreamed it, I thought.

"They were probably right. I just imagined it. The call came, I don't know, was it seven—ten? Ten days after he disappeared? He was already dead by then."

Just remember: It's not reliable.

This kind of hypnosis—I explained to Aqil—is looked on with suspicion. Many feel that it's a kind of quackery, I said. Though it can be very useful in certain therapeutic situations, you can't say these memories are real. I told him about the research of Elizabeth Loftus, about the misinformation effect, how our recall of episodic memories becomes less accurate because of post-event information. I'm sure he knew already about the case I myself testified in and how that turned out.

"I get it," he said. "Not suitable for a court of law."

"Well," I said. "Not suitable for a lot of things."

But Aqil only shook his head sadly. "What if she was right?" he said. "What if Allingham *was* being held prisoner? What if he might have broken away—got to a phone somehow? I'd guess he was pretty drugged, but he managed to remember his childhood home phone number. That's the one thing you don't forget, isn't it?"

"Well," I said. "They did check the phone records. Unless he was being held prisoner by a telemarketing firm in Texas."

Aqil shrugged. "Could have been a dummy phone number, maybe? Happens all the time."

"That seems far-fetched," I said. "And anyway, wasn't he already dead?"

"No, no," Aqil said. "Here's the thing that I'm thinking. I know you're not crazy about this thing with the dates, and I agree with you in principle. But let's for a minute pay attention to the dates.   What's the day after she talked to him?"

"Uh . . ." I said. "November eleventh?"

He raised his eyebrows and nodded. "What I'm saying is," Aqil said, "he *disappeared* in the early-morning hours of November first. But what if he didn't *die* on November first? What if . . . ? It's like I was telling you before—we know they drowned, but do we know that they were alive when they went into the body of water that they were discovered in?   I have this idea that he was held and that his captors kept him incapacitated with drugs, maybe some kind of re-straints that wouldn't leave a mark?

"Because I do think that they want to kill him on a certain date, for probably ritualistic or religious reasons. November eleventh, 2011: 11/11/11. I realize that it doesn't all line up the way I would like it to, but I still keep going back to it. You can tell me that I'm confabulating, Doctor; I need you to be my skeptic. But just let me lay it out."

"Okay," I said. I was not a fan of the ritualistic-dates theory, but I didn't object. You don't know what you'll find if you let a patient's story spin out. Sometimes something important.

"Let's say this," Aqil said. "They saw the opportunity to kidnap the young man on Halloween, and then they probably kept him caged or something until the time and then he was taken to some sort of sacred site. And he was ritually drowned. And then only much later was his body dumped in the river."

"Hmm," I said. And in some ways I could picture it all very clearly. I couldn't say that it was *factual*, but it was vivid. It was a way to ex-plain the discrepancies. Possibly there was a glint of reality in it, somewhere.

"The call placed to his mother on November tenth. Maybe he got loose for long enough to make a call. Or maybe they *let him* make it. Maybe they put the phone in his hand. *Call for help*, they told him. They knew he wouldn't get away, and they liked the *power* of it. They liked that he was crying, that he called out for his mom. They loved that he used the word *Mommy*."

"I'm not quite following you," I said. This is how it always seemed to go. I would feel almost convinced, and then Aqil would spin off into a new set of speculations, and I would think to myself, *he's making this up as he goes along.*

"I think maybe they drown them in some sort of ritualistic pool or fountain of some kind," Aqil said. "Possibly the boys are tied up and they put their heads down in some kind of container filled with water. And they do their chants and pray to the devil, or whatever. . . ."

"But I don't see—why would they hold them prisoner for such a long period? The chance of at least one of the victims escaping would be very high, wouldn't you think? What would be the motivation?"

Aqil gave me a frustrated look. "Really?" he said. "I thought you studied Satanists, man," he said, almost as if I'd hurt his feelings. "What does Satan want? Doesn't he want you to laugh at suffering? Doesn't he want you to lick the tears off the cheeks of the children calling out for their mommy? Don't you think there's a lot of people out there who would get their kicks out of this kind of thing?"

NOVEMBER 2012

No one expected her to die as fast as she did, and she was the most shocked of all. "This can't be right," she said to the doctors. "I think you need to recheck these results," and she was a prosecuting attorney to the end. The oncologists stuttered and equivocated like bad witnesses under questioning, mincing words, wincing, gesturing submissively, and looking toward me for help. "Are you fucking kidding me?" Jill said. "I'm only forty-three! This is not acceptable!"

But no matter the arguments and counterarguments, the disease ate her down swiftly and steadily. Between April and October, she lost sixty pounds. The color saturation of her skin faded and faded until it was almost gray scale.

She still insisted that we not tell the kids. "It's too much for me," she said. "We don't have to rush into things—we don't need to . . ."

In November, when the doctor said she should go into hospice, she shook her head. No!

No!   She was at the stage where she was mumbling; no one could understand her but me, and I stood there as she appealed to me hopefully. "Nuh," she said, "uh-uh," a mushy garble, not words. And our eyes met, and I knew that she really, really didn't want to die. There was no grace or acceptance.

"It's just for a few days," I said reassuringly. "You don't have to stay if you don't want to."

Her last breath.

It has been hard to breathe for a long time.

She is sucking air through her bared teeth, and there's only just a trace of oxygen in it. Her eyes rake back and forth along the contours of the ceiling.

Rictus.

Rictus.

It looks like a horrible, clownish, unnatural smile and that is the worst thing.

That in the end, her body forces on her the expression that she hates the most. The fake grin of celebrities and prom photos and pleased to meet ya's, and I'm pretty sure she is blind, she can't see me, and her hand scrabbles wildly for a moment across mine

And her eyes say: This isn't possible. Wait! Even as her mouth smiles her eyes plead with me and her body arches

Wait!

The boys are sitting in the TV room with Rabbit, and there's something about seeing Rabbit dressed up in a suit—this slump-shouldered, six-foot-four, two-hundred-fifty-pound boy, melting into his chair like a snowman, holding his paper plate of hors d'oeuvres, his face a mask of blank discomfort. And I don't know why this should be the image that makes my voice go tight, that forces me to press my teeth together to keep from bawling.

Dennis and Aaron stand up, maybe sensing it, alert and wide eyed as deer.

And I press the hams of my hands against my eye sockets and push hard and then I'm giving them a melancholy but together smile, I'm saying, "Boys, we're all going to gather in the living room and people are going to share some of their memories of your mom? And I was hoping you'd be able to join us?"

When Jill died it dawned on me that I had few friends. It was not something I'd noticed before. Jill—and to some extent, the boys—had taken up so much of my mental space that I honestly hadn't realized. I had a lot of pleasant acquaintances, who sent cards and flowers, and I sent thank-you notes.

It wasn't until my meeting with Aqil Ozorowski, two weeks after Jill's death, that I realized the extent of it. He was sitting in the waiting room and when I came in he stood and opened his arms and wrapped them around my shoulders.

It was a sudden, surprising gesture, and at first I just stood there with my arms at my sides. I don't, generally, like to be touched by random people.

But it also occurred to me that I had not been hugged—genuinely embraced—since before the death. There had been shoulder-patting and hand-rubbing and awkward quick busses on the cheek. Not

Do you believe in demons? Do you believe in bad luck? Do you believe that someone up there doesn't like you?

Retrospective patterning is the fallacy of seeing planning where there is none. A design that doesn't exist.

Do you believe that there is a cult of people who are drowning young men in Ohio?

There is a difference between stopping and concluding. Rain stops falling. A song concludes. Only one is deliberate.

Do you believe that Rusty killed your parents? Do you believe a mistake has been made?

"Sorry for your loss," Aqil said, and his voice was actually shaking with emotion, he put his arms around me and I found my face pressed against his shoulder.

"Sorry," he whispered into the hair near my ear. "So so so sorry, Dr. Tillman."

He was a kindhearted person, and I may have wept for the first time onto his shirt that morning.

"You're not okay," he said. "Doc, look at your face, you shouldn't be at work!" He released me from his grip and held my shoulders at arms' length. "Oh my God, you can barely stand up!"

Do you believe that what happened to you is real, Dr. Tillman?

I watch as Rabbit puts his hand to his thick neck and the fingers touch the knot of his tie.

So awkward. Unspoken thoughts floating, almost tangible.

"Yeah, sure, of course," Dennis says. And he and Aaron look at each other, and Aaron says, "Uh . . . yeah. Okay."

Aaron is holding his hands behind his back, and I'm aware of the smell of marijuana smoke in the room.

"Well," I say. "People are beginning to gather. So"

The gibben? The hands behind the back?

Do you think that the best way of killing yourself is to take pills and put a plastic bag over your head? In a bathtub, maybe?

Do you think that probably Dennis would be fine, but Aaron is so vulnerable—he *does* still need you, even though he'd like to pretend that he doesn't.

Pharaoh had commanded that all male Hebrew children be drowned in the River Nile.

And then you realize that in some versions of the story the river is the main character.

Her cremated remains in a clear plastic bag. About a gallon's worth of dust and stones. You think ashes, but in truth it is more like gravel, like the jagged little pebbles you find at the bottom of fish tanks.

The bag is cinched at the top and there is a tag that says: "Cremation certificate enclosed. This is not a permanent container."

A precious phone message from her saved on the cellphone, hoarded, listened to again and then even downloaded to the computer:

"Hi honey it's me I'm on my way home from work and just wanted to see if you needed me to pick something up—but since you didn't answer your phone, I guess I can't ask you. Okay. I love you. See you soon."

There are so many vases that flowers came in. Most of the vases are very pretty, made of glass, expensive looking, and when the flowers die the vases have to be cleaned in the dishwasher.

Maybe they should be saved? Maybe they should be taken to Goodwill, so poor people can use them?

The boys look at you blankly.

The cremation jewelry purchased from the funeral home. Tasteful small lockets that you can hang around your neck, and the boys and I kneel on the floor of her study and I try to use the tiny spoon the funeral home provided to scoop a portion of her ashes and pour it into the locket.

Little bits trickle out and spill onto the floor, and get tangled in the lint.

One of her hairs by the foot of the desk chair.

The boys sit in their room listening to Kendrick Lamar, Mac Miller, Bob Marley singing "Three Little Birds."

The odor of marijuana smoke fingers through the cracks in the doorframe, and you hesitate there, holding a tumbler of whiskey.

"Every little thing gonna be all right," Bob Marley is singing. And your children sing along.

"Dad, listen," Dennis says as we are watching TV. "Listen. I think I'm going to go back to Ithaca. I'm in good enough shape to finish up my finals and I don't want the whole semester to be, like . . . a waste—"

And the look on Aaron's face: reddening envy.

Because of course he has nowhere to go. He's stuck here.

<table>
<tr>
<td>

Driving down to the offices in Kent for the first time since she died, about 45 degrees and foggy and muddy the sky the same cement color as the interstate, textureless and dense. The sun and sky are underneath that thick sludge of cloud, invisible.

</td>
<td>

Three Little Birds:

The song that their mother sang to them as babies.

</td>
</tr>
<tr>
<td>

Lick the tears from the cheeks of

</td>
<td>

Lights a cigarette in the car, opens the window a crack. A constant smudge of condensation, icy mist, the drip that runs along the frame and trickles into the car, a restaurant called Bahama Breeze surrounded by bare sleepless trees

</td>
</tr>
<tr>
<td>

The flattened strip of commercial real estate as you enter Streetsboro: Fun Buffet Staples Little Caesars Space Available LoanMax

The rows of trailers in All Seasons RV peering out from behind their high hurricane fence.

Pain Recovery Center

</td>
<td>

Dear Ann, thanks so much for your card and the flowers, it was a very thoughtful gesture that we all appreciated

Dear Jason, thank you for the

Dear

</td>
</tr>
<tr>
<td>

Wait! Wait!

Wait!

</td>
<td>

At the stoplight, text Aaron:

Can you check in the fridge and see if we need OJ? Because I can't remember if we're out.

</td>
</tr>
</table>

AQIL EMAILED AND said he was going to send a couple of links. "I know this is a real bad time and I hope it's not an intrusion but this is very urgently important. . . ."

Hypnagogia: the transition from wakefulness to sleep, and you keep having the dreams that you are dreaming that you are dreaming, or that you are waking up when you are not waking up, and it seems to go on and on. *Anthypnic sensations. Phantasmata. Praedormitium.*

Waking up over and over, but not waking up.

And then I during the lucid moments I download the and there is a part of me that wants to be a good skeptic lucid and but absolutely he's right the absolutely the pattern it's so clear.

Apophenia, says another voice. Resemblances and recurrences: the the belief that belief that random and meaningless things are connected.

IT WAS MORNING and when I stirred, Jill did, too.   I felt the weight of her shift, the emanation of warmth and flesh that you can feel through your skin.

"Ugh!" I squinted my eyes open. Must have been seven o'clock by the color of the blinds. "I had a terrible dream," I said.

"Mm," she said noncommittally, and rolled over and pressed the front of her body against my back. Her nipples touched my shoulder blades.

"I dreamed you died," I said. "It was so morbid," I said. "You got cancer and died really quickly, like over a period of months!"

She reached around and put her palm against the curve of my bare belly.   She put her lips close to my ear, so I could feel the soft moist breath.

And then I opened my eyes but I couldn't move.

SEARCH CONTINUES FOR MISSING LAKE ERIE COLLEGE STUDENT
VERONICA VELLA, Daily News Staff Writer
Posted: December 4, 2012

Bryce Lambert is still trying to understand what could have happened. It was a normal Friday night, Lambert said. He and his childhood friend Slade Gable were celebrating their Thanksgiving vacation with a few beers at a local pub. Lambert had no idea that his friend was about to disappear without a trace.

"There was nothing unusual about his emotional state," Lambert said. "He seemed happy. We talked about how he felt very positive about the way his classes were going, and he was excited because there was an indoor track and field meet scheduled for the first week in December."

When Slade didn't come back from a trip to the bar for more beer, Lambert wasn't that surprised. Maybe Slade "got lucky" and went home with a girl, Lambert thought. At worst, he had passed out somewhere and there would be a funny story in the morning.

But when Gable didn't turn up for classes the next Monday, Lambert became increasingly concerned. On Tuesday, November 27, he called Gable's parents in Pennsylvania, who contacted the police.

"This is like one of those weird news stories," Lambert told the *Daily News.* "But you never think it would be a person you're close to."

Now Lambert is one of many northeast Ohio residents combing the Painesville area for Gable, who seemingly vanished into thin air early in the morning of November 24. Police have brought search dogs in and are looking high and low, including areas around the local river.

Gable, 21, was last seen at Nemeth's Lounge on N. State Street. He was wearing jeans, a green Lake Erie College Storm sweatshirt, and tennis shoes. He left his coat in the bar, in the booth seat across from Lambert.

"I should have known something was wrong when he didn't come back for his coat," Lambert says. "But I didn't think that much about it at the time. Slade is not a person you worry about. He's a guy that you figure can take care of himself."

Gable, a pole-vaulter for the Lake Erie Storm track and field team from Elysburg, Pennsylvania, is six foot one inches tall and 180 pounds. He has dark blond hair and blue eyes. At this time, no one has come forward to say that they saw Slade leaving the bar. Lambert was the last person to see him.

"It's hard to believe that it's real," Lambert says. "I keep thinking it must be a bad dream."

STUDENT ATHLETE REPORTED MISSING BY MOTHER
Posted: December 5, 2012
By: Timothy Rasheed
HIRAM, Ohio—

Hiram and Garrettsville police confirm they are searching for a missing Hiram College wrestler.

Investigators say 20-year-old Keegan Brewer of Worthington was reported missing on Saturday by his mother, Susan Brewer.

Keegan Brewer was last seen at about 2:00 a.m. early Thursday morning, November 29.

His mother says he was in his Bancroft Street apartment with his room-mates from 11:00 a.m. until about 2:00 a.m., when he told them he was going to go for a walk.

According to his mother, his phone was last pinged in the area of Garfield Road and Highway 305.   Brewer is described as being five feet nine inches tall and 170 pounds, with a weight lifter's build. He has fair skin and short, curly black hair, and was wearing a blue Columbia ski jacket, jeans, and hiking boots. Brewer did not show up for team practices on Thursday or Friday.

He was not carrying his wallet or ID and did not take his car, so he was presumed traveling by foot or was picked up by someone.

If anyone has any information regarding the whereabouts of Keegan Brewer, please contact Hiram Police.

"So WE'RE CLEARLY coming up on December twelfth," Aqil said. "And they're crafty motherfuckers, aren't they? Two missing guys. Same basic profile. I almost feel like they're taunting me, you know? And how is it that no one else in law enforcement has noticed? *How the fuck is it possible?*"

I cleared my throat. "Yes," I said. "It's troubling."

"*Troubling*," he said. "I love that."

We were in my office in Kent, and I felt as if I was focused on him, on what he was saying, I could hear it perfectly—though there was a small voice that seemed to be emitting from a distant radio station, barely audible.

Wait wait wait

"They may have got both of them," Aqil said. "But I think maybe the fact that there's two is just a weird coincidence. My strong feeling is that it's the Painesville one. There's not a good drowning river in Hiram, or at least not that I can see on a map."

I rubbed my eye sockets with my thumb and forefinger, let the sparking kaleidoscope swirling play for a moment. The high, jet-plane slice of metal in my left ear. I hadn't had an episode like this in years, not really since college, since I got married, this kind of   possibly experiencing panic attack or mixed state   mild schizoaffective symptoms?

"I imagine that they are holding them," Aqil was saying. "One or both of them—somewhere in the vicinity. We've got about six days, Doctor. Because I guess that they are going to be drowned on December twelfth. Probably at midnight."

"I wouldn't go that far," I heard myself say. "That seems like pure speculation on your part. But I *do* think that   yes, alarming.   Pretty certain that and   seems clear to me that this is the time to contact the   I don't think there's any doubt that   obviously"

Aqil smiled tightly. "Dustin," he said. "We talked about this a long time ago. I went to the FBI long before I ever went to see you. They're not interested. They've dismissed it. To them, the Jack Daniels stuff is an urban legend."

He put his hand over my hand, and his dry fingers tightened on my wrist. "The only way we're going to get the feds in here is if we have it already figured out and laid out for them. We need to lay it out for them on a fucking platter, right?"

"Uh-huh," I said, and I glanced up and I saw that we were in the car driving, and Aqil was in the passenger seat, and I was behind the wheel.

DECEMBER 7, 2012

PAINESVILLE IS A town of approximately twenty thousand people, a half hour east of Cleveland on the coast of Lake Erie. We drove there that morning without saying much. Without discussing what we hoped to accomplish, without questioning whether it was a good idea, I was at the steering wheel and Aqil was in the passenger seat, silently reading something on his phone.   And I was looking out at the interstate, at the horizon.

There was a kind of dimness about northern Ohio as it approached the winter solstice, a kind of suffocating lack of direct light. On days like this, you could scope the sky for the sun but couldn't pinpoint its location, the cloud cover was so thick. It made me think of the neurology class I took in college, the professor talking about *eigengrau*—intrinsic gray, brain gray. It was the color you "saw" when light was totally absent, a kind of visual noise, like snow static on a television. That was the color of the sky above us.

But Aqil didn't look up from his phone toward the landscape out-side. "Lake Erie College was a women's college up until 1986," he reported. "Now it's about fifty–fifty male–female. Their most popu-lar major is called 'equine studies.' Horses, right?"

"Yes," I said. "I would assume so."

"That's weird," Aqil said. "Why would that be something you have as a college major?"

I shrugged.   It was raining a little, and the wipers smeared through the freckles of water that appeared on the windshield.

In Painesville, Slade Gable's family was cooperating with police to organize a Saturday-morning search party, which was what we were going to observe. "I have a buddy on Painesville PD," Aqil said. "We went to the police academy together." And this turned out to be true.

We stopped the car near the park, where a center contact point had been set up, a card table with coffee and donuts, manned by an oddly jolly old woman and a hollow-eyed preteen girl.

I sat in the car as Aqil hopped out and strode toward a pair of policemen in uniforms. They looked up from their Styrofoam cups and conversation, and I watched as Aqil threw his arms up in a "hands up, don't shoot," and he and one of the cops clasped hands and shook enthusiastically and I watched out of the windshield.

"Sometimes I think I'm cursed," I told Jill once, back when we were first together. "I don't know anybody that's had as many weird, tragic things happen to them." We were sitting on a sofa on a porch, outside of someone's small house party. Dance music was coming from inside, and we were watching cars drive by on the street. My first year of graduate school.

"You should intern for a while with a public defender," Jill said. "You wouldn't believe the shit that rains down on people."

And then she put her arm around me. "You grew up *poor*, honey. Poor people don't have good luck." I rested my head against her shoulder, and her fingertip brushed the tip of my ear.

"We live in capitalism," she said. "For better and worse. Disproportionate numbers of bad things happen to people who are economically disadvantaged."

Aqil made a laughing face. In any other mammal, you would think it was a snarl. But the other men copied the gesture. It was a kind of masculinity that reminded me of growing up in Nebraska—I was awkward and unathletic, eager to please and easily tricked—and that kind of laughter made me think of jock bullies from middle school, of Rusty and his stoner friends, the way the noises they made sounded like pack animals. That distinctive sound Rusty taught himself to make when he thought he was funny. *Fuh huh huh.* The edges of his mouth pulled up in sharp points, and I had to wonder where he was right now. Still in Chicago, still homeless? Could he possibly know about Jill?

I rubbed my finger against my ear. There was a sharp feeling against the helix, a kind of pinch, and it reminded me of the way that Jill used to bite me, the way my body tingled and shuddered. The mind offers these little snapshots up to you when you least need them, slaps you with them, tases you with them. And you wonder *why did I just think of?* And then Aqil gestured toward me. *Come over here!* And I took a breath and turned off the ignition and got out of the car.

"I wasn't poor!" I said. "We had a lot of money for a while. My dad had a settlement. Because of his arm."

"Dustin," she said. "You went to college on a Pell Grant. Those are for poor people. Right?" She bent down and put her mouth on my ear. She took the cartilage very lightly between her teeth then let go. "I don't want to use the term 'white trash,' but," she said. "Everything you've told me is just—*yikes.*" She began to knead my shoulders, and she pressed her teeth against my ear again. The pleasant sensation that she could bite a piece off, and trusting that she wouldn't, and my back arching as the teeth tightened on the helix. I held my breath, and felt the tip of her tongue run along the groove. "You know what you learn when you study the legal system? *Poor people pass down damage the way rich people pass down an inheritance.* Most of their children don't get out of that, Dustin. But you did. You got away. And now you've got a really mean, crazy lawyer bitch who is madly in love with you.   And she is going to watch out for you. Nothing is going to hurt you while I'm around."

"This is my friend Dustin," Aqil said. "*Doctor* Tillman," he said, and emphasized the "Doctor" with an ironic gravitas. "He's writing a book about missing college students. He has this kind of wacky theory about how they may be connected, and I've just been consulting with him on it. Trying to keep his feet on the ground."

Aqil put his hand on my shoulder and gave me a conspiratorial look out of the corner of his eye. But for a moment his casual lies left me speechless. It took me a few beats to realize what he was up to.

"Consultant—that doesn't sound like a bad deal," said the cop named Ellison, squinting at me skeptically. "Anything you wrote ever got made into a movie?" he asked me.

"I'm not really a," I said. "Well," and I glanced at Aqil, but he didn't make eye contact. Officer Ellison seemed not to notice my awkwardness.

"Maybe if you were writing a movie you could make something out of it," he said. "But this isn't going to be anything interesting. Nine out of ten, he just went off somewhere without telling anybody. He'll call his mom from some state in Mexico and ask for money to get home. Or else a corpse will show up. There's a river a hundred yards down that way; maybe he fell in and drowned and got washed downstream. It wouldn't surprise me."

The other officer, Synnott, shook his head. "These kids," he said, with the tinge of a Dublin accent. "The level of binge drinking we see with these college kids. There's no mystery."

"I don't think they got a big turnout for their search party, unfortunately," Officer Ellison told Aqil. "Under ten, I would guess. The family's from out of state, and the college kids are in the midst of their final exams, so . . ."

"I don't know what they'd find, anyhow," Synnott said. "We had dogs out here. We already spent a lot of man-hours walking that riverbank. It's not like they're going to find a bloody glove or a mysterious footprint or some *CSI* bullshit."

"Well," Ellison said. "It's their loved one. Sometimes the family needs to do it, just to have something to do. I understand that."

188

Synnott nodded grimly, and he gave me a look up and down. "So what's your theory, Doctor? You been reading all that stuff online about the serial drowner preying on poor helpless drunken frat brothers?" He patted me on the shoulder, and I smiled, though I also flinched a bit. He showed his teeth at me. "I think the killer's name is Darwin," he said.

We stood there at the edge of the park and watched the cops drive away. Aqil lifted his hand and his grin fell off. "Dicks," he said to me confidentially. "*Darwin!* You know, it's interesting. You hear comments like that, you go online and read the comments on the news stories, and there's just not a lot of sympathy. From any quarter. People are kind of, almost, amused. Happy. I've heard that Darwin joke a couple of times now. Also—the serial killer's name is *Binge Drinking*. The serial killer's name is *Stupidity*. And then I realize that these murderers were so so smart to pick this particular demographic."

I cleared my throat. "Listen," I said. "Aqil, why did you do that?"

"Do what?" he said.

"Why did you transfer your theories to me, instead of taking ownership of them? That was very strange to me, that you wanted me to be the mouthpiece. And it made me very uncomfortable."

He shrugged. "Well," he said. "I thought they might take you more seriously. You've got the *Doctor* in your title. And there's enough rumors about me going around in the law-enforcement community as it is. I mean, if you're writing a book and I'm consulting, that seems a lot more legit than you're my *life coach*."

I just gazed at him. Nonplussed. There were maybe a few things that I should have broached at this point, things about the relationship between the therapist and the health-care consumer that could have been opened for discussion. But of course we were beyond that.

"I'm just saying," I said. "If you feel that role-playing is important to this—uh . . . I think you need to make that more clear to me. I felt a little taken off guard, and"

"Okay," he said. He flicked his finger against his forehead, like it was a melon. "My bad."

And he turned to gaze at the long grassy field that stretched out behind us, the woman and the girl sitting at a folding table with their sad box of donuts and their coffee urn. "Hey there, young ladies," he called. "Is this where we volunteer for the Slade Gable search?"

The Kiwanis Recreation Park appeared to be a few acres of cleared floodplain, a flat expanse with a baseball field for Little League and a small football stadium and a stretch of mowed green space that ran along the western bank of Grand River. A flock of Canada geese had settled on the lawn and observed irritably as we walked past, but didn't rise to their feet. In the distance, a lone figure was tottering along the edge of the cyclone fence wearing a Day-Glo vest, and we watched as he bent and appeared to examine something on the ground.

"Come on," Aqil said. "Let's go look at the river."

The edge of the park met the river just above the bridge of Main Street. There were some weeds and rocks, and the riverbank was lined with large broken slabs of cement. Pieces of sidewalk? A line of geese marched single file up from the muddy banks, and Aqil paused to watch them curiously.

"That's like ducklings—the baby brothers and sisters follow each other like that, right?" he said. "That's so cute."

"Yes," I said. "Goslings." And then he strode toward the water's edge, his arms swinging cheerfully at his sides. *Manic?* He seemed so happy. I watched him alight on one of the cement blocks with a graceful leap, and he shaded his eyes and peered up at the traffic passing by on the bridge above the river.

It was not an impressive river, in my opinion. About as wide as a suburban street, and the same dirty gray shade as the sky. Not water you would drink from. *Eigengrau.* It ran mildly across its silty bed, and there were narrow shoals of rocks and sticks and detritus. A ragged black plastic bag hung off a log, writhing dreamily in the current. Not a place to drown in.

"Aqil," I said. "This seems like it's too shallow to"

But Aqil only raised a finger, beaming at me. He pointed toward where a fly fisherman was standing, fifty yards down. The fisherman was in the middle of the river, which was about knee-deep, wearing hip waders and a black stocking cap. We watched as he cast his loose line and it unraveled with a sleepwalking slowness.

"Hello!" Aqil called. Cheerful and full of enthusiastic charm. "Hey!" he said, but the man kept fishing as we walked down the edge of the bank toward him. "Morning!" Aqil cried aggressively, and at last the man looked up. He was Caucasian, mid-fifties, with hard blue eyes and deep-etched frown lines.

"What're you fishing for?" Aqil said.

"Steelhead," the man said. He squinted one eye.

"Catching any?" Aqil said.

"Not yet," said the man.

And then he turned. Casting again. The conversation was over.

"If there was a body in this river, they'd have found it by now, don't you think?" Aqil said as we picked our way upstream, north toward Lake Erie. "I just want you to say now that it doesn't seem likely that there's a body in this river."

"It doesn't seem likely," I agreed.

"But there will be a body after December twelfth," he said. "You know that now, don't you?"

"I," I say.

I didn't quite want to answer yes, though maybe I   yes.

But my mind was drifting a little. I had done my share of grief counseling, and of course I'd previously experienced grief, as well, after the death of my parents and my aunt and uncle. For years I had taken a pharmaceutical regimen of mood stabilizers, which had always been effective.

But this startled me, whatever it was. The way it inhabited the body. It wasn't a mood; it was a physical sensation, not unlike drunkenness. The body both numb and hyper-real: the stony weight of the eyes in their sockets, the porcelain scrape of the teeth touching one another, a dull throbbing on the edges of the skin where it met the air. And the air itself had a viscous quality, thick, trudging through mud or snow. *Eigengrau.* Not atypical to lose chunks of time.

And when I lifted my head we were talking to the mother of Slade Gable. She was a couple of years older than I was—forty-four? forty-five?—long, wavy strawberry-blond hair, athletic of build, hazel-eyed, stunned—and I recognized the glazed disbelief, the look of someone who hopes that maybe it's a dream, and Aqil said, "This is my card. I'm not in any way associated with the police. My partner and I—we're investigators looking into this particular case, and other ones like it. And not for profit or anything. We're just here to help," he said.

Our eyes met, hers and mine. "Thank you," she murmured.

Nemeth's Lounge was the kind of place where locals were huddled together talking and laughing and they all looked up and grew silent when we walked in.   There was a smattering of working men— a laborer, mid-twenties, nursing a beer and whiskey; a road worker who might be his uncle, in an orange vest; a pair of bearded frowners in flannel shirts. There was a woman in a red Buckeyes sweatshirt, her graying hair still teased and feathered into the kind of bouffant a heavy-metal girl would have worn in 1987.

It was a narrow, boxcar room, a length of wooden bar counter on the left, a length of vinyl booths on the right, a pinball machine, a Ms. Pacman video game, a hall at the back that led to bathrooms and a backdoor exit.

Behind the bar was an elderly white man—aged seventy, perhaps; silver-haired, rosacea-nosed, with the wiry look of an old sailor—

and a younger Filipino woman, and the two of them turned toward us as we came in.

It was the kind of dive bar that had probably been around since the 1940s or '50s, the kind of place that had been ironically rediscovered by college students. Rockabilly bands played here on weekends. There were cheesecake nudes, old centerfold calendar girls hanging on the walls, the old-fashioned poses: kneeling, breasts bare and jutting, toes pointed.

We sat in a booth beneath one of these posters and Aqil considered it. "Is that Bettie Page?" he asked.

"I'm not sure," I said. The wooden surface of our table had been gouged with graffiti.

Brittany '09, it said. *Mot! Fangface 2010* and a crude sketch of a cat. I cleared my throat.

"Listen," I said. "Is there an issue with calling ourselves 'investigators'? A—somewhat—misrepresentation?   Impersonating a"

"Well," Aqil said. "I didn't say *'private investigator.'*   I didn't say *'licensed.'* I mean, we're investigating. That's what we're doing. I don't see the problem."

"Mm," I said, and the Filipino woman approached our table, smiling exaggeratedly.

"What can I get you, gents?" she said, with just the trace of an accent. A soft, high, musical voice. A round face made severe by heavy makeup.

"I'll have a Coke or Pepsi," I said, and Aqil ordered a beer.

"You got a menu?" Aqil said, and the woman touched his shoulder confidentially. "Hamburger or cheeseburger," she told him kindly. "French fries or potato chips."

"This is the bar where that kid disappeared, right?" Aqil said. "What's going on with that?"

"Ugh," she said. "College students are a lot of trouble! It's a business, so they're welcome here, but—so crazy." She gestured regretfully at the defaced surface of our table. "Look at this mess," she said. "Why would you do that?"

193

"I guess they have people out today searching for him," Aqil told her. "Down by the river."

She nodded gravely. "He's dead, probably," she said, and walked off with our order.

"I'd like to talk to that friend of his," Aqil said. "The one he was with at the bar when he disappeared. He's probably out there searching, don't you think?"

"Possibly," I said. "But I don't think we should be misleading people." I sipped my water. "I'm not writing a book, for example."

"Not yet," Aqil said cheerfully. "But anyway, all I want to do today is just try a walk-through. Just a pretend thing, like you do when you're hypnotizing people."

Pretend!   I thought.

It had always been my contention that guided confabulation could be a powerful therapeutic tool, but of course it was never a good course of action in a case where the health-care consumer was having difficulty distinguishing reality.

Was that, in fact, the case with Aqil? I realized that I didn't think so anymore. I realized that I accepted his basic premise—at least the core of it.   I believed that it was likely that the body of this boy would be recovered some time after December 12.

"Let's imagine," Aqil said, "just for the sake of expediency, that I'm Slade Gable, and you're his friend whatshisname. Lambert.   It's the Friday after Thanksgiving. Black Friday!—I didn't even think of that. So most of the kids have gone home for the weekend, I imagine. With their families. So why are Gable and Lambert at school?"

"They're both from Pennsylvania," I said. "And Gable has a track meet coming up, so maybe he has practice over the weekend."

Aqil nodded. "Okay," he said. "So. We're sitting here. It's a small bar—smaller than I expected—so probably crowded on a Friday night, but fewer college kids than usual. We're sitting here in the booth, drinking pitchers of beer.   We're drunk, right?"

"Yes," I said.   "But you have track practice in the morning. You wouldn't be overdoing it."

"That's right. We're not talking about a reckless person, are we?"

"No," I said. "Although—pole-vaulting. It seems like it might give you a certain kind of adrenaline, doesn't it?"

"Hm," he said, and nodded his head thoughtfully, and we were both holding this thing between us—this story. It was nothing but conjecture built on the barest of facts, but I could feel that we were there together. Aqil and I. It was as if we were both leaning over an arena, watching a play unfold, and yet also collaborating in directing its movement. Our brains were both in a shared imaginary space, and both of us could move around in it, we were watching it from above and acting in it at the same time, I was imagining Lambert and Gable as if they were in a movie but I am also sitting here as Lambert, watching my friend drain the cheap beer from his plastic cup and pour another and I surmise that neither one of them had girlfriends, and I see them as athletes but a little on the nerdy side, and I think *pole-vaulter.* It's just such an odd thing to want to do. Psychologically, what would be the attraction? Flying, I guess?

"So," Aqil said, "we've been talking about sports and classes and da da da, and then I get up and I'm going to go take a piss and get another beer and I'll be right back. And I leave my coat in the booth."

"And I'm sitting here," I said, "waiting for you to come back . . . sipping my beer and thinking and maybe running my fingernail over the graffiti . . ."

"You don't pay attention to where he went," Aqil said.

"No," I said. "If I'm looking at anything, I'm probably scoping around the bar to see who's attractive. I've probably already previously noticed several women and now I'll probably devote some time to watching them in earnest."

"*In earnest,*" Aqil said. "I love that. But how much time passes before you start to wonder why he hasn't come back? Five minutes?"

"More, I think," I said. "You'd probably start getting a little bored after ten, but it wouldn't be terribly abnormal. Maybe there's a line at the bathroom. Maybe he saw someone he knew and he's talking to them? I think it could be as much as twenty minutes before you'd really start to wonder what was going on."

"So how long before you go looking for him?" Aqil said.

And it struck me. "I actually don't think I would," I said. "I'd probably be annoyed and a little hurt, maybe, but I think I'd assume that he left for some reason or met somebody; I don't think I'd be *worried, though*. I wouldn't think he was in trouble or in danger—"

"Would you call him?"

"No. That would be too—I don't know—needy or clingy."

"Ha-ha! You're not his girlfriend, right?"

"Right. I might text him. And then if he didn't answer I'd just think, *fine, screw it*, and I'd finish my drink and go home."

"Yes," Aqil said. "Exactly. And you'd be annoyed enough for a day afterward not to be worried. I'll bet that's exactly what happened. But we've got to talk to Lambert."

I imagine that Slade Gable walks through a cluster of people toward the hallway at the back. There's a pair of café doors that lead to the tiny kitchen where hamburgers and cheeseburgers are made; and then there are the bathrooms, Men's on the left, Women's on the right; and beyond that, there are stairs leading down to a basement; and beyond that, there is the back exit, which opens onto a small fenced patio, and some graffiti-tagged dumpsters, and a parking lot.

1. Let's pretend Slade goes into the bathroom and there is a urinal and a stall and a sink, and the door doesn't lock.   There is a window the size of a bread box, a slot shape with opaque textured glass, and he couldn't fit through it. He has to come out again.

2. Pretend that Slade goes down the basement stairs and there is a narrow crowded storeroom stacked with beer

kegs, cardboard boxes full of liquor, file cabinets, cob-
webs, framed posters from rock shows long past, glass-
ware, silverware, napkins, cleaning products.

At six foot one, Slade would be ducking his head and feeling the wooden beams of the unfinished ceiling bearing
down upon him and he'd wonder why he'd gone down
here in the first place; maybe there was a shape a figure
something that caught his attention

3. Let's say that Slade goes out the back door and onto the
   small fenced patio, where a cluster of smokers has gathered. They are talking—someone is telling a story, and
   they are listening; the listeners all have one eye on the
   mouth of the storyteller and another eye is inside the
   story, picturing it. They don't turn as Slade walks wordlessly past them.

   He may be stumbling a little; he's surprised to feel so
   drunk! His head is very fuzzy, and he just needs some
   fresh air.   And he sees the short Mexican dishwasher
   standing by the dumpster, and the dishwasher is standing
   there with a plastic bucket of slop and gazing up at a
   three-quarter moon and draws on a little joint and holds
   the smoke and then lets it out in a slow cumulous plume
   and Slade thinks *Have I been roofied?*

4. Imagine that Slade walks into the parking lot and it's
   close to full, though it's not big enough for more than ten
   or fifteen cars. There is the freckled crud left behind by
   melted snow. The asphalt is full of lightning-bolt cracks
   that have been lazily patched with black tar, and he is
   aware of the ugliness, the dinginess, of the back ends of
   things.   The place where businesses hide their garbage
   bins, where the raw brick and metal siding are unadorned
   and the true nature of things—worn, trashy, economically
   sinking rust-belt decay—is not hidden by the Main Street
   façade.

There might be a figure at the far end of the parking lot. Someone he knows? Someone who beckons to him? Someone—a police officer?—who is an authority? He walks over. He gets in the car (or he is *placed* in the car, somehow?) and is driven away.

5. Or he just decides to take a walk. Beyond the parking lot is a slope that leads to a narrow, curving, ill-traveled street, the street that leads past the Kiwanis Recreation Park, where the geese are huddled dark shapes that shudder in their sleep, and a few raise their sleek dark curving necks to observe him as he passes.
Wait. Why would he go this way? His home is in the opposite direction.
Maybe he's feeling blue.   It's a darker mood than Lambert would have noticed, not something Slade wants to talk about. It's a feeling that has been bothering him for a long time, that he can't name, and he comes to the thin river and begins to walk along its banks, stepping along the cement slabs, picking his way through reeds and scrub trees, and above him the icy and merciless stars. He can see that his life is not going to work out the way he was hoping it would. Even something as simple as an upcoming track meet feels like a sign of expected failure, and he can see the old cemetery at the top of the ridge on the other side of the river, he can see the silhouette of the mausoleums and the bare, burnt lightning-struck trees, it's all like a bad angsty poem written by a sensitive middle school boy and he thinks: *I just need to keep walking.* Or maybe he starts to jog. There is a path that leads along the edge of the park, tracing the river toward where it dumps into Lake Erie.

6. Let's say he's been drugged. Something in his beer, probably, a drug of the soporific class. Yes, Rohypnol, perhaps. Before he gets to the bathroom, a pretty girl takes his

hand and maybe kisses him on the cheek. *Come on*, she says sweetly, *follow me*, and he can't quite focus his eyes but he grins because she is so pretty, and she likes him, they are holding hands, he can feel the soft lotiony dampness of her palm, which is a kind of promise, and they cross the parking lot into a copse of trees and just when they are about to kiss he feels a bag pulled over his head

7. "Slade!" a voice calls from the basement. "Slade, come down here. I want to show you something."

   Slade squints uncertainly.   He feels woozy—more drunk than he should be.

   "Who's talking?" he says. But he takes a step down the stairs. "Lambert? Is that you?"

8. He gets up from the booth and gives his crew cut an itch with his fingers. "Dude," he says. "I'm going to go take a piss. Do you want another pitcher?"

   "Yeah," Lambert says. "Sure. Why not?" "Okay," Slade says.   "I'll be right back."

DECEMBER 8, 2012

IT FEELS SO good to be outside yourself!   You press yourself into another life and it presses back into you, and then the pressure equalizes—some parts of you have been replaced, or diluted at least. All the things that have been crawling in slow, endless circles around the circumference of your mind have been washed down a drain for the moment. You're *investigating*, and it holds you in its arms and focuses your attention.

For example, I hadn't given much thought to Rusty for weeks. Not until Kate called me on Saturday morning.   I was sitting in the breakfast nook with my laptop, searching for news stories about Slade Gable, and I picked up the phone absently. "Hello, this is Dr. Tillman," I said curtly, and she said, "Dustin . . . ?"

It was a month since Jill's death, and Kate spoke in that soft, empathy-buttered voice people like to soothe on new widowers. "So how are you doing?" she said—an imitation of a therapist's intonation, one that I'd heard myself using often enough. But in the past weeks I'd come to recognize its awfulness. The way the voice lowered you into a jar of chloroform and sealed the lid.

"I'm fine," I said. "I'm back at work. I've still got a lot that needs to be taken care of. I haven't cleaned out her closet yet. I have to take her clothes to Goodwill."

"You should just," she said, "just take your time. There's no hurry, is there?"

"I don't know," I said.

Because I didn't know whether there was a hurry or not. I thought that there might be.

And then I heard Kate's breath against the phone's earpiece again, a soft exhale rendered into digital audio, and it occurred to me that she must be smoking. Maybe I'd buy some cigarettes?

"Rusty called Wave, I guess," Kate said.   "I think they might be in some kind of contact or conversation, I don't know. But she has talked to him at least once, apparently. She was very vague, as usual."

"What did he say?"

"God! I have no idea.   Talking to Wave is like talking to a Magic 8 Ball. There are no straight answers.   I'm just, like . . . he hasn't talked to *you*, has he?"

I blinked.   "Of course not," I said.

"Because he hasn't called me, either. And I'd just like to know what his game is. Calling *Wave*. Or whatever her name is now."

She cleared her throat. She always got quiet when the subject of Wave came up. The fact that she and Wave were estranged, that they were so alienated from one another—it was a kind of loss that wasn't that different from a death. The two kinds of grief had a kinship.

"How long had it been since you last spoke to her?" I said, and she didn't reply. Through the line, I could hear the sound of a faucet being turned on, and I guessed that she was getting herself a glass of water.

"Probably . . . five years?" she said.

I nodded. I glanced back to the Google search that I had been doing on Slade Gable, scanning through the paltry results. "Well," I said.

"Can I ask you a question?" she said after a moment. "Have you . . . ?"

"What?" I said.

"Have you told Aaron and Dennis? About the Rusty stuff?"

I looked up from the laptop. The question actually sent a spark of electricity through me. "No," I said.

I hadn't told anybody except Aqil about Rusty. But especially not the boys.

In truth, we had never even discussed the murders. They knew that my parents were dead, but Jill and I had never agreed about how to tell them the full details, or when. "We'll explain it to them eventually," she said. "When they're ready."

I didn't really know when that would be. How do you explain to your children that your parents were murdered? And at what age would they be mature enough to absorb the information? Age twelve? Age sixteen? Now—age seventeen and eighteen, just after their mother had died?

"It doesn't seem like a good time right now," I said.

"I know," she said. "But I just keep thinking: *What if Rusty tries to call them?* It's a scary thought!"

"What?" I said, and the electricity ran through my fingers and toes; I straightened up. "I don't think he even knows I have children. How would he know . . . ?   Unless . . . did Wave say?"

"If he can get in touch with Wave, he can get in touch with anybody. With the Internet—Facebook? I just think you should be prepared. *They* need to be prepared."

"What are you talking about? Why would he . . . ?"

"Dustin, he could do a lot of damage," she said. "He could do a lot of damage in a short time."

DECEMBER 9, 2012

HIRAM COLLEGE WAS about an hour southeast of Cleveland, about half the way to Youngstown along Route 422.   We crossed over the La Due Reservoir and Aqil regarded it. We were on a four-lane highway, passing across a stretch of water on a low bridge, but the air was so misty and the light was so dim that the lake was just a blurry flatness, still as a parking lot. The sky and the water reflected each other, horizonless, just a blank scrim beyond the low corrugated metal bridge fence that traced the edge of the highway.

"That would be a good place to drown," Aqil said. "But it's too far for him to walk there."

"Ah," I said.   I had been thinking about talking to the boys. Broaching the issue of Rusty with them. But Dennis was away at Cornell, and it wasn't a conversation to have over the phone. And Aaron was elusive at best—the only times I seemed to encounter him, he was on his way out the door, or on his way up to his room.

But maybe when Dennis came home for Christmas? I could order some pizza, and we could watch a movie—maybe a movie about prison? Or about foster brothers? Something that would give me a jumping-off point for further discussion. Would that be the way to do it?

I wished that I could consult Jill, but I couldn't prompt her to say anything, even in my imagination. All she ever whispered was *wait . . . wait . . . wait.*

I don't know how long I'd been quiet before Aqil cleared his throat. "Dustin," he said. "What do you know about isolation tanks?"

"I don't know," I said. I blinked. Had I missed some part of the conversation? "I've recommended them for some patients. I think the preferred term is *sensory-attenuation tank*. It's a," I said. "I think it's a good experience for many people. Which is—the word *isolation* has negative connotations, and I don't think it really reflects—"

"I was thinking that maybe that would be a good way to keep them incapacitated," Aqil said. "What if you kept them in an isolation tank? Their hands are tied, or maybe they've even been mummified in some way . . . but when they come out, they're so disoriented that it's really easy to sacrifice them. Don't people go crazy after a certain number of days in isolation?"

"There are studies," I said. And I pressed my forehead against the cool glass of the passenger-side window, and outside there was a yellow diamond sign that said RIGHT LANE ENDS and a three-armed telephone pole and a smatter of bare trees that clustered, staring like bystanders. "There are the Lilly experiments from the 1950s about sensory deprivation—which, yes, can lead to hallucinations and depression and so forth. But on a practical level"

"But if you fell asleep in an isolation tank, you wouldn't drown, right?"

"My understanding," I said, "is that you're in a very dense saline solution—probably Epsom salts? So it keeps you floating even if you were to go to sleep."

"Interesting," Aqil said.

"Well, I don't think," I said. "It would be very complicated to keep someone in sensory attenuation for more than a few hours. The captive would have to . . . urinate and defecate and so forth. So practically speaking that would be," I said, "a problem."

"A problem for who?"

"Well," I said. And I pushed the idea of that from my mind. "I suppose more importantly, if you were keeping them in a tank longer than a day, they'd have to eat and drink."

"Mm," Aqil said. "What if they have a feeding tube? Or maybe there's just rubber straws dangling near their mouth that they can suck on, and water comes out. Water laced with painkillers. Sometimes they get some kind of liquid protein.   Sometimes they get whiskey."

DECEMBER 9, 2012

IT SEEMED LIKE I was clear a lot of the time. Right now, for example, Aqil and I were in Garrettsville, Ohio, and we were sitting down to speak to the sister of the boy who went missing at Hiram College. And I felt very alert and present.

The disappearance of Keegan Brewer was less newsworthy, even, than that of Slade Gable. No search parties had been organized, however small; no one was combing the edge of a river, however shallow and unlikely. There was only a single mother, waiting in her home for news from the police.   The older sister, Ciara, aged twenty-two, worked as a waitress in nearby Garrettsville, and Aqil had somehow organized a meeting with her at a coffee shop. I imagined that Aqil had told her we were "investigating," and it was easy for me to settle across from her as if she were a patient.

"How are you doing?" I said.   Made eye contact.   Gave her a sympathetic gaze.   "I hope you're holding up okay," I said. "It's got to be a hard time for you and your family."

I can imagine that Aaron and Dennis would laugh if they saw me. They would think it was phony, this attention I was bending toward

this sister, *smarmy*, they might say, but it wasn't that at all. I was trying to direct my whole mind toward her—not an easy thing to do—
and if my approach would seem laughably obvious to them, that was
only because there was a certain kind of soft, calm voice that I knew
was relaxing.   Even if smarmy. Even if uncool.

She was a small, thin young woman with a sharp face that reminded me a bit of Kate and Wave. She had those thin hands, too,
but hers were chapped and cold, and she had the fingernails of a
severe onychophagiac. It was the kind of nail-biting that seemed like
the sign of an impulse-control disorder.

Ciara sighed, looked at me skeptically. "Well, we're not getting a
lot of support."

"That's a shame," I said. "You haven't had a good impression of
the police response?"

"Fff," she said. "I don't know what the cops are doing." She observed a hangnail on her index finger with dislike, and then plunged
it into her mouth and gave it a bite. "And there was, maybe, *one* article in the Akron paper. Nothing in the Cleveland news. Like it's no
big deal; I guess people go missing all the time."

I nodded. There were a lot of things I was making an effort not to
think about. I was not thinking about Jill.   I was not thinking
about her face, that last smile. I was not thinking about Dennis or
Aaron; I was not thinking about Rusty in Chicago. I was not thinking about the picture that Aqil had shown me, my dad with his prosthetic arm extended as if reaching out with his hook, his eyes and his
mouth still open.

"That's why we contacted you," I said, and I focused on the young
woman's flecked hazel eyes. "We just want to help you out in whatever small way we can. You should know that we're not associated
with an official agency of any kind, we're just privately investigating.
I've been . . . working on a book about these kinds of disappearances."

The girl regarded me. "What do you mean—*these kinds of disappearances?*"

And I acknowledged her concern silently with my expression. "Unexplained," I said. "Disappearances where the facts don't quite add up. Is that your own experience with this? Do you have some ideas about what might have happened?"

She looked at her cup of coffee. "He wasn't depressed," she said. "But he had a concussion about six weeks ago. Something from wrestling practice. And it took him a long time to get completely over it. And I think he wouldn't say how bad he really felt, because he didn't want to have to miss a wrestling meet. So that's something that worries me."

"I see," I said. I glanced over at Aqil, who was watching avidly, and he gave me an encouraging nod. "I wonder," I said. "Do you know whether he'd experienced any previous brain injury? With athletes, mild traumatic brain injury is often underreported. If there's substance abuse, that can prolong the symptoms. Did he seem more nervous or irritable than usual?"

"I don't know," Ciara said, and it occurred to me that she herself was nervous and irritable in the way of a concussed person—that, in fact, grief and brain injury had a lot of the same sets of symptoms. "I do know he was drinking. A lot. But not, like, alcoholic. Just—the way college guys are heavy drinkers."

She took a small sip of her coffee. "But why would he go out walking at eleven o'clock at night in November?" she said. "That doesn't even make sense. I mean, it's Hiram, Ohio. There's no place to walk to. I don't know. Was he in trouble in some way, and he had to skip town? I was close to Keegan, but there are probably things he wouldn't tell me."

I nodded, and Aqil and I exchanged looks again. He lifted an eyebrow.

"Have you ever heard of fugue states?" Ciara said. "I've been reading about it online. It's like you have amnesia? But at the same time you start traveling. Like you're running away from something, but you don't know what."

She paused. "I'm thinking maybe it could be a fugue state,"

she said. "I feel like I would know it if he was dead." I watched as my hand reached out and touched the back of her hand.   As a therapist I'd always felt that physical contact should be used sparingly: It could be a very loaded and psychologically complex gesture, difficult to gauge appropriately—but she didn't flinch.

Of course he was dead. That's what I told Aqil afterward.

"But I don't think it's a match," I said. "With the other profiles you've shown me, I think this one—he's not one of ours."

Aqil raised his eyebrows. "You got a little psychic glimmer, did you, Doctor?" he said, and I winced.

"No, no," I said. "Not at all. Just an intuition. And it might not be right. But I think she suspects he's dead, as well. I could tell that right away."

Aqil gazed out at the road, quiet for a long while. We listened to a song on the radio. "See?" Aqil said at last. "I knew you were the right one."

DECEMBER 10, 2012

I'D NEVER IN my life had a "psychic glimmer," as Aqil had called it. *I don't have psychic glimmers,* I said.

Though for years and years, I wished to. In middle school, I dreamed of having telepathy: imagined hearing people's thoughts and then perhaps creating subliminal suggestions that they thought were their own ideas. Also moving objects with my mind, making silverware bend and books fly off the shelves and locking doors so no one could get away.

I used to try to practice. In high school, after the murders, back when I was living with Grandma Brody in Gillette, Wyoming, I used to concentrate hard on the necks of fellow students as I sat in my desk behind them. Hoping to make them feel an itch or a sharp poke.

I wished for magic powers. I used to practice moving my hands as if I were a wizard, as if I were casting a spell. I used to pretend that I could turn people into animals—monkeys, pigs, chickens, rabbits, dogs. I would just form my fingers into rune shapes and the transformation would happen immediately. In the lunchroom, I once turned a student-council girl into a mole, and a shy ugly boy into a snake.   The mole and the snake both looked surprised at first, but then the snake turned to the mole and felt very happy. I almost burst out laughing!

I still remember that fantasy so clearly.   More vividly than any actual thing that happened during that time.

After Kate graduated from high school and moved away, I was very lonely.   An active imaginative life, but not much in the real world. No matter how hard I tried, I couldn't read anyone's mind. No matter what I wished, I couldn't make them sprout feathers or scales.

But I did, genuinely, have a good intuition.   I didn't know how I knew, for example, that blowing on Mrs. O'Sullivan's fingers would give her relief from her pain, but it came to me clearly, and in the same way, talking to this girl, Ciara Brewer, I could feel a sharp picture of her brother emerging.   He had a brain injury. He had been drinking heavily. He was likely using steroids or other performance-enhancing drugs.   There would obviously be severe mood swings, I thought, and if he hadn't killed someone else, I thought, he had likely killed himself.

And I saw that Ciara thought that, too, when I looked into her eyes. *I feel like I would know it if he was dead,* she said, and I thought, *oh, you know it.*   She was already in mourning.

Yes. *He's likely killed himself,* I thought.

I sat on the couch, eating carry-out Vietnamese food and staring at the news. The death toll in the Philippines from Typhoon Bopha was nearing seven hundred, and rebel forces had seized an army base near Aleppo, Syria, after weeks of heavy fighting. The governor of Colorado had issued a proclamation allowing the personal use of marijuana. There had been a murder–suicide at the Cleveland airport.

And yet most of the workings of the world slipped by incognito. CNN wouldn't broadcast the news of Keegan Brewer's death, or Slade Gable's; there were, no doubt, terrible tragedies in Nigeria and New Zealand that I would never know about. I could hear Aaron coming through the back door, and I looked up from the TV to see him pass briefly through my peripheral vision. A flit.

Have you told Aaron and Dennis? About the Rusty stuff?

"Hey, honey!" I called out. "What have you been up to?"

No answer.

DECEMBER 10–11, 2012

WOKE UP AND there was an image I couldn't catch. A memory? A dream?

I was sitting on the couch with my tumbler of whiskey still clasped in my left hand. TV going, the same news from the Philippines, no idea what time it was anymore, and I thought I had a realization. *The gibbeners!* I thought. As if I had just had a bolt of inspiration. I wrote it down.

"Here's the place where that kid drowned," Rusty said.

It was the irrigation ditch that ran along the neighbor's property.

You could see it from a distance because the banks of it were the only thing that was green in the flat gray-yellow sod: Wet, greedy grasses and reeds growing high on the borders. A barbed-wire fence along one side.

You'd think it was nothing. Not much wider than a sidewalk—with a running start, you could jump across it. The water was flat murky brown, moving steadily toward the sluice gate, but in a smooth, still way. You'd never guess it was deep.

But I knew that the boy had been swimming and had been caught by a pipe that was carrying the irrigation water. The suction was very strong, that's what my dad told me, which is why you should never ever play near it.

"You know what a gibben is, right?" Rusty said. "It's where they tie your hands behind your back and then they push you into the water. And then they just watch you drown."

He put his arm on my back and I felt the touch of his palm. We were alone together on weekends, after school. Just the two of us, Dusty and Rusty, going for a hike.

must've been eight or nine years old

"But," I said. "Why would . . ."

"That's the rule. If you talk, that's what happens," he said. "If you try to tell anyone that they exist."

"But who are *they*?"

"The gibbeners," Rusty said, and gave me one of his secretive looks, nudging me closer to the edge of the water, so that I stumbled a little. "The gibbeners. They get around you in a circle, with their hands behind their backs."

"What have they got behind their backs?" I said. I looked into the water. Eddies of mud, coursing sinuously but purposefully, too.

Rusty only smiled. "You should take a dip," he said. "I won't let anything happen to you."

"No way," I told him.

"Why not?" Rusty said. He put his hands behind his back. "Don't you trust me?"

And the radio in the car still playing   just a little of the tinnitus in the ear, a slow, high-pitched leak of air
                        behind your back

And then
    parking in the lot behind the Bay Village office,   spraying sharp, painful mint
                into my mouth to mask
                        the smell of cigarette
    and I also spray a little
                mist of fabric refresher onto my clothes
    And I have my session with Mrs. Goland at nine-thirty and
    This kind of thing has happened before. These sudden, hard jolts of memory—or half memory—the way you lift out of them dazed, in a state of vague, disconnected adrenaline.
    Look behind you.   *No, don't look behind you!*

You want to think that it must mean something. This dream, this memory—you have a temptation to do a sort of Freudian analysis. Is your subconscious trying to tell you something? And if so, what?
    He could do a lot of damage. He could do a lot of damage in a short time. Have you told Aaron and Dennis?

Debbie McCrae in the break room at noon, sitting there eating a vegan meal from a bento box and she smiles at me kindly. "Oh, Dustin, how are you doing," she said, in a voice that performed kindness and sympathy. She tilted her head and gave me a concerned, therapeutic look that was obviously practiced but not necessarily un-genuine.
    "Good!" I said. And then I didn't want to seem too glib, I didn't

want to seem like I was brushing off her gesture, so I shrugged and showed my palms, I grimaced wryly but let my eyes go sad. "It's a complicated process, of course," I said. "But I've got a good support system, and I'm working, and . . ."

"If you need to talk . . ." she said. She made her eyes larger, and it seemed that there was a very thin, moist layer over her pupils, like a contact lens made of water—not that she was going to cry, but that her eyes were welling with empathy. Such an expression, I thought, must be extremely effective during therapy.

"Sure," I said. "Yes. Absolutely."

Jill hated Debbie McCrae so much.

Debbie McCrae had once been a cheerleader for the Ohio State University Buckeyes football team, and she was still a very hearty, athletic-looking woman. She was a well-regarded grief counselor, with a number of lucrative gigs at hospices and intensive-care units in the area, and every time they'd met socially, Jill had a negative reaction.

"The cheerleader who became a grief counselor," Jill said. "It's just so exquisite that it's almost unbearable."

"Exquisite?" I said.

"Give me a *D*!" Jill said, and shook imaginary pompoms over her head. "Give me an *E*! Give me an *A*! Give me a *D*! Your husband is dead!"

"Oh, come on," I said. "She's really nice!"

"*I'm sure she is,*" Jill said.

And then I woke up and it was night and there was the sound of a skateboard rolling along the street outside my house.   The very distinctive sound of small wheels on asphalt.   And then the wooden *click* as the skateboarder jumped off the ground and landed.

I sat up in bed and pulled aside the shade and peered down. There was a halogen streetlight right in front of the house, and I could see the kid in that washed-out light. Caucasian, blond, his hair in dreads.

He was shirtless, wearing pants that had been cut off just above the ankle and big white high-tops.   Maybe fifteen years old?

He skated down the street in front of my house, then jumped. Then he went back and did it again. There was a little slope bump in the street, and he was using it for practice.

I took my phone off the nightstand and looked at the time.   2:27 A.M.

Really? There wasn't snow on the ground, but it must easily have been below freezing.

I got out of bed groggily and went to the bathroom, and even then I could hear the sound of the skateboard: *Rooooll. Slap. K-chint.* Then back to the beginning. *Rooooooooll. Slap! K-chint!*

I padded from the bathroom to the edge of Aaron's room and stood there in the threshold of the doorway. He was curled up, his face turned away, but I could see him breathing.

No one is skateboarding in front of the house, I told myself. *Not in the middle of winter.*

I went to Aaron's bedroom window and pulled aside the shade. The big maples in our yard bared their naked branches like fangs or claws.   Sleet swirled around.

And Aaron stirred irritably, shifting under the covers. "What?" he mumbled. "What are you . . . ?"

"Are you awake?" I said. "I thought I heard something."

He sat up and palmed his eye. "What?" he said.

"Do you hear something?" I said. And he squinted.

I felt like I could clearly see the skateboard rolling riderless down the street, the soft gargle of wheels rolling along asphalt, clear and sharp.

In a circle, with their hands behind their backs

But Aaron only sighed and settled back into the covers.

"There's some things I need to talk to you about," I said.

"Mm," he said.

"Let's have dinner together," I said, and then I lifted my head again and listened.

It was possible that something had been looking for you for a long time, and at last it was drawing near.

DECEMBER 11, 2012

I was in the process of hypnotizing Mrs. Kasso when my phone vibrated, and I couldn't help but glance at it. It was a text from Aqil.

> I need to talk to you

"You will walk safely in your way," I said, and Mrs. Kasso echoed. "I will walk safely in my way."

> This is important!

I put my fingers very lightly over Mrs. Kasso's closed eyelids, and then brushed the chakra spot in the middle of her forehead. "I'd like you to imagine a place that you'd like to be right now," I told her. "It might be a place from childhood that you loved, or a place from a book you've read, or a movie you've seen. It might be a place that you dreamed about . . ."

> Can you drive to Painesville when you get off work? It's almost December 12. I think we need to go out there tonight! Area near the river must be patrolled!!! Pls let me hear back from you ASAP

I GOT INTO the passenger seat of Aqil's car and I hesitated.

Some strange things had happened to me in the past twenty-four hours, but none of them felt as if they could be discussed.

I could ask him, I thought. *How can I explain to the boys about the murders? And about Rusty? Should I?*

I could tell him about the

What could I say about the skateboarder that wouldn't sound—

Or the gibbeners? The hands behind the back? The flat reflection of the water in the irrigation ditch?

He would make too much of it, I thought. He was still in a state where he could be led into confabulation and wild theories; he was susceptible to paranoia. You could both go further down that path. Wouldn't it be better if one of you still hewed to the path of reason and logic?

If Jill were here, I thought, *I would know what was real and what was not real.* But now I wasn't sure. I could feel a strong thrum in my chest, right in my breastbone, as if I knew something, as if I was certain, but was I?

Sometimes Jill would say, *that seems reasonable.* Sometimes she would say, *that doesn't really make sense.* And that had been my guidepost for the better part of my life. Now there was no one to tell me the difference, and so my thoughts bobbed uncertainly as Aqil drove.

THERE WAS A little park that ran along the eastern bank of Grand River, and when we pulled in, there was a chain barring the lot. A sign said:

GROUNDS CLOSED

during hours of darkness

And Aqil said, "We'll just park the car here." And he turned off the ignition and we got out into the purple-skied gloaming. He took a small flashlight out of his jacket pocket and handed it to me; then he retrieved another for himself. The flashlights were about the length of a hand and the width of a finger, smooth black metal—the kind you'd imagine a cop used to shine down onto a pair of teenagers in the backseat of a parked car. He flicked his on, and I did the same.

"Let's just walk down this way a bit," he said, and gestured. "Don't worry, we're not going to get in trouble. If security boys come, we'll tell them we're looking for a lost wallet."

We walked along the wood-chip-covered path that ran curving along parallel to the river. I passed my light across a tall, blackened bare tree that had been struck by lightning.

Here was a plaque that had pictures of PLANTS OF THE FLOOD-PLAIN. *Wild Rye. Bladdernut. Toothwort. Loosestrife. River Oats.*

Aqil pointed his light across the river. "You see that?" he said.

On the other side of the river, up an embankment, there was the vague glow of civilization.

Streetlights, the backs of buildings. "That's the back parking lot of Nemeth's Lounge. That's where our boy was last seen."

The trail continued along the river, winding northward toward Lake Erie, which lay about four or five miles distant. Sections of the bank were thickly sheltered by high cattails and reeds. "I just want to patrol up this way about a mile or so," Aqil said. "I don't even

216

know what I'm looking for. But most of them tend to be found near the site of disappearance." He passed his light along an old gravestone. GAGE, it said. The dates worn away. "I mean, you've read the dossiers. That's another crazy thing, how they suddenly show up in the exact place where people were searching when they went missing. They weren't there then, but suddenly they're there now? That doesn't make any sense, does it?"

"I noticed that, too," I said. I spoke in a low voice, because Aqil, I thought, was talking a little loudly, and he was walking at a pace that was almost bouncing, *brisk*, when it might be better to be a bit more   cautious.

But he didn't get quieter. He was keyed up—manic?—and he looked back at me and showed his teeth in that way, not really a smile. "I had an amazing revelation," he said. "This is something I forgot to tell you."

"Yes?" I said. The river was a ripple of moonlight, and I kept my eye on it.

"The moccasins. Peter Allingham's moccasins. What were they doing on his feet?"

"I don't know what you're saying."

"You fall in the water and you don't thrash hard enough to kick off *slip-on leather moccasins?* Are you kidding me?"

It was a startlingly good point, and it gave me pause. "Unless they were very tight," I said.

Aqil laughed. "Very tight," he said. "That's rich."

"I didn't mean to discount your observation," I said. "It's actually . . . very astute."

"Thank you," said Aqil.

He doesn't seem nervous enough, I thought, and I looked ahead where the shadows of trees appeared to be a pair of large cupped hands. And I observed as he shined his light on another plaque posted at the trailhead—this one about the importance of floodplains, written in the language of friendly grade-school science textbooks.

The floodplains between the Tigris and Euphrates rivers are home to some of the world's earliest civilizations and first cities, including Ur, Aqil read aloud.   He looked at me, raising an eyebrow. "Doesn't that sound weird to you?" he said. "*Ur.* That's like the name of a demon."

"It's an ancient city," I said. "Sumerian, I think. It was somewhere in the south part of what's now Iraq."

"Mm," Aqil said doubtfully. "I don't like it."

The trail tended upward, but not too steeply.   The river was now below us, down an embankment, and Aqil kept his light pointed low, a pool at his feet.   He was circumspect suddenly.

At last he said, "What do you think we're looking for?"   His voice was much softer. Not quite a whisper. "What's your intuition, Dr. Tillman? If you're going to do a ritual murder . . . a human sacrifice? Where do you do it?"

"Well," I said, and I couldn't help but think of

"Well," I said, "there is generally some kind of sacred site, something that can be desecrated. It depends. It might be a graveyard. An abandoned church? It might even be some spot   an underpass for example   that has been tagged with graffiti that represents the cult's symbols and that has been consecrated by animal sacrifice. Often dogs or cats"

Aqil peered at me. "*Sacred sites,*" he said. "I like that."

Down the embankment, on the branch- and rock-cluttered shores of Grand River, a black-pelted rodent bigger than a rat scurried into the water.

"They're going to kill him tonight, I think," Aqil said at last. "Or tomorrow afternoon. That's my crazy stuff with the dates, I know, but . . . yeah. My guess is they want to kill him at 12:12, on 12/12/12. That has some power, doesn't it? Even thinking about it as a nonbeliever, you have to say that you're going to at least notice it! Right?"

"Maybe," I said. "It seems like it would attract the superstitious. There's twelve signs in the zodiac. Twelve disciples—not just in Christianity, but in many occult sects."

I tried to say this blithely. I tried to banter like Aqil bantered, but my hands felt cold, and I shined my flashlight around because now it was coming on full darkness.

"Plus we've got that Mayan apocalypse coming up in a couple of weeks," Aqil said. "Did you read about that?"

"Yes," I said. "A kind of pop-culture eschatology. I wouldn't think anyone who's truly invested in occult practices would take it seriously."

"Eschatology, eh?" Aqil said. "I love your vocabulary."

I cleared my throat, blushing a little. "I'm just trying to understand your conception of this supposed cult. Are you expecting people to show up in black hooded robes?" I said. "And they'll— what—sacrifice the victim in front of the tomb?"

And even as I said this, I was hit by a vivid bullet of memory.

That night in the graveyard—

Me. Kate and Wave. Rusty and his friend. Rusty drawing the pentagram on the gravestone in chalk. I watch as he slowly unzips his backpack and spreads it open and the baby rabbits are inside, squirming and blind and pink, and he lifts one out and Kate says, "Guland, do not make us go to Yellowstone National Park. Let us stay here and celebrate your glory with our friends—" and that's when I see the figures. They are standing at the edge of the trees that circle the cemetery, and they are not robed and they are not necessarily even there, they are just a flicker, barely more than silhouettes. A tall man with a cape and a three-cornered hat. A short man with an unnaturally long nose, like a proboscis.

A dollop of water fell onto my glasses. And then a few more drops hit my face and I looked up.   "Is it raining?" I asked Aqil.

Aqil looked up at the sky suspiciously. "I don't think so," he said.

I held out my hand but no more water hit it. *Weird,* I thought, and I put images of the graveyard to the back of my mind. The memory, which had been acute, had now begun to desaturate and fade back, thankfully.

"I don't think they'll sacrifice him here," Aqil said. "They'll want to do that in a more private place, so they can take their time with it. But I'm thinking that they may have marked the area where they'll dump him with some kind of . . . like you say, an animal sacrifice, or graffiti."

I considered this. It made sense, of course. But I realized that there was some part of me that was imagining we had come here to stop them. To catch them before they killed the boy.

"There's not really any way to save him," I said. "Is there?"

But he wasn't paying attention. "Shh," he said abruptly. He had gone to the edge of the embankment, his body suddenly tensed, and he shined his flashlight down toward the river. Aqil's light passed through a long strip of scrub trees, and the shadows of their trunks stretched out, extending grotesquely, and he took a step down.

"Careful," I said.

It was quite a steep drop-off, not what you would call a cliff, but still not something you'd want to lose your footing on.

But instead of watching his step, he turned off his flashlight and motioned fiercely for me to do the same. "Shh," he said, and pointed.

A figure was standing in the silvery, shallow water of the river. The river was about as wide as a two-lane highway, with ambling curves and eddies running over large stones, and the shape—the person—appeared to be standing knee-deep in the middle.

He was fly-fishing. We watched him swing his pole, cast his line, reel it back. And then he repeated.

Aqil took another step down and put his foot in a gullet of leaves. He stumbled briefly.

"Careful," I said.

"Shh," he said.

There was something mechanical about the figure's movements—an uncanny sort of repetition, a stuttering quality to it, like a hologram or a splice of projected film that was being looped over and over. Was it possibly an optical illusion? Maybe, I thought, it was just a cluster of shadows—a tree stump, with a caught piece of string that was blowing behind it in the wind—that looked exactly like a fishing man?

And then, abruptly, there was movement at the periphery of my vision. It startled me, and I turned to glance back. In the distance, a collection of moving shadows was pacing around the circumference of my parked car. *A velociraptor?* It was taller than my car, with a hunched, tiptoeing movement.

There was the possibility of dopaminergic neurotoxicity with some of the medication that I had been taking. Possibility of acute amphetamine psychosis—paranoia, delusions.

I heard the soft, slow beat of hooves. *Clip, clop, clip, clop.*

"Aqil," I said.

I turned on my flashlight and pointed it in the direction of the thing, and that was when I realized that it was a person on a horse.

This appeared to be illuminated in my flashlight beam. There was a black horse and a rider in a uniform: a wide-brimmed hat like a Mountie, the glint of a yellow shoulder-sleeve insignia. A soldier from World War I on horseback? It seemed certain that I was hallucinating.

"Aqil?" I said.

And then the light hit me.   Aqil turned now, but he was a few feet down the ravine, and it was steep enough that he struggled to climb upward.

The flashlight trained on me was blinding—police grade, military grade, I thought—so I put my hands up to shield my eyes. Glowing, dazzling coronas expanded across my vision, but I could see the figure of the horse stepping lightly along the path toward us. *Clip clip clip.* And the rider swaying sleepily in the saddle.

"Are you lost?" a brightly Midwestern female voice said. "Sorry, this park closes at dusk!" she said, swaying closer, and I felt Aqil at my shoulder.

Aqil shaded his eyes with his palm and peered upward. "Officer?"

he said, and grinned ingratiatingly into the light. "Or—I'm sorry—Ranger? We're looking for a lost wallet," he said. "We dropped a wallet somewhere around this area."

"Oh! That's unfortunate," the woman said. She'd stopped about ten yards away from us, and I couldn't see anything but her silhouette. The horse's hooves tsked a couple of times on the asphalt road, and it lifted its head as the woman pulled on the bridle. "Well, you'll probably have better luck looking for it if you come back in the morning."

"You a ranger?" Aqil said. "I didn't realize this was a park. Is this area under your jurisdiction?"

She turned the full force of the flashlight's beam on Aqil, and he squinted his eyes shut, a hand in front of his face. "I'm afraid I'm going to have to ask you to leave this area," the woman said. "The park is closed. There's a sign, and there's a gate. Maybe you didn't see them."

"Do you mind if I ask you your name, ma'am?" Aqil said. "Do you have some identification that you could show me?"

"Sir," the woman said, and the horse shifted restlessly underneath her. "I need you to return to your car and leave this area.   This area is restricted after dusk, sir."

"Yeah," Aqil said. "I get that. But what's your name, Officer? I would really appreciate it if you could give me your badge number, if you don't mind."

The figure was silent for a moment—and it occurred to me for the first time that it was possible that this person wasn't a real officer, a real ranger, but whatever she was, she clicked her tongue and the flashlight shuddered along our faces as she began to approach at a trot.

I felt Aqil's hand clutch the ham of my forearm. "She's got a gun," he murmured. His breath against the helix of my ear. "She's got it drawn.

"I need you to jump," he whispered.   And then he shoved me.

I thought there might have been the sound of a gunshot, but I wasn't certain. A sharp crack—! And the   And

I thought I saw Aqil's arms fly back, pinwheeling, and then he fell down the embankment toward the river.

I started to run—it was a pure panic now—but then I fell, too, tumbling end over end, down the side of the ravine.

DECEMBER 11, 2012

THE SLOPE WAS about a sixty-degree angle, and there was no way to catch my footing in the mud and leaves and brambles; there was only the hope that I could avoid hitting the trunks of trees that were flying past me, that I could somehow not break my neck. But I was in the hands of gravity, and when I reached the bottom I landed hard. My thoughts went black.

And then Aqil was leaning over me, crouched, his gun unholstered and ready, and I could see that his shoulder was bleeding. The hand that held the gun was shaking so hard the movement was blurred.

"Fuck," he said. "Shhh. Shhh! Be quiet!"

His eyes were wide. He turned swiftly in a circle, holding his gun in both hands. "Don't move!" he hissed. "Don't move!"

I pulled myself to my hands and knees. The walking trail was a hundred feet above us, the hill a hunched shadow behind the net of bare trees that were angled along the slope. The horse and its rider were nowhere to be seen.

We were silent. There was the sound of the river and the sound of cars passing over the viaduct in the distance.   No hooves.

"Shh!" Aqil said. He held up his hand, and I saw that the entire left side of his shirt was soaked with blood.

"Oh my God," I whispered, but Aqil kept his hand out to silence me. "Shhh!" We listened together for a long time, both of us tense and waiting.

There was nothing. We were on the muddy banks of a river, and the light rain pattered and rustled. The fisherman we thought we saw was gone. There was no flashlight shining from above us, no ranger on a horse. After a long while, Aqil lowered his gun.

"Aqil," I said. "My God! We need to get to a hospital."

Aqil looked down at himself, puzzled. He wiped his hand over his bloody shirt and looked at the wet blood on his palm. "Fuck," he said.

"You've been shot!" I said, under my breath, and he turned to me scornfully.

"Shot?" he said. "I got poked by a stick falling down that god-damned hill." I watched as he grimaced and touched his shoulder gingerly.

"It's *cops*," he said hoarsely. "Maybe real cops, maybe people dressed as cops. But that's how they get them."

He touched his wound again and looked at his palm. More blood. He smelled it. "Okay," he said. "Take me to the hospital."

DECEMBER 11, 2012

BY THE TIME we left the emergency room, it was almost midnight. I'd been sitting in the waiting area, trying to piece the events together into something coherent.

Had we been attacked?

If so, why didn't they pursue us?

I put my hands in my lap, clasped them, fingertips against knuckles: the feeling of being in a dream when you are not in a dream.

Depersonalization. Derealization. It is a common symptom when you are experiencing an anxiety attack. I pressed my clenched hands against my chest, and an elderly black woman in a ski coat stared at me with disapproval.

I smiled and nodded, but she looked away, avoiding eye contact by pretending that she was considering the dull abstract paintings on the wall.

I took out my phone, and that gave me a little grounding. The online world reached out and gripped my hand. I heard the phone make its comforting musical sounds.

New text messages.   From Aaron.

11:51 PM December 11   WTF?

6:50 PM December 11   Didn't you make a big deal about having dinner together tonite? LOL Nvr mind.

DECEMBER 12, 2012

AND THEN AQIL emerged and stared at me sternly. He was still wearing his bloody shirt, though now there were bandages on his shoulder. "Let's go," he said.

We walked grimly out of emergency and into the parking lot, where it was still raining.

"Damn it," Aqil said. "They knew we were there. They know about us. I should never have talked to Ellison!"

"You think your friend Ellison is . . . ?"

"Pff," Aqil scoffed. As if the thought of Ellison being involved was ridiculous. "It's just that they all gossip among themselves, so they knew that we'd be looking around out there."

"I'm very confused," I said. "Who's 'they'? Who was that woman on horseback?"

"Must've been one of the cultists," Aqil said. He considered. "Or maybe she really was a park ranger. But I didn't like the look of her."

"Surely we can find out her name," I said. "If she's really a ranger. We could—"

"Mmph," he said. I felt his hand close over my forearm, and his fingers tightened. "I feel like I'm close to figuring it out. This has been really helpful."

I nodded uncertainly. I opened the door of the car, and then, I didn't know why, but I was abruptly aware of an absence. "Oh," I said. I touched the back pocket of my pants, and then I put my hands in my jacket.

Empty.

"I think I lost my wallet," I said.

DECEMBER 13, 2012

BACK IN THE late eighties, early nineties, we earnestly believed in these things. My professor, Dr. Raskoph, was an authority on recovered-memory syndrome, dissociative identity disorder, et cetera. There had been no doubt that Satanic Ritual Abuse, as it was then known, was a real and true phenomenon. It was a legitimate subject to explore in a dissertation.

It had been a hot topic for a while. How many people were living with repressed memories, we wondered? One in ten? One in *three*, perhaps? The image of the father leaning over the bed, your eyes opening, only half awake. The face looming toward you.

Or: The image of hooded figures encircling you, peering down at you. The sensation of being awake but unable to move, the voice box shriveled and hard as a walnut.

Some kind of violation by a powerful figure. A horned demon, clutching your wrists, forcing your legs open. A cluster of masked figures, exposing themselves above you, swollen, uncircumsized penises swaying pendulously. Your baby ripped live from your bleeding womb, your baby screaming and screaming, umbilical cord dragging behind it as the soft throat is slit, and the blood poured into cups. Various celebrities in the crowd, laughing. Sometimes it might be a powerful well-known figure—a senator, or a CEO of a Fortune 500 company, a pop star or talk-show host—watching from a distance as his bodyguards force you to strip naked.

It was a metaphor, of course. If the memories were not literally true, then they represented distorted versions of traumas that *had* truly occurred.

But as the claims became more extreme, the whole thing became increasingly improbable. Lawsuits began to be filed against psychiatrists who had helped their patients recover memories of Satanic abuse; convictions were challenged; according to FBI Special Agent Kenneth Lanning, *the number of alleged cases began to grow and grow. We now have hundreds of victims alleging that thousands of offenders are abusing and even murdering tens of thousands of people as part of organized Satanic cults, and there is little or no corroborative evidence.*

A professor from a California university testified that the theory of "repressed memory" was a myth unsupported by reliable scientific evidence. "It's the worst form of quackery in the twentieth century," he said. "These so-called therapists have destroyed thousands of American families."

Meanwhile, I had finished my dissertation and received my PhD, and I had started a small practice, and I had testified in a number of court cases that involved recovered memory.

I was aware, of course, that there was growing hostility to some of these ideas. I no longer spoke of "Satanic Ritual Abuse" but rather simply "Ritual Abuse," or "Sadistic Ritual Abuse." I freely admitted that Dissociative Identity Disorder had been wildly overdiagnosed for a period, even by Dr. Raskoph, who by that time had been stripped of her license to practice medicine and was on indefinite leave from her position at the university.

But I thought I was being very careful and conservative in my diagnoses. I felt quite confident in what I was doing, until a patient that I had been treating recanted her testimony on the witness stand during a trial. Gina Deleo. Her father had murdered one of her childhood friends while she watched, she alleged, but then during cross-examination she had suddenly balked.

"I don't know whether anything I'm saying is true," she said. "I think it might not be."

I had worked with her for over a year, and her disavowal shocked me as much as anyone. I had been convinced by the memories that she had recovered while under hypnosis. I had believed in them.

In some ways, I still believed in them.   The event was so vividly described! I could still see her father sitting there next to his lawyer, with his thick white hair and pale eyes, and he would always look like a rapist to me.

But her memories had come while she was under hypnosis, and the defense questioned whether these were even permissible as evidence.

Later, Gina Deleo said that I had "implanted" the memories.

"He made me think up the most horrific things," she said. "And then he convinced me that they were real."

There was a lawsuit afterward, which was settled out of court, but certainly the career that I thought I was going to have was ruined. I was married to Jill, and Dennis was three, and Aaron was an infant. Once again, I would need to completely reinvent myself.

More than a decade passed.

I thought I was safe.

But now here I was, circling back. Or else it was circling back around me. Maybe I believed again—or maybe it once more believed in me.

DECEMBER 14, 2012

On Friday, both bodies were discovered. Keegan Brewer was found in the basement of an abandoned building outside of Hiram, gunshot to the head, an apparent suicide, which, with his history, was exactly what I would have predicted; Slade Gable was in a gravel pit near the place where Grand River dumps into Lake Erie. Workers had found the corpse in a shoal of thick silt on the edge of a fence that surrounded Osborne Concrete & Stone Company.

I guessed I would have expected that, too.

The river snaked a shallow, irregular path from the Kiwanis Park, near where Slade disappeared, to the lake, but police were speculating that the remains must have been slowly pulled downstream for some time—drifting, then catching on tree stumps or debris, and then drifting again, traveling, traveling, before finally coming to rest in a heap of sand.

"That would be a pretty beat-up body, don't you think?" Aqil said. "I wonder if they're doing an autopsy. I'd like to see some photos."

We were on the pier, trying to get a look at the site where the body was discovered, but Osborne Concrete & Stone was protected by a high cyclone fence. If there was a crime scene that had been blocked off, it appeared that it had been taken down.

"Ha!" Aqil said. "They probably didn't even put tape around it. Probably just brought in an ambulance and picked up the corpse and hauled it to the morgue. This death isn't going to be investigated. I have no doubt it's going to come back from the coroner as an accidental drowning."

"Really?" I said. "I mean, there will have to be . . . some kind of inquest, right?"

"Hm," Aqil said, and looked at me sidelong. How naïve was I? "I'll tell you," he said. "A body is found in a waterway and there's presumed alcohol consumption involved? The coroner isn't going to be looking too deeply into it. I told you. That's what makes these killings so smart."

"But the parents could insist," I said. "If they think foul play may be involved."

Aqil shrugged. "Yeah, maybe," he said, and made a wry face. "I haven't had much luck with that. The cops usually finesse them, get them convinced pretty solidly. That's one of the reasons I wanted to bring you on board, Doctor. I thought maybe you'd have more in common with these folks than I do. Thought maybe they'd be more likely to trust you."

He gave me a look that I found inscrutable, and we walked for a while in silence along the parking lot at the edge of the beach.   The waters of Lake Erie were choppy, bleakly hostile, like the eye of a fish.

"It makes so much more sense now if I imagine that it's cops," he said. "God! Do you know the mischief even one corrupt cop can make, just by being a *little bit* careful?"   Aqil shook his head.   "My guess is there's dozens.   All over the state."

"Really?" I said. "That seems like a lot." And I glanced toward the horizon, the line between lake and sky almost indistinguishable.

"So—what? These cultists just decided they'd infiltrate police departments? It's not that easy to become a cop, is it?"

"Of course it is," Aqil said. "A person goes to the academy for a few months, takes the test. Hell, *you* could do it, if you wanted. As a matter of fact, I think it might be useful if you tried."

"Hmm," I said. "The thing is, Aqil, almost all of the typical victims of Satanic abuse are young children, very occasionally teenaged females. Young adult males—I can't think of anything that isn't primarily associated with sadistic gay serial killers. Like Gacy or Randy Steven Kraft."

"But that's what's brilliant about it, right?" Aqil said. "It's not going to make much of a splash in the news. A drunk college boy drowns? It's a lot less conspicuous than babies or children or teenaged white girls. I mean, why not? Sacrificing a young dude might please the dark lord just as much."

I considered this.

In the summer, I imagined, Fairport Harbor might be a pretty place, an easy weekend drive from Cleveland. There might be sunbathers on the sand, and children chasing one another, inner tubes bobbing in the water, and people wading and swimming. There was a quaint lighthouse in the distance, looking out over Lake Erie.

But in December, the sky and the lake were the same featureless steel gray. The shore rippled with dull, unfriendly waves, and the sand was washed out, colorless. Twenty miles down, the hazy stacks of nuclear power plants were exuding thick white steam from their chimneys.

The rails on the sides of the pier were lined with seagulls, hundreds of them perched in a row that extended all the way down the boardwalk, and they lifted up as we passed and then settled back, hardly ruffled or even curious about our presence. "Creepy fuckers," Aqil said. "This is Hitchcock movie material."   A gull held its mouth open soundlessly, as if to say, *I bite!*

"I'll bet these things made a few meals out of poor Slade," he said. "Probably made a mess of that corpse."

I grimaced. It was not an image I wanted to picture. "Well," I said. "What do we do now? If your theory is true, it's going to be a year before they"

"Take another victim?" he said.   "Maybe. But we've got more information than we had before. And we've had some kind of contact. Maybe now they know about *us*."

DECEMBER 15, 2012

DENNIS WOULD BE home from Cornell at the end of the week, and I hadn't done anything to prepare. There was no Christmas tree, I hadn't bought any presents, the refrigerator was full of old leftovers and aging fruits and vegetables that neither Aaron nor I would really eat, though I kept replenishing the supply every time I went to the market. There was a lot of unused kale.

It was only six weeks since Jill's death, and I wondered—were these rituals necessary? Did anyone even want them? I didn't know. My mind felt like a shipwreck, a clogged lagoon with broken pieces of flotsam bobbing in it, a clamor of voices speaking urgently.

Do you believe, Aqil said in my head, even as I sat down with another patient to talk about compulsive eating behaviors, even as I scanned briefly through websites, looking for sweaters for young men that might make appropriate gifts for the boys, even as I sat up in bed and listened: the sound of a skateboard?

Then I lay there, silent. *Think of the constellations,* I thought. The little speech that I had made up for my patients, I repeated it in my head like a prayer I had memorized. *We look at them in one dimension, and it seems that they are all connected. We think that there's some image we can make out if we connect the dots. But more than likely the dots are not connected.   They're on separate geometric planes, light-years apart.*

But now, with my eyes opened in the dark, the clicks and hums of the house settling, the radiators stirring, the appliances doing their secret nighttime work, with my heart beating in an uncomfortably noticeable way, I couldn't help but think: *What if the dots* are *connected?*

DECEMBER 18, 2012

THE PACKAGE WAS in the mail when I got home from work. It was a padded manila envelope, nine by six inches, with my name and address printed out on a label. No return address. But I noticed that the stamps on it looked oddly old, like something robbed from a philatelist's collection.

The stamps were lined up, each with the picture of a bald white man etched in blue-gray ink. *Eisenhower. USA. 6c.* There were three rows of five, and they'd been hand-canceled, aggressively, no doubt by a bored and irritated postal employee.

I opened the envelope with a knife and my wallet fell out. At first, I felt only vague irritation. All the credit cards had been canceled already, and I'd spent a dull three-hour stint at the DMV to replace the driver's license.

And then I opened the billfold and saw that my money was still there—seventy-eight dollars in twenties, tens, fives, and ones—and I felt a twinge of guilt.

This was a nice person, who took the time to mail your wallet back to you! Without stealing from you, without even asking for thanks! How many people are there like that anymore?

I sifted through the mail for a moment. A water bill. A Christmas card from Jill's law firm. A flyer from the grocery store.

They must have gotten my address off my driver's license? I thought.

I opened the wallet, and, yes, the license was still tucked behind its plastic protector. There was a photo of Jill and me and the boys there, too, and I felt a pang of unease. *They know what all of you look like. They know where you live.*

I lifted my head and glanced toward the front window. Our street was not a main thoroughfare, and though our block was not close-knit, we were considerate neighbors. We loaned each other tools, we kept our lawns mowed and scooped our sidewalks right away after it snowed. We noticed if there were strangers in the neighborhood. I didn't have a house alarm, but I kept the doors locked and dead-bolted.

Then I noticed that a thin rectangle of plastic had been inserted into one of the folds in my wallet. I took it out.   It was just a plain black plastic USB flash drive.

SANDISK: cruzer   *micro 1GB*

DECEMBER 18, 2012

I OPENED THE door and Aqil was standing on the steps, his hands balled in the pockets of his oilskin drover jacket. The porch light was off. Aaron was staying over at Rabbit's house—studying together for a final, he said.

234

"Come in," I said. I whispered—I didn't know why. But he glanced over his shoulder, as if he, too, thought someone may be watching.

It was the first time I'd ever had a patient inside my house, and it was awkward. From the beginning, I felt strongly about this—I never wanted to practice out of my home; I was very careful about any kind of overlap between the professional and the private.   I had developed a few semi-fictional personal anecdotes that I would occasionally trot out to humanize myself, but for the most part I felt that borders were important. Lines needed to be drawn between the different aspects of our lives. The idea of a patient walking into my house was as unnerving as encountering a character from a television show coming down the sidewalk toward you.

But Aqil, I realized, was no longer really my patient. We shook hands, and I ushered him in, and it occurred to me that I probably needed him more than he needed me. There was not another person I could talk to.

No doubt, he was as uncomfortable as I was. I noticed him glance around in short flicks of his eyes. He wiped his boots on the mat, and, seeing the shelf for shoes in the foyer, he asked me if I wanted him to take his shoes off.

"Well," I said. "Generally. We do. Leave the shoes in the"

"Front porch," he said.

"Yes."

There was still a wilting orchid on the dining room table, something someone sent for the funeral, and he took note of it. He looked at the big framed family photograph from two years ago—me, Jill, the boys, standing in front of the blooming wisteria in the backyard.

He looked at the Christmas tree in the living room, which I'd decorated the night before with small, winking yellow lights. No help from Aaron. There were a few presents underneath it.

"That's a nice-looking tree," he said.

"It's HARD TO explain what it is," I said. I was in a state that I recognized as being close to panic—the kind of hollow, jittery dread that might come from too much coffee and no sleep. "It's—I don't know what the purpose of sending something like this is," I said.

"Let me take a look at it," he said, in a firm, calm voice.

He watched as I knelt down and plugged the flash drive into the back of my computer, and then the two of us sat side by side in chairs and looked at the big screen attached to my PC monitor. There was a single file on the drive, an MP4 video, and when I clicked on it, it opened in Windows Media Player, full screen.

It starts with darkness, low-end static, and then light opens up in a rounded cone. The image is blurry, gray scale, but you can see some kind of movement—quivering, almost gelatinous. It might be an image of a distant galaxy, or the inside of a cell, the shapes pixelating and growing fuzzy and then sharpening abruptly, briefly.

"What is it?" Aqil said. "Night vision?"

"Actually," I whispered, "I think it might be an ultrasound."

Beneath the static is a distinct, irregular thrashing.   At first it seems as if it might be some kind of musical instrument, but it slowly becomes clearer. It's the wet, hollow squeaking sound of a hand rubbing a window, a bare foot on the floor of a bathtub.

Then the shape of a human hand passes through the darkness and swirling white flickers. The image is distinct for a few seconds, though it seems as if it's partially translucent; it appears that you can see the bones of the fingers through a film of skin.

But it's clear that we're watching a creature that is thrashing and struggling. It appears to be curled up like a fetus in a womb, but it's not a fetus. It's an adult human figure, and there are flashes of limbs, a hand, the sole of a foot, an openmouthed face half-obscured in darkness.

And all the while, under the hum of static, there is the sound of water splashing, and a young man weeping, calling for help, choking.

PART SIX

The future is fixed
The past ever-changing—

—LYNDA BARRY

FALL 1983

WHEN THE TRIAL was over and Rusty was sent to prison forever, Kate and Wave and Dustin were remanded to the care of their grandma Brody, in Wyoming.   No one listened when Kate protested. Their house was the only home they had ever known! It was their senior year of high school! They had been planning to graduate with all of their friends.

"Wave and I are seventeen!" Kate exclaimed. "Why couldn't we just be declared legal adults? We could take care of Dustin; it's not that big of a deal."

But no. Apparently nobody was willing to negotiate.

It had all happened so quickly—much more quickly than Kate thought it was supposed to.

The prosecutor was a balding, spidery man who smiled at her as if he were on a children's show and she were a puppet he was supposed to pretend to talk to. "Our community is eager to be healed of this incident," he told her. "Our first priority is to make sure justice is meted out as quickly as possible." He showed her his small white teeth, which to Kate looked like baby teeth.

They thought there would be money, but there wasn't.

"Don't you get paid if your parents are murdered?" Dustin wanted to know. Plaintively.

"I guess not," Kate said.

They had been imagining that they would get to continue living on in their own houses, in their own rooms. It turned out that their homes weren't even owned by their parents! Their houses were owned by a bank, which their parents paid monthly. The cars, the camper, the appliances—all were purchased on credit. There was no life insurance.

Because they were minors, many things were decided for them—very abruptly, Kate thought—and she was suspicious of the social workers and lawyers who began weaving webs around them. But what could they do? They had no money, no car, no place to go. As it turned out, they didn't own *anything*.

What had happened to all the money that Uncle Dave had gotten as a result of his accident? No one alive could tell them.

And so they were sent away, broke and orphaned, and they sat silently on the bus as it traveled toward Gillette, Wyoming. Dustin slept heavily beside Kate, curled into a ball on the seat, his legs tucked under him, his face smushed against the window. Wave sat in a different aisle, because of course one of them had to sit with Dustin.

Wave would glance over her shoulder from time to time; their eyes would meet. Wave kept making expressions that suggested she thought she was owed an apology.

They arrived in Gillette at about midnight, and they were dropped off on the outskirts of town. There was a Kum & Go convenience store there, and a sign for Smart Choice Inn, but instead of a motel there was only a gravel lot with some broken-up car parts and a rusted backhoe.

They stood blinking in the halogen lights, watching the semis rush past. It was the middle of September. They each had one suitcase.

After a while an old four-door Buick came rolling slowly up and stopped. They watched as the driver's side window slid down, and a thin, hollow-eyed man in a cowboy hat peered out at them. His glasses were tinted a yellowish-brown, as if they'd been stained by cigarette smoke.

"You the Tillman kids?" he said. He had a surprisingly deep voice for such a small man.

"Who are you?" Kate said.

The man stared at her wordlessly for a moment, to show her that he didn't like her tone. "My name's Dolin Culver," he said at last. "I'm your social worker."

He lifted a can of Pepsi to his mouth and thoughtfully spit tobacco juice. "Get in," he said. "I'll take you to your grandma."

They sat in the back of Dolin Culver's car, with Dustin between them, and they didn't speak.   They were driving out into the countryside beyond the lights of Gillette, and soon there was nothing to see outside the window but darkness and stars. Kate had never understood why people liked to look at them, constellations and whatever. They were so boring and random.

I don't have anything to apologize for, Kate thought, and she took Dustin's left hand and clasped it. Were she and Wave at the stage of actually "not speaking"? Kate wasn't sure.

"So," Dolin Culver said, after they had driven in silence for a while. "I reckon that you kids have had a rough time of it. I want to let you know that, anything you need, you should call me."

He turned around to look at her. She couldn't see his eyes behind his tinted glasses, but she guessed that he was sizing her up and down. He was younger than her parents, maybe thirty or so, but still old.

"Why are you wearing sunglasses," she said, in a tone that was polite but still made it clear that she thought he was gross.

"It's them photosensitive lenses," he said. "It's only supposed to go dark in sunlight, but they stopped working."

"It makes me uncomfortable," Kate told him.

She could feel Wave staring over at her, probably giving her another judgmental look, but they didn't make eye contact.

And then they pulled up to the old house.

It was a few miles outside of town, on a barren stretch of county road, a two-story farmhouse from the 1920s, and Kate recognized it right away.

The girls had come here when they were little, when they were five, six, seven. They used to visit in the summers; they used to come for Thanksgiving or Christmas.

Then, after Grandpa Brody died, the visits had stopped. Their mother and Dustin's mother—Vicki and Colleen—had gotten into a disagreement with their mother over some belongings of their father's that they wanted to have as keepsakes. Grandma Brody had refused, and eventually heated words were exchanged. Things were said that couldn't be undone.

The place had changed a lot since the last time Kate and Wave had seen it. Ten years had passed, and from the outside it now looked abandoned. One of the front windows was boarded up, and another had plastic sheeting tacked over it.   There was a dead crabapple tree in front of it—which, as Kate remembered, had once held a tire swing.   The grass had long ago turned to weeds.

Grandma Brody came out of the front door when they arrived, leaning on her cane. She lifted her hand, squinting into Dolin Culver's headlights, and Kate remembered how Vicki and Colleen used to complain about certain things she had done when they were teenagers.

She would lock them in their room at night, and there was a big thorny rosebush below their second-floor window, so they couldn't escape that way, either. She had taken jewelry that their father had given them and worn it herself. She had burned letters that Uncle Dave had sent Colleen from Vietnam.   "She set the letters on fire in the sink," Vicki told them. "And then when they were burned, she turned on the water so the ash washed down the drain, and then she smiled at poor Colleen." Vicki shook her head. "That was just pure sadistic," she said. "And after a while we came to realize that was the core of her. It made her happy to see other people miserable."

Kate and Wave hadn't remembered her that way. She had been nice to them when they were little girls, as they recollected, made them good food and sat with them at the kitchen table and they made dream-catcher wind chimes out of yarn.

She didn't look that different from what Kate recalled. More wrinkles. A more pronounced hunch in her back. But her hair was still short and permed into a puffball on top of her head. She still had that large, unfeminine nose that belonged on a truck driver or a plumber, and wide ruddy cheeks, and long earlobes that the girls used to like to stroke, when they were small enough to sit in Grandma Brody's lap.

And she still had the same voice. Even if she was a strikingly ugly woman, her voice was quite lovely. She called out to them as they opened the back door of Dolin Culver's car and stood in the drifting exhaust, tinted red from his brake lights. "Oh! My poor babies," she called, and if you closed your eyes and didn't look at her, you would have thought her voice was the alto of a mother from a long-ago television show, the kind of mother who would stroke your hair as you fell asleep, the kind of voice that could sing a lullaby.

"Oh my Jesus!" she said. "You poor babies."

And the three of them stood in the gravel driveway under the wide stars, and Dolin Culver drove off without another word.

Hugs were exchanged. She told them all how grown-up they looked, even Dustin, who was thirteen but looked like he was ten.   She apologized for making them take the bus. "I have a gal down the road that gives me rides to the grocery store and to church, but I couldn't ask her to drive all the way to Nebraska. That would be too much."

Grandma Brody didn't drive, Kate remembered. *Refused to,* Vicki and Colleen said. This had been one of the sources of disagreement between Grandma Brody and her daughters. They had wanted their father's car after he died, but Grandma Brody refused. The car was a beautiful blue and white 1957 Studebaker that Grandpa Brody had loved, that Vicki and Colleen had loved, as well. "But she'd rather let it sit in that garage and rust," Vicki said. "Spiteful old witch."

Kate glanced over at the garage—which leaned at such an angle that it seemed about to fall over. She imagined the rusting Studebaker hunched inside.   She could sense it there, just as she could sense the house, and the dead tree, and the pulse of crickets—all of them beaming out a soft, malevolent glow.

"Oh! It's so late," Grandma Brody said. "Almost one in the morning! I'm usually sound asleep by nine!"

Fuck, Kate thought.

And then she and Wave and Dustin followed Grandma Brody into the house.

Based on the condition of the outside, it was about what Kate expected. Maybe a little worse. The living room was like someone's old attic or storage shed—stacks of magazines and junk mail, furniture that seemed to have been set down haphazardly in various corners, dishes, cardboard boxes, knickknacks, a fuzz of dust on the lampshades that made the light seem dull and dirty. Smell of mildew and some kind of baby powder.

"There's a bedroom down the hall where you kids will be staying," Grandma Brody said.

But it wasn't until they opened the door that they realized that it was the bedroom of their two dead mothers: Twin beds, a vanity dresser with a large oval mirror. Some old stuffed animals resting on the white chenille bedspreads. "Your grandma always bought us the ugliest things she could find," their mother had told them once. "If she saw something in a catalog that she knew we'd hate, she'd buy it for us."

Wave was the first one to enter the terrible room. She went silently to one of the beds and lay down without taking off her clothes. Kate and Dustin looked at one another.

"I can sleep on the floor," Dustin whispered, but Kate shook her head.

"No, no," Kate said. "I don't want to sleep in that bed by myself. There's enough room." She took his hand and held it. "It's going to be okay," she said.

That night, she dreamed about the morning when they discovered the bodies.

They were asleep in the camper, and she was a little hungover. Dustin was next to her, and she could feel his damp mouth against the side of her arm, and at first she thought the sound was a bird or a dog that had been hit by a car. Shrill, almost mechanical shrieks.

And then she realized it was Wave's voice. She sat up and Dustin cried, "What? What?" and she went running toward the sound that Wave was making. This awful, high, rasping eeeeeeee sound, repeating over and over.

Being murdered? Raped? Tortured?   No matter what happened between them afterward, she would always remember this: *My sister was screaming and I ran to save her.* It was a deep, deep instinct, maybe it was what soldiers got when they were in battle, but she was going to kill whatever was hurting her sister, that was all she knew.

She saw Aunt Colleen dead on the porch, and she heard Dustin call out. "Mommy!" he screamed, and she was aware that he was on his knees, shaking his mother and trying to revive her, but Kate kept running forward. Maybe she would be able to get the shotgun out of the hall closet, she thought, and she saw Uncle Dave in the living room, dead, and she thought, *oh my God they are raping Wave*—she had a picture in her mind of Charles Manson and his followers, killing people and writing words with their blood on the walls, and she thought about turning back, she pressed herself to the wall and held her breath, listening for the sound of mean male voices.

And she saw her sister standing in the kitchen doorway.

Just standing there. No one was near her, and Kate took a step closer.

"Wave," she whispered. But her sister didn't turn. "Are they gone? Did they hurt you?"

The murderers were gone, apparently. If they hadn't killed Wave by this point, they probably weren't going to.

"Did you see who did it?" Kate said. She tried to put her arms around Wave, but it was like Wave was possessed. She went rigid and thrashed, and her eyes were blank.

But Kate held her tightly. She could see now what Wave was looking at. Their mother was dead under the kitchen table. Their dad was sitting on the floor, leaned against the counter. She could tell it was him because of his hands and his haircut. His face was just a hole.

Whatever creature was possessing Wave, it wouldn't leave even when Kate shook her and shook her, and then Kate had to walk across the kitchen, she had to walk barefoot through her parents' blood so that she could get to the phone and dial 911.

By the time she'd gotten Wave to stop screaming, the police had arrived. She put her hands over Wave's eyes and pressed as close as she could against Wave's back, and she told her that they were going to walk out.

"I can't," Wave said. "I can't move, I can't move!" And Kate put her mouth close to Wave's ear. She pressed her palms tightly over Wave's eyes.

"You can't see it," she said. "It's not there. Just walk with me; I'll lead you."

And she had guided Wave out of the house, away from the murder scene. Little tiny steps.

She startled as the journalist snapped the picture as they left the house. She took her hands off Wave's eyes.   The picture that would be in all the papers.

What was the photographer even doing there?

Just a bit of luck, as it turned out later. He was working on a piece about western Nebraska for *National Geographic*, and he happened to be doing a ride-along with the county sheriff when the call came in.

And then she woke up.

Dusty was breathing thickly against the side of her arm and she

248

was in Grandma Brody's house, sleeping next to him on his dead mother's childhood bed.

Fuck, she thought.

Wave was already awake. She was downstairs, sitting at the kitchen table, eating a bowl of oatmeal, and when Kate came in, Wave looked up and said nothing.

"The bus is going to stop right out there by the mailbox," Grandma Brody was saying. "First thing on Monday morning. I made all the arrangements. I talked to the principal, and he knows all about what happened to you three."

The old woman looked up and saw Kate. "Oh," she said. "Katelynn! I'm glad you're up. I was just telling your sister. I think it would be good if you three could start school on Monday morning. You've missed a lot already, and I think you need to get settled in right away."

She sat down next to Wave, but Wave didn't look at her. *Oh, come on*, she thought. "Stop it," she whispered into Wave's ear, and Wave glanced at her dully.

"Stop what?" Wave said, gazing back down at her oatmeal. Grandma Brody stood at the filthy old oven, stirring a pot. There was a clock in the shape of a cat on the wall. The cat's tail was the pendulum, and its googly cartoon eyes moved back and forth with each tick. It grinned and looked down.

After the murders, Dustin came to her.

They had spent hours and hours in the police station, and then afterward they had been "sequestered" at the house of one of the town's councilmen. Kate and Wave had wanted to stay over with one of their friends, but the police said it was out of the question.

Instead, they were in a part of town that Kate had never really visited. The councilman had a house in the hills above St. Bonaventure, in the very richest part, and when Kate went out to have a cigarette she saw that they had an actual built-in swimming pool in their backyard, which—in Nebraska—seemed like an insane extravagance. How many months of the year was it even usable?

There was a "patio" and a high fence around it, and Kate rummaged through her purse until she found a half-empty pack of Merit Ultra Light 100s. The pool emanated a chlorinated glow.

She was reclining in one of the deck chairs when she heard the sliding glass door open and Dustin came out. He came over and sat down cross-legged next to her. He was barefoot, wearing pajamas that someone must have given him, a man's pajamas that were too big for him.

She took a drag on her cigarette. She saw, from the way it wobbled, that her hands were shaking, but whatever she should be thinking about she was carefully unthinking.

"I," Dustin said. "I need to talk to somebody."

"Yeah?" Kate said. She breathed some smoke and watched it dissipate, and she stared at her feet, she stared at the blue water.

"I think Rusty killed them," he said. "I'm pretty sure about it."

Dustin was the last to awaken that first morning at Grandma Brody's. He came down sleepily, wearing those creepy men's pajamas, and Grandma Brody said, "Well, it's about time you got up, Dusty! You're sleeping your day away!"

Kate and Wave watched as Dustin ate his oatmeal. First, he moved his fingers above the bowl, as if he were pretending to sculpt something. Then he took a spoonful of oatmeal. Then he lifted the empty spoon to his mouth and pretended to eat something off it. He was playing some imaginary game in his head, Kate figured, but it was freaky, nevertheless. It made her uncomfortable.

He might be sick, she thought. *He might be having a mental breakdown.*

She glanced at Wave, to see if Wave was seeing what she was seeing. But Wave's face was hooded. She seemed to be observing Dustin with a kind of irritated boredom. Almost impatient.

Dustin wiggled his fingers over his bowl of oatmeal again, and they both observed him. "I'm nervous about him," Kate whispered to Wave. "Do you think he's all right?" Wave gave her a stern, eagle-like look, but she didn't say anything.

"Please," Kate whispered, her lips close to Wave's ear. "Don't do this."

The cat clock grinned. The dirty curtains on the window above the sink stirred and billowed. There was a shelf of salt-and-pepper-shaker knickknacks, and she could see a boy skunk with an *S* on his belly kissing a girl skunk with a *P* on her belly, and they both leered suggestively.

And then Grandma Brody told them that she was going to be reading her Bible and that they should go outside and play.

The night after the murders, the night they spent at the house with the swimming pool, Dustin told her about the things that Rusty had done. They were sitting side by side with their legs dangling in the water, and she put her arm around him because he was crying. Once in a while she turned her head to blow her cigarette smoke away from his face.

He told her that Rusty did drugs—which of course she knew—and that Rusty once pressured him into doing LSD—which she *hadn't* known, and which shocked her a little. She had never heard of a kid as young as thirteen doing LSD.

He told her that Rusty and some other people had tied a boy's hands behind his back and drowned him in an irrigation canal. It was a gang called the Gibbeners, he said.

"Did he *tell* you this?" she said. She didn't completely believe it, but she didn't want to sound skeptical. His back was shuddering underneath her arm, and she rubbed her palm in the space between his shoulder blades. "Maybe he was just bullshitting you."

Dustin wiped his eye roughly. "It wasn't just that," he said. "It was a lot of things."

He told her that Rusty said his real mother was a part of a Satanic cult, and that she had slept with a demon, and that Rusty said he was, himself, half demon. Rusty said that the cult had made his mother go to prison and they had her sacrificed there.

"He told me that, too," Kate said. "I don't believe it. He's such a liar."

"But sometimes there's a grain of truth in what they say, you know," Dustin said solemnly. *Grain of truth?* Kate thought. Was that something he'd read somewhere? "Some stuff is a lie. But maybe some stuff is true, too. Like—how his foster family before us died in a fire? And how he said that a cult did it? But I think it was actually him."

Dustin said that one time, when he was eight, Rusty tried to talk him into burning the house down. Rusty wanted to shoot Dave and Colleen and set the house on fire and take off in the truck.

"Are you serious?" Kate said. "Why didn't you tell?"

"He would just say I was lying," Dustin said dully. "And then he would kill me."

"God," Kate said, and kissed the side of Dustin's head. "I'm so sorry," she whispered.

But did she believe it? Could it be that Rusty was, like, really a psycho? It would make so much sense. All the things he had told her, which she thought were just fake stories to impress her.

There was one time—this was when she and Rusty were together, and they were sitting on the couch at her house, watching a video of the movie *Friday the 13th*, and he had his legs spread wide and his arm draped across the back of the sofa so that his fingers touched her hair, and her parents came in, along with Dave and Colleen, and Rusty looked at her sidelong and whispered.

"You know they all have sex together, don't you?" he said. He grinned and narrowed his eyes, in a way that she found devastating at the time.

"Shut up," she said. "You're so gross."

"They're part of the same cult that my mom was part of," he said. "The Order of Dog Blood. Why else do you think they adopted me?"

She stared at the TV. A boy was having an arrow pushed through him by someone who was hiding under the bed.

"I don't know why anyone would adopt you," she said. "You're such an ugly baby."

And he grinned more broadly. "They screw in all kinds of crazy ways," he said. "Brother touching brother. Sister touching sister. Sisters and brothers touching brothers and sisters they shouldn't be touching. And the stuff Uncle Dave does with his hook—it's unimaginable!"

She laughed. "Shut up!" she said. "You're making me nauseated."

This memory came to her as she and Dustin were sitting there in the backyard of the St. Bonaventure councilman. Their legs made soft sluicing sounds in the water of the pool, but Dustin had grown very still.

"He does," Dustin said. "He did . . . stuff to me."

She heard her legs moving nervously through the water and she made them stop.

"Like . . ." Dustin said. "Sex stuff."

"What do you mean?" she said. She felt Dustin's back muscles tighten, and her own spine stiffened in alarm. "What kind of stuff?"

"Not for a while," Dustin said softly. "Not since I was . . . nine or ten, maybe."

He looked down, and the pool lights glinted off his glasses. "He would get into bed with me," he said. "And he would, like, rub his"

Kate felt her hair tingle.

"Against my stomach sometimes," Dustin said. He put his hand over his belly button. "Or, like, my back. You know. The place where your butt starts?"

She didn't say anything.

She took her cigarette out of her mouth and gritted her teeth behind her closed lips. She knew exactly what Dustin was talking about, because it was one of Rusty's favorite moves—one of the things that originally made him seem kinky and exotic and experienced.   He'd push his cock back and forth against your belly button, or slide it along the crack of your ass, and at first she thought: *This is wild!*

But then he just, like, spooged on her skin, and at first the cum was warm, almost hot, but it cooled off very fast, and shortly it was like gross gelatin drying on you. She had to look around to find her panties to wipe it off.

And meanwhile, as she was cleaning his sperm off her body, he had fallen asleep.

He was a child molester. Basically a rapist.

She felt the slow realization bloom in her stomach and then branch outward to her limbs.

Maybe he was even thinking about little kids—about Dustin— when he was doing that stuff to her.

It made a shudder of revulsion go through her. Who could do something like that to a kid? And she had let someone like that— a pervert—put his dick in her?

Her face grew warm. Blushing, blood rushing to her cheeks, whatever. Her eyes were staring so hard they felt tingly. *Slow realization:* It made your mind feel like it was moving.   People said things like "my thoughts were reeling," or "my head was spinning," but up until this moment she hadn't understood that it wasn't just a metaphor. It was an actual physical sensation.

Her brain wasn't traveling as fast as "spinning" or "reeling." It was more like a bobbing.

As if it had detached and was now turning in a slow current.

So many things were clicking into place.

And now they stood outside Grandma Brody's house on a Saturday morning in September and nobody was sure what to do. Their parents were gone. The trial was over. All the little pleasures they had been anticipating about their senior year of high school had been taken away.

Their whole lives turned to ash, and she looked over at the garage, which lurched to one side and seemed to peer at her.   She thought of the dead Studebaker inside it.

They were so far outside of town that they couldn't even see houses. Just prairie, rolling slopes of it, and Dustin went wandering along the dirt road, looking for rocks. She and Wave stood there watching him.

Kate sat down in the grass by the front porch and lit a cigarette. "This is bullshit," she said. "We can't watch TV while she's reading her Bible?"

She waited for Wave to agree with her, but Wave said nothing. She folded her arms over her chest and sat down on the steps in front of the house, staring out at the mailbox, which sat on a post along the dirt road. Dead apple tree, still puzzled that it had been planted in this barren place.

"And did she really say, 'go outside and play'?!" Kate said. Trying again. "What are we supposed to do?   Jump rope?"

"Mm," Wave said.

Kate had been pulling up blades of grass and forming them into a little bowl, which she put her cigarette out in.

"I wish we had our car," Kate said.

"Yeah," Wave said.

Kate looked at her pack of cigarettes. She had ten left, and she considered before lighting another one. "I don't even know how I'm going to get cigarettes," she said. "I don't even know how far out of town are we?"

Kate blew smoke into the morning air.   She suddenly wondered if Grandma Brody would be against smoking? She wondered if she had a Chiclet or something in her purse?

"Do you have any gum?" she said, and Wave gave her a look.

"What?" Kate said. "Are you mad at me? Or do you just not want to talk?"

Wave shrugged.

And so then they were silent. Dustin was crawling along the berm of the dirt road on his hands and knees, and Kate kept an eye out lest a semi come along; he would never notice it until he was flattened like roadkill. *Fuck*, she thought.   *What is he looking for?   Rocks? Really?*

But he was very engaged. Talking to himself, it looked like. He picked up a stone and sat up on his knees and held it up to the light, tilting it and giving it careful consideration.

"I hope that's a fucking diamond he's got," Kate said, and Wave looked over at her.

"What?" Wave said. She'd been lost in her own thoughts; she wasn't even looking at Dustin.

"Nothing," Kate said, and she hated that she had said something funny that no one would ever laugh at. Things were going bad between them, she thought.

She blew smoke from her cigarette and put it out in the grass house she had made. Now there were four cigarette butts, like four little people, twisted into poses of decease.

"I don't have any proof," Dustin had said. It was probably long past midnight, but the two of them were still sitting by the pool on the night after the murders, talking. "It's just a feeling. So I don't know whether I should, like, say something to the police?   Or"

And Kate had considered for a long time and very thoughtfully. She had started writing things down in a notebook.

Proof that Rusty is the killer

1. He had once tried to get Dustin to burn their house down. His previous foster family had died in a fire, too. Coincidence? Not likely!
2. He had killed baby rabbits in front of Dustin: sick and without mercy.
3. Claimed he was the child of a demon. While this was obviously made up, it showed that his mind was deranged. Also that he didn't know who his father was and his mom

was a prostitute and maybe also a member of a cult. Many serial killers have moms who are prostitutes. Plus, who knew what cultish beliefs had been taught to him? No doubt he was a mental case.

4. Told Dustin that he was in a gang/cult and that they had committed a murder. Probably a lie but shows that he has been thinking about killing/murdering for a long time.

5. Had done sex stuff to Dustin when he was a kid. Proof that he was a predator and perverted. Was also a sex addict? Had sex with her and Wave and how many others? Also, how many other kids had he molested? More proof that he had no morals and was twisted.

6. Talked about Satan and Satanism all the time. Was a fan of bands like Black Sabbath, Venom, Judas Priest. Drew pentagrams on stuff. Took hallucinogenic drugs.

7. The night before the murders performed a Satanic ritual in a graveyard while high on peyote. Danced and sang to Satan. A girl sat down on a grave and spread her legs and said, "O Guland, please don't make me go to Yellowstone!" And then the parents died, so the girl didn't have to go to Yellowstone. Could Rusty have killed them because he wanted to make her prayer come true in some fucked-up way?

It was #7 that seemed most convincing, and Kate didn't particularly like that.

She didn't like that she herself had been the drug-addled girl who had taken off her panties and spread her legs in front of two boys. And then prayed to Satan, or a demon, or whatever.

It made it seem like she was possibly on Rusty's side.

Could she be blamed? Could they frame her as one of Rusty's accomplices? It made her seem like one of those Manson girls, she thought.

That's how they could make her look if they wanted. They could possibly make all kinds of awful things about her appear.

Was it weird that Kate and Dustin slept together at night in his dead mother's bed? *You're fucking right it was.* He was just starting to go through puberty, and so there were the beginnings of smells. Underarm smell. The awful sour odor of teenage-boy feet. The slobbery mouth against her arm, the disturbing thirteen-year-old erections that he got and pressed against her thigh unintentionally in his sleep. The way he would whisper. "O Guland," she thought he was saying. "O Guland, Guland."

But she had no choice. She knew he would be scared otherwise. If she made him sleep on the floor, he would see the ratty stuffed animals that she and Wave had stowed underneath the beds; he would see their button eyes looking at him through the darkness.

If he was on the floor, there would be more sleepwalking, which had been worse since the murders—night after night, this zombie of Dustin would rise and try to wander around if he wasn't woken up. If he didn't sleep beside her, he would be able to wander off in the night and she wouldn't wake up to stop him.

She had a good idea of what kind of boyfriend he would become when he grew up. He would be the horrible baby boyfriend that some poor girl would be tricked into taking care of. The boyfriend who was always experiencing some kind of inexpressible longing and unexplained sadness.

Some girls really dug that. Kate didn't.

But it was what she had to do, she thought. Otherwise—

Otherwise what?

It was a question that she considered frequently. What *did* Dustin remember? What would he eventually remember in the future? He sat next to her on the bus and made the signs with his hands, gnarling his fingers into shapes like a wizard casting spells. "Sssss," he murmured, and she hoped no one could see them.

They rode to school on a bus with children of all ages. Country kids in cheap clothes. They traveled up and down dirt roads where children stood at the berm of a driveway, waiting to be picked up. The whole process took about forty-five minutes, and Kate sat there next to Dustin as the school bus poked along, and it seemed endless.

She remembered how she and Wave used to drive to school in a car their dad bought them.

An orange Mustang hatchback that they called "Tiny." They took turns being the driver and the passenger, and sometimes they took long detours, driving up and down Main Street several times before they finally pulled into the school parking lot, knowing they would get a tardy slip.

Wave was the more reckless of the two of them. Once, they'd taken the Mustang out onto some back roads and Wave had got it up past 80 miles an hour, until the frame of the car started to actually shake and they thought it might bust apart.

If it wasn't for the murders, they might still be driving to school. *If it wasn't for Rusty!* she thought. She sat there on the bus next to Dustin and looked at the back of Wave's head, a few seats in front of her. *Would you really choose* Rusty *over me?* she thought. *Really?*

She didn't like her new school. It was a lot of rough, stupid low-class white kids—their dads all worked construction, building the new power plant, or in the strip mine—or else it was standoffish Mexican kids who spoke Spanish to each other in the lunchroom.   Kate and Wave were not assigned to any of the same classes, so they rarely saw each other during the day.

Sometimes Wave would be spotted in the hallways, talking and even *laughing* with her new friends. The new friends looked like druggies, trailer-park girls who were trying to look punk but they didn't even know what punk *was*, Kate thought, they were just copying someone they saw on MTV.

As for Kate, she didn't make any new friends. She felt weirdly self-conscious. She had the idea that people *knew*—she was the murder girl, they thought. She'd been in that Satanism trial, and did you hear that she was raped on a grave?

No way!   *Yes, way!*

Probably they didn't know anything, but Kate felt like they did; she didn't want to talk with them or interact like Wave apparently did. She had so many new friends! She was such a popular new girl!

For a while Kate actually tried writing little notes. It was pathetic, really. She wrote the word *Foxy* in elaborate bubble letters and colored it in with marker and folded it and put it in Wave's jacket pocket. She wrote *I love you* and put it in Wave's shoe.

She tried to think of things that Wave would like, that would make her laugh like they used to. But it became harder and harder to remember what such things might be.

When they were little, Kate and Wave had loved being twins. There had never been much psychic anything between the two of them, though of course she could hear Wave's thoughts now, for sure:

Liar,   Wave was thinking.   *Liar liar liar liar liarliar*

She was not a liar.

There had never, never been any doubt in Kate's mind that Rusty was the killer. After that night at the pool, when Dustin talked to her, there wasn't any question. She had written all of the evidence down in a notebook, numbering it, trying to make it sound official. Every time she remembered something incriminating that Rusty had told her, she kept adding it to the list.

She had reached #20 when she finally decided to talk to Wave about it. A few days had passed since the murders, and the three of them were still "sequestered." Being "questioned."

But things had not been going well between Kate and Wave. For some reason, Wave seemed to think that she was more deeply affected by the deaths than anyone else, and she had begun to act very melodramatic. She slept, like, eighteen hours a day, and when she was awake she traipsed around in their mother's white nightgown, padding slowly on bare feet down the hall with a sort of sleepwalker-y slowness. She would give Kate these stricken, accusatory looks.

Kate knew why, of course. It was because of that one time that she said that she hoped that Vicki got cancer. It was because she told Wave that Dave had a nice ass and because she gossiped about the idea that they all—Dave, Colleen, Lucky, Vicki—were screwing each other. It was, no doubt, because Kate had prayed to Satan that she didn't want to go to Yellowstone. Wave thought that just because Kate wasn't *performing* her grief like a silent-movie actress, she didn't care. Wave sent out ripples of judgmentalness whenever they looked at one another.

So it was awkward when Kate gave her the notebook. It was a Sunday afternoon, and they'd been forced to go to church that morning with the councilman and his wife. More theater: People had gaped at them, and they all had to try to look like you were supposed to after your parents were murdered.

They were sitting in the grass alongside the cyclone fence, on the edge of the garage, just beyond where the trash cans were, and Kate watched as Wave read her notes. *Proof that Rusty is the killer.* Wave made a little frown and then turned a page. Her eyes crawled along the lines of Kate's handwriting and then her eyes stopped and she let out a soft grunt of disagreement. She flipped the next page with quiet disdain.

And then finally she lifted her head. Blank. No expression, no acknowledgment. She handed the notebook back as if it was a joke that was more disgusting than funny.

"Well?" Kate said, frowning. Their eyes met for a moment, and Kate tried to hold the gaze but Wave didn't want to. She looked down grimly.

"What do you want me to say?" Wave said. "It needs to be proof-read for spelling and grammar if you're going to try to publish it as a novel."

Kate was sitting cross-legged, plucking blades of grass and piling them, and she shrugged. "I think he did it," she said. "Dustin and me want to go to the police."

"Oh, *please,*" Wave said, and her look was wounding. It had seemed like they had been close not that long ago, but it was suddenly clear that they weren't anymore. Kate felt herself actually flinch.

"Are you kidding me?" Wave said. "More than half of this is lies."

Kate felt herself blushing, getting red, whatever—it was a sensation she hated. She had the kind of skin that showed her emotions more than most normal people, she thought, and it was maddening that her own face would betray her whenever she was angry or embarrassed.

So now she tried to give Wave a reasonable, thoughtful expression. *I'm listening to you,* the expression said, even though her cheeks were hot and probably bright red. *I'm interested in what you have to say!*

"What do you think is a lie?" she said. She thought she did a good job of keeping her tone neutral and calm. But then Wave actually made a soft scoffing sound.

"Pfft," Wave said, and Kate knew the color in her face had grown brighter.

"For one thing," Wave said, "most of the things that Rusty says about his family or Satanism or whatever—that's just a joke. That's, like, him trying to show off. It's obviously fake. He's just copying Ozzy Osbourne or somebody.

"And . . ." Wave said. "Well.   The stuff that Dustin says? I mean, I *am* grossed out by it, but . . . it's Dustin. He once told us that he saw a grizzly bear walking down the road! And he believed it, right? You remember that mean game we used to play with him. You know how gullible he is."

Kate said nothing.

"None of this is *true,*" Wave said. "I was there. You weren't in a trance. And they *didn't* put a fucking crucifix in your vagina. How disgusting! You took off your panties and showed your pussy. That's it. We were tripping. You danced with Rusty. Then we went home."

"You don't remember everything," Kate said. "You were tripping more than I was."

"Ha-ha," Wave said. "I'm not as easy to screw with as Dustin is."

Fuck you, Wave, she thought. She was not screwing with anyone. Why would she lie if she didn't believe it? It was so clear, that was the thing. So clear that Rusty was guilty, the rest of it didn't matter.

She guessed that Wave didn't see it that way. The next day, riding home on the school bus, Wave sat across the aisle, three seats ahead as usual, and no matter how long Kate gazed at the back of Wave's head, she didn't turn. Wave thought Dustin was somehow Kate's slave or something.

There was a game they had played with Dustin ever since he was little. Kate couldn't even remember when it started. Was he six, that first time? Seven?

He was an adorable little boy. So happy and wiggly and tiny— small for his age, always mistaken for younger until he spoke. Then people were astonished by how smart he was. *Where did he get that vocabulary?* they wondered. He liked to read children's encyclope- dias, and he could recite facts from them. "He's the funniest little guy!" said their mother, who was not prone to exclamation points.   "Such a chatterbox! He'll tell you anything you want to know about dinosaurs. And God! Such an imagination! I don't know where it comes from. He sure didn't get it from Colleen!"

The girls were ten or eleven. Eleven. They took him like a pet, like a doll. He was so small that he could fit into the Easter dresses that the girls had worn when they were three. They took him up into the tree house and made him try them on, and he didn't seem the least concerned. He sat there in a lavender chiffon dress and told them about dinosaurs, reciting long lists of names.

"Dustin," Kate said. "Make a duck bill with your lips. And close your eyes." She put her hand firmly on the top of his head to hold him still. Behind her, Wave readied the tube of their mother's lipstick, like a nurse preparing a hypodermic.

They thought he would resist being made up, but he seemed to be hypnotized. He opened his eyes and gazed up at Kate's face the way a cat would stare at the moon, and she held him firmly by the scalp as she drew a line along the upper lip.

"Dustin," Wave said. "You look just like your twin sister!"

Kate had just started on the bottom lip, and she was very focused on his face, so she saw his eyes widen.

"I don't have a sister," he said.

Kate and Wave exchanged looks, and Wave gave her a little smile. They were able to do that then—to communicate with just their eyes, just their expressions.

"You probably don't remember," Wave said. "You were so little when she got sent away." Dustin frowned, and Kate hesitated before she started on the lower lip.

"We shouldn't be talking about this," Kate said. "He's too little to understand."

"He doesn't remember, anyway," Wave said.

"I remember!" he said: offended to have his memory questioned. He stared up into Kate's face—maybe to see if it was a joke—but Kate didn't return the gaze.

"I don't think so," Wave said. "You couldn't." Dustin shifted a bit in his chair.   His brow creased.

"Poor Desirée," Wave said. "They had to give her to the circus."

"Wh—?" Dustin said. Kate held his jaw between her fingers and ran the lipstick along the plump skin of his bottom lip.

"It's better that you don't think about her," Kate said, because Dustin's eyelids were fluttering, and she could see his face tightening—as if he were having a memory. His lower lip trembled, and she stumbled out of the lines as she was drawing lipstick on it.

"Why did they send her to the circus?" Dustin said, and Kate looked deeply at his face. She could see that he was "remembering," and it fascinated her.

He *believed* it.

"Well, obviously," Wave said.   "Because she was so deformed. She had to go to the circus because she was a freak."

"Wave," Kate said. "Don't say 'freak.'" She smiled at Dustin. "I thought she was beautiful," she told him.

Dustin nodded. His lips parted as Kate touched the edge of his mouth with a tissue. "I thought she was beautiful, too," he murmured.

"But you don't really remember," Wave said. "You were so little when they sent her away."

"Yes I do!" Dustin said. He grimaced, and Kate gave Wave a hard look. Did she really want him to spaz out and run crying to his mom and dad, and then they'd get in trouble?

"Of course he remembers," Kate told Wave. "It was his sister." And then she leaned down and spoke gently to him. "Tell us," she said softly, and tucked his hair behind his ears, so it looked more like a pixie cut. "What do you remember about her, honey?"

His eyes dreamed up at her. "Well," he said. "She had red eyes. Like a white rabbit has red eyes. And she had long white hair. And she had a hole in her stomach where she put her food."

"Oh," Kate said. "Interesting."

"But I was sad that she had to leave," Dustin said.

"We all were," Kate said, and she and Wave widened their eyes at one another with astonished pleasure. "But we can't talk about it, because it makes your mom cry. She couldn't have any more babies after you were born."

"I know that," Dustin said.

It was a mean thing to do, they both agreed later. But it didn't really hurt him, either.   It was just . . . so interesting and funny.

"*She had a hole in her stomach where she put her food,*" Wave said. "Oh my God! Do you think he's crazy?"

"No," Kate said. "He's just a spaz."

"It's going to be terrible for him when he gets older," Wave said. "The boys are going to murder him."

Kate shrugged.

"Well," she said. "We have to protect him."

The next time she saw Dustin—a few weeks later—she was alone in the tree house. She had stolen a pack of her mother's cigarettes, and she was teaching herself to smoke. Wave didn't know, and she liked that fact, though it also worried her. What if Wave also had secrets?

It was then that she heard Dustin talking—if that's what you wanted to call it. It was a kind of noisy mumbling, like listening to the sound of a cartoon in another room. She peered over the railing and he was standing in the yard not far below, talking to himself and dancing around.

After she observed for a while, she guessed that he was pretending. He was whispering, mostly, though his voice rose and fell. He gestured while he talked, and then ran a little ways and pretended to hit himself on the chin, and then made the sound of a cartoon explosion, and then he drew himself up and squared his shoulders. "Why you . . . !" he exclaimed, and then he put his palms above his head in the pose that Superman makes when he is flying.

He was acting something out, she guessed. Maybe a TV show? But he was playing all the characters, and making all the sound effects, and sometimes singing the music, and it wasn't *that* abnormal— all kids played pretend—but it seemed more fervent and urgent than the usual kid.

Spazzy, Kate thought.

She put her feet up and watched him for a while, smoking cautiously and flicking the ash in the way she'd seen in movies. She framed Dustin's capering between her feet and curled and uncurled her toes. She had painted her toenails the color red that was called Soul Mate—it was a kind of dark magenta—but she felt that they still looked like boy's toes. They were wide and squarish, and the big toes were especially fat and inelegant. And her legs had hair on them. Her mother said they couldn't shave their legs until they turned thirteen.

Dustin was still involved in his performance when she came down from the tree house, down the slats that had been nailed into the trunk to form a ladder, and he didn't notice when she dropped the empty pack of cigarettes onto the grass. He was still babbling to himself when she walked right up to him.

"Dustin?" she said. "What are you doing?"

And it was as if she had snipped a cord and a helium balloon suddenly floated off into the sky. He stopped talking and gesturing and his face went completely blank for a second, and a little shudder went up his spine. She could see his body quiver with whatever was leaving it.

"Huh?" Dustin said. "I'm not doing anything."

Kate considered this for a moment. "I was looking for you," she said. "I wanted to talk to you. Wave is really mad at you."

"Wave?" Dustin said. "But? I didn't do anything?"

"She says that she saw you spying on her," Kate told him. "She was smoking some of our mom's cigarettes, and now she's afraid that you'll tell. She thinks you're a tattletale."

Dustin made a hurt face. "I won't tell," he said. "I'm not a baby."

"We'll see about that," Kate said. She crossed her arms and frowned. "But you really *did* see Wave smoking?" she said. "You saw it with your own eyes? Why were you spying?"

"I—" Dustin said. "I didn't mean to! I was just playing."

"But you saw it," she said. "You saw Wave smoking a cigarette in the tree house."

"Yes," Dustin said. "I saw her. But I won't tell."

It was the first time that she realized that Dustin's imagination could be useful to her.

She loved him, though. *She loved him.* He was at the forefront of her mind during those months, those first months that they were living with Grandma Brody.

Sometimes, she would catch him doing his little weird gestures, pantomimes: pretending to feed himself, or patting his eyelids with the pad of his index finger—left eye, right eye, left eye, right eye—as if making sure they were still there; putting his index finger to his lips like someone who is saying *shhh*, except that he would softly blow air up and down the length of the finger, as if he were trying to cool it off.

She wished she could talk to Wave about it, but there was no warmth from that quarter. "I don't know," Wave said with disinterest. "He seems fine enough."

The three of them sitting there together, peaceably, watching *Soul Train* on TV. Maybe things between them were improving, Kate thought?

And then Grandma Brody came limping down the hall with her cane. "Katelynn?" she called. "Waverna? I'm looking for you. I have some things I need you to do."

Sooner or later, Kate thought, Wave would give in and they would make up. Even though she had new friends at school, Wave was stuck at home after school and on weekends. There was no way to get out. They were miles from even a gas station, and they weren't allowed to talk on the phone. Kate watched with interest as Wave and Grandma Brody did battle over it.

"It's too expensive to have you girls a-chatting and gossiping on that phone. That's not what it's for," Grandma Brody declared, and Wave, who was holding the phone, looked stunned.

"It doesn't cost anything to make a local call," Wave said. "It costs zero!"

"Do you pay the bills in this house?" Grandma Brody said. "When you pay for your own phone, then you can just gab and gab to your heart's content!"

Afterward, the three of them sat in the old bedroom of Vicki and Colleen, Kate on one bed, Wave on another, Dustin on the floor, and they stared at one another.

If I could think of something that would make her laugh, Kate thought.

She just couldn't believe Wave would be so stubborn forever! She would have to soften eventually, Kate thought.

"God!" Kate said after a while. "I can't believe we aren't even allowed to use the phone!" It was a kind of invitation: a shared complaint.

Let's talk about things that we both agree on. Let's start a conversation.

But Wave wouldn't take the bait.

"It doesn't matter to me," she said. "Why? Do you have someone you need to talk to on the phone?"

"Yeah," Kate said. "I wanted to call the stick up your ass? I have a message for him."

Wave snorted. It wasn't a laugh, but at least it was an acknowledgment. At least it meant that she was listening.

They sat and watched as Dustin dug through the haunted closet that had belonged to their mothers. He had found a cache of board games. He pulled out Yahtzee, and Operation, and Parcheesi, and Monopoly.

"What's *Mystery Date*? Have you guys ever heard of that?"

"No," Wave said. "Not interested."

"How do you pronounce *O-U-I-J-I*?" Dustin said.

"Don't touch that!" Wave said. She stood up, and she was very alert all of a sudden. "I fucking mean it, Dustin. Don't you dare touch that!"

And Kate agreed. Open up a Ouiji board in this room, who knew what would come?

Kate and Dustin sat by the swimming pool, and as she looked up at the sky she could feel her mind orbiting slowly around a slow realization.

Rusty killed our parents, she thought.

There was outrage, of course. Revulsion. But also the steadily chiming dread that if Rusty *was* the killer, she could be connected to him. That stupid pentagram, her acting out a scene from *Michelle*

Remembers. Dancing with him to Black Sabbath. People would say that she was his accomplice. His accessory—wasn't that what they called it?

Kate reached her hand out of the chlorinated water and put it over Dustin's. "I think *both* of us have been abused," she whispered.

She arranged herself so that they were kneeling on the cement beside the pool, their knees almost touching, and she took his hands in hers. Her palms up, his palms down. She stared into his eyes.

"Do you remember any of it?" she said. "When we were at the graveyard?"

His hands jolted a little against her palms, and he blinked a few times. For a moment, she thought he was going to protest—*what are you talking about?*—but then he just stared at her.

"Yes," he said at last.

"It seemed like," Kate said. "It seemed like you were almost hypnotized. Like you didn't even know where you were. Like you thought you were just at home, watching TV."

"Um," Dustin said.

"It seemed like you were drifting in and out," Kate said. She'd had years of practice in lying to him, and she knew where to pause, the places that she could let him fill in the blanks with his imagination, the places where she would need to prod or cajole him. "You took a lot of drugs."

"Well," Dustin said. His brow creased. The look of someone who is trying to remember.

"I tried to fight," she said, and she leaned in, her hands tightening lightly around Dustin's fingers. "I thought I tried to call out to you to help me. But it seemed like you were just . . . paralyzed."

"I don't even know if I remember it," Dustin whispered. "I mean," he said, "I kind of remember. In little bits and flashes."

She woke up one night in the bedroom in Grandma Brody's house and Dustin wasn't there. She had never before had trouble sleeping, waking up over and over and feeling like something was watching, waking up with Dustin asleep beside her, mumbling and breathing against her like he was maybe dreaming of having sex? Dreaming of running from someone or chasing someone? Short, hitching pants.

And then waking up and he was not in the bed at all.

She sat up, blinking.

Wave was sound asleep in the bed across from her. Dustin was gone.

She heard the wooden slap of the kitchen screen door, and she got up. There was something wrong with him, she thought. Whatever had once been odd and kooky and kind of cute about him had become more pronounced. Like, almost a mental illness, she thought.

Downstairs, the kitchen was aglow with moonlight. The little table had a plate on it and an almost-empty glass of milk, and several of the cupboard doors were ajar. So was the back door.

It was wide open, and the old wooden screen door wavered, tapping lightly into the frame at intervals. The September wind blew some dry leaves and flotsam over the threshold.

She could see him in the yard, wading through the weeds around the apple tree, walking like a sleepwalker with his arms held out in front of him, his palms up as if he were holding an object in each hand. He was singing in a high, clear choirboy voice. "Luckenbach, Texas": It was a song that their parents had all liked. Mostly he didn't sing the words of the song, just the tune. "Come to Luckenbach, Texas," he crooned, and swayed. "Loo loo loo loo." He swayed like one of those sea creatures, an anemone or a jellyfish, almost floating. The moon was out, staring blankly down at him, and she felt a prickle down her back.

O Guland, she thought. She didn't know who Guland was— a demon of some kind from Rusty's Satanic Bible—but she wondered sometimes if she actually *had* summoned him when she called his name in the graveyard. He granted her wish: They had not gone to Yellowstone. And in exchange, she lost everything. Even now, she was still losing it.

Guland, she thought. How delighted he must have been. She had done something terrible.

But she had not!

She had done the right thing!

Did it matter that Dustin hadn't actually been there with Kate and Wave and Rusty and Trent? Did it matter that the story she told was a little exaggerated in places? That she pretended, at times, to be an innocent damsel?

It didn't—because she was very certain that Rusty killed their parents.

She had been reading *Michelle Remembers*. Looking at the grainy black-and-white photos that were on stiff paper in the center of the paperback. One caption said: *Michelle told Dr. Pazder of being taken to Victoria's Ross Bay Cemetery. The lid of an old grave, such as the one above, was pried back, Michelle was lowered into the grave, and the lid was replaced.*

She said to Dustin: "Do you remember when you told me that Rusty and Trent put you in an open grave and wouldn't let you out?"

"Yeah," Dustin said.

"Are you sure that really happened?" she said, and Dustin stared for a long time.

"Yes," he said. "I definitely . . . I can picture it really clearly."

She thought that most of the last part of *Michelle Remembers*, where Satan finally appears, was too extreme. Satan spoke in kind of awkward rhyming poetry, and she remembered the night that Rusty had snatched the book from her and started reading aloud from it in a fake English accent.

"He was reading this weird poetry," she told the police later. "He said it was something that Satan had spoken to him."

In *Michelle Remembers*, when the woman begins to recover repressed memories, she speaks in the voice of a five-year-old girl, and Kate thought this was kind of interesting. She tried on a childlike voice herself—not in a corny way, but just a little puzzled, softer and slower than she'd usually speak. Like she was in a trance as she was recounting these terrible things she remembered.

They were sitting there in a room at the St. Bonaventure police station. It didn't look like the interrogation rooms you saw on TV. It was like a little narrow break room, with a couch and a counter where there was a coffeemaker.   She sat on the sagging velour sofa, and the two policemen sat in folding chairs, and the social worker stood by the door with her arms folded.

She had been worried that they would be questioned separately, and that was exactly what happened. They brought them in one at a time—Dustin first, then Kate, then Wave.

She and Dustin had gone over the important points. She had written it down in her notebook, and she read it aloud to him so they would both remember it right. So they were both in agreement about what had really happened.

"There might be trick questions that people ask," she told Dustin. "They might not want to believe what we're telling them, so we have to match up."

1. That they had both heard Rusty, on numerous occasions, talk about killing Dave and Colleen. They had both heard him talk about burning the house down, and they both remembered that his previous foster family had died in a house fire.
2. That Rusty claimed to be a member of a cult, and that his biological mother was a member of a cult, and that he listened to Satanic music and drew Satanic pictures, including pentagrams and pictures of the devil's face. That he claimed to have been part of a cult that drowned a kid in a ritual at an irrigation canal.   And that he also participated in cattle mutilation and animal sacrifice.
3. That he had driven them to the graveyard and tricked them into taking drugs that he gave them in Kool-Aid.

4. That Rusty drew a pentagram and baby rabbits were sacrificed on it and they all were forced to pray to Satan.
5. That Dustin was thrown down into an open grave.
6. That Kate had been forced to take off her panties and spread her legs on the pentagram and Rusty and Trent put a crucifix between her legs and smeared the blood of the baby rabbits on her face.
7. That Rusty had called on Satan to kill their parents.

And she believed that most of this was not untrue. It was in the spirit of the truth, at least; it represented the essence of what they knew about Rusty and what he was capable of, even if it didn't necessarily happen in that order.

Wave was another issue. She might not remember things the same way.

"But she might be kind of prejudiced," Kate told the policemen and the social worker. She put her hands over her eyes, shuddering with embarrassment. "She was—I think—having sex with him. I don't think she had anything to do with the murders, but I *do* think . . . she's under his . . . sway."

Kate doubted whether Wave remembered much clearly, anyway. They were all on peyote, and Wave seemed to be tripping harder than anyone.

According to Wave, there had been another girl there at the cemetery. "I think her name was Montgomery?" Wave had said.

Kate looked at her skeptically. "Oh, really?" Kate said. "Are you sure?" She had been confident that Wave would eventually agree with her.

She would have never believed that she and Wave would grow so distant so quickly. As if they'd never been sisters at all.

By the middle of October, Wave had stopped riding the bus. There was a boy who would give Wave a ride in the morning in his truck, sometimes driving up when Kate and Dustin were standing there by the mailbox waiting for the bus, and Wave would get into the passenger side without a word and leave them there. Sometimes Wave would be dropped off after school by a carload of girls, and you could smell the pot smoke seeping out of the windows from a hundred yards away.

"This will not do!" Grandma Brody said, and limped after Wave as she went up the stairs to the bedroom. "I called that social worker, and he's going to have a talk with you!"

"I hope that they put me in juvie," Wave said. "It would be better than living here!" Kate and Dustin sat in front of the television, watching an old rerun of *Bewitched*.

Dustin was entranced by it, didn't even seem to notice the drama going on behind him. But Kate watched with fascination as her sister turned and faced Grandma Brody.   It reminded her of the fights that she and Wave had once had with their mother, which seemed so long ago. It felt like Wave was her old self once again.

"You're not my mother," Wave called from the top of the stairs. "My mother hated you, you old witch!"

Wave didn't even slam the door, just closed it firmly, and Grandma Brody went to the forbidden phone and called the sheriff to complain. On TV, one of the witches had turned the husband into a chimpanzee. Dustin was watching with an openmouthed smile.

Kate went upstairs. She knocked very lightly on the door and said: "Wave?" No answer. "Wave? It's me. Can I come in?"

"I can't stop you," Wave said from behind the door, and so Kate opened it gingerly.

Wave lay on the bed, facedown on her folded arms. There was a bedside lamp with a base in the shape of a prim ballerina, and it gave off an oddly garish yellow light. "What do you want?" Wave said.

"I just want to talk," Kate said. She sat down on the floor not far from where Wave was lying, but not so close that it would be intrusive. "I wish we still talked. Like we used to."

"Mm-hm," Wave said. "I know."

"It doesn't have to be like this," Kate said. "'Cause I'm on your side."

Wave looked down and smiled almost sadly. "Kate," she said, "I don't really want you on my side. I'm not interested."

"Why are you being like this?" Kate said. "We used to be so close. We used to do everything together. I don't know what happened."

It was the first time she'd said something that made Wave laugh in months. But it wasn't a nice laugh. "Oh, really?" Wave said. "You don't know what happened? Maybe you need to recover your repressed memories."

Kate felt the hated color rise in her face. She was kneeling meekly on the floor like a child saying prayers, and she tried to will the blush away. She kept her face turned downward, and she could see a pink stuffed octopus staring at her from under the bed, an octopus made of felt with glinting white shell buttons for eyes. "I just want things to go back the way they were," she said at last, and Wave let out another sharp laugh.

"How far back do you want to go?" Wave said. "When would you hit the reset button?"

"I don't know," Kate said. "I mean, last year? Remember driving around in Tiny and all the parties and everything? Like, how we would always have great talks? We were best friends."

"No, we weren't," Wave said, and she leaned back, crossing her arms over her chest. Downstairs, the closing music of *Bewitched* began to play.

"Last year was terrible for me," Wave said. "And you didn't even notice. It's probably not even your fault. You're not able to see outside of your own self, I guess. But I was miserable. I just don't like the person that I have to be when I'm around you. And I think about what a better person I'd be if I'd never had you for a sister. Like, all the life I wasted trying to mold myself for you."

"You're lying," Kate said, but she felt like she was being shot or stabbed. "I know that you loved me. You know you did. You're just being stupid."

But Wave only closed her eyes. She ran her palms down her face.

"You know what I thought when I found them?" Wave said at last. "When I found their bodies?" And she chuckled, or whimpered—Kate couldn't tell which. "The first thing I thought was that *you* killed them. I mean, I definitely thought you were capable of it." She shook her head. "I still sort of wonder, actually. Maybe it *was* you. I sure as fuck don't think it was Rusty."

Kate was now at the ugliest shade of red that she could possibly be. She could feel her face glowing; even her eyes hurt.

"You're in love with him, aren't you?" she heard a nasty voice say from out of her mouth. "You'd choose that piece of shit child molester over your own sister."

It sounded hollow and melodramatic, even as she spoke. They were both silent, and the stuffed octopus eyed Kate ironically from under the bed.

"I don't think I've been able to love anybody," Wave said. "You're always blocking me whenever I try to feel anything for myself. And I just—I don't want to be around you anymore. You know when you and Rusty prayed to Satan because you didn't want to go to Yellowstone? You know what I prayed? I prayed that I wouldn't have to be your sister anymore. *O Guland! Please let me not have a twin sister!*"

She'd sat up and was leaning on her palm on their dead mother's bed, and she seemed almost sort of sorry. She was lying, Kate thought. Kate was sure she was lying, but even as the words came into the air she could feel them hardening into the truth.

"You sacrificed them, Kate," Wave said. "And this is your reward."

By late October, Wave wasn't coming back to Grandma Brody's house at all anymore, and by November she was gone altogether. Vanished.

She'd run away from home: That's what Kate told Dolin Culver when he summoned her to his office. She spoke dully, though there were all kinds of fires burning in various parts of her brain. She felt wronged and tricked and heartbroken and dizzy and so incredibly angry, all of it smearing together like paint on a palette.

"Do you have any idea where she is?" Dolin Culver said. She hated his stupid yellow-tinted glasses so much that they felt like a personal affront. "You haven't heard from her at all?"

Kate kept her head down so that she didn't have to look at him. "No," she said.

"Okay," Dolin Culver said.

His mouth twitched like a rabbit's, and she could feel his distaste for her. She imagined that he thought she was a certain kind of stupid, slutty teenage girl. *He knew her type.* She was wearing an open-necked, *Flashdance*-style sweatshirt that revealed her bare shoulder, and she pulled it up self-consciously.

He was silent for a moment. "So," he said heavily. "What makes you think she ran away? Did she . . . express to you any kind of unhappiness about her situation? Did she discuss any sort of . . . plan or so forth?"

Kate shrugged. "I don't know. Not really," she said. She looked out the plate-glass window of his office, which was in a mall, and there was the blinking neon light of a cheap-jewelry store nearby. "We weren't really talking that much," Kate said. "She was hanging out with a different crowd."

"But you're *sure* that she ran away?" Dolin Culver said. "If she's missing, any number of things could have happened. And I, personally, am concerned about that."

She shrugged again. She didn't know why but it made her sort of happy, how much Dolin Culver loathed her. It was satisfying. "I don't think anybody kidnapped her," she said.

"Honey," he said. "We may be needing to go out to the sheriff, to fill out a report. And I'm going to have to tell them that a young woman—who was previously involved in a murder crime—has disappeared. And the sister doesn't seem upset about it. So you will definitely be coming down to the sheriff's office with me. I know you don't want to go through that again."

Kate glanced up at the reflective surface of his glasses and then looked off to the side. There was a postcard taped to the wall that said: *Greetings from Yellowstone National Park!*

Which she guessed was a coincidence.

"I know she ran away, because she took her clothes," Kate said. "*All* of her clothes. And her jewelry, and toiletries, and whatever mementos she saved from home. And her suitcase. So that's why I think she ran away."

He looked at her, and she looked at the postcard on the wall. She was aware that there were terrible storms moving through her body, lightning and blizzards and torrential rain, but she also felt as if she were looking at them from a distance. Dolin Culver shrugged and turned away from her.

"What about you, Dusty?" he said. "Did your cousin Waverna confide in you at all?"

Kate shook her head silently. If Dolin Culver had been a decent human being or even a competent social worker, he would have noticed that Dustin was not mentally normal. If Culver was the kind of person who cared about his job—which was to be a liaison for orphans and foster kids—he would have looked into Dustin's eyes and felt as alarmed as Kate did.

But Culver's expression didn't shift. He tapped his pencil lead lightly against his desk, while Dustin sat there like a ventriloquist's doll, his eyes fluttering weirdly, as if he'd just woken up.

"Dustin?" Dolin Culver said.

"Huh?" Dustin said.

Culver sighed, and then he repeated himself slowly. "Did Waverna tell you that she was thinking about running away from home?" he said. Kate realized that he must have thought that Dustin was retarded.

"Uh?" Dustin said. "No?"

She watched as Dustin put his fingers to his mouth, as if he'd just snuck a bite.

This had become a sort of "tic" of Dustin's; it seemed like he did

279

it unconsciously, and then his eyes grew dull, and he slid down into himself.

If she were a social worker, Kate thought, she would be seriously concerned.

There was something kind of frightening about him. Didn't other people notice? Was Kate the only one who saw? Since they had come to Gillette, he had almost completely stopped talking, as far as Kate could tell. Sometimes she would hear him whispering to himself under his breath as he did his homework, printing the right answers on worksheets in his careful, ugly, boyish handwriting, but mostly he was silent. Sometimes she would catch him doing little weird gestures, like a wizard casting a spell.

Maybe Dustin should go to a hospital, she thought.

But Dolin Culver's main interest was in the disappearance of Wave. It was probably something that would cause him trouble—losing one of his wards, or clients, or whatever they were to him. He'd probably have to fill out lots of paperwork. She watched as he picked up a can of Orange Crush soda and positioned it under his mouth. A little stream of brown tobacco spit trickled from his pursed lips.

"I hope for your sake that you kids are telling me the truth," he said.

And so Wave had escaped somehow. Kate tried to imagine how it had happened. Did someone drive her somewhere, did she have money, somehow, to buy a bus ticket? Or hitchhiked maybe? Kate understood that it was possible, but it didn't make her feel any less trapped.

For her own self, she couldn't quite imagine a way out. Sometimes, she would go out to the shed and look at her grandfather's old Studebaker. It was clear it would never be drivable again. She thought of their old Ford Mustang, Tiny. Where was he now?

In any case, she probably couldn't leave Dustin. Somehow, it felt like he was her responsibility.

Meanwhile, it was too far to try to walk to town in the cold, and she had made no friends that could give them a ride. Most of the time they couldn't even watch TV unless they were willing to watch the same thing Grandma Brody wanted to watch. *Hee Haw; 60 Minutes.*

Upstairs, she and Dustin played the old board games they'd found in their mothers' closet. They lay on the bed, side by side, and read paperbacks that they'd brought home from the school library. They did chores that Grandma Brody came up with.

Sometimes she wondered if Dustin had lost his mind—if some part of his brain had wandered away and couldn't find its way back. He seemed calm enough, though. He would sometimes talk about books he liked—*The Lord of the Rings, Dune,* the sort of thing Kate found impossibly boring, but she listened because it was better than silence. They never spoke of Wave. They never spoke of what had happened.   They never spoke of Rusty.

The truth was, Kate sometimes thought, even though Rusty had been convicted of murder and sentenced to life in prison, he may have gotten the better deal. Her family was dead. She had lost all her friends. She had lost her sister.   She had lost her home and everything that she had once believed that she "owned."

And then it was full-on winter, in Gillette, Wyoming.

The day of Christmas was very bad. There was something haunted about it. When she went outside to smoke, the sky was a kind of dead color. Some grackles perched in the bare apple tree, watching her, and she opened her pack and saw that she had only three cigarettes left.

She walked along the edge of the highway, and the wind blew into her face whichever direction she turned. She had to crouch down on her haunches with one hand cupped across her face just to get her lighter to work. She'd woken that morning and found herself thinking about their family photograph albums. What had happened to them? she wondered. Neither she nor Wave nor Dustin had thought to bring them. There was a whole drawer full of Kodak Instamatic pictures she and Wave had taken and that she once really enjoyed looking at.

She could remember the pictures they took last year on Christmas. There was the formal one of all of them in front of the Christmas tree: Kate and Wave on either side of their parents, Dustin in front of his. Rusty off to the side, grinning. All the presents splayed out in their garish wrappings. There was the one of Wave putting sardines onto a condiment plate and making a hilarious grossed-out face. There was the one of Dustin solemnly wearing a Santa hat. Uncle Dave holding up a bottle of Johnnie Walker and grinning. Rusty showing off his new .22 hunting rifle, holding it out in both his palms and making a mad-scientist grimace of goofy joy. "It's alive," he was screaming, she remembered. He was imitating the scene from *Frankenstein*, which he loved. She didn't really get it, but she thought he was cute.

There was a photograph of Vicki and Colleen having an argument in the kitchen, both of them with their mouths open, pointing their fingers at one another, and Kate remembered the exhilaration she felt when Vicki had turned to her and screamed: "Get the hell out of here with that goddamned camera! I'm going to smash that thing!"

There was a photograph of her dad sitting beside Dustin, with his arm casually draped over Dustin's shoulder, and Dustin was hunched over, putting batteries into the electronic game—Atari—he'd been given.

There was a photograph of Kate and Rusty sitting next to each other on the couch, and Kate was flipping the bird with both hands.

It made her wince, thinking of this picture.

She turned and looked over her shoulder, looked back at Grandma Brody's place in the distance.   There were no cars on the road, and the wide prairie and the sky stretched out emptily in all directions, but there was still the distinct feeling of being watched. It gave her a superstitious feeling, and she dropped her half-smoked cigarette and began to walk quickly toward the house.

She could hear the TV going in the living room.

There was a weird moment when she was certain that she heard Dustin say the word *Rusty*.   But when she walked in, he was sitting on the floor by Grandma Brody's easy chair, and they were watching *It's a Wonderful Life*. Grandma Brody was dabbing her eye with a tissue.

There was a weird moment when Grandma Brody had raised her hand and gestured: *Come join us!* And Dustin had looked at her with the blankest eyes.

There was a weird moment where she thought, *You sacrificed him. And this is your reward.*

When she went back to their room, she saw that the Ouiji board game was open on the bed.   The box was open, and she could see the contents.

There was the game board, with the alphabet on it and the moon and sun, and there were dozens of rocks that had been polished, and stamps, and coins. There was also a revolver.

She thought it was her father's pistol, the one he'd kept in the kitchen drawer for "protection."

Fuck, she thought. She didn't touch it.

She backed out of the room and she could hear the actor from *It's a Wonderful Life* screaming ecstatically. "I want to live again! Please, God, I want to live again!"

Even after Wave left, they'd continued sharing the same bed. She didn't know why—except that neither of them had suggested doing anything different. Even a simple change in their arrangements would have felt huge.

But when Dustin got into bed with her that night, she stirred uncomfortably. She sat up in bed and looked at him, and she felt herself flinching from his touch when he climbed under the covers.

"What?" he said.

She shuddered. "I had a bad dream," she said. "I'm scared."

He sighed sleepily. "What are you scared of?" he said.

"Just that—" she said. "What if we made a mistake?"

"Mmm," Dustin said. He yawned. "Don't be scared," he said. He pressed up against her and began to sleepily stroke her hair. "There's nothing to be scared about," he murmured.

If there had been any lingering doubts about Rusty's guilt, the trial put them to rest.

The first astonishing thing that happened was that Trent testified against Rusty. They questioned him and questioned him, and finally he broke down. He said that he and Rusty were high on PCP and that Rusty told him that he planned to kill everyone and burn the house down. Rusty told him that he was going to move to Los Angeles, Trent said, and start a metal band.

Then there was Dustin's testimony. He told them about the baby rabbits and his voice broke, and then he talked about being forced down into the open grave and he actually started crying. The courtroom was silent, and he gasped in a couple of hoarse, sobbing breaths.

Rusty took out a comb and ran it through his long hair, as if he were distracted.

Kate decided to tone things down a little, to be very soft-spoken and to only describe things very vaguely. She kept her head down a lot; she was a traumatized girl. But she didn't cry.

She only glanced up once. The prosecutor was looking through some papers, and it seemed like he had lost his place. "One moment, your honor," he said, and Kate lifted her head.

She looked at Rusty, and their eyes met before she could stop. He stared at her with a softly bemused look. Then he lifted his hand, his pinkie and forefinger raised: the bull sign, the *rock 'n' roll forevah* sign. He raised his eyebrows at her: *I toast you.*

She never understood why he didn't testify himself. If you say you're not guilty, shouldn't you at least try to defend yourself? But maybe he had given up. Maybe he saw it was hopeless.

When classes started again in January, she rode the bus to school, but she didn't go inside. When she got off the bus that first day, she stood on the sidewalk, staring at the kids milling around in the courtyard.

Then she turned away from them, putting the school to her back, and began to walk in the direction of downtown. She was wearing a blue down parka, and she put the hood up. A circle of fawn-colored synthetic fur framed her face, and she lit a cigarette as she walked.

Her makeup was modeled on Joan Jett. Heavy black eyeliner, almost to the point of raccoon eyes. Bright-red lipstick.

But now she regretted it. It was the kind of look that construction-worker guys would hoot at, and Gillette was full of those kind of men.   A boomtown, so people said.

So she kept her head low and she tried to walk in a way that expressed quiet hostility and gloom, so that the worst that she might expect from the men outside the bars were a few catcalls. *Hey, don't be depressed, what are you sad about? Lift your head up, honey. Let the world see that pretty face.*

Knowing that making eye contact would be an invitation to pursue her.

For a while she stood outside a pharmacy and thought about shoplifting. She was low on makeup, but she wondered if she could get away with it, and eventually an old man came out to shoo her away.

Literally. He waved his arms at her the way you would at chickens. "You go on, now," he said. He was a thin, white-haired man in a white lab coat, wearing a name tag that said AMOS. He actually stomped his foot at her on the sidewalk. "Git!" he said. "No loitering!"

And so she moved grimly down the block and settled against the wall of a storefront Chinese restaurant called Oriental House, and no one bothered her there. She leaned against the wall, smoking, and finally at around ten o'clock some short, skinny Chinese guys came to the door. They were talking—maybe arguing?—in their native language, and when they saw her standing there shivering, they stopped.

"Hi," she said. She brought her cigarette to her lips, and her hand trembled.

"Hello," said one of them, and the other made a quick bob of his head, like a bow. Then the first one took out a key and unlocked the door.

She stood and watched snow fall. Cars went by in the street and ground the snow into muddy slush. She would be eighteen in March. Then . . . what? She could leave somehow. How had Wave managed it, with no money? She looked at the quiet Gillette street, the row of one-story brick storefronts with their worn awnings bent with snow and icicles. A station wagon drove by with the chains on its tires rattling. A long black Pontiac rolled past, and the driver stared at her. A bearded guy, maybe late twenties. If she wanted to, she could get a ride, she thought. But she knew that she couldn't leave Dustin. Not ever.

Then the door to the Chinese restaurant opened and a boy peered out. This was Vincent Cheng. He was maybe nineteen? Twenty?   Wearing jeans and a T-shirt and black Converse high-tops, with straight black shoulder-length hair and tan skin. He made her think of a surfer. He grinned at her: big white teeth.

"Hey," he said. "Are you here about the waitressing job?"

"Oh," she said. She blinked. Speechless for a moment.

She would always remember Vincent fondly.   Years later, when she was living in Los Angeles, she once thought she saw him on the street. She started waving and grinning at the poor kid, until it occurred to her that Vincent Cheng would be a man in his fifties. And even if she saw him she probably wouldn't recognize him.

But he had saved her life. If he hadn't opened the door of the

Oriental House, who knows? Would she have gotten into a car with some letch or rapist or worse?

Would she have killed herself outright?

Well, she didn't. She stood now at a window of an apartment in Hollywood that looked down onto the grand old hotel that was now the Scientology Celebrity Centre. She was still alive.

You sacrificed them, she thought. *And this is your reward.*

She wasn't even sure what Wave meant by that. Who had she sacrificed? What kind of reward had she gotten?

It was the spring of 1984. She was very involved with Vincent Cheng, working at the restaurant, et cetera. And Dustin seemed okay. He had friends at school, other nerdy boys, and it seemed as if he didn't think about any of that stuff anymore.

It seemed like he came back to himself by not remembering. It seemed that he had found some kind of powerful formula that allowed him to unremember things; it seemed like he was—what? Better? Cured? Free?

Whatever had happened to him, she never dared to ask. She never found out.

PART SEVEN

January 2014

Unfortunately there can be no doubt that man is, on the whole, less good than he imagines himself or wants to be. Everyone carries a shadow, and the less it is embodied in the individual's conscious life, the blacker and denser it is.

—C. G. JUNG, *Psychology and Religion: West and East*

1

My DAD SAID that Rabbit was the victim of a gang of serial killers.   He said that he and Aqil had been investigating the murders
for over a year now, and he widened his eyes in that awful expression. *Wonder*, Uncle Rusty called it.

We were sitting in the living room, and I was not in a good frame
of mind. I didn't feel like it was cool for him to make Rabbit a part
of his insanity. It seemed kind of offensive, actually, and I balled my
hands in my lap.

He brought out charts and folders full of photographs and notes;
he showed me a time line he had made and transcripts of interviews
that they'd done. Meanwhile, Aqil stood at the front window facing
away from us, and from time to time he would rock up onto the balls
of his feet.

Like he was pretending to be a Secret Service agent.

"This is all making me really uncomfortable," I said.

He opened his laptop and showed me a video that he'd been sent:
in it, black-and-white blobs moved around the screen, and there was
a sound that might have been breathing or sawing or the sound of a
microphone being licked. But my dad felt that it was clearly an
image of one of the "victims" being held before they were
"murdered—sacrificed."

And I was like: blink.   blink.

He believed it was a cult of some kind, religious or otherwise, and
that it might have ties to the Fraternal Order of Police. He said
maybe the video was sent to him as a way for the cult to let him

know they knew he was snooping. That it was a way for them to boast but also to warn him.

"But I never thought they would do something this close," he said. "I think they killed Rabbit to let me know that anyone I knew could be next.   It could be you. Or Dennis. I should have told you sooner."

2

HE HAD ALREADY been dead for a while when I found out about it. Xzavious Reinbolt texted a link to an article, and for a while I just sat there on my bed looking at it.

> Cleveland Police report that a nineteen-year-old Cleveland Heights man found dead beneath Hope Memorial Bridge appears to have been the victim of an accidental drowning.
>   Police say that Bruce Allan Berend, a recent graduate of Cleveland Heights High, had drugs in his system when he apparently stumbled into the Cuyahoga River, just a hundred yards from the Ohio & Erie Canal Towpath Trail.   The body was discovered on the west bank of the river by volunteers from a local homeless advocacy group, who were distributing coats and blankets to homeless residents in the area.

I smoked some weed, and then I crushed up an Oxycontin and snorted it, then I read it again. *January 6, 2014.*

Which, when I checked my phone, turned out to be eight days ago.

Wait, I thought. *Did they have a funeral?*

I did a bunch of Google searches.   *Funeral Bruce Berend. Funeral Rabbit Berend. Death Rabbit Berend. Death Bruce Berend. Body Bruce*

Berend. Bruce Allan Berend. And the only thing that came up was that stupid two-paragraph article: Body of Man Recovered from River's Edge.

Otherwise it was just his Facebook page, which he hadn't touched since 2012, and a Google+ that he'd never really set up, and an ancient Myspace page from middle school.

"I don't know what I'm supposed to do," I said to Uncle Rusty. "I was thinking I should call his dad, because do you think they notified him? His dad's in prison, and I'm not even sure how you go about calling someone in prison. Do they have phone numbers?"

Uncle Rusty was quiet for a moment. "Listen," he said. "I'm not sure why you think you need to do anything."

"Well," I said. "His mom's dead. She was alienated from her family and not in contact with them much. She didn't like his dad's parents. His dad is in, like, jail. So I don't know who else is going to do it."

"Somebody will get the body taken care of," Uncle Rusty said. "It's a corpse. They won't just leave it lying around. And maybe the rest of it is none of your business. You don't even know his dad, and you're going to try to make contact with him in prison? That doesn't seem like a good idea, for about ten thousand reasons."

"I guess," I said.

But I thought back to that moment when I looked up from kissing Terri and Rabbit was standing there in the door, watching us. It seemed overdramatic to say that I was a contributing factor in his death, but I couldn't help but think that I was.

"Look," Uncle Rusty said. "Let's look at it from Rabbit's perspective. Say that Rabbit knew how he was going to die, and he's making a list of things that he wanted you to do. Do you think calling his dad would be on it?"

I considered this for a second. "Oh," I said.

3

IF YOU ARE very high and watch the "captive murder victim" video that Dustin showed you, it is like watching a lava lamp.   It is like watching a lava lamp with fuzzy close-ups of body parts projected onto it.   Is that someone's fingers? Or a vagina? Is that water? Or just a silvery pixelation that glints in the way that water does?

I tried to describe it to Uncle Rusty over the phone. "Whatever it is," I said, "it's not what he *says* it is. It's not anywhere near as obvious as he seems to think."

"Mm," Uncle Rusty said.

"Do you think he's, like . . . unsound?" I said. "I mean, I think he might be for real crazy." He was silent, and his silence was like a frown traveling through satellites.

"I don't think it would be cool for me to comment on that," he said at last.

4

DUSTIN OPENED THE door without knocking and I slid my pipe under my thigh; it was like a high school cliché . . . and he stood there blinking in the drifting cirrus cloud of smoke, and in any case the smell of marijuana was plenty strong as it floated over him.

His face was ridiculously transparent. I could see him shuffling through a whole series of responses, his expression practicing different opening lines, and finally he settled on a look of blank cluelessness. He decided it was easier to pretend he didn't notice.

It felt like he was inviting you to perform in some kind of play. He was going to pretend that he wasn't aware that there was a still vaguely smoking glass pipe under my leg, and I was supposed to pretend . . . what?

"Hey," I said. "What's up?" I raised my head and met his eyes. He didn't look crazy—just kind of sad and puzzled. He looked, I thought, like a gambler whose winning streak had vanished and now he was in debt; he looked like a guy who was pretty happy a couple of years ago and then had all the things he was happy about stripped away.

He thought he could remake his life and become a detective and a celebrated author of investigative books.   He thought that maybe his life wasn't over.

It could have been worse. He might have been doing Civil War role-playing, or Zen Buddhism, or online dating. There was a part of me that felt sorry for him; I could feel it crawling over my skin like an ant, and I thought I should squash it but I didn't.

"So," he said. "I just wanted to . . . check in with you.   To see how you're feeling. I know that we put a lot of very"

He made his palms-out gesture again. "Disturbing," he said. "Disturbing material. And complicated."

"It's a lot to take in," I said at last.

"It is," he agreed. "I know I could have done a better job of . . . presenting it to you."

I shrugged.

"You have a right to be confused," he said.   "And even angry! I understand that I didn't do this perfectly. He was your childhood friend, and there have to be," he paused, "many different emotions."

I nodded, and then he came forward awkwardly and sat down on my bed. It was something I remembered from childhood—lying in bed and my dad sitting on the edge, reading to me, or talking to me about my day at school, or just running his fingertips along the hair-line at the edge of my forehead, which was how he used to put me to sleep.

Of course none of those things had happened in many years, but they were ghostly presences as he settled near the foot of the bed. I shifted, and I felt like he was thinking about putting his hand on my leg, which was under the covers. But, thank God, he didn't.

"I would understand if you thought it was," he said. "If you thought it was too speculative, and you just didn't want to get involved."

My laptop was open but he couldn't see it. I didn't think he knew that I was watching his insane video. Which, you had to ask yourself, why would someone send to him? If they were this powerful network of serial killers, why would they send it to him as a "warning"? Why wouldn't they just kill his ass?

I looked down and it was paused, and for a second I thought I could see a face in the blurry black-and-white blotches and dapples. A pair of wide eyes, scoping blindly; an open mouth.

"I guess," my dad said,   "I wanted to make an appeal to you.   We've been interviewing people for the past year. The victims' families and friends and so forth. But there are obviously issues of trust and—who are we, why are we asking questions, and we do reach a kind of dead end with these   after a while   it's not"

He thumped his head with his forefinger.

"You know," he said. "But!" he said. "I guess the question is.

If you were willing to

You'd be uniquely

Maybe canvassing people that Rabbit knew and

"Well," he said.

5

"You know," Uncle Rusty said. "I'm not sure it's a good idea to get involved in Dustin's—I don't know."

I was out driving and my phone was mounted on its little throne on my dashboard. His voice came out through the car speakers. "Dustin's fantasies," he said at last.

"I mean," Uncle Rusty said, "his imagination sent me to prison for close to thirty years. I wouldn't want to be the next guy he testifies against."

"Yeah," I said. I couldn't think of an answer for that. I glanced over to my phone as if it were a figure I was talking to, although it was just a thin, blank rectangular screen. I nodded at it.

"Part of the time I think he believed it," Uncle Rusty's voice said from my speakers. "He was brainwashed, maybe. They, like, 'implanted memories' when they questioned him at the police station. That social worker was a . . . piece of work.

"But then I'm like . . . I don't know. A part of him must have known that it wasn't true. I mean, don't you think that there's really a reality, and we all know it is *reality*?"

"Huh," I said.

And then I pulled into the grim old strip of storefronts that sat across from the ancient Richmond mall, glided into one of the many empty parking spots in front of Taj Palace Indian Cuisine, and I said, "Wait, I've got to turn the Bluetooth off for a minute," and then I went in and the lady brought out a plastic bag with the carry-out, and I pulled up the wad of twenties that my dad had given me and I realized that it was about twenty dollars too much. Maybe some of it was meant to be a tip, I thought, but tough luck. I'm not going to tip you for walking a bag from the kitchen to the front counter.

Still, it felt nasty to pocket the money. I was aware that I was sort of stealing from my dad, yes, but also from that Indian lady that I could've tipped. There was a vase with a tulip opening, and an index card taped to it: *Gratuity Welcomed!* But I was beginning to need every cent I could get my hands on.

I sat in the parking lot and I laid out a line of dope on the side of my hand. If you make a fist, you can make a nice little surface between the base of your thumb and the knuckle of your pointer finger, and then you bring it to your nose and pinch one nostril and it snorts up perfectly. Rabbit used to tease me about this. "Dude," he said, "you'll never really experience heroin until you shoot up. It's like fucking with a condom."

I thought about what Uncle Rusty had said. *Don't you think that there's really a reality, and we all know it is* reality? It was an excellent point. But I was also feeling like, hm.

So was he saying he just didn't believe my dad on principle? Because Dustin's presentation did have some good points, too. And there were plenty of other people besides my dad and Aqil who believed it. It was an actual meme on the Internet.

I looked at the phone on the dashboard and I still didn't call him back.

I closed my eyes and found that I was having a pleasant memory of the book series that my dad used to read to me. The Three Investigators. There was one kid who was fat but brainy, and another one who was athletic, and then another who was good at fixing things. And they solved mysteries. *The Mystery of the Stuttering Parrot. The Secret of Terror Castle.*

And then—I wasn't sure. I reached over to the passenger seat and touched the bag of food and it wasn't warm anymore.

It must have been eight o'clock.

"Shit," I whispered.

6

I STILL HAD Rabbit's phone. Xzavious Reinbolt had given it to me weeks ago, when I met him at House of Wills, and at the time it hadn't even occurred to me to look through it for clues. It was only when my dad suggested that I "canvass" some of Rabbit's friends that I realized that I actually *had* Rabbit's contacts list.

This was not to say that I was eagerly joining up as the junior investigator with my dad and Aqil. I was not, like, *Yeah, Dad, let me be Robin to your Batman! We can fight crime together!* But I found myself thinking about the stuff he told me. The folders full of pictures of drowned guys, and the pattern of the dates, and how there was always something suspicious about the way they seemed to suddenly disappear without leaving any witnesses, and then it's always days or weeks before the body is discovered. Always dismissed as an accident, every time.

I plugged in Rabbit's phone and let it charge. It had been dead for a long time, so it took a while for it to wake up.

Finally, the Apple symbol began to apparate, solidifying and brightening in the center of the screen. And it occurred to me for the first time that the apple had a bite taken out of it, and I realized that it was, like, a reference to Adam and Eve, the apple in the garden of Eden.

Forbidden knowledge.

He had a background photo I'd never seen before. It was a calm blue pond with ripples in it, like you'd just tossed in a pebble and made a wish. Very disturbing in a way, I thought, given how he died. And also not really what you'd imagine Rabbit would choose.

It was weird to be inside Rabbit's phone. I had seen him type in his security code thousands of times, so it was easy enough to open it. But once I was there, I was aware that he wouldn't be cool with me touching it, and it felt invasive and uncomfortable to slide my thumb through the pages of his screens. Something dirty about opening up his texts, as creepster as reading someone's diary.

I put my index finger on the last text he ever sent.

To Xzavious Reinbolt. Amy.

Be there in 5 min

7

"I REMEMBER THAT night, actually," Amy said. He was wearing khakis and his green Whole Foods Market polo shirt, which was a little too small for his upper-body muscles. You could see his pectorals flex when he smiled.

"I had just gotten this really good dope," he said, "and Rabbit was really excited about it, so he drove over to my place. It was, like, about a week before Christmas? He was in a bad mood, but . . . I wouldn't say suicidal."

We were standing in the produce section near a stack of avocados, and Amy had one of those plastic tulip glasses with some pissy-looking white wine in it.

"You should get some if you want," he told me. "It's free. Friday is the Single Mingle."

And then the scene around me kind of clicked into place. I could see that some people were shopping but others were standing, holding wine and scoping for someone to converse with. There was a little cluster of singles mingling around a folding table where an employee was dispensing Chardonnay.

"I'm not into wine," I said, and Amy nodded sympathetically.

"It takes work," he agreed. "But once you start learning about it, it can be pretty cool." I was aware of the weird, uncomfortable heaviness of his arm as he draped it over my shoulder.

"So," I said. "Have you ever heard of the serial killer thing? The Jack Daniels thing?"

"Oh my God!" he said, and he grinned broadly, giving my shoulder a squeeze. "Jack Daniels is actually one of my favorite serial killers!   I mean, for me, Gacy will always be the king. But in terms of contemporary ones . . ."

"Uh-huh," I said.

He took a sip from his wine.

"I wouldn't say that Rabbit fit the profile for Jack Daniels, though," he said. "He's the right age but way too fat. And the circumstance doesn't really match up, either. He wasn't, like, an innocent college boy. He was a depressed junkie who was on a towpath that no one in their right mind would walk down alone at night. That's not Jack Daniels material.

"Still," he said. He smiled as a young blond woman with a toddler pushed her shopping cart past us, and his gaze followed her as she rattled along toward the lettuces. "It's an interesting idea," he said.

"But you don't think it's . . ." I said, "like, likely."

"I'd say it's ninety-five percent that it was some combination of accident and suicide," he said. He took in a slow breath, and I wondered if he was pretending to vampire my aura, like he did at House of Wills. "Junkies are always on that edge, you know?"

"I guess," I said. He let his arm slide off, and it was like there was a distinct feeling of a shadow moving across me. He glanced again at the young mother and her kid, thoughtfully.

"Anyway," he said. "I'm guessing you want to get hooked up. If you've got cash, I've got some baggies out in my car."

8

RABBIT KNEW A lot of people. After I parted ways with Amy in the parking lot of Whole Foods, I sat there and scrolled again through the contacts. It was weird. Even though we hung out practically every day, it seemed like at least 50 percent of his calls and texts were to people I'd never heard of.

There was, for example, this one contact named Gergely. Rabbit had called Gergely fifteen times in that last week that he was in possession of his phone, and it seemed like he and Gergely were talking regularly, stretching back for months.

I'd thought about asking Amy about it, but I wanted to be cautious, too. I didn't want him to have the idea that I was trying to play detective. That tends to be a turnoff for drug dealers.

But then I heard myself bring it up as we were on the way to Amy's car. "Oh," I said, very casual. "By the way, I meant to ask you," I said. "You ever heard of somebody named Gergely?"

"*Jurgily?*" he said, and looked at me sidelong. "You mean *Gairgely*?" And he raised his eyebrow in this way that was like, *Are you serious?* But I didn't know exactly how to take it.

"I don't know," I said. "It was somebody that Rabbit mentioned."

"Really?" Amy said. He made a half grin, as if he were calculating. "Mentioned how?"

"It was just somebody he talked to, I guess," I said, and Amy tilted his head dubiously.

"Huh," he said. "I guess I didn't realize that was the road he was going down."

"What does that mean?" I said, and for whatever reason he laughed.

"It means," he said, "that's something you should keep a distance from, little brother."

Which, now that I was thinking about it, kind of pissed me off. *Little brother*, I thought, as I pulled out of the parking lot and onto Cedar Road. *Little brother.*   It was so condescending.   And also the implication that he thought I was less badass than Rabbit, that I was in need of protection. And the way he leaned over me, the way he would deliberately make me aware that he was six feet or more and I was five foot four, just a wee hobbit to his Aragorn.

And of course *little brother* wasn't my favorite because I *was* a little brother. I had grown up with an older brother who was always a few yards ahead, who was always better in school and funnier and more likely to attract girls and so on, and though we had been pretty good friends in high school there was always the sense that Dennis was the leader and Rabbit was second and I was always going to be the follower. Even if I was by myself.

I got home and my dad and Aqil were sitting at the kitchen table, drinking coffee.   Not talking, at least when I walked in. Aqil was scrolling through his phone, and my dad seemed to be seriously involved in reading *The Atlantic.* When you walk into this kind of scene, it kind of automatically activates your paranoid gland, and a part of you assumes that they have been talking about you up until you opened the door.

"Hey," I said, and my dad did a performance of man-reading-magazine-is-interrupted.

"Oh," he said. "Hey, buddy!" And Aqil glanced up and gave me a terse nod.

"What's going on?" I said.

"Nothing," my dad said.   He gave me his *warm-and-loving-father* expression. "We're just doing a little"

He gestured at his magazine. "Reading," I said. "Research," he said.

"Yeah." I cleared my throat. "So," I said. "I've been meaning to ask you. I guess I should have thought of this before, but have you talked to Dennis recently? I mean, did you tell him about Rabbit?"

"Well," my dad said. And the question seemed to startle him.   "Of course. I talked to Dennis," and I watched as he touched the tip of his nose three times, the way he always did when he wasn't going to tell the truth. "I talked to him a few days ago. But I didn't"

"You didn't tell him that Rabbit was drowned by a serial killer."

"Right," he said. "I just thought . . . I don't know. Dennis isn't . . . and you're more . . ." He hesitated, and Aqil gave me that look he liked to cast off occasionally.

It was his cop look: cold evaluation. He thought he knew me. He thought I was probably a drug addict of some sort, he recognized something in my face or my posture that he'd seen before, and then at the same time he had to keep his opinion to himself because I was his best friend's son. And he wanted something from me and was a little repulsed by me at the same time.

"The thing is," my dad said.   "The, well. I don't really want Dennis to know about the issues of possible. I mean, the possibility of a 'serial killer' being involved in Rabbit's—I don't think that's a good thing for Dennis to"

"Know about?" I said.

I was aware that a manipulation was probably being perpetrated upon me, but I was helpless against it. The idea that he had confided in me and not in Dennis. The idea that I knew something Dennis didn't. The pleasure of that was almost as good as a hit of dope.

And of course there was manipulation from my direction, too— now that I was part of his detective posse, now that I was his confidant, it was going to be easier to ask him for money.

9

IT WAS EARLY afternoon when I tried to call Gergely, and he picked up after two rings. "What?" said a deep male voice, and it's kind of startling when someone answers the phone abruptly like that, and I heard my voice come out kind of weak-ish and uncertain. "Hey!" I said. "I'm a friend of Rabbit's . . ."

I don't know how many words I said before he hung up, but it wasn't many.

I sat there in bed, staring at my phone. It was a Saturday in the middle of January, the weekend before Martin Luther King Day, and I was still under the covers in my sweats, the dim light of a Cleveland winter day pouring through the window.   I checked email on my laptop and scanned through Netflix to see if there was a movie I wanted to watch, but everything seemed boring. It was that dull mood where you kind of felt the angsty life-is-meaningless vibe but you were too lazy to get very worked up about it.

I thought about calling Dennis. But at this point—almost two weeks after Rabbit's death—it was going to be awkward. Why hadn't he talked to me right away?   Why had he not talked to me at all since he went back to Cornell?   He and Rabbit and I had grown up together; we had been best friends. I mean, why would he *not* call me? We hadn't had a falling-out that I knew of.

But I guessed that we must've. That was the only way I could figure his silence. I must have done something that really pissed him off before he went back to college, but when I tried to run back over those weeks there was so little I could even remember.

10

I WAS SITTING in Mike Mention's apartment and we were on the couch, passing a blunt back and forth, watching some old videos on his laptop: Mike and Rabbit and I, goofing around. It was hard to believe this stuff still existed.

We were thirteen when we made this, and at the time we thought it was so hilarious that we were busting out laughing throughout the filming, and now it was so sad and unfunny that it was actually hard to watch. Meanwhile, Mike Mention was crying. "Oh, man," he whispered. "Look at this. We were just kids!" He put his face in his hands and genuinely sobbed for, like, two minutes.

And it was so uncomfortable for me, that kind of emoting. The thing about Mike Mention: He had a certain kind of tall body that got on my nerves. The long arms that hung down floppy like tentacles, and the thin legs that seemed like the femurs must be abnormal, a long narrow skull that was almost horse-like, and so I just sat there stiffly as he wept. I didn't say anything.

After a time, Mike Mention composed himself. He took a very long pull from the blunt and held it with his chin raised and his hand over his chest, as if he were saying the Pledge of Allegiance. Then he expelled smoke in a slow plume. "Oh, man," he said. His eyes were still wet from crying. "You don't expect it. This is what happens in life, and we all know it's coming, but for some reason you don't expect it."

"Right," I said. But I wasn't actually sure what he was saying. *It* = Death?

For a while, we sat around listening to sad hip-hop: Cage's *Depart from Me*, Lupe Fiasco's *The Cool*, Capital Steez.

I handed over Rabbit's phone and Mike Mention took it silently and formally, like the way that the parents of a dead soldier will take the American flag his coffin has been draped in.

"Oh, man," he said. "Where'd you get this?"

"Xzavious Reinbolt gave it to me," I said.

"That guy gives me the creeps," Mike Mention said. "*Amy.* What is up with that?"

"I know, right?" I said. "But look at Rabbit's contacts. I don't know half of those people."

I watched as Mike Mention put out his long stick finger and respectfully touched the screen of Rabbit's phone. His face was grim as he scrolled through the alphabetical list, and his hand shook a little. It was almost as if he were touching Rabbit's dead body.

"Dude," he said. "I don't know most of these." He cleared his throat. "Oh, wait. That's a drug dealer," he said. Pointing to *Blake B.* And then he went down slowly, letter by letter. "That's another drug dealer," he said: *El W.* "She does dabs and edibles, I think."

"So what about this," I said. I put out my index finger and touched *Gergely.* "What the hell? Gergely? That's freaky, isn't it?"

"Not really," he said. "It's like—Hungarian.   It's basically the same as Gregory."

"Really?" I said. "It looks made up."

"No, honest," Mike Mention said. "It was my great-uncle's name. It's totally like a normal Hungarian name."

"Oh," I said. "Okay."

11

UNCLE RUSTY'S FACE came up on my laptop. It was the frame of a Skype window, severely pixelated, but I could see his face for the first time. He peered down at me as if he were looking through a hole, his eyes wide, nervous, or surprised. The connection was fuzzy, but you could see that he had shoulder-length brownish hair with white streaks in it and a square face with a thick tattooed neck and broad shoulders. Not exactly what was expected.   His image sharpened for a minute and then dissolved into a blotchy portrait that had been done in watercolor.

"Hello?" he said. "Can you hear me?"

"Yeah," I said. It was weird to look him in the face. He was squinting and confused by the technology, but it was the actual person nevertheless.

"Ha-ha," he said. "I can see you! You look so much like your dad!"

He was in his apartment. Some people at the support group he'd been going to had helped him out, and now he had an efficiency on the northwest side of Chicago, and he had been saving his money to buy a cheap laptop and a Wi-Fi plan. At last, he could experience the shoddy magic of the twenty-first century. "This is amazing," he said, and beamed out a blissful grin. "Like science fiction. Now all I have to do is get me a hover car and I'm really in the future."

"Ha," I said. I never understood why people from the 1980s thought there would be flying cars. It just seemed really dangerous and impractical to me, but they all talked about it, so it must have been a thing. Meanwhile, my dream for the future was that it wouldn't involve mass extinction and large-scale water shortages and cannibalism.

"So what's been going on with you, man?" he said. "How's it been going?"   I watched as he folded his arms in front of him. He had tattoo sleeves on his forearms—red and black decorations of some sort, though it was impossible to tell, with this blurry connection, what they were of. *Hopefully not swastikas*, I thought.

I shrugged. I was surprised by how unnerved I was. Seeing him at last, after all these months of talking on the phone, I somehow hadn't expected that he'd look like a fifty-year-old guy who had spent the last thirty years in prison. I realized that I had been picturing him as if he were still nineteen or twenty, because that's what his voice was like—that deep, scratchy, hard-rock stoner intonation.

Now it was as if his voice was being ventriloquisted out of the head of a mean-looking old redneck, and it freaked me.

"Nothing," I said. "Just . . . hanging out."

"Staying safe, I hope," he said.

"Yeah."

"I've been thinking a lot about our last conversation," he said. "And the stuff about your friend Rabbit. It worries me."

He shifted his laptop as if he wanted to get a better look at me, as if he thought he could bring me closer by moving his camera, but all that happened was his face loomed larger in my screen. There was a thick scar above his eye that had split his eyebrow in two, and it ran crookedly up his forehead and disappeared into the hairline.

"I mean," he said, "a serial killer who drowns young guys? That sounds a little far-fetched to me. And your dad and this guy are investigating this for whatever reason, and suddenly one of your friends dies and the serial killer did it. Does that not sound fishy to you?"

"I guess," I said. He raised his chin, and for a moment the Skype image resolved so that I could see the letters tattooed there in that Olde English–style font. **ƐMƐMƁƐ**

"What do you know about this Aqil guy, anyway?" Uncle Rusty said. "Who is he?"

"He was a cop," I said. "He was a patient of my dad's."

"A patient for what?" Uncle Rusty said. "What was wrong with him?"

"I don't know," I said, and I backed away a little from the screen even as Rusty pressed in closer. "Probably nothing that serious. Nothing you'd have to get pills for, because Dustin can't prescribe medication. He's just a psychologist."

"Hm," Rusty said.

"I don't know," I said again.   "The more I've been looking into it, the more I feel like—maybe there are some things about the way Rabbit died that don't make sense. I don't think I believe that he just drowned."

He was silent. Then he sighed. "Look," he said. "There's some stuff I've been wanting to talk to you about. And I've just been trying to figure out how to broach it. I wanted us to get to know each other better. You don't really know me, and I don't want to . . ."

He made an agitated movement that sent the Skype connection into fat, blocky pixels. The place where his mouth should have been was a thick, glowing square that pulsed as he spoke.

"Listen," he said.   "Have you ever talked to your aunt Wave? Have you guys ever had any contact with her?"

"You mean Aunt Kate's sister?" I said. "The one that lives on the commune or something? I always thought her name was Waverna."

He put his hands up and tucked his hair behind his ears, and I could see that there were letters on all eight of his knuckles, though it wasn't clear enough to read what they spelled.

"I've got her number," Rusty said. "I think you should call her."

12

THE MAIN INSTINCT was to run away from him as far as I could. Maybe it was the fault of a bad Skype connection, but his face had really freaked me out. *Disturbing*, I thought, so I went out in *your mom's car* just to clear my head.

Either I believed my dad, that Rabbit was murdered, or else I didn't believe my dad, and Rabbit died by accident.

Or else there was a third path: I didn't believe my dad, but I did believe Rabbit was murdered.

I choose the third path, I thought to myself, and I cruised down the curve of Cedar Hill. It was snowing on top of the snow that was already layered on the ground, and a salt truck rumbled along in front of me.

Maybe because there was something so screwed up about Rusty's eyes. There is a part of our brain—the amygdala—that knows things we don't, but it has no words. But it can recognize danger, and that was what I felt when I saw Rusty's face.

I choose the third path, I thought. And so I brought up my phone at a stoplight outside the dreadful towers of Cleveland Clinic. I texted El W with Rabbit's phone.

> Hey where r u?

It took a while for her to respond. I had passed the battlements of the hospital complex and was back in the post-post-industrial rubble of old mansions that had been abandoned and then converted into beauty parlors and convenience stores and so forth and then those closed and were boarded up and now the mansions were covered with dead vines and dirty snow and looked like they were returning to the earth. There were acres of vacant, snow-drifted lots that might have once been the parking for a warehouse or a factory. And then finally my phone blooped.

> Who is this?

And I was rolling past this place that was called, seriously: Fresh Start, Inc. It was one of those cinder-block things from the 1970s, and all the windows were broken out, and it looked as if there may have been a bad fire a long time ago.

> A friend of Rabbit

Really, I knew I shouldn't be driving and texting. I shouldn't have been driving at all. But the road unfolded out the window pretty smoothly, and my hands did the things they were supposed to do when operating a vehicle, and besides, this was a part of the city where you were not likely to see pedestrians, or police, or even other drivers. Seeing a car on this street would be like seeing Rusty's face. Certain alarms would go off. But then another text came from El W:

You know the hookah bar on Euclid?

Yeah. What do u look like?

Green dress

13

SHE WAS SITTING by herself at one of the low booths and there was a hookah on the wide coffee table in front of her. Maybe thirty years old, white girl, and, like, twenty or so pounds overweight. She was wearing a green dress, without a doubt. It was like a dress from the 1950s or something, a deep cleavage neckline, and made of that kind of shiny material—satin? Silk? The hose of the hookah wound its way over her stomach and across her breasts and she drew from the mouthpiece and blew out a cloud of the flavored vapor. The hose was kind of intestine-like, umbilical. It wasn't sexy. More like body horror.

"You're the friend of Rabbit," she said. She had short dark hair and a kind of harsh face. I was very aware of her nostrils.

"Yeah," I said. And when she gestured, I sat down across from her. I could sense the snake of hookah pipe, and I made a conscious effort not to look at it. "I'm just making the rounds," I said. "Rabbit was a really good friend."

"My condolences," she said. The tip of the hookah pipe was like the reed of a bassoon, and she put it to her lips as if she were drawing in a note.   "He was in terrible shape," she said. "It's too bad nobody was able to help him sooner."

"Yeah," I said. My hands twitched a little as I reached in my pocket and took out a hundred-dollar bill. I set it down on the table next to the hookah pipe, but I tried to make the gesture casual. "Like," I said. "Like, I'm just still trying to process my, like, grief. You know? And I was just wondering if you'd be willing to look at his phone. Maybe I'm not seeing everything that needs to be seen, you know?"

She was motionless. You'd think that she was the sort of person who would wear heavy makeup, but she didn't.   She looked thoughtfully at the phone, and then at the hundred dollars that I'd set down. She brushed the hose of the hookah aside. She took the money first, then Rabbit's phone.

"What am I looking for?" she said. "I don't even know what we're talking about here."

"I guess," I said. "I'm just trying to understand his contacts. Because there's so many people I don't know, and I was, like, his best friend and I'm just . . ."

"Oh my God," she said. "Are you the guy who kissed his mom?"

She started laughing, and then it turned into coughing, and then she put the pipe tip into her mouth and sucked up some more hookah and blew out the flavored smoke or vape or whatever.

"Oh, honey," she said at last, and her voice softened. "I'm so sad for you." She gave me what seemed like a genuinely sympathetic look.

I was blushing, but I didn't say anything. Suddenly I realized that probably most of our friends and their friends and acquaintances had heard the story of Rabbit walking in to see me kissing his dying mom. His version of it.

"Look at you," she said. "Your heart is broken." She said this matter-of-factly, as if she were telling me that I had a stain on my shirt, and I didn't say anything. Was my heart broken? I didn't know. Maybe.

She leaned back. She had expended her sympathy, and now she relaxed again, settling into the gaudy pillows. She regarded the screen of Rabbit's phone. "So what am I looking for?" she said. "I'm not going to go through every single contact."

"I don't know," I said. "I just want to figure out. I mean, he sort of disappeared, and then he turned up dead, and I just . . . I'd like to figure out what happened to him."

"Oh," she said, and looked at me brightly. "You think he was murdered."

"Not necessarily," I said. "I just want to know."

El W regarded me. Her eyes were lavender—colored contacts, I guessed—but it gave her a supernatural vibe, like she was a psychic or something, which I supposed was what she was going for.   I figured if I asked her to read my palm, she would know how.

"That's really sweet," she said. "When I die, I hope there's somebody who loves me enough to think that I must have been murdered."

"Gergely," I said, and tried to pronounce it the right way, the way Mike Mention had. *Gair-gel-ee*. "Do you know who that is?"

She raised her eyebrows. "Oh, *Rabbit*!" she said softly, as if he had done something surprising and dirty. "That's too bad." Then she looked at me and shrugged. "Gergely," she said, "is a creature of the night."

"What does that mean?" I said.

"He's just a mild sicko," she said. "He likes to tie up teenage boys. So he'll give you dope if you let him tie you up. Straight white boys preferred."

She smiled at me apologetically. "Oh, sweetheart, you look so stricken!" she said. She gave my hand a pat. "You don't want to think of your poor dead friend that way, I know. But Rabbit was pretty desperate."

14

WHEN I GOT home my dad was awake.   He was sitting on the
couch in the TV room with the old afghan draped over him and a
space heater blowing. Watching a chef competition on the Food
Network. It was always kind of sad and disturbing to come across him
in this state, because his eyes were so bright and attentive and interested in the moronic action onscreen, and he had the gentle smile
that you might wear if you wanted to signal: *oh! please tell me more!*

Maybe the kind of look he gave his patients? The kind of smile
that convinced people that he was listening? And maybe a part of
him was. A part of him was genuine and caring and compassionate
and really wanted to help.

Then there was another part. Something as blank as a reptile, and
I could see that, too, in the way he cocked his head as, on TV, one of
the chefs was about to be eliminated.

I had been noticing it more and more, that blankness. Maybe
because I was getting older—when you're a kid you just accept that
your dad is the way he is; you don't question it when your mom calls
him "spacey" and makes a beloved family joke out of it.

I could remember this one day. I was about eight or nine, and my
mom and I came across him in the dining room. We were standing
in the threshold and my mom suddenly stopped still. She put her
hand out and softly touched me so I didn't go forward. "Shhh," she
said, and pointed. *Shhh*. As if we had encountered a rare woodland
creature.

Dustin was standing in front of a houseplant that was on a stand
near the front window.

He had the watering can in his hand, but you could see that he'd
forgotten that he planned to use it. He was just staring at this fern,
apparently mesmerized by it, smiling his thoughtful smile, and my
mom leaned into me confidentially. "Look," she whispered. "Astral
traveling."

Astral traveling: A part of his mind wasn't in his body anymore, and when my mom was alive she made this seem secret and mystical and kind of funny. Now that she was gone, it wasn't so charming anymore.   If a part of his mind wasn't in his body, where was it?

I cleared my throat. "Hey," I said from the doorway. I had been standing there for a few minutes by that time, and I didn't want to startle him. "I'm home."

He looked up, startled anyhow. Though I didn't know if he was actually startled, or just pretending to be startled, or whether, for him, there wasn't any difference between the two.

"Oh!" he said. "Hey! Did you just get in?"

"Yeah," I said. "I was just out for a while. Talking to a friend."

"I'm glad to hear that. You really need to . . . cultivate a support group in times of"

"Right," I said, and then the music on the television indicated that something dramatic was going to happen, and his eyes shifted. He stared and then seemed to catch himself. "Oh! Do you want to watch TV?" he said. "We can change the channel."

"It's fine," I said. "I'm not in the mood."

"Oh?" he said, as if my mood was of interest. He looked at my face attentively. "Have you been," he said. "The things we discussed, have you been"

"I don't know," I said.

"I'm not trying to pressure you," he said. "That's the last thing I want."

"I'm thinking about it," I said.

And he gave me that same smile.   That same interested smile he gave his TV show, and his patients, and for the first time I realized that it was not a human smile. It was a protective coloration. An adaptation of some sort. He would project it equally at a television, or a son, or a houseplant, but whatever was really inside him was crouched and peering out stealthily. "Let me know," he said, "if you'd like to talk."

15

I WAS IN the parking lot of Kaiser Permanente in *your mom's car* and I was trying to call Dennis, but he didn't pick up.

Why was I in the parking lot where I used to wait for Terri to get out of her sessions in the infusion room? No doubt Dustin would find it very psychologically symbolic, but the truth was I knew it was a place that had great privacy. You could sit here all day at the edge of the lot, where the fence was overgrown with vines and small trees, and no cop would ever hassle you.

Dennis's voicemail: "Hey, it's Dennis; leave me a message. Or better yet, send me a text." So I texted him.

> I really need to talk to you

> I guess u know Rabbit is dead. I don't know why u havnt called me maybe ur mad? But weird stuff is happening at home and I rly need 2 talk 2 u.

I started to say: *I need your help.* But then I decided I wanted to hold on to at least a little dignity, so I erased that.

I waited.

I turned the ignition on and let the heat blow for a little while. It was late afternoon, but the parking lot's halogen lamps had already come on in the dim January light. I was the only car parked in the far back row, and feathery pieces of snow occasionally dropped from the trees. The thick honeysuckle vine that gripped the fence was coated in a film of ice, and parts of it were formed into hunched shapes by the accumulated snow.

I sent Dennis an email.   *WTF? You're not going to respond?*

I called his phone again.   *"Hey, it's Dennis; leave me a message. Or better yet, send me a text."*

> Where are u? Are u OK?!?

That feeling of calling and not being answered. That particular, peculiar sinking. The image of Rabbit thrashing around in the dark water of the Cuyahoga River.

I checked Dennis's Facebook page, and there was a picture of him partying with two girls that had been posted two days ago.   *Fuck you, Dennis,* I wrote in the comments section.

16

IT WAS AFTER nightfall, and I was still sitting in the parking lot.

I smoked cigarettes and snorted a little of the dope that I'd gotten from Xzavious Reinbolt, and I felt this weird sensation of being trapped—like, kind of a panicky hesitation that you couldn't get out of, looping around and around in your mind until you felt like you'd been entirely mummy-wrapped in indecisiveness.

I don't know why I felt so nervous.   I took out the number that Rusty had given me. *Aunt Waverna.*   *Wave,* he had called her. The back of my mind kept whispering: *It's really not a good idea.*

It was a male voice that answered, and I almost hung up. The voice was deep, gravelly, blunt—the first thing I imagined was an old construction worker with a shaved head—and it surprised me to hear myself speak.

"Hey," I said. "I'm looking for Wave?"

There was a long silence.   And then the hostile voice said: "Who is this?"

"It's her nephew," I heard myself say. "My dad is her cousin?"

"Is that right?" the man said. "I don't think you know what a nephew is."

"Um," I said. I had no idea what he was trying to get at, and I hesitated. I only heard my voice distantly as it spoke. "My dad's name is Dustin Tillman. She'll know who that is. And I'm his son. Aaron. I guess I kind of really need to talk to her."

Another pause. "How'd you get this number?" the guy said.

"I found it in my dad's address book," I said. Which seemed like a good enough lie.

"I kind of doubt that," the man said. "But tell me what you want her to know, and I'll give her the message."

"It's not a message," I said. "I guess I just need to talk to her. To ask her, like, advice? I mean, I think it's kind of urgent."

"Hm," the man said. "What kind of urgent is it? The urgent that she's-inherited-a-million-dollars kind of urgent? The kind of urgent where your dad's dead and you need to know how to clean up the body?"

"Um," I said, and put my hand through my hair.

"Listen, son," he said. His voice was almost kind, in an unfriendly way—like a boss who is trying to gently explain to you why you're so stupid. "First of all, you're not her nephew, you're her first cousin once removed. She doesn't know you. She hasn't been in touch with your dad for thirty years. What do you think would inspire her to come to the phone and give you urgent advice?"

"Rusty gave me her number," I said. "Rusty said I should call her."

I guess that was the right answer, because it seemed to give him pause. A long silence emanated from his end of the phone line. Then, at last, he sighed.

"I'll take down your information," he said. "If she wants to talk to you she'll call you back."

"Okay," I said.

"Let me get a pencil," he said.

17

I GOT TO Rabbit's house at about midnight.

It was hard to park in his driveway—so many bad vibes—but it seemed like the best way.

The most unobtrusive, because of Cleveland Heights cops. You don't want to run into them.

The driveway had been cleared, which was strange since the walks hadn't been scooped. But I guessed maybe they had a service that was still clearing the drive, even after both of them were dead. That was a creepy thought.

His mom's car wasn't in the garage, of course. I was aware that he had probably driven it that night.   *That night:* I guessed that he must have parked somewhere near the path below the bridge, and probably the car had been towed away at some point. Now, most likely, it was sitting in a west side junkyard.

So I slid *your mom's car* into the garage and turned off the lights. The neighbors' houses were all dark, but still when I got out of the car I crouched and crept a little. The one neighbor was a mean old Irish cat lady who had once called the police on me and Rabbit and Dennis because we were sitting in Rabbit's yard listening to hip-hop music she found offensive. The other neighbors were an aloof religious black family who generally pretended that Rabbit and his mom didn't exist.

I tried to be stealthy as I troll-footed my way through calf-deep drifts into Rabbit's backyard, which now of course was so haunted I almost lost my nerve. There was the old trampoline, still set up, though we hadn't jumped on it since probably sixth grade. There were the lawn chairs we'd sat in on summer nights, the three of us and Rabbit's mom, getting high and listening to her old Black Sabbath records; there was Rabbit's bike, leaned against the high wooden fence and so coated with snow that it looked like it was an ancient, worn statue. It made me think of those old gravestones where the engraving has been smoothed away by the years of rain and wind. I didn't know who would come into possession of the house now that Rabbit and his mom were dead, but I figured that whatever little piece of them was still here was going to be gone soon.

So why was I here? I dug through the hard crusted snow on the back stoop until I found the broom thatch of the welcome mat, and I turned it over and there was the key, where it had been for as long as I could remember. I scraped it up out of the ice and put it into the dead bolt. *Why am I here? Why am I here?*

I guess I was looking for clues.

A part of me that wanted to think that my dad was right. A part of me that wanted to think there was some way to make sense of the idiot world.

It was a small house. One floor plus an unfinished basement, a little square ranch house type thing. The back door opened onto the kitchen, and then there was the dining room, where Rabbit's mom spread out her bills and papers on the table, and the living room with the sofa facing the TV.   I used my phone as a flashlight and ran a dim illumination across the walls. A shelf of knickknacks— mostly Día de los Muertos skeletons that Terri had collected over the years. A cheaply framed painting of wolves howling at the moon above the couch where Terri and I had kissed.

On the coffee table, a mug with the thin slime of evaporated coffee in it. I shined my light on it, and I was mesmerized for a moment. *Someone's last cup of coffee,* I thought: Terri's, or Rabbit's.

I didn't know what I was looking for, but I figured that Rabbit's room was the place to start.

I held my phone aloft like a girl in a fairy tale, holding a candle.

Wasn't this the way it always went? You put your hand slowly on the doorknob, and there was the room that you thought you knew, the room you'd been in so many times before, but now bathed in an aura of eerie hostility.   Rabbit's little twin bed, the same bed he'd had since I met him in third grade—how had he even slept in it? The bongs lined up on the shelf, along with the model ships he'd been obsessed with in fifth grade, and the action figures from *Game of Thrones*, and the framed photo of him and his mom, right there on his nightstand, the sweetly grinning Bruce Berend and the proud Terri, set up like a guard to watch him while he slept. And I thought: *Oh.*

The bed was unmade, a mass of tangled blankets, and the closet was open, and there were some dress shirts on hangers and his one suit jacket. I knew if I reached into the side pockets I would find a bundle of hypodermics with the caps still on the needles, and if I reached into the vest pocket I might find a little baggie of dope.

Well, it turned out the pocket was empty. But I couldn't help but look.

And then down at last to the basement, where we'd spent so much time in the last year, the two of us side by side, wasted, holding our game pads even though the game had been paused for so long it seemed that it hadn't ever started. Just staring.

And there was that sense that heroin gave you—not happy, not hopeful, not even interested. Just free from thinking that things were logical. Free from thinking that the world was benevolent or something, or that it cared at all. I always thought it was how you would feel in the womb, before you knew that there was such a thing as being born.

So there were the game pads, laying there on the coffee table like a pair of severed hands with a wire extending from the wrist. There was evidence that he'd been cooking before he left. A spoon. A piece of aluminum foil. There was a bottle of cheap whiskey, and a tumbler glass.

Go ahead: Sit right down and contemplate suicide with him.

The worst thing: Rabbit's fish tank was still going. Still lit up, still bubbling and filtering, and the little plastic treasure chest opening and closing. The fish themselves were long dead. It had been a month since they'd been fed, and their corpses were floating at the top of the tank.

And then I saw it.

It was a three-by-five note card, tucked underneath the ashtray. Rabbit carried these note cards around with him in his pocket, because he liked to use them to write down observations, or draw sketches, or whatever. It was the one way that he still allowed the smart, eccentric, poetic nerd he'd once been to draw an occasional breath—though mostly he was fastidious about tearing the note cards into tiny pieces or even burning them up with his lighter.

But this one on the coffee table was whole. It was just a simple card with an address written in the middle of it in Rabbit's neat block letters.

18

IT WAS ABOUT four in the morning and I was finally asleep in my bed when the phone rang. It was Aunt Kate, my phone said.

"What the fucking fuck?" said Aunt Kate. "You've been talking to Rusty?"

I had been pretty sound asleep. I'd had a complicated night, and quite a bit of drugs had been consumed, and so it took me a while to try to calculate what was going on.

> Aunt Kate + Rusty = ?
> Aunt Kate (Waverna) > Rusty

"What?" I said groggily.

"Are you an idiot?" she said.

"I don't even know what you're talking about," I said.

She made a scoffing sound through her nose. "Honey," she said, "I'm trying to protect you. I'm just asking you: Do you want your life to be completely fucked?"

"No," I said. I sat up in bed with my phone to my ear and my other hand holding a blanket to my neck. "No. But there's a lot that's been, like . . . obscured from me. I mean, I didn't even know about—"

"What did he tell you?" Aunt Kate said. "What did he say about me?"

"Nothing," I said.   "We never talked about you."

"Right," she said. "You just became phone pals to talk about sports and video games."

I put my hands over my eyes and rubbed my upper face. You could tell it was almost morning, because birds were beginning to cheep monotonously outside, even though it was dark. There was the sound of a salt truck lumbering down an artery road somewhere in the distance.

"What would I tell him?" I said. "I don't know anything. I didn't even know that your parents were murdered until, like, a year ago. I'm not exactly a great source for family secrets."

"Yeah," she said. "But you're the little hole that he can squeeze into. You're his point of entry. You don't get it, Aaron. You don't have any idea."

"You're right," I said. "I don't get it.   I mean, first, there's this guy that calls me and says he's my long-lost uncle, and he's been released from prison because of injustice, and so I get that story, and then he says that you and my dad won't talk to him, and so I'm the only person he has a connection to in the world, and so we just talked. That's all. I thought I was doing a decent thing."

"But I also know that it's more fucked up than that. Whatever happened between the four of you—whatever, I don't know. I'm just like, okay, so, Rusty tells me to call Wave, and then Wave must have called you, I guess, and then you called me, and it's like some kind of weird chain letter. What do you want from me?"

"Mmf," she said. And then she was silent for a while.

"So tell me what I'm supposed to know," I said. "What does Rusty think Wave is going to tell me about my dad?"

"I'm curious about that myself," she said. Her voice had grown calmer, or at least she'd decided she was going to take a different tack. "I'd like to know what he thinks he's doing. Because I can tell you this, Wave is never going to call you. So whatever game or scam he's playing on you, it's a way to get to me and Dustin."

"I'm not going to turn against my dad," I said. "Or you. I'm not that easy to manipulate."

"Really," she said.

"And Rusty . . . it seems like he basically took responsibility for what happened. He admits that he was, like, really abusive to my dad, and my dad was a kid, so it was easy to get him to believe in this stuff about cults and witches and demons and so on. I mean, he more or less said that he brought the whole thing on himself."

"That's very big of him."

"I'm not saying that I totally trust him, either," I said. "Because I don't. Which is why it would be nice if you would be straight with me."

"About what?" she said.

"What should I know about my dad?" I said. "What should I know that I don't know?"

"That's an impossible question to answer," she said. "How am I supposed to figure out what you don't know? Or even what you *should* know?"

"Okay, then," I said. "What do you think Wave would tell me?"

Kate made a short, unkind laugh. "I don't think she would tell you anything," she said. "But I'm guessing maybe Rusty hoped she would say that she thought Dustin and I framed him. And she would probably tell you that I maliciously lied because I'm evil and that Dustin lied because he's delusional and crazy."

I caught my breath. "What do you mean by crazy?" I said softly.

Kate was quiet, seeming to consider. "I don't mean anything. I'm just telling you what I think Wave might have said. Which is that Dustin was very . . . impressionable? Imaginative? Gullible? More than normal. And he had a hard time telling the difference between what was real and what was not real. That's what Wave would tell you, and it's not untrue."

I heard the sharp snap of a lighter's flint being hit and then heard her exhale.

"What *I* would tell you," she said, "is not to talk to Rusty. Not to trust anything he says. He's telling you, *oh, I'm soo sorry I was abusive to your dad,* but I can guarantee that he hasn't told you the half of it. Maybe he didn't commit those murders. I don't know, I wasn't there. But he's definitely not innocent."

He woke up as she said this. My dad.

He made a few phlegmy coughs, and then I heard the creak of his bed as he sat up, the sound of his bare feet on the floor. Bathroom light went on, bathroom door closed shut. It was quiet enough that I could hear him pissing, the trickle of water on water.

I was aware that I couldn't trust him. I couldn't trust Rusty, or Aunt Kate. Dennis?

Maybe he was hiding things from me, too?

"I have to call you back," I said to Aunt Kate. But she had already hung up.

19

MY DAD WAS eating cereal in the kitchen when I came in. He was very involved in the newspaper, and there were a few droplets of milk clinging to his goatee.

"Hey," I said. And he looked up, sleepy and surprised and pleased to see me. It felt painful to have him beam a smile my way.

"What are you doing up so early?" he said. "That's fantastic. Getting on top of things!"

"Yeah," I said.

"College starts back up this week for you, doesn't it?" he said.

"Yeah," I said. And I had to wonder: How could he investigate a serial killer if he couldn't even figure out that I wasn't going to college. That I'd never even been to college once.

"Have you talked to Dennis recently?" he said. "I guess you saw on Facebook that he has a girlfriend?"

"Yeah," I said.

I took a bowl from the cupboard. There was a part of me that must have been exhausted, but I couldn't make contact with it. It was like that one period when Rabbit and I were doing Adderall, that sort of hunter's focus, that tingling in the front of your brain, knowing that there's something you're chasing, even if you're not quite sure what it is. I poured Wheaties into my bowl and poured milk over them and then a couple of spoonfuls of sugar and then I began to shovel it into my mouth in a very determined way. My dad watched me as if what I was doing was really interesting, an unusual and complicated experiment. *Astral traveling.*

"So," I said. "Can I ask you a psychology question?"

"Of course!" he said, and he seemed so flattered that I was paying attention to him, and it was both sad and creepy. He made a "curious" look.

"Are you taking a psychology class?" he said.

"Yeah," I said.

"Neat," he said.

"So," I said. "The thing I wanted to ask you. What do you call it when someone can't tell the difference between what's real and what's not real?"

He didn't flinch. "Delusional," he said. He picked at his goatee thoughtfully. "But it's a spectrum. At the far end, of course, it's schizophrenia. But everyone has occasional glitches."

"Yeah," I said.

"I was reading this interesting article," he said. "Apparently, most people have a fold in their prefrontal cortex called a paracingulate sulcus. And this fold seems to help us distinguish between the real and the imaginary. But only about seventy-five percent of people have the fold—and there's some circumstantial evidence that people without the fold are more susceptible to schizophrenia. And they tend to be more trusting and gullible."

I took a moment to finish my last bite of cereal. "Uh-hum," I said.

IF SHE WERE alive, my mom would help me.   It almost made me laugh, it was such a wussy, pansy-ass thing to think, but it was also true: None of this would be happening if she were here.

It was snowing again, and I woke up out of a mid-afternoon doze and stared out at the gray-and-white streetscape. It could've been dusk or dawn again. A certain kind of loneliness magnified inside me. A kind of terrible, unsolvable homesickness—for the home that doesn't exist. That maybe never even was. But there's no path back. In a fairy tale, there would be a witch you could make a deal with, the same witch that stole away everyone you loved, and you could ask her: *What can I give you to be with them again?*

I pulled the covers up to my chin and closed my eyes. It would be so nice if my mom came to me in a dream and told me what to do.

And then at the same time I knew exactly what she would tell me to do. Stop taking drugs. Consider rehab. Don't be involved with the people you're messing with. *Get out of the situation you're in, Aaron.* So of course I fell back to sleep and ignored her ghostly advice.

When I woke up again, it was full-on dark. My phone had pinged the arrival of a text, and when I picked it up I saw that it was 10:01 P.M. A message from Xzavious Reinbolt.

> Hey! Saving some good shit 4 U! HOW, 2NITE.

I stared at the message for about five minutes, and I was like, "HOW?"

What's HOW?

And then I was like, "Oh." House of Wills.

So when I head out I am thinking about my mom's advice, I can feel it chasing me even though I have muffled it with a small hit of fentanyl and I turn the music on loud. It's my mom's Bob Marley CD, her constant companion ever since I was a kid, and I remember how we would sit in the back seat when we were little and sing along, and years later I was surprised to find out that the songs weren't written for children.

"Could you be loved," he is singing, and it makes my nerves feel a little less jangled, though there is still the edge of an anxiety attack underneath the drugs and the music and my left leg is twitching but not to the beat.

"Only the fittest of the fittest shall survive," Bob Marley tells me.

"And then, in the end, not even them," I tell Bob Marley.

That night Rabbit leaves the house—you guess that he's desperate—maybe he's made an appointment with Gergely, maybe he's been drinking Jim Beam whiskey even though he hates alcohol, maybe he's getting up the courage for something he can't turn back from.

On his phone is a selfie taken on December 18, 2013, which was the day before his mom's funeral. Which was also the last day that anyone saw him alive.

And he looks like a person who's going to die. Even though it's just a head shot, you can see that he's lost a lot of weight since you last saw him in November, *gaunt* is the word that comes to you, and his skin is grayish except around his eyes where it's dark, bruised-looking. Stretched and hollow-looking like a real actual junkie. Yet he's trying to smile as if he's posing for a graduation photo, displaying his upper teeth in that unnatural way that means *I am smiling*—

Which reminds me of something that Terri told me once. I was driving her back home from the infusion room and she started laughing to herself, and I said "What?" and she said, "Do you know the funniest thing about dying? It's that you have to live through it."

"That's weird," I said, and I felt her put the pads of her fingers on the back of my hand.

"You know how, when you realize that everyone dies, and it's like: You realize that you can't get out of it, you can't escape. You've had that thought, right?"

"Yeah," I said.

"But then it kind of dissipates, and you're like, *ok, I can't worry about it, nothing I can do,* and you stop thinking about it. You just keep going along."

I nodded.

This was the photo he texted to Gergely. 10:01 P.M.

He wrote down an address on an index card. He was completely out of dope, and so he decided to try some whiskey.

No good.

And then he texted Xzavious and made plans to spend whatever money he had left. His mom had been dead for three days by that point, and he was in a certain frame of mind.

When someone you love dies, you die, too, of course. There's a freeze frame, a pause button, and you're stuck in an endless GIF, the same fifteen seconds looping around and around in your head.

"And I think it might be like that all the way to the end," Terri said. "Even if you just have five minutes left, you're still moving into the future, you're still thinking about what you're going to do next, making plans, there's a part of you that's still saying *everything's going to work out somehow . . .*"

I felt her fingernails blanch the skin above my wrists. "And then it stops," she said. "I think that you might be alive up until the very second that you're not."

One of the images might have been the moment you walked in and your best friend was kissing your dying mom in a sexual way. Let's make a GIF of that one. Let it play for eternity while Bob Marley sings "Three Little Birds," *every little thing gonna be all right*

Rabbit pushes the garage-door-opener-button and watches the wall lift, listens to the metal rattle.

Even then he isn't alive anymore, probably. He gets into the car. He turns the ignition. But he is already leaving the living part of himself behind.

22

I pull around to the parking lot behind House of Wills and I walk toward the employee entrance with a certain kind of loping gait that is confident but wary. The kind of walk that tells other people that you're minding your own business but they shouldn't mess with you. Probably not convincing, but I do my best, put my hoodie up, my arms loose at my sides like a gunslinger. As a regular customer of street drugs, I have gotten used to walking in blighted neighborhoods, dangerous places, but this is also a business district of a sort, and as long as a white boy is shopping he will probably not be harmed.

Rabbit must have parked in the back just like you did and you do a quick scan of the cars just to be certain that his isn't among them. You can see the ghost light of a blunt being passed around in a 1980s' Lincoln, and a Kia with a cap of snow on top of it a half foot high, and only the driver's-side windshield has been cleared. There is a car that vaguely resembles Rabbit's, you think, but when you get closer you see that there is a girl with long bejeweled fingernails in the passenger seat, delicately stroking the screen of her phone with her clawed finger, and she looks up at you balefully as you glance in at her.

Rabbit recognizes the House as an example of Georgian architecture; it's one of those weird bits of knowledge he soaked up somehow, he doesn't even remember. Three stories, a line of gabled windows at the top. The skeletal framework of an awning leads from the sidewalk and up the front steps to the red wooden doors of the entryway. *Come in the back*, Xzavious said, and so he parks his car in the nearby strip mall which is full of ghetto-y storefronts— a cellphone place, a place to buy hair extensions and beauty products, a place called Manhattan Fried Chicken Fish Shrimp.

For a while, Rabbit told me, they were running ghost-hunting tours out of this place. It got mentioned on websites about "Haunted Places," but it was hard to make money when you found that you were more likely to discover drug deals going down or junkies fucking or meth heads tweaking hostilely than you were to encounter some misty spirit vapor shit floating down the hallway in olden garb.

I don't believe in ghosts, but I believe in . . . ? What?

Malevolence?

A girl and a guy are kissing right next to the back entrance. She has her back pressed to the wall and his legs are spread wide apart as he leans into her, and you don't look at them until one of them says, very distinctly: "Aaron?" And then you turn and say, "What? Did you say something?" And the guy doesn't stop kissing his girl but lifts his hand with his middle finger extended and puts it right in your face.

Maybe this is the first of the night's hallucinations?

Rabbit doesn't like the idea of going into an abandoned funeral home on the night before his mother's funeral, but there's really no other choice. It's not like he's going in alone. He watches as a car pulls up and a dude gets out. Teenager. White. He's got his hoodie pulled up and he's trying to put on a kind of menacing, faux-street-smart walk, and Rabbit feels a little shudder of recognition.

"Aaron?" Rabbit says, but the guy doesn't turn.

I believe in bad places.

I believe that there is a part of your brain that knows things but cannot speak. That feeling of the hairs rising on your neck, that sense that someone is watching you, the way a building can contain a presence that is observing. I open a door and there are stairs going down, probably down to where they embalmed the bodies. I back away.

Even though you've been here before it doesn't seem familiar at all. Doors and hallways, stairs going down or up, and you keep hearing the sound of voices but you're not sure where they are coming from. You open a door and all the carpet has been pulled up and rolled into a lump against one wall, and there is a single folding chair in the center of the room, waiting.

Labyrinthine. It seems like it was built to get lost in. He walks along an empty hallway and opens a door and there is a clutter of chairs, along with a life-sized plastic Santa—why would a funeral home need Christmas decorations?—and a collapsed ceiling with the asbestos hanging down like kudzu. The sound of someone talking in another room.

I can hear voices out of the corner of my ear, which may or may not be my imagination. The sound always seems as if it's coming from several rooms away, and when I open another door it stops altogether. The hallway I am in now is lined with round wooden columns that seem to be sort of Egyptian in their designs. The carpet is still red, with a pattern of green fans or fronds, though there is a path through the middle of it that is worn black from the soles of dirty shoes, scattered with garbage: hypodermic, gum wrapper, a dead mouse, a used condom, a naked Barbie whose hair has been burned off.

It feels like it's laid out like a maze, which makes sense: Back in the day, they might have had three funerals going on at once, and they had to keep them from running into one another. They'd need all these side-hatch rooms to put people in when they started losing it. And you realize that if there are ghosts, they are not the ghosts of the dead. The ghosts are the ones who sat in these little waiting rooms. The bereaved. They are the ones who can't help but return, over and over—they remember every detail of that couch they sat on while they were weeping; they are the ones who can't leave.

"Oh my God," says the girl. Rabbit thinks she must be talking on her phone. "I just saw Xzavious Fucking Reinbolt, I can't believe it." And she draws in a noisy breath. "What an asshole," she says. "He's over there with some little chick who looks like she's fourteen. He's probably talking his vampire shit. The creep." She listens for a moment and then she scoffs. "Oh no I didn't," she said. "Who told you that?" And Rabbit moves toward the sound of her voice; he opens a door and there's a little room with a bar. The girl isn't in the room, but her voice is coming clearly from a vent.

The sound of voices in the corridor. A young woman exclaims, "Oh no I didn't! Who told you that?" And then she laughs in that softly mean way that girls have when they are talking about one another. "I've actually been pretty good about avoiding him," the voice says, and I stand in the dark hallway listening.

In the distance, at the other end of the corridor, is the sound of human grunting, male and female, sexual, and in the other direction a white boy with a hillbilly accent calls out: "You guys! I'm fuckin' lost!" His voice plaintive, starting to get scared. "Guys?"

That hospice where your mom died, for example. She's not there anymore, but *you* are, you walk down that mentholated hallway practically every day, you know how to get from the front desk to her room, you can make your way to the boardwalk that looked like a grape arbor. *I don't think she's going to make it.*

Try to focus. You're here to buy some dope or else you're here to investigate a mystery, or possibly both. But you have gotten turned around again, and you open the door to the room with the folding chair. An old camping lantern on the floor glows dully.

"I've actually been pretty good about avoiding him," she is saying. "The last time I saw him, you will not believe it, was in this place called Club Eros? I know, how embarrassing." And Rabbit moves hesitantly into the room; there is a mirrored shelf behind the bar with one bottle on it. Crème de menthe.

"But there had been a lot of buzz on social media about this event. Because apparently this girl, this stripper, had agreed to be, like, flayed. And I admit I was curious about it." She laughs. "Shut up!" she says to the person she is talking to. "I am not!"

But when I walk in that direction, the frightened hillbilly is nowhere to be seen, and I find myself at the base of a balustrade, a formerly elegant staircase with a thick, curving rail, the kind of staircase a woman in a ball gown would descend in an old movie.

Maybe this is the right way?

Echoes of people talking in the distance, a woman's voice, hollow and tinny like it's coming out of a barrel. Is it an auditory hallucination, maybe? It seems like it's probably coming from the room at the top of the stairs, faint and wispy like some plant that grows underwater. I can't help but think:

Ghost?

For a second you think you see someone standing in the corner. *A figure* with their back to you, facing the wall, very still, as if they are looking at a painting in a museum, and you turn on the flashlight app on your phone and hold it up and say "Hello?" and take a hesitant step forward.

"Excuse me," you say, but the figure doesn't turn, and then when you step closer it's not there anymore. Your light shines onto a water stain on the wallpaper, which might be said to vaguely resemble a human shape. But that wasn't what you saw.

And you guess that may be the second hallucination of the night.

The woman's voice appears to be coming from the room directly above him, and Rabbit looks around to try to identify what part of the house he's in.

But there are no windows, and practically no light. Just a candle burning on the liquor shelf next to the crème de menthe.

"It was *very* theatrical," she says. "You bought a ticket and you got taken down in an elevator to a basement—they were calling it a 'dungeon,' but the set design was so corny and conventional and the girl was really not attractive. Like, folds of flab coming off of her ribs and severe cellulite. She was probably, like, thirty-five?"

But, no, when I open the door it's just another empty room and the voice is coming from a vent in the ceiling so I think that I just have to go up one more floor somehow. I look down a hallway lined with doors, like a hotel.

Rabbit used to talk about "dissociating." It was a word he used a lot. He "dissociated" in English class when this one asshole student started talking. He "dissociated" in the grocery store in front of the salty-snack aisle. I thought he meant he "spaced out."

How many drugs have you taken? You actually need to start reading up on drug interactions and so forth; you actually need to start parceling things out a little more or you're going to die of an overdose.

But maybe that's part of the plan. It's not *your* plan, but there's more than one person running the good ship Aaron, and several of them are pretty fucking feckless. Some parts of yourself don't care if you die. They are just in this for a good time, and they'll evacuate when it goes bad.

"So she's strapped to this wooden X-bar, right? And a shirtless dude in crotchless leather chaps he's cracking a whip around and showing off like a cowboy at a circus. So lame! And that's when I saw Xzavious.

"Just standing there in the group of people who are watching, and he's acting so cool like he's so fascinated and this is so deep, right? And he looked over at me and gives me that stupid fucking grin?

But actually it's more like the feeling of being detached from your body. Or the feeling of having more than one body, all of them moving along in different universes, unaware of each other, three different films playing on three separate screens and you happen to be acting in all of them.

There is another staircase at the end of the hallway, and I move toward it past the rows of doors. Some open, some shut. Some dark and some with a bit of light coming out. I'm trying to keep an eye on my surroundings. Be aware that a grinning meth head could pop out of a door holding a broken bottle above his head. Someone could creep up behind you with the intention of robbery. Be aware of the need to beware. Don't dissociate.

Pot. Fentanyl. A little heroin. Ritalin. Possibly one or two others that you can't remember. Your body is awake in ways that it probably shouldn't be, and all your worst instincts are having a party together. All of them have an oar, rowing toward opposite shores.

Oh, shit! Maybe you're dying? Maybe the last pill you took set some bodily process in motion that will end with your functions shutting down, and when you come to the bottom of the stairs you feel your muscles tensing and the endorphins pinging and you can hear your teeth tighten against one another. You can hear the soft, squeaky rubber sound the teeth make as they grind, and you do it over and over for a few moments. Fascinated.

"It was a very triggering moment! I didn't want to see him. I didn't want to think about his bleachy-tasting cock, or the way he kept trying to bite my clit when he was giving me head, or that time that he talked about trying to get pregnant so we could eat the fetus.

"God! He was such a poseur! And then he gives me that stupid gaze. You know what I'm talking about. Where he tells you that he's 'drinking from your aura,' or whatever, and then suddenly Flabby the Stripper starts, like, shrieking when the guy hits her with the whip. And a splatter hits me? Right in the face! Right on my, like, mouth, and honestly that is the one thing that I thought was well done. Because it tasted like actual blood. Not corn syrup or something.

At last, I think I recognize where I am. A light at the end of the hall opens up into a chapel, wooden pews facing an altar where the coffin would've been displayed and some dudes of my type are sitting around passing a glass pipe, and I pause at the edge of their circle: "Hey, do you guys know where I can find Xzavious?" and one of them squints at me and points to a door.

Third hallucination: two dudes. One in a long cape with a three-pointed cap that has a feather in it. The other one is a midget, except instead of a nose and a mouth he has a long pointed beak like a bird. "Hey," I say, "do you know where I can find Xzavious?" and the taller one points with his gloved hand. He speaks to me in a foreign tongue.

"But I wasn't about to hang around with Xzavious in the same room. And so, you know—the whip cracked again, and the victim screamed, but I didn't look at it anymore. Some of the BDSM biddies were giving me a judgmental look, like they thought it was too heavy for me and I couldn't handle it, but fuck them. I was out of there."

23

"Aaron!" Amy says, and waves me over. He's in a bare room with an elaborate fireplace, and I watch him feeding various items of trash into the flames.

Pieces of furniture. Paperback books. A Beanie Baby. A pair of tennis shoes. A hairbrush. The smoke coming off it smells upsetting.   He and this girl are standing there watching the fire and when I walk in he turns to me.

"Hey, Sweetroll," he says, and hugs me unpleasantly. "I've been thinking about you, man. I've been a little worried, actually."

Worried? I think. "What do you mean?" I say, and he shrugs.

"Well, you know. Things get around."

"Hey, Amy," Rabbit says. He is not even sure how he got to this room. It's like someone shoved him from behind and now he stumbles into his place. Amy looks up.

His girl stands over by the fireplace, and she taps a wooden spoon against the edge of the iron kettle. She looks fourteen, skinny and flat-chested, silver halter top and a pair of cut-off jeans that barely stop at the edge of her legs. Barefoot.

"Hey, my bunny!" Xzavious says, and gives Rabbit a bear hug. "Damn! You've lost weight! Have you been working out?"

"Not really," Rabbit says. Being hugged— being touched— undoes him for a moment, and a tear volunteers itself at the bottom of his eye.

"Rabbit," the kid whispers, which was my dog's name. And that wakes me up. I burn a little brighter.

For the most part I am aware of them as lights and shadows, lumps of meat that give off heat and stink, their sad, dirty anxieties. We are not awake enough to notice them, most of the time, nor to notice each other, nor to haunt, in the traditional sense.

But there's a little jolt when you're near someone who is going to die soon, particularly those who are going to die horribly, and so I drift along behind the kid for a while, out of curiosity. *Curiosity:* like the time I went to Club Eros, to see a woman flayed. I remember standing right here, telling my friend Eve the story when

There is an iron pot suspended on a spit over the fire—the kind of thing you'd see at a cowboy campfire in a movie—and the girl stirs it with a wooden spoon. "It's nothing," I say. "It's just some very fucked-up family shit that I'm trying to figure out." And Xzavious/Amy nods his head vigorously, showing off his perfect white teeth.

"Well," he says, "this dope that I've got will definitely help you pack up your troubles."

"Oh, man," Xzavious says softly. "Dude, I heard about your mom. That sucks, I'm so sorry," he says, and looks sidelong at the girl.

"I always admire people who love their parents. 'Cause I hated mine. I actually hired someone to kill them, you know?   But I always wished that I had parents that I loved."

"Yeah," Rabbit says, and when Xzavious releases him he feels a little dizzy and bleary.

I had this terrible dream about my dog, and in the dream the dog ran under a barbed-wire fence and he tore his skin, he ran to me crying and his skin was falling off his body and you could see the raw muscle of him beneath the fur coat, and I picked him up and tried to carry him and his coat kept slipping off, I tried to put it back, to cover him with it like a blanket. The high-pitched cry that dogs make when they are dying. That's the sound of prayer.

A bug lands in my hair, and I swat vaguely with my fingers as Amy makes some lines on his CD jewel case and breathes one in with his silver snorter. Then he hands it to me, and I bend and take a hit.

And my brain makes a perfect, chiming chord. Something in the major key. I pass my hand over my mouth and the salt on my palms tastes amazing, I feel it running brightly through my veins and the beat of my heart lays down a track that goes along with the chiming. I feel an easy smile spread on my face. *You don't know, you don't know, you don't know*, I think, I don't know why

Did Amy just say that he killed his parents? Rabbit thinks. But the girl comes forward and extends her hand with her fingers straight and tucked together as if she's going to insert it into a small space.

"Have you heard the good news?" she says. "The Lord is coming."

"Oh," says Rabbit. "Cool." He shakes her hand and then wipes the edge of his eye with his index finger. His legs feel wobbly and he sits in one of the ancient, dirty wingback chairs, which once upon a time was some kind of bright mustard color.

When I was stabbed to death I called out for my mother in my last moments. I said, "Mom, I'm sorry, I'm sorry," as if the knife wounds were just a mistake I could somehow be forgiven for.

You don't know, you don't know, you don't know. The man who stabbed me kissed me as I was dying, and I think it was meant as a final insult but it wasn't. It was a mercy. He wasn't even there anymore when he pressed his lips to mine, he vanished and I felt a hundred other kisses that I'd had in my life, all of them happening at once, chiming together like a chord.

"It's good, right?" Amy says, and I nod. And then the three of us all laugh softly for a while.

And then I'm like: *oh.* "I was supposed to ask you something," I say, and my voice sounds like it's being filtered from underwater. "I was, uh," I say.

"This guy," I say. "This Gergely guy?"

"Ugh," says the girl, who is stirring her soup or whatever over by the fire. And she and Amy exchange glances.

"I'm sorry," Rabbit says. "I'm not really doing that well. I'm feeling kind of shitty, actually," he says.

"That's natural," Xzavious says. "Under the circumstances, right?"

Rabbit sits there and the two of them stand looking down at him. Their eyes are avid, and Xzavious flexes his weight-lifter pectorals. The girl scratches a mosquito bite with her toe.

"I think I just realized that I'm truly fucked," Rabbit says. He looks up at them, as if he's surprised. As if he's had an epiphany.

Some people are lucky to die this way: Your life splits into hundreds of hallways, and you can briefly grasp all the lives you've had and all the people you've been, even in your short span on this earth. You can see the infinite, never-ending math equation of it, and you realize that any way you tried to tell your life story would be wrong. You weren't even one person! You *aren't* even one person, even now, even as you

I touch the boy who whispered "Rabbit" and he shudders and slaps at the air like there are insects around him.

"I think," I say. "Maybe he might've been the last person to see Rabbit alive? I think, I don't know, I don't know. I just wish I could—just some things that don't completely make sense. Do you think Rabbit killed himself?"

Amy smiles kindly. "Does it matter?" he says. "I mean, you can't help him now. I don't even know if you can help yourself at this point."

"Oh, wow," Rabbit says, and he puzzles for a moment, as if he's trying to do a math problem in his head and it won't come out right. "I'm really not going to make it, am I?"

"Don't freak out," Xzavious says gently. "It's okay. What can we do to help?"

A lot of people die screaming, and I'm not passing judgment on them. Some of them hold onto that one thread all the way to the end, clinging to that idea that there is a "me" to keep intact.

I think of the bright shrieks of my dog. *Why won't you answer? Why won't you help me?*

That's his only question.

24

"DON'T THINK ABOUT a hamburger," my mother said. "Don't think about a bear. Don't think about a bear dancing on a washing machine in a tutu."

My brother and I laughed, because of course we imagined the bear dancing; we couldn't help it.

It was a game my mom used to play with us. The don't-think-about game, and of course it was a fun sort of brain teaser. How do you *not* think about something? The only way was to try to swiftly imagine something else, so quickly that it tackled the other thought.

And now I am playing it again.

Don't think about Rabbit. Don't think about Jim Beam. Don't think about Jack Daniels.

Don't think about Gergely.

"I don't know that much about him, really," Amy says. "All I know is that he pays guys to let him do various kinds of bondage and domination stuff. Duct tape. Mummification. Crucifixion. And apparently a lot more-extreme stuff, too. I think he actually had a streaming porn site for a while but it got shut down. It was on the border of snuff films."

"But Rabbit didn't say anything about him? The last time you saw him?"

"The last thing Rabbit said to me," Amy says, "and I remember it, he said, *I think I just realized that I'm truly fucked.* And I was, like, no you're not. It's all right. Et cetera. But he was in a very worked-up state."

"And you think he killed himself, right?"

Amy looks over at the girl again, and she lifts her eyebrow like she's giving him permission to say something, and he shrugs. "I don't know," he says. "Probably. He was going to die soon, one way or another."

Our eyes meet. He doesn't drink from my aura this time; he doesn't seem that mysterious even. He's a drug dealer who works at Whole Foods and fucks fourteen-year-old girls and pretends to be a vampire.

"Look," he says. "I don't know the answer. I think that it's seventy percent that Rabbit killed himself. And even if it's like, 'Oh shit, Gergely is a murderer!'   It's still basically the same thing. I mean, you open that door and you made a decision, right?"

The young girl in the silver halter top looks over at us and licks her wooden spoon thoughtfully. She makes a face as if it's bitter, and I watch as she lights a cigarette. "People say he's a cop," she says.

"So?" I say, and she smiles at me a little sadly.

"Did you ever hear on the news where the heroin junkie was sexually abused by a cop, and then he got a lawyer and went to trial and the cop eventually went to jail?"

"No," I say, "I don't think I heard about that."

The girl shrugs. "Because that would never happen," she says.

"Um," I say, and for a few seconds I try to untangle the riddle she's just told me. But I'm too high. "I don't think I get it."

"I know," she says sympathetically, and she puts her small hand on my arm, and the pads of her fingers are very warm and damp like clay. The fire crackles as it reaches the insides of the Beanie Baby and the stuffing begins to pop and glow.

25

AMY HAD GIVEN me a lot of dope for a surprisingly low price, so I was happy about that.

Truth was I felt almost giddy, which was kind of depressing because it made me realize that I was more of an addict than I thought.

"Shit," I whispered. I was sitting in the car in the parking lot of House of Wills, a user among users, all of us lined up in our little private cells with our motors running, and I pulled out the index card with the address written on it. *Rabbit left this for you to find*, I thought.

So why not just drive over there and look at the place? I thought. "Stake it out," isn't that what the cops said?   And if it's nothing, you haven't done anything wrong.

Bridgewater Road. Lyndhurst.

It's on the east side.   Not that far from home, actually, kind of almost on your way, and so you pull out onto East 55th and drive a few blocks to the interstates until you've pointed yourself east.

When you're high, driving feels so good. You have your hands on the steering wheel and the world outside looks like a video game that you are controlling, and your eyes are sharp and focused but your mind is sifting out behind you like sand blowing off a dune; you feel it rolling away from you even as you move forward steadily.   You are speeding along at 65 miles per hour and you can feel your tires hissing over the salted asphalt and see the blur of the corridor passing, you change lanes, you pass semis, the green interstate exit signs fly over you, but you are also not moving. You are sitting on the couch in your house playing a video game in which you're driving along the interstate, and you are dozing in a warm bath imagining that you are sitting on the couch playing a video game. There are layers of thick, porous time between each of these things. You are aware of your eyelids lowering to blink, and when they raise again, you've traveled miles.

And then here is the place. Bridgewater Road. Who knows what time it is? After midnight, surely. The house is tiny, a white little box with vinyl siding and a red door, no trees on the lawn, no shrubs like the neighbors'. Nothing scary about it except it seems anonymous and abandoned. The kind of place that has a FOR SALE sign on the lawn that has been there for years.

I sit there and listen to Bob Marley sing "Waiting in Vain." Which Rabbit would have said was too on the nose, and if he were in the passenger seat he would have reached over and turned the CD off. *Come on, Sweetroll,* he says. *Why don't you make your way back home?*

And that is when my phone rings, and I fumble with it, press it to the side of my face.

"Aaron?" says my mom's voice.

26

"AARON?" MY MOM said,   and I said, "Uh?"

But I didn't say anything else, because I was freaking out. I looked down at the cigarette I was holding and it was vibrating between my fingers, but otherwise I had nothing. No voice, no thoughts, just the bouncing cherry of my cigarette, and my chest getting tighter and tighter.

"You called me," my mom said, and I couldn't help it. I started to cry.

Wouldn't that have been a breakthrough, back in the day? Back in the day—how long ago?—when my dad didn't think I'd shed a sufficient number of tears, and he wanted me to see a shrink, he wanted me to take some medication that would help me get through it. He wanted me to process my grief.

"What the fuck?" my mom said. "Are you crying? Are you on drugs?"

"No," I said defensively. I put the hams of my hands against my eyes, and a bunch of sparrows shot out of my forehead with a loud flapping of wings.

She sighed. "Aaron?" she said. "I hope you don't think this is some sort of reunion, because it's not. The only reason I'm calling you is because you phoned a number that you should have never been able to find. And I'd like to know how my number came into your possession."

And then she spoke very slowly. As if to a child or an animal. "My name is Waverna Tillman," she said. "You left a message for me."

"Oh," I said. "Right."

And the world tilted sort of back into position. "I'm sorry, I'm . . . uh," and I blotted my eyeholes with my knuckles.

"My husband said that you told him that Rusty gave you my number?" she said.

"Yeah," I said. And I took a breath, because the disequilibrium was washing away from me only very slowly. "He, uh," I said. "He said he thought I should talk to you, and he . . . gave me your number. He just gave it to me; I don't know how he got it."

"Okay," she said. "But I don't get why he would be talking to you in the first place."

"I don't know, either," I said. "He called me. That's all. He was out of prison, and . . . apparently you guys didn't want to talk to him. He didn't have anybody else, and so he called me, I guess. I wasn't looking for this, you know?"

"Mm," she said. It was the sound that you make when you have a pain in your sternum.

"I don't even know how I got into this," I said. "I really don't."

And it surprised me that she laughed. "Yeah," she said. "That's how we all feel."

We were silent, and then her voice softened a little. "Shit," she said. "I can't believe I'm doing this. But you know what? Maybe I'll just play along with it for a while. Because this has been eating away at me for a very long time. God! I'm coming up on fifty years old, and maybe I'm a little bitter. I hope you don't mind if I'm bitter," she said.

"Uh," I said. "No? I'm not really . . ."

"You're not really anything, right?" she said. "Of course you wouldn't be. It's so funny. Was he a good dad?"

"I don't know," I said. "I think maybe. Not terrible in any obvious way."

"Yeah," she said softly, and her voice was breathy but still very much like my mom's. "That's exactly right," she said. "He was never terrible in an obvious way, but I *do* think—ugh," she says.

"What?"

And I heard the movement of the phone as it shifted from one ear to the next. "Okay," she said. "You know how my parents died, right?"

"Yeah."

"Have you seen pictures of the crime scene?"

"I guess so. Yeah. Some of them."

"And what do you think is missing from those pictures?" she said.

"I don't have any idea," I said. But I thought: *Wow, she might be crazier than my dad!*

"Do you know that I've hired people over the years? Investigators. Private detectives. Forensics people. And they all tell me the same thing. It was a murder–suicide. I have had some ideas over the years about why that might have happened, I think I have some solid theories—but it doesn't matter. I don't think that anybody will ever really know, exactly, but I'm pretty sure about the basic facts.

"The truth is this: My dad killed his brother, and then he killed my mom, and then he killed Dustin's mom as she was trying to escape. In that order. And then he killed himself. The whole scene is really obvious.

"Except that there's no gun, is there? The gun that my father must have put in his mouth and pulled the trigger of? It's not there."

"Um," I said, and tried to fit a cigarette between my lips, but I kept missing the mouth hole.

I could hang up if I wanted. I knew she was going to tell me something bad. I could choose if I wanted to know it, or not.

"Your dad was the one who found them that morning," she said, after a little pause. "I think he moved them around a little bit, probably. But the gun that was in my dad's hand? He definitely removed that from the scene."

"Why . . ." I said. "Why would he do that?"

"That is the question, isn't it?" she said. "What was the motivation? I don't think he realized what he was going to do when he took it. I think that he and Kate decided to frame Rusty later."

She was quiet for a moment, but I could hear her breathing. "Uff," she sighed. "Yeah, I'm still bitter about it, I can't believe it. They did it all behind my back, and it took years—maybe my whole life—to try to sort it out. And honestly I can't forgive them for it. Maybe he was a good dad to you, maybe he and Kate are really different now, I don't know. Maybe they've changed. But they did something very, very evil back in the day. You want to know the worst thing about your dad?" she said.

I finally fitted the cigarette between my lips, and it made me aware of the way that my fingers were still fluttering.

I could have told her to stop. But maybe it was just a sort of Bluebeard's wife thing. You can't help yourself: *Open the door, you stupid bitch. Go ahead.*

"What?" I said.

"The worst thing is that he thinks he's the hero of this story, and he's never, ever going to find out that he's actually the bad guy."

I considered this. Was it the worst thing to think that you're a hero when you're not? Was it even worse to never find out that you're a bad person? Maybe it was a mercy.

I stared out at the house with its faded FOR SALE sign, the bright circle of porch light. "One of the things I keep asking myself," she said. "When did he die? I think that's an important question to ask, if you care about him. And it's sad, because there's no way for you to find out. He was dead long before you were born, I know that for sure."

"Um," I said. "I'm actually having kind of a hard time following you. I mean, literally, my dad's, like, alive."

"Really?" she said.

"I hope so," I said. "Last time I checked. He was breathing, and walking around, and I—I get that you're talking metaphorically." *The Death of the Heart:* That was a book that my mother loved, a book that she was always telling me I should read, though I never did. "You mean like the death of the. The death of the heart."

She laughed. And I could swear that she had the same laugh as my mom. I guessed they were about the same age, and maybe there were a lot of women who were born in the sixties who learned the same intonations, something viral went across the generation and they all started making that sleepy, sweet, thoughtful laugh as one, but oh my God it sounded so much like her.

And then I noticed a weird thing.

The front door to the little house was open now.

A figure crossed through my peripheral vision, and without thinking I hung up on Wave. I was sitting in *your mom's car,* and I was trying to take a three-sixty-degree look around myself when knuckles tapped on the driver's side window.

PART EIGHT

January 2014

1

IT'S GARBAGE NIGHT, and Aaron is supposed to take out the trash, but he's not home.

I realize I have a little obsessive–compulsive thing about it. For whatever reason, it's a chore that I hate more than any other, it upsets me, and I can only manage to do it if I break it into stages.

So I bundle up the newspapers with twine, and then I put on my overcoat and boots, and I step down the poorly scooped sidewalk. The yellow porch light reflects off the piles of snow, and I move quickly to drop off my parcel at the edge of the curb and then I hurry back to the house, glancing at my phone: 10:36 P.M.

He can do the rest of it when he gets home, I think, and I imagine some of the things that I could say about following through with your responsibilities, about maintaining order. I can be overbearing, and I don't want to be overbearing. *I realize that there's a lot going on for you right now,* I picture myself saying. *There's a lot going on for all of us. And we all have to pitch in.*

Pitch in: Ugh! It sounds so awful and chipper. *Cooperate?* I think. But that sounds worse. Like something a thug would say to a prisoner he's tied to a chair.

And then it's after midnight, and I turn off the television, and he still hasn't come home. It's not that unusual, though it would have been considerate for him to text me.

I never thought he'd be the one who would be hard to communicate with. When he was little, he used to love to be close to me. We used to sit side by side on the couch, watching TV, and he'd lean his cheek against my arm, and then he'd take my hand and press it against the side of his head, pushing it to the exact spot that he wanted it to be. And I would hold my hand there in the exact spot and he would smile and nuzzle closer against me.

I know he loved me. I know he did.

Okay. I guess I will do it.

There are two garbage bins along the north side of the house, and I pull the large black plastic bags out of them and they're heavy and frozen stiff. I drag them along behind me down the driveway, letting them slide like sledges, leaving a groove behind them.

I don't know why I hate the idea of my neighbors watching. I'm sure, of course, that they are not—not really. Yet for some reason I feel self-conscious. I've got a coat over my pajamas, and I've stuffed my bare feet into winter galoshes, but I feel exposed. The fact that I have two big bags of trash makes me feel weirdly ashamed. Wasteful. I drop the bags off quickly on the snow berm at the edge of the drive and then hurry back into the house.

No one is watching you, I think, and as the leafless, snow-covered branches shake their shadows across my path, a figure assembles itself in the periphery.

Or—not a figure. Just a sound, just the memory of noise and movement—that night when I woke and heard the boy skateboarding in front of the house. Just the barest echo of it.

    rooooll. Slap. K-chint.   *rooooooooll. Slap! K-chint!*

And then I wake up in bed and I look at my phone and it's 5:14 A.M. I get up to go pee and I notice that Aaron's bedroom door is still open.

I stand in the doorway and look at his tangled covers, the piles of unwashed clothes leaning against the laundry baskets full of clothes that are clean but unfolded; the Wu Tang Clan poster and the Jamaican flag with a marijuana leaf superimposed over it. He didn't come home last night.

Not that unusual, I think. He used to sleep over at Rabbit's house, for example. But he would always text.

That ache when you realize that you've reached the point where they don't even text. Maybe I'm an overprotective parent. He'll be nineteen in February, so legally he can do whatever he wants. Maybe he's spent the night with a girl. Maybe he had a few too many beers and he slept on a friend's couch. It's none of my business.

Nevertheless, there is still the recycling left to do. He won't be doing it, so I go downstairs to the basement. This is what I hate the most, the clinking jars and rattling cans and hollow, echoing plastic bottles. Something eerie and skeletal about the sound. Xylophone music.

I pull the recycling down the driveway in my slippers, and the snow and ice and salt soak through immediately. So stupid! Why would I not put on the boots? But I make it to the end of the driveway and I throw the clear blue bags of recyclables onto the pile and there is a percussive tinkle and clink as the bag hits the hard snow.

There's nothing to be concerned about; it's nothing, I think.

2

HE'S STILL NOT home when I leave for work, and, yes, I'm a little annoyed but it's normal. He's almost nineteen, flexing his independence, and I shouldn't hover. I shouldn't panic.

So I just send him a polite text.

> Hey Honey!

> I'm stopping by the market after work. Is there anything you want me to pick up?

Will you be home for dinner? If so, is there anything special that you'd like to eat?

And then, after I hit the send button, I regret it. Too pushy, I think. Too, too pushy.

3

WHEN I ARRIVE at the Cleveland Heights office, Mrs. O'Sullivan is already sitting in the waiting room next to the waterfall sculpture. Deeply engaged with her phone, so I tap the doorframe lightly so as not to startle her.

The hypnosis seems to gives her temporary relief from the pain, but it returns every few months. I hold her hand in mine, and we sit there for a while. Staring together at her hand.

Possibly, I think, there is actually something physically wrong with her, even if the doctors can't find it. But there's no swelling or redness, nothing from a visual or tactile perspective that indicates

If it's psychosomatic, it must have some sort of powerful traumatic origin. *Some sort of repressed memory?* I think briefly.

But, no, I'm not going down that path again.

Afterward, I go out to the parking lot for a cigarette. I smoke a little surreptitiously—I don't really want a patient to spot me—so I hold the lit end palm inward, and smoke trickles out from between my knuckles. It looks kind of cool. Kind of supernatural. I hold out my hand and pretend that I'm casting a magic spell over the rows of salt-streaked cars.

I was a good dad when I was pretending. The boys used to love it when I would twist my fingers up and tell them I was casting a spell. We'd be sitting at a stoplight, and they'd be in the back, and I'd lift my hand. "I'll make this car in front of us turn right," I said. "How much do you want to bet I can do it?" And they liked it. I think they sort of believed.

I raise my hand and at the far end of the lot an old van is running, the exhaust from its muffler denser, even, than the smoke from my fingers. I can see a silhouette in the passenger seat.

Then my phone vibrates and I reach in my pocket because of course it's Aaron. About time!

But it's Aqil.

> Don't we have an APPT?

I look at my watch: 1:05. I've kept him waiting for five minutes.

I turn on the microphone for speech recognition and try to talk slowly and distinctly at the phone. "I. Will. Be. Right. There," I say. And I watch as the phone pauses and does its magic, converting my words into text, and even now this is still remarkable to me. I can't believe it is actually the future, where such things exist.

4

WHEN I OPEN the door, Aqil is leaning back on the couch with his eyes closed and he keeps his eyelids shut when I come in. It is a trust exercise that I invented, and I think it's been helpful.

The idea is simple. I will not be present in the office when he arrives, but he should sit down and close his eyes and not open them. "Try to make your mind as blank as possible," I told him when I first came up with it. "Once you've turned off the visual sense, then see if you can slowly turn down the audio . . . and then the senses of taste and smell . . . and, finally, focus on your skin. Try to forget that your skin is touching anything."

"I don't think that's possible," he said.

"Probably not," I said. "We don't need to be attached to results. Think of it as a challenge." And that had caught his attention: a challenge.

Now, as I enter, I know that he can hear the soles of my shoes against the floor and the springs of the couch as I sit down across from him. He doesn't open his eyes. He can hear me take out my notebook; he can even hear the pen marking the date on the surface of the paper.

The first time I'd suggested the exercise, he'd given me a hard, quizzical look. "Doc," he said. "You realize that there's a horror-movie aspect to this, right?"

"I don't know what you mean," I said, and he laughed.

"In the horror movie, I'd have my eyes closed, and my therapist would come in, and I'd start talking . . . and then at some point, I'd crack open an eye . . . and I'd see you holding your Dr. Tillman mask in one rotted claw."

"Well," I said, and I looked down at my hand ruefully, wondering why he might imagine it as a rotting claw. "It *is* a trust exercise, so . . ." I noticed the veins on the back of my hand. "So it's going to tap into some," I said, and my nails were clean and manicured. I cleared my throat.

"Look," I said. "We're just attempting to find ways to break down some of the issues that you've been having. You've described your-self as a very suspicious person. A wary person—always, as you say, 'hyperaware,' to the extent that your upper-body muscles are con-stantly tight. To the extent that you wake up five to ten times a night. To the extent that you feel abnormally alert in public. You're always keeping an eye open for the person who's going to try to kill you: Isn't that what you told me? And that's not healthy for you.

"If you still want to do therapy, we have to find some way to get you to let your guard down.

"So this is just an idea. Close your eyes and try to imagine that you're alone. Almost asleep. I'm only a voice in your head. And I promise that if you crack open an eye, I'm not going to be the bogeyman."

So now he sits there on the couch with his eyes closed and I lower myself into the couch across from him.   *There are so many layers to this guy*, I think. Though we've known each other for almost two years by this point, though we are actually, in many ways, close friends, there are still things that he's never spoken about.

I know next to nothing about his childhood, about his family. There has been no discussion of his romantic life, no mention of girlfriends or dating, rarely any mention of social interaction of any kind. I know that he lives in Lyndhurst, but I've never been to his home. What does he do with his days? I sometimes wonder. He goes to the gym. He says that he's been working on getting his private-investigator license, says that he's been setting up a website to advertise his services, but nothing concrete has materialized that I know of. He watches a lot of sports and a lot of movies. Once he talked about re-watching an entire season of the television show *Dexter* in a single weekend, and that struck me as troubling. "How many hours was that?" I said, and he shrugged. "Thirteen?" he said. "Something like that?"

There was no discussion of what was going on between us. We met twice a week for therapy sessions and just as often to socialize as—what—friends?

I'd never really had a close male friend that I could think of. Many male acquaintances, of course, but I generally didn't have much in common with them. I've always felt more comfortable with women. With Jill. With Kate. Women seem more trustworthy.

After the police discovered Slade Gable's body, Aqil wanted to go out for a drink. This was something I generally didn't do—go out to bars. But I'd agreed, and we met at a little place not far from my house in Cleveland Heights. Parnell's Pub. The place was almost empty when we sat down, and a young blond woman named Liz came over and gave us beers and I said to Aqil, "I don't think I should be your therapist anymore."

"What?" he said.

"I feel like our relationship has changed," I said. "We're working together. We're—"

I didn't say *friends*.

"What are you talking about?" he said, and lifted a pint to his lips. He tasted the foam and raised an eyebrow. "I don't have romantic feelings about you, Doc," he said. "If that's what you're suggesting."

"No, no," I said. "Of course not. But there's a line that's been crossed," I said, "a—"

"A what?" he said. He regarded me blankly. "I don't see what the problem is."

And then months passed. We did a few interviews with the relatives of victims, we looked at some police records and autopsy reports, but it seemed that whatever discoveries we had come close to in Painesville had slipped away. By June of 2013, seven months after Jill's death, we had begun to meet more casually. We went out to the bar together once a week, even though I was still also ostensibly treating him. We went to movies, and once to an Indians' game. We pored over news sites together, looking for drowned young men.

There were swimming accidents, of course, and drunk boys fell in rivers and died, but there wasn't anything that had the particular frisson of Slade Gable.

Sitting at the bar in Painesville, when we were trying to walk our way through his disappearance, the two of us were connected as we told each other this story. That feeling. Being able to *see* something together that others could not. "We're alike," Aqil said. "Or—" he said. "Actually, we're opposite, but we're compatible. I feel like I've been looking for someone like you for a long time."

And then it was fall. There was hope that a death might occur on 10/3/13, or 10/13/13, or 10/31/13. Then, possibly, 11/3/13, or 11/30/13?

"It's going to happen soon," Aqil said. "I'm sure of it."

We *wished*, I thought. Which was awful. But—yes. A part of me was eager for a new death. A new murder, a piece of the puzzle that could bring us back to

5

I TEXT AARON again after my last appointment, and then I call him. I leave a message on his voicemail. "Aaron," I say. "This is your dad. Please call me."

I'm in the kitchen making dinner. Frying two turkey burgers with horseradish, the way he likes them—as if that might conjure him. I press on the meat with the spatula, and then I stand at the center island, making a beet and kale salad, which of course Aaron probably won't touch. But beets and kale are considered "superfoods."

I'm listening to a podcast on my headphones. *Pop Culture Happy Hour,* it's called. They are talking about the movies that have been nominated for the Oscars, and they make pleasant conversation as I chop. The beets give off beautiful juice, the droplets like garnets.

For a moment I remember the pleasure of feeding people. The image of Jill and the boys at the table, talking companionably, waiting for me to put dinner on a plate and bring it to them—a simple, easy feeling of contentment. Everyone would be sitting in their specific chair. Who knew that would be the most beautiful memory? The thing you most long for?

"Now it's time to talk about the things that are making us happy this week!" says the earnest young woman of the podcast, and I look up.   Did the door just open?

I take off the headphones.

"Aaron?" I say.

6

I'M SITTING IN front of the television with my burger and my beet salad and I have the phone pressed tight to my ear.

"Hullo," Aqil says, the way he always answers the phone—his voice deep, unfriendly.

"Can I talk to you?" I say. On the TV, there is a channel that plays soft instrumental music and videos of playful puppies.

"I think Aaron is missing," I hear myself say.

There is a long pause.   And then Aqil says suspiciously: "What?"

"I imagine I'm losing my mind over nothing," I say. "But he hasn't been home since last night. I've left a number of messages for him that he hasn't answered. I guess I'm a little"

"Concerned?" Aqil says.

I pick up my burger and hold it. It's shaking a little, and I start to put it to my mouth but then I remember that I'm talking on the phone. So it just hangs there in my hand, and roly-poly bulldog puppies bound through a meadow in the background behind it.

"Yes," I say. I clear my throat. "Quite concerned."

"Have you talked to anyone?" Aqil says.

"I," I say. "Not yet. Who should I talk to?"

"I'll be right over," Aqil says.

7

AQIL SITS ON the couch in the TV room. He's wearing sweatpants and a T-shirt, and he looks as if he just woke up, though it's only seven in the evening. There is the glow of the television on his face, and the soft gurgle of the water in the radiator.

"I would say that there's probably a simple solution," Aqil says. "Maybe his phone ran out of juice and he doesn't have a charger?"

"Right," I say. "That's what I'm hoping."

He tilts his head and scratches near his eye, squinting thoughtfully. "You guys didn't have a disagreement, right? There's not any reason to think that maybe he's not returning your calls because he's unhappy, maybe?   I mean—I'm sure you're a great dad, but young guys get sick of their parents. It's part of nature."

"I don't think so," I say. "I had a very nice talk with him only a couple of nights ago. And—no, I didn't get the sense of any animosity or—"

I clear my throat. "Who knows?" I say. "He's not good at communicating his emotions."

"What about his brother? Did he say anything to Dennis?"

"I haven't talked to Dennis yet," I say, and Aqil nods thoughtfully.

"Well," he says, and he gives me a sympathetic smile. "That's a place to start. Before we call the police in.   What about friends? Have you talked to friends? You've checked his Facebook status, all the social-media stuff?"

No, I haven't done that. "I . . ." And what do I know about my son, really?

The fact is, now that Rabbit is dead, I don't know who his friends *are*, and it didn't even occur to me to call Dennis. The things that I haven't thought of are surprisingly basic, and for a moment I feel my worry shrink to something more human-sized and manageable.

I look at Aqil and I'm aware that, maybe, he is the more level-headed one of the two of us. I had diagnosed him as paranoid and conspiracy-prone, but in a dire situation he is much more reasonable than I am.

"I think I've been looking at too many autopsy photos of dead boys. I just—"

"I know, right?" he says. "And I'm not saying that I'm not worried."

I watch as he shifts on the couch. I am petting the dry, almost crisp hair of my beard, and I take my hand away.

"Dustin," he says. "Can I be straight with you?" I nod.

"What do you know about Aaron's drug situation?"

"I don't . . . I'm not sure what you mean."

"Is Aaron a drug user, to your knowledge?" Aqil says.

I stare out the window at the backyard, and the   dark shape of a bush coated with snow

"Uh," I say. "Marijuana, I guess," I hear myself say. "Probably other recreational   I don't have any specific"

On the couch, Aqil crosses his leg, and I watch as he glances uncomfortably at the puppies on the television screen. Which I realize is still playing: It's apparently a channel that just shows puppies, the same puppies over and over, in a loop.

"Maybe I should have said something sooner," Aqil says. "But I wasn't sure if it was my place. I mean, I don't want to interfere with you and your son's relationship, right?"

I look at him and nod.

"So I was a cop, right? I'm very familiar with the ways that different kinds of drug use present themselves. And . . . I don't know. Aaron set off alarm bells in me with his behavior. His countenance?

His coloring, and his weight? The constriction of his pupils? My guess is that he would possibly be using an opiate of some sort?" He shrugs. "My guess would be heroin?"

"What?" I say.

But of course the things he mentions play over in my head. *Coloring, weight, pinpoint pupils.*

For some reason, I had thought it was a fashion choice—that he was trying to be what we used to call "Goth." It was a good way for him to channel his angst and grief, I thought.

But now I recall the time in October when Aaron fell asleep. We were talking out on the porch, and I remember looking down and noticing his hands resting on his thighs. He was still holding a cigarette, and there was a black, burned circle on the cloth of his jeans where the burning ember was touching.

"I don't think *heroin*," I say.

Aqil doesn't say anything for a while. He just looks at me, and it sinks in.

8

It's almost eleven when Dennis finally answers his phone. This is the eighth time I've tried to call him after leaving a number of messages, and he sounds irritated when he answers.

"What?" he says curtly. "Dad, I'll call you back tomorrow; I'm busy."

"Aaron's missing," I say. "He didn't come home last night, and he doesn't answer his phone. I'm very worried."

"Ugh," Dennis says, and lets out a long sigh. "It figures," he says.

"What's that supposed to mean?" I say.

Then it appears that he is muffling his phone. I imagine that he covers it with his hand, and I can vaguely hear voices. A girl's voice, also irritated. She sounds like she's giving him instructions.

"Dennis?" I say. "Hello?"

I'm sitting on the bed in Aaron's room with a laundry basket beside me, folding the clothes that seem to be clean.   When he was little, five or six, I used to sit on this bed for hours because he was afraid to go to sleep without someone watching him. It would get to be so aggravating! Even when he seemed to be fully unconscious, any move I made toward standing up and leaving the room could wake him. So I would always test the waters. I would whisper in the softest voice I could: "Are you asleep?"

And he would whisper back, even more softly: "No."

"Listen, Dad," Dennis says at last. "I haven't really talked to Aaron since Christmas. We haven't really been . . ."

"But do you have any idea where he might be?" I say.   I hold up a wrinkled black T-shirt: *Horny Goat Weed!* it says, and I fold it in half. "I'm extremely concerned, so . . . anything you can think of . . . that might shed light on the. On the. On the, uh"

"Situation?" Dennis says, in an unkind voice.

"Well," I say.   "Maybe we should try calling his friends?   I want to make a careful. A careful inquiry before I"

Dennis sighs. "I really don't know," he says. "I mean, Aaron and I don't really travel in the same circles anymore.   Have you talked to Mike Mention?"

"Mike Mention?" I say.   I'm not entirely sure I can place him.   I have an image of the boys playing hoops in the driveway. "The . . . basketball . . . ? He was the one who"

"You don't remember who Mike Mention is?" Dennis says. "Really?"

"Do you happen to have his phone number?"

"No," he says. "I don't. But his mom's name is Carol Mention?"

She was very good friends with Mom; I guess you don't recall that? Aaron and I went to school with Mike from, like, kindergarten on?"

"I'm sorry," I say. "I'm drawing a blank. What does he look like? Is he tall?"

"Uff," Dennis says, and I pull up another black T-shirt; this one says *Keep Calm and Fuck Off*, and I fold it and then Dennis says, muffled, *I'm trying.* And then I hear the girl say, quite sharply: *Just hang up on him.*

"Dennis," I say. "Listen. Do you think Aaron might be on drugs?"

He makes a short sound—part laugh and part spitting, and it's so close to a slap that I flinch. "Fuck," he says. "Dad. How far up your ass does your head fit?"

I open my mouth and then close it. Because it's so abrupt, this hostility. So unexpected. Weren't we getting along great just a few weeks ago?

"He's a junkie, Dad," he says. "Him and Rabbit. Jesus. I tried to spell it out to you, like, ninety-nine ways over Christmas break, but you're so focused on your buddy Aqil and the stupid book you claim you're writing, it's ridiculous. It's—obscene, actually. There is no such thing as the Jack Daniels serial killer, Dad. It's an urban myth."

He takes a breath, but I don't speak. I notice my hand is pressed to my throat—like some shocked lady clutching her pearls—and I lower the hand slowly and put it on my knee. I make an effort to gather my thoughts. "I think," I say. "Listen. There are a lot of things that—there are some things that"

"I think you're out of your mind, Dad," Dennis says. "You need to get help. Seriously. If Aaron isn't answering your calls, there's probably a reason—something you *should* know, but you don't know, for whatever your own weird reasons are. Honestly, Dad, if Aaron left, he's probably safer than if he stayed around you and your buddy's insanity."

"Wait," I say—

Wait   wait   wait

But there is a rattle and thickening and I guess the phone is taken out of his hands.

The female voice comes on the phone.

"Why can't you leave him alone?" she snaps. "He's just starting to heal. He's trying to get better! So enough—enough!—with your toxic family, okay?"

Then: disconnected.

9

You will walk safely in your way, and your foot will not stumble.

In the bathroom, I turn on the hot water and let the shower run, and I sit there on the toilet, watching it, still dressed in my sports jacket and jeans and loafers, taking long slow breaths of the steamy air and repeating the mantra until my mind has slowed.   Then I call Aqil. Straight to voicemail. It's past one in the morning, and the sound of Dennis's short laugh keeps coming back to me. The laugh that felt like a sudden snarl and a bite, the sheer dislike in his voice, sent a dull, pins-and-needles sensation across my skin.

> *You will walk safely in your way, and your foot will not stumble.*
> *When you lie down, you will not be afraid; yes, you will lie down and your sleep will be sweet.*

I have had patients whose children hated them, and I can think of words that I would tell them, various kinds of advice. *React with calm, rather than hurt or anger. The mask they are putting on you is not your own face.   But they may need it at this stage in their fledgling adulthood. It may be exactly what they have to believe in order to*

You will walk safely in your way, and your foot will not stumble.

I rest my face against my palms and close my eyes and listen to the white noise of the shower spraying against the surface of the tub. The worst thing is that, of course, I should have seen. I'm a psychologist; I should recognize the signs of heroin abuse, I've counseled people about it. I can see Aaron displaying each of them, posed like the pictures on a deck of cards. Constricted pupils—weight loss—inappropriate nodding off. They fix into place in my mind with a distinct, ratcheting click.   And then my phone rings.

10

"I NEED TO talk to you," Kate says.

I'm still seated on the toilet, still in the sports jacket and jeans and loafers that I wore to work in the morning. The shower is running.

"Kate?" I say. Completely disoriented for a moment.

"Are you asleep?" she says. "I forgot how late it is there."

"No," I say. "I'm up. I'm actually having a very difficult time. I can't talk now."

"What's wrong?" she says.

I shake my head.   The shower has been running so long that the small bathroom is opaque with steam, and I wipe sweat from my forehead. "Aaron didn't come home last night," I say. "He doesn't answer his phone. I haven't said anything, but I've been concerned about potential drug issues for a while now."

She's silent. Then she says *oh*, in this way that sends a trickle of dread through me. The hiss of the shower spray makes my neck prickle.

"Oh," she says. "Oh my God."

And then she doesn't say anything. The phone is silent, and I press my hand against my free ear to muffle the noisy whispering of the shower.

"Are you okay?" she says. "Can I be truthful with you?"

Can I be truthful with you? It's a terrible question to be asked, and I think suddenly of Grandma Brody's house, of sitting on the bed with her in my mom's childhood room, and

"I should have called you two days ago. There's been some . . . weirdness. And I should have called you. I should have called you right away."

I feel that I should get up and turn off the shower, because a bead of sweat runs down from my eyebrow and along my nose and when I breathe I accidentally pull it into my nostril. But I don't get up. The shower keeps running, and the room has a kind of foggy cast at this point.

"I guess," she says, "that Aaron is talking to Rusty? It's all very murky to me still—which is why I didn't want to call you. I can't tell you exactly what's going on. What Rusty's told him . . .

"But apparently they've been in contact for a while now. There's been this whole, like, back and forth, because I guess Rusty somehow told Aaron to call Wave, and then Wave called me, and

11

The things that Rusty might say about me.

I picture them talking together. Aaron reclining on his bed, his phone at rest on his pillow next to his ear, high, drifting, and Rusty's voice comes through his earbud headphones.

Listening to Rusty talk about prison. About his life now. About just wanting a chance to talk to me and not understanding what my problem was. Rusty makes a self-deprecating joke. *Fuh-huh-huh*.

That laugh: the way it had a certain note in it, a certain music, that made people think that they liked him. My parents did.   So did Kate and Wave. So would Aaron.

Jill and I had decided that it was not something we wanted them to know about, at least not until they were adults.

"It's like a monolith," Jill said once. "You don't want that looming over them."

The boys were only toddlers, and we were in a cheap Italian restaurant. Aaron was in a high chair, eating buttered pasta. Dennis was using crayons on the paper place mat.

"You don't want it looming over *you*. You're a completely different person when you're not thinking about that stuff."

Little did Jill realize that Aaron would hear the story for the first time from Rusty.   Up until the moment that Rusty called him, he thought that my parents had died in an "accident," and he hadn't ever been particularly curious about it.

But Rusty—Rusty has a practiced version of the story. He's had years to work it out. He told it to the grad students who worked for the lawyers who won his release, and then it made the news; he told the story to the press, how he'd almost given up on anyone believing him, how he was not angry about the past, not blaming anyone at all. Rusty was just feeling grateful. Feeling "blessed." Smiling that sheepish grin. *Fuh-huh-huh*.

He starts very humbly. "I wasn't such a good person," he admits. "I was into drugs and heavy metal music, and I was a wild teenager."

Maybe he even confesses to some of the ways that he used to hurt me.   "I was just a mean kid," he says, and Aaron, listening to the voice on his pillow, nods. He understands.

Rusty doesn't mention the sexual stuff.   He doesn't talk about that night that he tried to convince me to burn the house down. *We'd probably have to kill them, you know. Dave and Colleen. I mean, we could get the gun while they were sleeping and it wouldn't even hurt them.* The way he grinned. *Come on. Don't you want to get out of this dump?*

He doesn't talk to Aaron about things like *the gibbeners.* The murders he claimed to have participated in.   The rituals that he told me that his biological mother's coven would perform, the time he showed me what they had once done to an infant. "They put it on the altar," he said. "Like this." And he used some baby bunnies I had found as an example.   "They put it on the altar, and they raised the brick . . ."

Whatever he does say, it's probably kind of vague, but with enough specificity to demonstrate that I had a grudge against him.

He says how he used to like to scare me. He talks about how gullible I was, and there would be enough of my personality in his description that Aaron recognizes it.   "Yeah!" Aaron says, like a patient on a couch who is in a deep hypnotic trance. "That sounds just like him!"

After Aaron talks to Rusty he looks it up on the Internet. There are at least ten or fifteen things that he'd find with a Google search. Victim of Satanic Ritual Abuse Hysteria Released from Prison. That's one of the headlines.

"The thing I learned in the group home," Rusty once told me. "I can get along with anybody." This was in the time right after we'd adopted him, and I was in awe of the breadth of the people that he'd met. "Like, I can talk to one kid that's completely into Nazis and Hitler and White Power, and we'll get along fine," he said. "And then at supper I'll be sitting with the Mexican gang kid, and he'll be teaching me Spanish. And then, you know, I'll be smoking cigarettes with the kid that wants to dress like a girl. It doesn't matter. I can relate to anybody."

I can relate to anybody: I imagine him telling the same thing to Aaron. I can imagine Rusty hearing that Jill died and telling the story of his own mother's death: murdered in prison. *He could relate to what Aaron was going through.* And Aaron, stunned, grief-stricken, adrift. It would have been easy for him to latch onto this charming stranger.

Rusty on the phone with Aaron: sad, funny, wronged. Rusty making Aaron his confidant. "What's your dad up to right now?" Rusty asks, and Aaron lifts his head and listens.

"He's just up in his study," Aaron says. "I can hear him talking to himself."

"Dude!" Rusty says, and laughs. "He still talks to himself?   Ha-ha! When he was a kid he'd have the craziest conversations with himself! Like, he was never quite in touch with reality."

They talk together once a week, twice a week? Rusty gets to know Aaron's interests, his hobbies, his likes and dislikes.   And after Jill dies, it is Rusty that Aaron turns to. Not me.

I remembered how I'd tried to insist that Aaron get some grief counseling. "I just think you need to talk to somebody," I said, and he'd glowered.

"I am talking to someone," he'd said. We were sitting out on the porch and I watched as he flicked his cigarette. He was smoking in front of me at that point. "I talk to plenty of people. Just not a fucking therapist."

"What's your dad doing right now?" Rusty asks him, and no wonder I had goosebumps on the back of my neck, no wonder I had the sensation of being watched.   *They were talking about me, just a few walls away.*

"He says he's writing a book," Aaron says, shut in his room, reclined on his bed with the TV mounted above him, playing some violent video game while they chat.

"Oh yeah?" Rusty says, and laughs his sleepy laugh. *Fuh-huh-huh.* "What about?"

I feel myself blush. It is such a vile, vile, awful thing to imagine that I sit there frozen. My phone is vibrating in my hand. I can see that Kate is trying to call me, and I watch the screen as the phone rings, as it sends her to voicemail, as a pop-up appears to tell me I have a missed call.

I think about a night not long before my parents died.   I had been interested in geology, and I'd just ordered a kit with a steel Plumb hammer and a leather sheath for the hammer that attached to your belt and a magnifying loupe, and I had a book about the geology of Yellowstone National Park, and I was sitting at the kitchen table looking through it when Rusty and his friend Trent came in.

"Whoa," he said. "What have you got there, Dusty?"

"Nothing," I said, and when he picked up the hammer I said, "That's mine." But he only smiled. "Dustin really likes rocks," he told Trent.

"He does?"

"Yeah," Rusty said, and gripped my hammer. He held it thoughtfully, as if he was thinking of using it as a weapon. "Yeah," he said. "He really loves rocks."

And then Rusty handed the hammer back to me, though now, of course, he'd poisoned it.

Each time he talks to Aaron, there is just exactly that kind of poison, a little edge of disparagement, a seed planted between them and growing. If Rusty didn't do it, who could have murdered those four people? Why won't I talk to him? What do I have to lose? It would have happened gradually, but there would come a time when Aaron and Rusty were on one team, and I was on the other. Eventually, Rusty would have made Aaron "realize" that I was the murderer.

And Aaron would have believed it.

At a certain point, we are repulsive to our children, we parents. It is a stage of development. At such a stage they might be willing to believe anything that confirms

12

I DID NOT do it.

I *know* I did not do it. When I looked at it logically, I had no reason to kill them. I had no motivation, I actually loved my mom and dad a lot, and my aunt and uncle were fine.

Yet there have been fragments of things. Contradictory images. The truth—my real memories—had always been infected by fantasies or daydreams; the two things kept flipping, shifting, so I had never been certain what was being recalled and what was being imagined.

This was the thesis of my dissertation, in some ways: that experience is so subjective that multiple things actually *do* happen. That we can't experience objective reality. Not exactly a useful stance for a court of law, my professor, Dr. Raskoph, said.

The mind has its unknown mercies and ministrations, many sealed chambers, she said once, and she smiled and put her palm on the back of my hand. We were talking about self-hypnosis, about hypnosis as therapeutic practice. *Some people's entire lives are directed by trying not to remember something.*

And so now, of course, it comes to me. When I think of what

Rusty might have told Aaron, the old dream comes back, settling itself around me, and it's still as vivid as it ever was.

June 12, 1983, and I wake up in the middle of the night. In the trailer, in the driveway. Maybe the sound of shots?

But I don't know. Wave is snoring. Kate is asleep beside me, and she smells bad. Sharp summer sweat and musky teenage-girl body odor.

I'm thirsty. I decide that I'll go up to the house and see if I can find a Coke in the refrigerator. I get out of bed and open the door of the trailer, and I step out barefoot onto the gravel. I can feel the round stones beneath my feet. I can hear the soft crunch they make, and I look toward the front door of the house and the June bugs are losing their mind around the aura of yellow porch light. June bugs—flying beetles that Kate and Wave and I used to catch and put into jars—are making clumsy arcs around the bulb, buzzing in a kind of ecstasy or craziness as they make their loops and kamikaze dives, or they miscalculate and hit the side of the house near the light with sharp, surprised ticks and then fall to earth. Tumbling down to where my mom's body was lying.

And here is the part that doesn't ever make sense. I see her body, but I'm not there. There is no jolt of fear or horror or sorrow. I look at my mom's corpse and I don't feel anything.

Nothing except a calm, dreamy curiosity. I don't scream. I don't call for help. I don't kneel at her side and shake her; I don't try to talk to her or check if she was still breathing.

It seems impossible to me that this is the way I would have responded. Every time this moment comes back to me, it feels as if I am watching it from far outside my own body. As if I am watching a movie that doesn't make sense. It doesn't seem plausible that I would just stand there, looking down at her.

But in this bad movie, I see her. She is lying on her side. Splayed out in the way you'd be if you'd been shot at close range and you fell, and there is a lot of blood around her.

There was a series of snapshots that would play over in my head. For a time, when I was in college, it was almost all I could think about. The images are laid out in front of me like cards in a losing game of solitaire, and I try to think of how I could move them differently:

She is on her side with her arms hugged close to her stomach, and I touch her with my bare foot and she slides over onto her back.

It is a clear night. The moon is out, floating above the television antenna on the roof.

I look at her and her eyes are open but sleepy. Bored.   Her lips are parted as if she's listening to someone drone on and on.

There are dead June bugs around her. One is on its back, stuck in her blood, and its serrated beetle legs are grasping at the air.

And then I just step around her, I guess.

Because I am in the living room, and the music is playing from the record player.

It is an old box stereo, a wooden bureau with sound speakers instead of drawers, and the song "Luckenbach, Texas" is flowing out over my dad's body. My feet find the thick carpet, and the soles sink into it. I see my feet moving, as in a photograph of feet moving. My dad is on his stomach; I don't see his face at all. I see his prosthetic arm reaching out as if he is trying to use it to point at something. The door, maybe?

I just keep walking toward the kitchen because I need to get a Coke.

Here is where the memory—feels—what? Unbelievable?

It is possible that I go into a kind of dissociative, numb state. Almost like sleepwalking.

But I also feel a kind of weird contentment. There is an uncanny glow around the scene. Not fear or horror or numbness. A sense of inevitability.

From the doorway of the kitchen I see my aunt underneath the kitchen table. Later, I learn that she had been shot the most times: four.

But I only notice that the left side of her hair is red and wet and the tips of her curls are matted and dripping blood onto the floor.

Her face is stern. Frowning, but peaceful.   Her eyes are open, like someone in a painting who is looking off to the sky and thinking a patriotic thought.

There is blood all over. My uncle is sitting in a pool of it, sitting there on the floor with his back against the cabinets. Gunshot wound to the face, at very close range, but I don't ever picture the face.

I only see the gun. It's an old pistol, maybe from a war, I think. Simple, black, almost like a toy, but made of metal instead of plastic, and I stare at it and then I reach down and take it out of his hand.

The gun is a kind of charm, maybe—some little memento that you'd want to keep, something you'd put in a cigar box with your other treasures: a real arrowhead, a baby tooth you'd kept, a buffalo nickel, a stamp from the 1890s. It is just a nice thing to touch, the gun. The handgrip has a pebbled texture, and it is cool and heavy.

I might need this, I think. I don't know why. I hold it loosely in my left hand and I open the refrigerator and take out a Coke.

How can any of this be so? It's not me. I never would have behaved this way.

The emotions are so odd and muted and distorted, so *dreamy*. Later, I would diagnose it a vivid fantasy, something that began afterward—after the murders had begun to settle into my conscious-ness, after I'd begun to try to process the

A guilt dream: That's what I would call it later. This . . . this de-lusional stroll through the crime scene—to get a Coke!—it's a way for my unconscious mind to exert some control over the narrative. A fantasy I made up at the time to share the guilt and blame for the murders.

The real story, the official story, went like this: Wave discovered the bodies in the morning. In the morning, in the trailer, we hear her screaming, and Kate and I come running, and I see my mom's body there on the porch among the scattering of dead black June bugs, and I fall to my knees and I pull her into my arms and I say, "Mom! *Mom!* MOM!" And inside, Wave is letting out shrieks that I will never forget. These high, shrill, bird-like cries. "Eeeeee! Eeeeee! Eeeee! Eeeee! Eeeeee! Eeeeee! Eeeee! Eeeee! Eeeeee! Eeeeee! Eeeee! Eeeee! Eeeeee!"

13

WHAT I REMEMBER: I am stepping out of the house and I see him.

I am stepping out of the house, and I have my can of Coke in one hand and I am carrying the gun in the other, and I am wearing a pair of shorts and nothing else.

He is in the driveway. He's just pulled up in his pickup and his headlights illuminate me. And I know he is sitting there in the cab smoking. I smell the pot smoke.

I walk up and I see him through the windshield; I see his jaw slacken. He is mouthing: *"Wha—?"*

I bid his mouth to close, and it does.

I raise my hands like a sorcerer.   The can of Coke. The gun.

Things will change soon. It will be better in the future.

The pickup begins to quickly back out of the driveway.

What happens when you are not there, but someone from real life sees you?

Rusty saw me, I thought.   I knew that's what he would tell Aaron. *Stood out in front of the house holding a gun in the air. Holding a gun and a can of Coke. With a little smile on his face.*

14

"Rusty's been talking to Aaron," I say. "I don't know what kind of lies he's been telling about me."

"Jesus!" Aqil says.

It's Friday morning, and we are sitting in the breakfast nook, and the January sun is shining grayly through the window, and my hand is shaking as I push the plunger on the French press coffeemaker. It gurgles. It had started out as a joke, the French press, Jill and I chortling over how pretentious it was, but then we tried it and found that the coffee was actually really.

Aqil looks at me uneasily as I fill two plain white mugs. "What would he say about you?"

"How would I know?" I say, and he looks at me ruefully, and I realize that my voice has been sharp and condescending.

"I don't know," I say, more softly, more reasonably. "He claims to be innocent of the murders. He—obviously—has been acquitted. I testified against him at the trial."

"So he's telling Aaron you're a liar, right?" Aqil says. He takes up his mug of coffee and gives it a sip.

"Mm," he says. He tilts his head skeptically. "I'm not sure I'm seeing the connections."

"I think Aaron might have gone to visit Rusty," I say. "I think he might have gone to Chicago. Maybe Rusty convinced him, or *lured* him in some way . . ."

Aqil frowns. "I don't think that makes sense," he says. "Why would he do that?"

"I . . ." I say. "I guess . . . I think the idea that Rusty wanted him to call Wave . . . thought Wave would say something . . . that she might . . ."

"Are you okay, Dr. Tillman?" Aqil said. "You seem a little confused."

He says that the first thing to do is to file a missing-person report. "He's a legal adult, of course," Aqil says. "And there's no evidence of foul play. So it's not exactly going to be high priority, but it will go into the NCIC database. And that's something, at least."

"So," I say, and I glance up at the fluorescent light on the ceiling, which has an unpleasant, uncertain flicker.   "I just go into the police station and say"

"Yeah," Aqil says. "They'll walk you through it." He tilts his head, peering into my eyes with concern. "And you've talked to his friends? You've looked at his Facebook and—"

"Apparently he has to accept my 'friend request' before I can view his page," I say. "But I did talk to his brother. And Dennis—actually, he confirmed the possibility of drug use, so"

Aqil nods and gives me a regretful, sympathetic look.   "So," he says. "There's a good chance that he's just on a bender. But there's definitely going to have to be rehab in his future."

Could I have done it? I think.

I don't remember killing them, but I remember the walking part, walking through the scene. I remember how it was not scary.   I remember how I felt peaceful.

My mom on the front steps. My dad in the living room, the music playing. My aunt under the kitchen table. My uncle against the counter.

"What about his room?" Aqil is saying. "You did a thorough search of his bedroom?"

I nodded.   "He must have taken his laptop with him," I say. "And maybe a duffel bag?"

"Uh-huh," Aqil says.

"Which is why I think he," I say, and I think: *I should tell him.* And then: *Tell him what?*

15

IT'S LATE AFTERNOON—THOUGH it could be dawn or dusk, the cloud cover is so thick and the sun is so dim and distant. Aaron has been gone for a day and a half, maybe more. It's Friday afternoon now, and I last spoke with him on Wednesday.

After I got back from the police station, I had begun to compile notes.

"Wednesday, January twenty-second," I tell Kate. I'm sitting at the window in my bedroom, looking down at the driveway. Waiting—for what? I don't know.

It was breakfast time, I tell Kate, and he was up unusually early, and I felt pleased. *You're getting on top of things,* I said.

He was very pale. There were dark circles around his eyes. *He looks so tired,* I thought. I was aware, too, that he had lost a lot of weight. I had spoken to him on several occasions about his eating habits.

But at the same time, I didn't think anything was wrong. There was just a vague unease, and I smiled and made some small talk.

College starts back up for you this week, doesn't it? I said, and he said, *Yeah,* which I know now was a lie, because he wasn't registered for classes. I'd called Cleveland State after I'd filed the missing-person report and discovered that in fact he'd never enrolled. He hadn't attended classes in the fall, either. They said he'd withdrawn. He'd gotten most of the tuition money refunded, apparently.

"He probably used it to buy drugs!" Kate says. "Oh, Dustin, this is so fucked up."

And I stare down at the driveway, hastily shoveled. Aaron had cleared just enough so that he could get his mom's car out of the garage and onto the street. Where was he going at such an early hour? In such a hurry?

I clear my throat. "How long have they been in contact?" I ask Kate. "Do you know?"

"I have no idea," she says. "Dustin, I literally found out about this on Tuesday.   And I called him. I called *him* instead of you, which I know I shouldn't have done. Fuck," she says earnestly. "I feel like this is my fault."

So do I, though I don't say it. I am trying to keep my voice calm. I have made out a list of questions that I want her to answer, and I need to stick with them.

"I just want you to go through the conversation again," I say. "Wave called you . . . and she told you . . ."

"Not much," Kate says. "She never says much. She just told me that Aaron had gotten her number and he'd called and left a message saying that Rusty told him to get in contact with her."

"But how did Rusty have Wave's number? Even *you* don't have it," I say.

"And I'd love to know the answer to that," Kate says. "All I can think is that he's been staking us out for a long time. All of us. Maybe he had access to the Internet when he was in prison, and he spent hours and days searching out every little thing. And it also occurred to me that maybe he and Wave had been in touch at some point, and she gave him her contact information.   I just—I don't know."

I look down at the list I've written.   "What did Aaron say to you?" I say. "When you confronted him?"

"He didn't really say anything," she says. "He said that he and Rusty hadn't talked that much about us. Which I didn't believe. He told me that Rusty said he felt guilty about how abusive he was to you. And I told him not to trust Rusty. And then he goes, 'Well, why would Rusty tell me to call Wave?' And he says, 'What should I know about my dad? What should I know that I don't know?' "

I blink. The notes I have been making have gone swimmy beneath my pen, and so I take the tip and press it against the back of my right wrist until I feel the focus come back into my eyes.

"And what did you say?" I ask. I try to make my voice soft and neutral, as if I'm talking to a patient.

"I sort of—I tried to be honest," she says. "I told him that you were impressionable when you were a kid. Gullible. I told him that you believed what you said but that what you said might not be entirely true."

I don't say anything. I blink. Here is the poorly shoveled driveway, with the shovel still stabbed into a snowbank at the end of the path.

I can remember the last thing Aaron said before he left.

"So," he said. "Can I ask you a psychology question?"

"Of course!" I said.   I grinned. "Are you taking a psychology class?"

"Yeah," he said.

"Neat," I said.

"So," he said. "The thing I wanted to ask you. What do you call it when someone can't tell the difference between what's real and what's not real?"

16

"THAT'S SO WEIRD," says this boy I don't remember. Mike Mention. It's a little past six in the evening, and I'm sitting at Aaron's desk, looking through the drawers. "I just talked to him, like, last weekend," Mike Mention says, in the polite, pleasant voice you might use to speak to an acquaintance's father. "We watched some of these old videos that him and Rabbit and me made. I don't know whether you remember back when we were in middle school and we were doing all these little movies?"

"Not distinctly," I say.

Aaron's desk is a cheap computer desk from Staples, laminate over engineered wood, and when I pull out the keyboard shelf there is a dried Mountain Dew spill that has grown a pelt of dust, and a Skittle is stuck to it. There are some rolling papers. A plastic straw. A souvenir eraser from Mammoth Cave, which we'd visited when he was twelve.

A three-by-five index card, with Aaron's sloppy, spiky, teenage-boy handwriting:

R.
3216 N Sissaro Ave
Chicago IL 60641

"So we were just reminiscing about Rabbit, basically," Mike Mention says. "But that was really the last time I talked to him."

"Can you," I say. "Can you think of anybody else he might be staying with, maybe?"

Mike Mention pauses for a moment, thoughtfully.   "Umm," he says. "Not really. I don't know that much about who he hangs out with now that Rabbit—passed away."

He hesitates again, then sighs, and I open the large bottom drawer on the left—the one that's meant to hold hanging files. There is a high school photo of Jill on top of a pile of haphazardly stacked papers.

"Listen, Mr. Tillman," he says. And his voice is surprisingly kind. "Look, I know that you and Aaron were, like, really close or whatever, but, you know. Sometimes I don't talk to my mom for, like, weeks. I don't think you need to be really freaked out or anything. It's just, you know. Like I tell my mom, she gets so mad when I don't call her back and I'm like, 'Mom, I grew up.' You can't stop it from happening."

I lift up the photo of Jill.

I'm aware that somehow the phone call has ended, and I put the phone down on the desk and peer into the drawer.

He has accumulated a little cache of Jill's possessions.   At first the word *stolen* comes to me, but then I think—*stolen from whom?*

He has collected a few casual snapshots from Jill's high school and college years—the kind of fuzzy, poorly lit photos you'd get when you and your friends snapped pictures at a party on a disposable camera. You'd drop them off at the drugstore and pick up a packet of glossies a couple of days later, and a third of them would be nothing—a blurry close-up of a finger or an overexposed group shot where everyone's eyes are red and their teeth all look like the teeth of skeletons.

But I can see why he wanted them. They're not posed. No one is looking at the camera. It's almost as if he could get a glimpse through a pinhole of a time when his mom was alive and he wasn't, a time when she was his age. Jill, barefoot and in shorts, drinking beer on someone's porch. Jill, sixteen years old, laughing as if she has heard the funniest joke. Jill in a dorm common room, sitting on a couch with a boy and pretending like she's squeezing his breasts. A different part of his mother's life, which he would never know. That I hadn't really known, either.

He has taken her law school diploma and the chunky, brightly colored necklace that had been made by natives of some tropical tribe in Africa or South America or Malaysia, which the boys had given her one Mother's Day. There is a Christmas-tree ornament that Aaron made when he was four or five, a turnip-shaped piece of construction paper that had been decorated with glue and glitter, and in Magic Marker is written: MERCIFUL TO FORGIVE OTHER

Here were a handful of letters that she'd kept.

There is one from the college years in which photo collages have been taped to the envelope, and there is one that is obviously addressed in her mother's handwriting, and there is one that is more recent, the addresses printed in anonymous laser-printer font, and I pick up that one because I don't know the sender.

It is dated September 27, 2009.

Dearest Jill, it says. *Wake up! You say that you're going to confront the problems in your marriage when the boys are out of high school, but that is literally years. The things that you've shared with me about Dustin have made me concerned that*

And I stop reading and put the letter in my pocket.

17

"WHAT DO YOU think Rusty told him?" I say to Kate.

"I don't know," Kate says. "What do you think?"

"I don't know, either," I say.

It's about eight o'clock now and I'm sitting in the living room with my laptop and my phone and my Moleskine notebook spread out on the coffee table. The desire to feel as if I'm accomplishing something. There is a fire in the fireplace. There is the large thirty-by-forty studio portrait of our family, taken about four years ago now, and Jill looks down at me. We are both silent for a long time. Uncomfortable. My eyes find the ceiling and up there I can see a bullet hole.

Or—no, it's smaller than a bullet hole. My guess is that someone had once mounted a hook of some kind. For hanging a plant, or a mobile. Some kind of pendant light. Odd that I never noticed it before.

"You would think," I say, "that he told him something about the trial."

We were on the border of a territory that we hadn't crossed into since the early days when we were staying with Grandma Brody. After Wave left, we had deliberately stopped speaking about it; it was a tacit agreement, as they say, and broaching it gives me a woozy, nauseated feeling.

"I guess he would say that we lied, right?" I say, and Kate makes a disapproving sound.

"Everything we said was basically true," she says. "At worst, maybe a little poetic license."

"Hm," I say.   I look at the fire, and then back to that hole on the ceiling. I wouldn't have been surprised if an insect with a lot of legs came crawling out of it. "Have you thought about—"

A mud dauber wasp? That was the insect that I hated the most. They make these horrible nests—clusters of tear-shaped cells, made of mud but as smooth as if they'd been cast on a pottery wheel and baked in a kiln.   The wasp paralyzes its prey and lays its eggs on it, and then seals it into one of the mud chambers. The trapped prey will still be alive when the eggs hatch.

"What?" Kate says, after my silence has extended. "Have I thought about what?"

"Well," I say. "If Rusty didn't do it, who did?"

She sniffed. "I still think he did it," she says. "I don't care if he was acquitted. I tried to read about—the documents, about *why* he was acquitted? Dustin, they don't even make sense. I don't know whether you looked them up online?"

"No," I say. And I'm aware that I have gone for a year and a half without reading a single thing about Rusty's release from prison. Maybe if Jill hadn't died, maybe if I hadn't gotten involved with the investigation, I would have been able to force myself to read it. But even in ideal circumstances, I'm not sure.

"You'd have to be a lawyer to understand it," Kate says, and I look away from the hole. I try to imagine her apartment. What's she's doing right now?   Looking out the window?

And I touch the envelope. It's still in my pocket. *Burn it*, I think. She's quiet.

"Besides which," she says, "I thought we'd decided we weren't going to talk about it. That was sort of the rule, wasn't it?"

"I wish there was some way for me to talk to Wave," I say.   "I just feel like—if I knew what kind of contact she had with Rusty, and with Aaron, if I knew what they were saying, I would be able to have a better sense of what was going on in Aaron's mind."

"I have her P.O. box number," Kate says. "In Wonder, Oregon. So you could write her a letter. She says she doesn't have a phone. She calls people from a pay phone on the highway."

I can picture Kate at the front window of her apartment. A limo is pulling up in front of the Scientology Celebrity Centre hotel. She brings the filter of her cigarette to her lips, and she French inhales, letting the smoke drift out of her mouth and into her nostrils, and I let this play in my mind's eye for a while because that particular kind of movement of smoke is beautiful. Billowing.

"I think he might have told Aaron that I did it," I say at last. "That's what I'm worried about."

She doesn't say anything. And I can't imagine what she's doing. I don't know if she's standing at the window. I don't know if she's at the kitchen table, or reclining in bed with the ceiling fan turning slowly over her, or on the couch with her remote pointed at the TV. The hole looks down at me from the ceiling.

"Well," she says at last, pensively. "Did you?"

"No," I say. "I'm pretty sure I didn't."

18

EIGHT IN THE morning on Sunday and Aqil calls me. I shift under the blankets and brush up against the shape of Jill, and I know that it's just a pillow that occupies the space she used to in our bed but I still touch it apologetically, as if the phone might have awakened it.

I blink.

The letter—the unread letter—is folded in half on the nightstand next to the old lava lamp that doesn't work anymore.   *The things that you've shared with me about Dustin have made me concerned that* If I was smart I'd have burned it before I had the chance to wake up and reconsider.

I remember talking to Mike Mention.   I remember talking to Kate.

I think he might have told Aaron that I did it

I have a mug that Jill got me for Father's Day. It says, BEHIND EVERY SUCCESSFUL DAD IS A FAMILY WHO LOVES HIM! and the mug shows a cartoon father being followed by a loving mom, who is followed by an adoring older son and an eager younger son and a tail-wagging dog, and they follow the father all around the circumference of the cup. And even though we didn't have a dog, I always felt connected to that image. To that idea. The memories of happiness.

"So, listen," Aqil says. "I have some information for you."

"Okay," I say. I sit up, and I can see myself in the mirror of Jill's dresser, sitting up and holding my phone to my ear.

"I entered your wife's car's license plate into the database," Aqil says. "And this morning I got a couple of hits. Traffic and parking violations, from the last few days."   He cleared his throat.   "In Chicago."

It is not that unexpected, I guess.   It clicks into place the way a game of solitaire can; you know the cards will all begin to move toward their final pile, and there is that tingle of recognition.

We had known Rusty was in Chicago for a long time. We knew his whereabouts, his address. Aqil had told me that summer before Jill died, well over a year ago. *I'm a cop; I have my sources,* he said.

I'm aware of the index card that Aaron had in his desk. *R. 3216 N Sissaro Ave Chicago IL 60641*

I know that he's been talking with Rusty for a long time—*bonding* with Rusty, I think.   And then Rusty told him to call Wave. And Wave—maybe? Wave told him—what?

What do you call it when someone can't tell the difference between what's real and what's not real?

What has Aaron heard about me? What have they been telling him? There is that feeling when your own story is out of your hands. Someone else is making you up behind your back, and it gives you a shiver of

The folded envelope looks at me. Folded into a hunched, sullen origami troll. It had been in Aaron's room. He'd read it.

"I think I'm going to have to go there," I say.

Aqil lets out a breath—maybe exasperated. "Dustin," he says. "Why would you do that?"

"It's not true," I say. "What Aaron thinks is true is not true."

"Well," Aqil says. "If Aaron is in Chicago—if he's visiting this guy, your brother? Do you think he might—would you say that Aaron is in any danger? That your brother might harm him?"

Strange that this is something I never considered. Even though I'd thought of him for years as a murderer, even though the abuse—for some reason I don't imagine that he would hurt Aaron.

I think that Aaron has gone there of his own free will—that he knows something, believes something about me. *Something Rusty told him.* He's a pawn, not a target. I feel my head shake.

"No no," I say. "I don't think—I don't think he'd hurt Aaron. That's not what he's . . ."

I hesitate. "The tickets," I say. "Are they on Cicero Avenue?"

"Yeah, that's right," Aqil says. "Some of them on Belmont."

"I guess I need to go there," I say.

"What?" says Aqil. "You think he's actually *with* your brother? Sleeping on Rusty's couch or something? Why would he do that?"

I imagine Aaron: *I am talking to someone. . . . Just not a fucking therapist.*

"Because they're friends," I say. "They've been talking for over a year. I'm guessing that Rusty's the closest friend he has now that Rabbit's gone."

"And how do you know that?" Aqil says.

"I have a good intuition for these things," I say. "You said so yourself."

"So," Aqil says. "You're just going to drive—what—six hours? Just to check on a hunch?"

What else can I do? I think. *Wait here?*

"I'm going to get up and shower," I say. "And I'm going to pack a little bag. I want to go there today."

"Um," Aqil says. "Really?"

"Would you be willing to come with me?"

19

WE ARE TRAVELING along. Driving in my car.

I am behind the steering wheel and we pass through a tollbooth and then we are on I-90 west, and I try to focus only on the road. When the semis go past me in the left lane, they send a blinding sheet of muddy slush across my windshield, and it feels aggressive, it feels like one of the video games the boys like to play in which you are being attacked but you have to keep pressing forward.   White, snow-covered, et cetera, on either side. No scenery.

The memory of happiness: I am driving and Jill is in the passenger seat and we're playing some kind of license-plate game. "Keep an eye out for pornographic messages," she says.

The boys are in the backseat, still very young—under five—asleep, and I keep a lookout until I see a truck that says VIB3 R8R, and we both start laughing even though it isn't that funny. We'll stop at a motel and rent a room with two double beds and we'll carry the babies in so softly that they don't even stir and then we'll try to have quiet sex on the bed across from them, but she keeps whispering in my ear—"Vee one bee three arr eight arrrrrr"—and I chortle so loudly I wake up the kids, but it doesn't matter.

I believe she loved me. I believe it in every part of myself.

Aqil is silent. He is very involved with his device, and out of the corner of my eye I see him frowning, swiping his thumb to the left across his screen. Once, twice. Six times. Then a swipe to the right. Maybe he's playing a game?

He clears his throat.

"I need to stop at a rest area," he says. "When the next one comes up."

"Yes," I say, and I brace myself as a semi carrying a rack of cars appears in my rearview mirror. "Okay."

"Do you want me to drive for a while?" Aqil says.

Yes. Okay.

I lean my head against the cold passenger-side window, and I can smell the thick dusty warmth of the defroster. He plugs in a CD and mumbles along with it.

"What is this?" I say, and we are passing Cedar Point amusement park, and I used to take the boys there. There was a water park.

"Modest Mouse," he says, and I nod.

I take the letter out of my pocket and unfold it. The return address tells me that it is from someone named Alice Fish in Buckingham, Pennsylvania—whom I have never heard of, though apparently she and Jill shared close personal information.

Wake up! You say that you're going to confront the problems in your marriage when the boys are out of high school, but that is literally years. The things that

you've shared with me about Dustin have made me concerned that he is not just
emotionally unavailable but incapable of

And I glance up and we are hurtling through a landscape of white and black. Asphalt, snow, fences. A bare tree in the middle of a field. A sudden explosion of grackles, curving through the air. A frowning, dead Pizza Hut, watching us with arched eyebrows from an abandoned mall. *If you read further, all of your happiest memories will be taken away.* All of it will be stripped and recolored.   All of the moments that you think of as important will suddenly shift and distort, and whatever you thought you remembered will be gone.

But at least you will know, I think. *Right?*

When we cross through the tollbooth at the edge of Ohio and into Indiana, I take out my wallet and hand Aqil a twenty and he pays.

"Can we stop for something to eat soon?" I say.

There is an oasis just off the interstate with a combination Taco Bell and Pizza Hut, and when I get out of the car I can see the overstuffed trash can, with its square robot head and the flaps for a mouth, full to bursting with fast-food bags and scattered uneaten French fries, dried drips of ketchup and neat little baggies of dog shit, and when we get close I push the folded letter into the opening of a wax cup that is still half-full of Coke.

Aqil doesn't notice. We walk quickly toward the glass doors as the wind blows sharp particles of snow across us.

2 0

I AM DRIVING and trying to dream myself into it.

"I hope you have a plan," Aqil says, and I do. Vaguely. I am going to find Aaron and I am going to convince him to come home and then he will go into rehab.

"Okay," Aqil says. "Run me through it, brother."

"I can't," I say. "I won't know what I'm going to say until I see him. When I see his face, I'll know. It can't be a planned speech."

"So," Aqil says. "You're just going to hope that roses come out of your mouth?"

"Yes."

"Hm," he says. "Kind of stupid but kind of badass."

I have gotten as far as the expression that will be on my face when I see him. I want to look at him the way I did when he was first born—I think about the surprised grimace on his face, the way he squinted at the light as I held him and cut his umbilical cord, the way he gasped but didn't cry, the way his tiny translucent fingers made grasping gestures as he rested in my arms. I was so astonished, and I want to see him that way again. I want to feel that kind of wonder.

I want him to remember me from that moment. When he was just born, and I held him, and we were connected forever.

But this is not what I say to Aqil, of course.

"Seriously," Aqil says. "Let's walk through it, Dustin. Let's pretend we go to Rusty's apartment building. You walk up to the door. Do you ring a bell and have to talk to an intercom? Do you go straight up and Aaron opens the door and looks out at you through a door chain, and you hypnotize him with the words that are just going to come flowing out of your mouth?"

I picture it. The door opens a crack. Aaron's eye, and the chain running taut just beneath.

"I don't know yet," I say, and I hold the steering wheel and stare out at Indiana.

"Okay," Aqil says. "I'm rolling here with what you're saying. I'm respecting it."

He runs his hand across his hair.   "But you *do* know that Aaron is not going to open the door, right? Rusty is."

"Yes," I say.   And even as I say it, I can picture Rusty's eye in place of Aaron's, and I recognize his eye even though it is fifty years old and he's been in prison more than half his life.

There are rows of uninteresting billboards passing us. We are part of a row of cars, a line of insects following each other at 73 miles an hour, which is the speed that most of us have agreed to. We hurry along, bobbing against a current, and I think, *If I'd been brave enough to*

The version of your life that can be taken away from you. The story of yourself that you tell yourself as you go through the daily routines, the story that you think other people would tell about you, your wife, your children, your loved ones.

"This is what he wanted all along," I say. "He wanted to make me talk to him."

"Does it occur to you," Aqil says, "that he might be luring you somewhere to kill you?"

"No," I say. I shake my head, and a semi looms in the rearview mirror, speeding up to pass me. "He won't do that. If he'd wanted to, he would've done that already."

21

THERE IS THE long death strip at the end of Indiana, Gary and then Hammond, an apocalyptic peninsula of half-ruined hangars and weedy marsh, the feeling that some country lost a war.

And then we find ourselves on the long steel Skyway Bridge, one hundred twenty-five feet above the mostly frozen Calumet River. I wonder, briefly, how many young men have drowned down there.

And then the towers of Chicago appear in the distance out of opaque January mist, cold and austere and yet with a fairy-tale quality nevertheless—an Emerald City in black and white and gray.

The memory of happiness.

"Well," Aqil says. "We're here."

22

IT'S AFTER SIX when we arrive at 3216 Cicero. Dark already.

The building is an old rectangle of brick, five stories. *The Elinor Hotel*, it says on the awning above the door, not quite as shoddy as I was expecting.

The neighborhood is quite a ways from the skyscrapers of downtown. In fact, the towers don't even seem to be visible in the distance. Instead, we are on a strip of mostly low-lying storefronts. The Elinor Hotel is next to a liquor store, and across the street is El Nino de Oro, "For all your special needs," and Mimi's Mature Book

Store: "Exotic Films—Marital Aids—Novelties—Latex" and a pawn shop called Easy Cash. *WE BUY GOLD*, the storefront advertises. Down the block, an elegant old movie theater front has been converted into a place called Golden Tiara: Chicago's Finest Bingo and Raffle.

The street isn't busy. Aqil drives around a block and we find parking almost directly across from the place. He wedges in between a small Toyota pickup and a salt-stained Pontiac, right in front of an establishment called Alliance Behavioral Services: D.U.I.

He puts the car into park, and we sit there, idling for a few minutes in silence. "Are you sure you want to do this?" he says.

"Let's just sit here for a minute," I say.

And we do. A monstrous salt truck approaches, a sound of grinding and lurching, and then it goes by. I look up and the windows of the Elinor Hotel look down. Four windows vertical, three across, all of them dark, empty, staring. There is a stone gargoyle face sticking out his tongue above the front entrance.

I can see now how stupid I've been. This is possibly the most idiotic thing I've ever done, in a whole lifetime of sleepwalking into one disaster after another.

Nothing I'm doing makes any sense. It is what Aqil has been trying to tell me all along. I look over at him and he looks back and raises his eyebrows. He's sympathetic: He understands an obsession and a series of disconnected hunches, but I can tell that even he doesn't have any faith in this one, this impetuous trip.

But Aaron's mom's car was nearby, I think. That's the key. Jill's car—somewhere nearby.

And then I see him.

23

I RECOGNIZE HIM by his walk. A certain kind of focused light appears in the scene: I see him moving down the block, and there's that particular way that he swings his arm, a certain gait, and I think: *Rusty*.

He's wearing an old dirty ski jacket, no hat or scarf, and he comes around the corner with his head down and his shoulders hunched. He has somehow become a middle-aged man, and his face looks heavier and more jowled than it used to be. He's got an unfortunate neck tattoo, and his long hair is lank and tied into a halfhearted ponytail.

But he is still the same person. *I know him*, I think.

I watch as he slouches his way into the front entrance of the Elinor Hotel with his plastic grocery bags swinging from his right hand.   As he disappears inside.

I sit up, and Aqil looks over at me. He's been involved with his device, but now he's alert. "What?" he says, and I lift my chin to point.

"That's him," I whisper. "Did you see him?" Because it seems possible that he wasn't there.

24

I REACH INTO the glove box and take out the gun. It's the gun that Aqil gave me a long time ago, Colt .380 Mustang XSP, and he watches me curiously.

"Dustin," he says. "Don't you think you better reconsider the weapon for a minute?"

He watches as I put it in the pocket of my coat.

"I'm not going to do anything," I say, and he clears his throat, gives me a skeptical squint. "I'm not thinking any kind of violent thoughts," I say. "I'm just going to talk to him. But you don't think I should have protection?"

He smiles, but sadly. He puts his hand on my hand, the hand that is holding the gun, and I feel the pads of his fingers rest on my wrist.

"If you take a gun, it's not imaginary anymore, brother," he says softly. "It's real."

And then he leans down and presses his lips to the back of my hand. "Thank you," he whispers.

And it occurs to me that Aqil is probably the only true friend that I have ever had.

PART NINE

January 2014

1

Yeah, I was a bad person. I knew it from the beginning, from the days when I was living with my real mom back in Grand Island, Nebraska, back before she went to prison, before the foster homes and the group homes; even my own mother knew something was wrong.

Today I am standing outside in back of the restaurant, in an alleyway by the grease dumpster, smoking a cigarette and taking a little break, when from out from the blue I find myself thinking about the peanut butter man.

He was one of my mom's boyfriends. One of *our* boyfriends, I realized later. He liked to sit with me on his lap and feed me peanut butter from the jar with his finger. He would put his finger in my mouth and I would lick the peanut butter off. My mom sat at the kitchen table across from us, watching. I guess I was about five.

I remember the peanut butter man had an unshaved face, not quite a beard. He ran his chin across the top of my head while he fed me, and I could feel it scratching. The taste of his finger was like old meat, and his aftershave was sweet and vinegary. It was my job to sit there and be fed.

"This is a very naughty boy," the man said to my mother, and she agreed with him. She took a sip of coffee. I was a bad boy, she said.

The man wanted to watch her give me a spanking, and so she did. It didn't hurt that much, but I blushed and tears came to my eyes because he was laughing at me.

She would never leave me alone with them.   That's what she told me once, after one of the boyfriends had left.   We were in bed and she was running her hand across my hair. "Don't worry, Rusty," she murmured.   "I won't let anything get out of hand."

Fuck, I think. *So many people I should have killed, and never got a one.*

I don't know why this should come back to me now. It hasn't crossed my mind in years, but now here I am and it time-travels its way into my head.   *Hello, bad boy,* the memory says, and I flick my cigarette against the trod-down slush of wet garbage and dirty snow, wincing a little. I look down at my shitty black canvas sneakers— wino shoes—and the wet cuffs of my checked pants.

I take out my cell phone and look at it. Polish that screen so that it lights up. That was the most amazing thing about getting out of prison.   I knew about cell phones, of course, but I never expected to see all the people of the world walking through the streets with their little black rectangles held out, stumbling along like the phones were leading them. Stroking their phones, poking their phones, staring at them lovingly and asking them questions. I heard the voice of the robot lady coming out. It was fucking crazy, man. Unbelievable.

Nobody's called me today. Might have expected to hear back from Aaron but he hasn't called me since we "Skyped," and I wonder if I scared him somehow. The neck tattoo probably didn't help. Maybe he was imagining somebody different.

2

GET ON THE blue line train after work and take it to Belmont station. Nobody's alert on these trains, all bundled up in their coats and scarves and hats like fat birds, plugged into their earphones, staring at their screens.   You see someone who's watchful, you figure they must have been in prison or they're on their way there soon. Keep an eye out for the ones who are looking.

Step off the train and onto the underground tunnel platform and the conductor's voice echoes metallic and incomprehensible, it kind of feels like you're underwater because the light has that blue, swimmy quality, and you move with the other fishies in your school toward the escalators that will take you to the surface. Faint smell of piss and ice.

Emerge into the aboveground and it's after midnight.   There's a little awning area where you can wait for the #77 bus to Cicero, a couple of people sitting there so you don't want to smoke near them. Across the street an old-fashioned drive-in called Mic Duck's, a couple of black teenagers loafing around outside even though it's about ten degrees; they're having a great time teasing one another. You light a cigarette and keep your eye on them.

And then the phone in your pocket starts buzzing and it scares the shit out of you for a second. You didn't have such a terribly rough time in prison, not like some of them, but you can be easily startled. You shift your head back and forth as if suddenly all eyes will be upon you.

They're not.

You've seen plenty of people answer their phone in public. They walk down the street laughing like wackjobs, or dictating stern instructions, arguing, calling out "I love you, too, sugar" in a babyish croon. Doesn't seem to bother them.

But you can't imagine doing it. Having a private conversation on a bus, on a train, in a public place, with other people able to listen? Might as well pull your pants down and take a shit on the sidewalk.

But then you pull the phone out, thinking that there's a button you can push to make it stop ringing, and you realize you fucking have to answer it.

It's Wave.

3

"So," WAVE SAYS. "I talked to the kid."

I look around me, feeling exposed, hunching down over my phone. "What did he say?"

"Why are you whispering?" she says. "Are you still at work?"

"I'm waiting for a bus," I say.   I raise my voice a little and put the phone closer to my lips, as if it's something I'm trying to warm my face with. "What did you tell him?"

"I told him what I perceived to be true," she says. "Wolf didn't want me to do it at all."

"Oh, wow," I say. "Okay." Wolf is her "mate," as she calls him. At some point in the history of things, they legally changed their names to Wolf and Galadriel Bluecloud. I can't really get behind it, but it's also not really mine to judge. I have gotten checks in the mail from Galadriel Bluecloud, and they did not bounce. Galadriel Bluecloud privately donated fairly large amounts of money to the Innocence Project group that was handling my retrial.

"What's your game, Rusty?" she says.

I feel myself shrug. "I made friends with his son," I say.   "I thought it was important that he heard stuff from another perspective.   So it didn't just seem like I was vengeful."

"Because you're not vengeful, right?" she says.

"Nah," I say.   The #77 bus has arrived, and I watch the people getting on it. But I can't picture myself getting on a bus while talking on a phone. Paying the driver while talking. I watch as the bus doors close.

"It's just—I would personally be interested in hearing Dustin tell the truth," I say. And I sit down and hunch over a cigarette, protecting it from the wind as I light it. "What is *his* truth, as he knows it? I don't think that's so much to ask for twenty-nine years in prison."

"Oh, Rusty," she says. "*The truth as he knows it?* What could that possibly be? It's not going to help anything."

"I'm not expecting it to," I say. "And I'm not vengeful. I'm not. But come on, Dusty, be a man. Admit what you did. It doesn't have to be in the newspapers. It doesn't have to be a notarized statement. I'd just like to hear him say it," I tell her. "And if he can't explain it to me, maybe he'll explain it to his son."

I always think of the way he looked when he came out of that house.

There's this one movie I saw when I was a kid, and it's about this girl who's an outcast but the popular kids trick her into thinking that she's queen of the prom. Then when she gets up on the stage and they give her the flower bouquet and crown and so on, they dump pig blood on her. It just goes all down her hair and her face and over her dress and drips off the hem onto a pool on the floor. She's like a statue made of pig blood. And then she opens her eyes through this thick red syrup, and they're really wide and white and surprised. But then she looks at the camera and you can see that they are the blank eyes of the goddess that kills everyone.

That's what Dusty was. That kind of monster.

His eyes were open so wide but they weren't seeing anything, and he had a can of pop in one hand and a gun in the other, and he was moving them in his hands like they were sacred priestly fucking icons, and I was just in my truck smoking a J and I looked up and here he's coming toward me. The revolver kind of wobbling in his hand, and his eyes completely dead.

Yes: The scariest thing I've ever seen. The way his face was fixed and rigid. Eyes stretched open. Puppet-like twitching of the body. I literally thought he was fucking possessed, and I booked it out of the driveway, drove all the way back to Trent's house.

Trent was tripping on PCP so he didn't really understand what I was trying to explain to him. Later he told the police that he vaguely remembered that I'd told him that *I* killed my family.

I told the police what I'd seen when they arrested me but wasn't believed. Told the lawyer, too, and I don't know whether he believed me or not. He didn't want me to testify—he said that I wasn't sympathetic, that it wouldn't make things any better if I got up on the stand and accused a traumatized thirteen-year-old. "They'd decimate you on cross-examination," he said, and held up his hand when I tried to say something.

"They're hanging themselves, anyway," he said. "The stuff those two are saying is the most asinine crap I've ever heard in my life. Prayers to Satan. Sacrificing baby bunnies. It's absurd. What adult in their right mind would find any of this credible?"

And I was like, "Actually, I did kill some rabbits. But it was, like, four years ago."

And he was like, "That's why you're not testifying."

4

NEXT #77 BUS won't be for forty minutes so I head along Belmont, marching west toward my destination. My apartment on Cicero is about two miles away, and I'm trying to walk down the street and talk to Wave on the cell phone at the same time. I've never tried this before and it's an upsetting experience.

First and foremost, you want to pay attention to your surroundings—which, at this time of night, in this part of Chicago, seems like a wise thing to do. Not that anything is going to happen to you, walking past Walgreens and some row houses and an Asian lady pushing a baby carriage.

Mounds of piled snow scorched black with mud and filth. You're fine, you're not in danger.

But with a cell phone, it's a complicated balance, because you think you're staying alert but at the same time you're conversing, you're pulled by her voice into some hippie parlor in Oregon and also into your wayback machine of memories, and you stop in front of an auto body shop and think, *Fuck, this is impossible.* How do people walk and talk on these things at the same time? Read on them? Play games on them?

It's because they are not walking, I realize. *They are not in their actual bodies.*

"The concern that Wolf has," Wave is saying. "The house phone number should not really be in the hands of strangers. We don't know this person. Dusty's son. And you tell me he has drug problems?"

"He's going through a rough time," I say.

"The point is," Wave says, "now we have to go through the whole rigmarole of changing the number, and contacting clients to let them know that the number has changed, and then the possibility of some lineman from the phone company coming out here? Wolf is beside himself."

"Sorry," I say. "I wasn't thinking when I gave him the number."

There's an old guy standing by the entrance to an indoor car wash, and I don't want to walk past him, because I'm afraid he's a beggar, so I cross the street. My shoes sink into the salted slush and I can feel the icy wet begin seeping through to my socks.

"I should have asked your permission and I did not and for that I apologize," I say, and I flinch because my feet are already beginning to sting. *Fuck. Fifty-year-old-man feet.*

"Well," she says. Maybe my tone makes her raise an eyebrow. "What's done is done. And I did what you wanted. I talked to him and I told him the same thing I would tell you."

"I hope he listened," I say.

I stand there on the sidewalk, panting out puffs of steam from my mouth and nose. The lifelong smoker, breathless from running across the length of a street.

"He did or he didn't," Wave says. Galadriel says. She has the voice of a stern Elf Princess. *All shall love me and despair!*

"You know," she says, "I want to be supportive. But I think this thing with Dusty's son is a bad idea. I don't know what you were thinking, but if I can be honest with you I think you need to be a little smarter. This could be considered stalker behavior."

"Oh, wow," I say. "Huh. I never thought of that." And I limp along the block, past the Laundromat and Fragrantica perfumes, and I can feel the melting ice water begin to soak into the skin of the soles of my feet.

"It's funny, though," I say. "I mean, I'm not completely a stranger, you know? The truth is, I'm still his uncle. Not by blood, but they did adopt me, you know? So he's still officially my nephew. Dustin's still officially my brother. Even you, Galadriel. You're still my cousin. We're still related."

"You don't need any bad publicity," she says. "I can just picture a think piece in *The Wall Street Journal*. 'The Dark Side of the Innocence Project.'"

"Yeah," I say, and for the first time I add her to the list of people I might kill. Dustin's on the list, for sure. Kate, definitely. Trent. Uncle Lucky. The first foster family I stayed with: all of them. My mom's boyfriends. The people who killed my mom when she was in prison. My mom herself. Me.

I never once thought about killing Wave, though. Until now. I could probably kill Galadriel. Even though I think she means well. Even though she's generous. She can't help but talk to me like she's my benefactor, though the truth is she didn't come to my aid when it mattered.

"You *do* have a life ahead of you," she says. "It doesn't all have to be about the past."

I look out west. I'm coming up on North Central Park and a 7-Eleven that's closed. A few flakes of snow are hanging in the air, mesmerized as fireflies. There is a long corridor that leads, eventually, to my bed, and I begin to walk in that direction.

Poor me. A murderer who got caught before he could murder anybody.

5

I GET BACK to my little place at the Elinor Hotel, and climbing the stairs I think that actually I probably wouldn't kill Dustin after all. I might put his head down in a toilet until he stopped bubbling and blacked out, but then I'd yank him up by his hair so he could take a breath.

I sit down on the couch and take off my shoes, peel off my wet socks—there must be holes in the soles of these fucking sneakers?—and I lower my feet into a tub of warm Epsom salts. Take the remote from the coffee table, let the TV light up.

Think about that one time you tried to show Dustin the Big Dipper.   This was the night that they said that they wanted to adopt you.   You were fourteen; he was seven or eight? You put your hands on the sides of his head and he was warm like a dog, you tilted the head like a telescope, you steered it in the right direction.

"There it is," you said. "Do you see it?" And there was the feeling of wanting him to be your little brother. Knowing you were going to hurt him very bad, but also hoping not to.

For a while in prison you would go to the group therapy. There was this one guy you felt friendly toward. Dr. Sharp.   A young guy—younger than you, by that point you were thirty or so, and he was maybe twenty-four, twenty-five?—and he took you aside one time after a session and he said, "You're smart, Russell. But you need to understand something. When you've been abused in the way you were, you have a virus. And the virus will demand that you pass it on to someone else. You don't even have that much of a choice."

I remember that I grinned at him, and laughed, and cocked my head.

"Good to know," I said. "I'll keep that in mind for future use."

But by the time I got back to my cell I was feeling very low. I laid down on my bunk, facedown, covered my head with my arms. Pressed my mouth and nose hard against the pillow.

It wasn't that I felt that sorry for the things that I'd done to Dustin. I didn't, really. I didn't give a shit about Dustin.

But the idea that I passed on a virus, and the virus would turn around and it was my own doom?

That was so fucking funny. That was so sad and so funny.

6

IMAGINE ME IN the third-floor window of the Elinor Hotel, looking down toward you. You poor thing: A streetwalker. Lady of the night, I reckon. Wearing a silver halter top and Daisy Dukes hot pants, not a coat on or a hat, and even from here I can see that you're almost my age. Poor woman on the long end of her forties, I'd guess. Sipping a cup of coffee from Starbucks under the streetlight. Reminds me of this girl I used to play Dungeons & Dragons with back in Nebraska, fourteen-year-old redhead, looked just exactly like the girl who was naked on the cover of the Blind Faith album. We'd get so stoned and this girl would come up with the craziest shit. I was an orc, name of Murder Mook. Carried a two-handed battle-ax, +2 against undead.

Ha! Dungeons & fucking Dragons. They actually brought that up at the trial. It was "Satanic," I guess—and the gal in the halter top gazes up toward my window, as if she sympathizes.

I had been having a lot of fun. For some reason, I thought the gibbeners weren't going to catch me. Finished high school, working as a driver for 7Up, stocking the shelves with the refreshing Uncola. Smoking a huge amount of weed but never doing the kind of heavy shit that poor Aaron was into. We did peyote that one time. LSD a few times. Psychedelic mushrooms—well, actually, quite a bit.

I partied, but I still got up for work in the morning. I was a productive citizen. If not for me, the people wouldn't have the delicious carbonated 7Up that they craved.

But then I look down and my lady has moved on.

I reckon she saw that neck tattoo, maybe? Didn't like the look of it.

Had a roommate in prison who was a tattoo guy, name of Lincoln Kelly. He was a murderer like me; he killed his wife and two little girls. Very quiet. Did a lot of drawing. I could probably count on my fingers the number of words we exchanged the whole time he was inking me, and it took a good long time to put that tattoo on. It was supposed to say REMEMBER, but he got distracted or something so actually it said REMEMEMBER, which actually I liked better. It was in a font that was based on the logo of Judas Priest on their album covers, and first he did the outlines of the letters and then it was a month, off and on, coloring the letters in.

I sat in a chair with my head tilted all the way back, open and exposed in a way that even a child would think: *Someone should cut that dude's throat!* Yes, it did hurt.

I mostly kept my eyes closed, tried not to wince. He filled in each letter in thick black, so it is the first thing that anyone who ever looks at me will see.

He put his fingers on my chin and pushed my head back, so I could feel the skin on my neck stretching. There are certain kinds of muscles in your neck that get warm in this position, and then hot. You can feel the blood in your jugular vein.

The good thing about Link Kelly was that he never asked me why. *Hey, man—what does* REMEMEMBER *mean? What are you trying to say?*

That poor fucker had REMEMEMBER tattooed on every inch of his body, on the inside of his skin. He didn't need to ask me a thing about it.

7

"So TELL ME what you remember, Dusty," I say, and I pretend he's down there by the streetlight, looking up at me. I look down out of my third-floor window give him a little nod and play a *ZZZMM!* chord on my electric guitar.

Yeah. The sound waves hit him hard and electrocute him, and he stares up openmouthed. "Tell me how you remember it, Dusty," I say. *ZZZMM!* I hit the guitar again! "Because I'd really like to know!"

I know what I remember.

I remember sucking peanut butter off a pervert's fingers. I remember the smell of my mom when I put my face against her neck; I remember being four and drinking milk from her titties. I remember a little rat terrier we had named Bibi, and the way she slept on her side, the way you could tell she was dreaming about running away because of the way her paws twitched.

I remember what it felt like to wake up with a house on fire, and a room full of smoke, and when you get outside they think it's maybe your fault.   I remember bringing a brick down on naked baby rabbits that Dustin had stolen from their nest, and they would have died anyway, less mercifully if he'd gotten his chance to take care of them. I remember making use of him, running my cock along the crack of his ass until I came on his back.

I remember the night in the graveyard, putting the ketchup on the baby doll and arranging it and saying, "I pray to you now, O Guland," because that was the name in the book.

If you look it up, you will see that he is mostly a very minor demon. Guland. The one we called up. Guland, lord of disease and drowning.

I remember the trial a little bit, but mostly I remember the moment I got put in prison. I remember being escorted to my cell. My footsteps, *tifty tifty*, in my orange slip-on boat shoes.

Exactly as I expected it.

I remember the time that Wave came out to visit me in prison.

I was in my thirties by then, and so was she. She flew out from Oregon and sat at a table in the visitor center: one of the tables that we made at the penitentiary—nice laminate table, eighteen inch by seventy-two—not exactly made by slave labor, available for purchase now on the Tecumseh State Correctional Institution website!

She looked like a ghost of herself.   Gaunt. Her hair colored. She had markings on her hands, which she said was henna, and fuck me, I did start crying when I saw her.

She told me that my dad—Uncle Dave—was fucking her mom and my adopted mom, Colleen, at the same time, and I was like, *yeah, I told you that*, I remember the time I saw him kissing on Vicki—Dave was such a horny badass—and she was like, *I think my dad killed them.*

I remember that when we were in the graveyard, Kate called upon the demon Guland to kill her parents.

I remember that I finally accepted that Dustin probably didn't do it himself. That was a hard one to give up, but I never could come to grips with why he *would* kill them. Even if he came walking out of the house with a gun, I couldn't figure what would make him shoot his own parents. There was nothing that suggested he had the kind of nuts it would take for such a performance.

Yeah, it was probably as Wave said. Lucky killed them all, the fornicators, the crazy swingers, and then Dusty came in and moved shit around, so that the crime scene was fucked, and then he walked out glowing ecstatically and fingering the gun in my direction, and I thought he wanted to kill me.

Well. He probably *did* want to kill me. I had tortured him for a long time, after all, and he probably would've done it, too, if he'd gotten close enough. But I put the truck in reverse and backed out of there so fast. Should've kept driving all the way to Mexico.

I remember the first time I talked to Aaron. That kid's voice, so sleepy and stoned and gentle. You knew from the beginning that you could fuck him up.

Though that's not exactly what you meant to do.

I liked him. Didn't I? Didn't I want to help?

8

FRIDAY AFTERNOON, AND I'm at the prep table, deveining shrimp. Slice along the back and pull out the string of dirty intestine, flick it into the can, repeat repeat repeat and try to do it fast enough that you don't get yelled at by the cook and slow enough that you don't devein your fucking thumb by mistake.

Thinking about Aaron. So weird to see him on that screen; he has that round face like Dusty, same wide eyes, but he put a ring in his eyebrow and dyed his hair black to make himself look a little less like a Raggedy Ann doll.

Probably going to kill himself with the drugs that he's taking.

Standing out in the alley on break, hunched up over a cigarette, and trying to call him. You put the phone to your face and your hand smells of shrimp veins.

"Hello?" says the voice that answers. It's gruff and deep: not Aaron.

"Hello?" I say.

"Who is this?" the gruff voice says.

"It's Rusty," I say. "Aaron?"

"Oh, good," the voice says. "I'm really glad you called." And you can picture him smiling.

Friendly, almost like he knows you. "You should watch your back," he says.

And then he hangs up.

9

FREAKS ME A bit.

Try calling him back but it goes straight to voicemail.   *Yo what up this is Aaron leave a massage.* Try again. Same.

After work, waiting for the blue line train on Clark and Lake: *Yo what up this is Aaron leave a massage. Yo what up this is Aaron leave a massage. Yo what up this   Yo*   The "massage" thing was funny the first couple of times, but now I hang up the minute he says *Yo.* Keeping an eye on my surroundings. There's a black cop with a hat like a Russian would wear. Two girls in hooded coats and short skirts, an old white crazy lady cruising for change.

You should watch your back.   That's upsetting.

More than likely you got a wrong number, and somebody took an opportunity to screw with you. *I'm really glad you called,* they said. If it *was* a wrong number, what a shitty thing to do. If it wasn't, even worse.

What if it was Dustin?   It seems impossible that his voice sounds like that now—harsh and purring at once, gravelly, deep. I just can't picture it.

But let's say Dustin picked up Aaron's phone for some reason. Answered it, and you said, *It's Rusty.*

Would he really say, *You should watch your back?* Maybe. Maybe if he didn't want you talking to Aaron.   Could be he's hired somebody to kill you and they're watching you right now.

Glance around and up comes the crazy white lady with three teeth in her head. Begging for change. She's wearing a parka trimmed with dirty pink fur and she's wearing a pair of pink plastic clogs. Maybe your age? Maybe younger? She's got eye makeup like Joan Jett, but otherwise she looks like hell, so you give her a dollar and then you turn to your phone again.

Never been to Vegas, but you can imagine you'd be one of those old men that sit in front of a slot machine and pull the handle over and over.

Yo what up this is

In the distance you can see the lights of a train coming along the elevated track, a glimmer through the icy fog.   Maybe it's your blue train.

Think of Dustin strolling toward you across the platform, slow and delicate like when he walked out of the house holding the gun. His feet barely touching the ground, his eyes wide, the gun and the can of Coke moving in his hands as if he were making them into puppets, pretending they were walking, too.

Watch your back.

10

OLD IRISH GUY at the front desk of the Elinor Hotel. Wavy hair of pure white and red nose shaped like an ace of clubs, and though you've been living there over a year and a half, he looks like he only half-recognizes you. You slouch past and he watches you take the stairs, not the tiny creepy elevator, and arrive at last in your little furnished room. Vanessa Zuckerbrot, your Innocence Project lawyer, found it for you, and even paid for the first three months' rent. Though now that you are in Chicago, she is careful to keep her distance. If you thought that she maybe was on the prowl for fifty-year-old prison-dude cock, you were sadly mistaken. Sweet Vanessa! She's already moved on to the next victim she's going to rescue, working tirelessly.

But Vanessa can't help you now anyway. You have to be a man, and you pause at the fire door to your floor, you look out through the little portal window with its chicken-wire glass, nobody waiting in your hallway, nobody by your front door.

You should watch your back: What a cruel thing to say to someone just out of prison!

11

SATURDAY AND YOU'RE like fuck it. Back at the restaurant early in the morning, you're making a vegetable stock in a 120-quart pot, chopping onions, garlic, parsley, carrots, celery.

If he calls you back, he calls you back. You never want to hear that message on his phone again, as long as you live. *Leave a massage.* Yeah, I've got a massage for you, you little shit.

The other bit of it is not so easy to shake, though. That little stab: *I'm really glad you called.*

You should watch your back. Somebody who knows how to screw with you. Not Dustin. Not Dustin, it doesn't seem like Dustin.

You've got to consider that maybe something went very wrong in that last call. The video call, the Skype. Something you said? Something about the way you looked?

I've got this crazy uncle that keeps calling me, Aaron tells his friends. *I don't know how to get rid of him.* They're sitting around some crappy apartment getting high, and Aaron's phone rings, and one of his friends says, *I'll get rid of the fucker for you.* The friend puts on a deep voice and takes up Aaron's phone.

Maybe Galadriel was right. "Stalker behavior," she said, and sure, why not, let's say that's what it is. You're just obsessed with the past, aren't you, Russell? Just can't leave well enough alone.

So let it go. You've got some kind of life in front of you, right? Lifelong smoker, fifty years old, completely without skills or resources. You could live another ten years! Twenty even! Why not fucking enjoy it, rather than dwelling on the past?

I think this, I feel this in my heart, and then as I'm cutting a stalk of celery I slice the tip of my left pointer finger all the way off.   I feel the knife go through the skin and bone, and I see the fingertip sitting there on the cutting board, a little piece of meat with a fingernail attached to it, and the blood spurts out like my finger is a water gun.   I put my other hand over it and blood trickles out of my fist.

"God damn!" I say.   "I just cut off my finger."

And the guy who is doing prep work at the next station, Alphonso, looks up.

"*¿Qué?*" he says.

So ALPHONSO DRIVES me to the emergency room but they don't reattach my fingertip like I think maybe they will. Nope. My finger meat is now medical waste, being hauled by semi to a landfill in Indiana.

And I—fully bandaged and gauzed and prescribed with painkillers, am sitting at a bus stop and waiting for the chariot that will bear me homeward.

Up until now, I have been pretty judicious about the use of substances. I have a beer now and then, or a shot of bourbon. I'll buy some weed from time to time from the kid who hangs around at the bus stop on the Belmont corner.

But nothing like this sweet painkiller. I'd forgotten what drugs could be like, and riding along in the window seat of a bus I think: *Hell, yeah*. This might be the motherfuckin' answer.

Get home and the thing continues to bleed like a house afire. Soaked all the way through the gauze and so I change the bandages, take just a quick glimmer of what the tip of a chopped-off finger looks like.

Exactly as you would expect it to look.

And so wrap it back up as best you can. You'll never get the mummy wrap as tight as that kind nurse got it, little brunette Hispanic lady. You said something funny and laughed and she liked you. When the doctor told you to get over-the-counter pain medication, she raised one eyebrow, then later slipped you a handful of goodies.

WAKE UP AND it's afternoon.   Sunday, the restaurant is closed—not that you would have gone back anyway.

You pick up your cell phone and look at the time: two-fifteen in the afternoon, as a matter of fact. You just slept for about eighteen hours, and your bandage must have shed at some point, because your bed is covered in blood. One place soaked through to the point that the mattress is wet.   Blood on the cook's shirt you slept in, the pants—you *did* manage to take off your filthy bum's shoes, good job!

Blood in your hair and on your face. The creases of your left palm, stuck together as if you'd let a piece of red candy melt in your hand.

Starving, and in pain. So wash your face off and take a half of one of those pills the nurse gave you, and then head out the door. Pull on your shoes and your ski coat, don't even change your fucking bloody duds.   Just want to get something to eat, because otherwise you're going to have some upsetting times.

Trudge your way to Burrito King, which is the closest possible food, just a couple of blocks; get in there, order the Special of the Day, and sit down at the table with it and promptly fall asleep.

Awakened and ejected by the stern old Mexican owner, and you see that the cute little teenaged waitress, maybe his daughter, is looking at you with her arms crossed over her chest, her face scared and sad, and you look down and see that your finger has bled all over their table.

"Oh, wow," you say, and you sound a little mushmouth. You take some paper napkins from the dispenser on the table and smear through the grue. "Let me clean up this mess for you," you say, groggily smearing blood into a finger painting. "I don't want you all to have to do it."

"Just go," the man says. He gestures, and poor teenaged daughter makes the kind of sad face that babies make right before they begin bawling.

On the street, stand under the sign that says KUPUJEMY ZTOTO, whatever that means, and then you make a hobbling jaywalk across Belmont to the Walgreens. Wherein you plan to purchase more gauze, bleach, a box of assorted chocolates, lunch meat, and a forty-ounce Cobra malt liquor.

You keep your poor left hand in the pocket of your coat, still bleeding, *copiously* as they say, and then you get to the front of the checkout line and put your items on the counter and the librarian-like white-haired white lady gives you a look of horror.

She sees that your hand is in your coat pocket curled in the position of a gun, and she is fully prepared to be robbed. She puts her little old hands up, and in turn you slowly raise your bum hand out of your pocket and show her your wound.

"Somebody bit off my finger," you tell her. "I need to buy this gauze. And these chocolates."

14

So IT APPEARS that I look pretty bad.   I keep my head down and try to find a clear path down the sidewalk back to my place. Left hand in pocket, still bleeding. Right hand with two Walgreens plastic bags swinging back and forth by their handles.

The injured finger throbbing to a fucking disco beat. "You Shook Me All Night Long," by AC/DC. That song sucks.

Get up to my apartment and put the bags down on the table and open the box of gauze with my teeth, because my left hand now feels like it's roasting over an open fire. Very red and swollen, not at all what I'd like to see happening right now.

More than likely means a trip back to the emergency room, an hour on the bus, another four or five in the waiting room.

I look at my phone. Seven o'clock at night? How is that even possible?

And then I see that I have a text message.

From Aaron.

It says:

And then somebody knocks on my door.

15

OPEN THE DOOR and there he stands.

I recognize him right away, though he should by all rights be unrecognizable. Hasn't aged well. Those kids that look like they are fresh-faced and freckled and ever-young? Round about forty, I imagine, it starts to get jowly and puffy in the jaw, the skin kind of plucked chicken–like. He also looks like he hasn't had much sleep.

"Hey," I say, and I let out an awkward laugh, which seems to be a bad choice, because his face hardens even further.   He shudders.

"Is Aaron here?" he says hoarsely.

There's blood up and down my shirt, and I watch as he assesses the scene.   Here's my bags on the little table. My kitchenette, with microwave and mini-refrigerator. My TV on the dresser, my laptop on the nightstand, and a little animated Windows icon is bumping drunkenly back and forth across the screen.   He stares at my bed. Just an ordinary cheap twin bed, but the sheets have big bright red stains of blood on them.

And just like that he draws a gun.

"Okay," I say, and I lift my hands.   "Look," I say. "Fuck. I cut the tip of my finger off at work.   Aaron's not here, man," I say.

He closes the door behind him with the back of his shoe. "You've been in touch with him recently?" Dustin says.

And I'm like, "Fuh! I just got a fucking crazy text from him.   All those little pictures, like comic-book pictures? What are they called? Emojoes?"

He looks puzzled, but the gun is very steady in his hand. Holds it like he knows what he's doing, and the eyes are wide and bright.

Remember would not be the right word for what is happening when he steps forward with that gun.

I take my phone and hold it up to him, so that he can see Aaron's text. "See?" I say. "He just sent this to me a second ago."

"His car was parked on this street two days ago, and now it's been towed.   Where is he now?"

"I don't know," I say. "He has never been here. Ever. I talked to him on Skype on Monday. That's the last time I saw him."

I hold up my sore hand, because, I guess, I'm going to stop the bullet with my palm?

"What did you tell him?" he says. "You told him to call Wave, right?"

"Yeah," I say. "I did."

I glance behind me, but there's nothing in my vision that looks like it could be weaponized to defend against a revolver.

"But he never came here," I say.   "I don't know what he's playing at, but I have been trying to get in touch with him for three or four days, and I literally just got a text from him with an exclamation point and a picture of a gun in it."

Dustin cocks his head. "I don't believe you," he says. "I don't believe you're innocent."

"I'm not innocent," I say. "I'm not innocent, I was never innocent. I never said I was."

Just a second and he comes out of whatever trance he was in.   You see his eyes sharpen, you see—what?—some little shred of the kid he was when you first shared a cot in his bedroom, back when you were fourteen. Back when they thought they would adopt you and make you well. Some shred of the kid who laughed his head off when you let crawdads pinch their claws to your earlobes and you wore them like jewelry. Some shred of the kid you took to the abandoned shed and let suck your nipple.   Some shred of the kid who stood with you at the canal, and you told him about the gibbeners. They were the men that would come for you, that's what your mom always said.

Especially if you couldn't keep secrets.

He looks at me, and he probably sees his own version of that stuff, too. After all this time, you're both on the same page.

"I'm sorry," I say. By which I mean: *I feel bad about abusing you, man.*   By which I mean:

Please put the gun down. Please don't kill me. By which I mean: *I can't even guess why I ever lived.*

What if the last thing you think before you die is not even regret? What if it's just, like, puzzlement? Why would they put you on this earth and then make your life so pointless? Who wished you alive? How dare they? The whole thing just seems accidental and random.   Throw a baby that no one asked for into the world, grin as it fumbles its way into the shitty arenas you made for it.   Watch it fight.   So much less cruel if you'd just taken a brick to it when it was born.

"The reason I was calling you," you say. "I just really want to know what happened," you tell him. "For a while, I thought you might know. But I think you probably don't, right?"

He doesn't reply. Just stares at you, the way a cat stares at the moon. His lips move for a second, but you can't read them. His eyes are wide like they were that night when he came out of the house carrying the gun. Blank or full of wonder, you can't say which, but you feel a keening go down your back.

He is dangerous, of course. Maybe he's always been dangerous, but you only see it now clearly for the first time. "Easy," you whisper soothingly. "Everything's going to be all right."

The gun moves back and forth in his hand. For a second, it seems like I could just reach right out and take it. Just snatch it away from him, and then I could fuckin' beat his ass and put his head in the toilet and then send him home. We'd be more or less even.

My hand twitches, and I make a move to reach toward him.

He flinches back. He still has the instinct of when he was a little kid, when I'd sometimes snatch something out of his hand, just out of pure meanness.

Flinches full body, and pulls the fuckin' trigger.

Oh.

The bullet enters somewhere in my torso and I have time to register the surprised look on Dustin's face. I have time to register the echoing ricocheted bang. So much time to see everything.

And I think: *Wait*

R e   m e   m e   m b   e r

PART TEN

WAKE UP.

Darkness. You think your wrists and ankles might be   you think you might be imprisoned.

You can't see or hear.

You're floating down a river but you can't move.

Last thing you remember: the rap of knuckles against the car window. Great. It's the classic policeman gesture, *tap tap tap, roll down your window, sir, license and registration,* and you already have your cop face on before you even glance up.

But instead it's your dad's friend Aqil.   He peers in at you, frowning, squinting one eye. Makes a twirling motion with his finger that means "roll down your window." And so you obey and he says, "What are you doing here?"

And you're like, blink. Blink. "Um," you say. "What are *you* doing here?"

"Mm," he says. And you get the hostile vibes that you've always gotten, ever since he started hanging around your dad. *Aqil Ozorowski.* He has the kind of face that always seems to be studying your expression, as if he's heard some rumor about you that he won't mention.

"I'll be honest with you, Aaron," he says. "This is a place that your dad and me have been scouting for a long time."

Scouting? What did that mean? "That's weird," you say. "I found this address when I was over at Rabbit's house. Is my dad with you?"

"Yeah," Aqil says. "He's inside."

"Oh," you say. "Isn't that, like, breaking and entering?"

He gives me a salty look. "Technically, maybe," he says. "But it's been abandoned for years, and we're not doing any damage. Just looking around."

"If you say so," you say, and he cocks his head, his smile full of teeth.

"Come on," he says. "Let's go talk to your dad."

Truth is you're not really sure you want to talk to your dad at this point, given the conversation you've just had with his cousin, given that letter you read, given all the things that are starting to emerge. But what can you do? And so you turn off *your mom's car* and follow Aqil across the street toward the house. Watching as he looks left and right as if he's afraid of anyone seeing him. *They're definitely breaking and entering*, you think. *They're going to end up getting arrested.*

"It's cool that you've taken an interest," Aqil says. "Makes your dad really proud."

"Uh-huh," you say, and when the two of you get to the edge of the curb he takes another scope around. It's probably like three in the morning, so you're not sure who would be peeping, but whatever. Then he heads up the sidewalk, moving quickly. The front stoop of the house has been recently shoveled, which makes you kind of wonder how "abandoned" it is, but Aqil moves fast and so you follow suit.

"I think we're making some progress," Aqil says. "We hit a fallow patch after that drowning in Painesville, 'cause we got *so close*, I feel like, and then 2013 was very dry for us; there was just nothing that fit the pattern. But this came up, and we're really back on the hunt again!"

"Cool," you say, but also realize again why you dislike this dude. *This came up.* "This," meaning Rabbit's death. As if he's completely oblivious to the fact that Rabbit was your best friend, that Rabbit was a person who died. *On the hunt again.* What a douche.

He opens the screen door for you like you're a lady, and you're like, okay, fine, and you go in first. He follows close, shuts the front door behind him. "Dustin?" he calls. "Aaron's here!"

But your dad is nowhere to be seen. You're in the living room of one of those little box suburban houses, and it looks like the kind of place where somebody's Polish grandma spent her last years. There is a horrible sofa facing the front door, looks like it's covered with the kind of material that Velcro sticks to, and there is a poster-sized family photo from the early nineties hanging on the wall, with a carved wood frame. There is a glass-topped coffee table with an ornate doily and some china knickknacks. Sort of the opposite of the kind of place that a BDSM dude would lure you to and tie you up.

"Whose house is this?" you say, and you take the note out of your pocket and show it to him.

"Look," you say. "This is the right address, isn't it? Rabbit was texting this guy named Gergely. Kind of an . . ." you say, and even as you speak you realize you are falling into cop lingo from TV. "An unsavory character," you say, and Aqil raises an eyebrow. He smiles.

"You've got Rabbit's cell phone?" he says. "That's good news."

"Yeah," you say, and you glance around again. The place doesn't look abandoned. There are vacuum-cleaner lines on the carpet. There isn't any dust.

"Hey, Dustin?" Aqil calls again, and gestures you toward a hallway. "Dustin!" he says, more loudly, and gives you a conspiratorial shrug. *That wacky Dusty! So spacey!*

"What are you guys doing here?" you say, and you feel a glimmer of puzzlement. Is this Gergely's house?

Have you been somehow following a thread that is connected to the thread they have been following? Is it possible that Gergely is the serial killer they've been looking for? You step hesitantly down the hallway. You figure that the door at the end probably leads to a basement? "Whose house is this?" you repeat.

Aqil raises his eyebrow again. "Well," he says. "We have a new theory."

And as you pass the first bedroom you can see out of the corner of your eye that there is a setup in there, a staging area for filming. A tarp has been draped over the window, and there are photographer's lights pointing toward it.

"Your dad's idea is that this may be an 'event cluster.' That's his term. Some of the deaths may be accidental drownings. Some of them may be opportunistic murders. But then—as they begin to accumulate they begin to attract people who *want* them to be a pattern. And once people begin to believe in something, it starts to become more true."

"Um," you say. There is some equipment hanging from the ceiling of the bedroom, a structure made of pole and wire that looks like a giant version of the controller for a marionette. The poles are limp and tilted, but you can see that they have cuffs hanging from them. Is that blood on the floor underneath?

"That's what happened with the whole Satanism thing in the 1980s," Aqil is saying. "That's what happened with the school shootings, too, I think. Once an interesting concept comes into the world, some folks will want to take a ride on it, right? It attracts a certain kind of—"

He shrugs. "A certain kind of energy, right?" he says, and I feel him coming up closer behind me, almost touching.

"It's kind of like your dad, you know?" he says. "He's like a little bratwurst walking through the dog pound. He attracts a certain kind of interest."

"Um," you say. You're aware that even though he's talking he's not actually talking. He's just murmuring words. Like he's trying to hypnotize you.

And then the sound of a gun being unholstered, a kind of metallic rattling that you recognize from movies, one of those Foley sound effects that you hear over and over in every cop show and thriller.

And you start to turn around and Aqil has taken out a pistol.

"Dad?" you call. Your voice high and hoarse, like an old chicken in a cartoon calling out for water. "Dad?" you say.

"He's just up ahead," Aqil says, and the two of you look at each other. "Hey, Dustin," he says. He puts the barrel of his gun against the hollow of your lower back. "Aaron's here."

Let's go over this scene again.

Let's say it's you, and your dad's crazy friend is holding a gun. Let's say you've been taking some serious drugs all night, and your reflexes are shit. What do you do?

Do you start crying or begging? Even while your entire body is unsolidifying and you can feel the liquidation running down your spine and spreading its branches through your nerves? Do you try to negotiate? Even though you don't actually have anything to trade?

"Hey, man," you say. Surprisingly reasonable. "Come on. We don't have to do this."

But he doesn't respond. The barrel of the gun presses where your spine meets your coccyx. "Put your hands behind your back for me," he says. "Wrists together."

Maybe there's someone who would have found a way to break off and make a run for it. Or maybe there's the person who would start talking fast and dazzle him with some sort of clever bit of dialogue. Maybe there's someone who knows some sort of magician's way of getting out of cuffs, and they just wait for the chance.

You don't have any of those skills, though your mind considers them anyway, runs you through the heroic scenarios. You wish you hadn't dropped out of tae kwon do in first grade.

And that's exactly what you hear your brain saying. *It's all right, it's all right*, you tell yourself, even as Aqil nudges you down the stairs. He won't kill you, you think. He's your dad's friend. There's a solution here.

"You will walk safely in your way, and your foot will not stumble," he says. "When you lie down, you will not be afraid; yes, you will lie down and your sleep will be sweet."

"What?" you say.

"It's a mantra your dad taught me," he says. Then he calls down the empty hallway. "Hey, Dustin! Aaron's here."

In the bedroom is a kind of oblong spaceship thing, and the first thing that you think is that it's a car. Or a time-travel device, possibly? You remember Uncle Rusty talking about his dream of flying cars in the future.

"Um," you hear yourself say.   "Just don't kill me, okay?"

"Okay," he says, and he steers me toward the Thing, which seems to be a kind of egg-shaped bed with an open lid, and blue light was coming from it.

"What is that?" you say, and Aqil presses the gun against your back.

"It's called a sensory-attenuation tank," he says. "Get in it."

Darkness.

Wake up.

The last thing you remember: the rap
of knuckles against glass.

Then darkness again. Fuck!

You know you're floating in the tank. Hands and feet tied.

Thrash.   Thrash thrash thrash.   Not really very
useful. Must be earplugs in your ears, because you can't even hear
the water sloshing. The water is the same temperature as your body
and the air, so it's hard to tell where one ends and the other begins.
Some kind of tube in your arm, you think, keeping you fed and hy-
drated, but your mouth is so dry. You call out: "Help! Help!" and it
echoes distantly like a voice in a jug.
    You think about being rescued.   The cops break in and open
up the lid, and behind them is—who? The last person you talked to
was Wave, and she's not going to do shit.
    Who will rescue you? Uncle Rusty? Aunt Kate? Dennis? The
ghost of your mom, the ghost of Terri?
    What about your dad? You know that's not going to happen. He's
probably sitting up in his study right now with Aqil, smoking cigarettes and sipping on whiskey, talking away about the "serial killer"
they're chasing, and Aqil so happy he's about to bust in his pants.

What did he say about your dad? *A little bratwurst walking through the dog pound.* He had Dustin picked out a long time ago.

You lie there, breathing. Darkness. You know you're in a tank, but it feels like it might go on for miles in every direction.

Your dad's never going to figure it out, of course. You run through it again and again, and even with what you actually know, it still doesn't quite come together. How many people has Aqil killed, you wonder? Is he Jack Daniels?

Probably not. Those killings started in the nineties, when Aqil was only a kid.   More likely he's just riding on them, just like he said, like a roller coaster at a theme park. He's done a few, you think—Rabbit, for sure, maybe the kid who died in Painesville, maybe the one before that at Kent State. It was something he got interested in at a certain point, and he just must have decided that it would be fun to pursue. He's just another parasite. *Some folks will want to take a ride on it, right? It attracts a certain kind of—*

Aqil. That's not his real name, you think.

He probably has lots of avatars, and you figure that one of them was Gergely. Maybe he has been playing a whole bunch of games at once. Running scams on people like your dad, people who attract a certain kind of interest.

You wonder what he's going to do to you. Drown you somehow, you guess? Will he hold you down under the water so he can watch your face as you gulp and gasp? Maybe just fill up the tank you're floating in? He gets off on it, so he'll make it last.

You think about the joy of seeing someone else suffering. It's sort of like the opposite of grieving.

Wake up. Darkness. You think your wrists and ankles might be   you think you might be imprisoned. You can't see or hear.

You're floating down a river but you can't move. Faceup? Face-down?

Thrash.   Thrash.

The things that they say about withdrawal from heroin are true. Legs so restless. Bad abdominal cramps. Eyes keep on watering. Terror. Hallucinations.

Not sure whether that's part of withdrawal or part of the fact that you're confined to a sensory-deprivation tank by a serial killer. You try screaming again, and your throat hurts like hell.

And then dream on.   Float on down the river.   Impossible to tell how much time has passed. Impossible to tell if you're awake or not.

Somewhere above you, you can hear Amy and his girlfriend talking in low voices. You have the idea that somehow the tank you are in has been moved to House of Wills. You are in that room where you last saw them—the red-haired girl in her silver halter top, smoking and stirring a pot by the fireplace.

"You open that door, and you made a decision," Amy is saying. "That's what I told him."

"He got a lot more chances than most of them did," the girl says.

You imagine that Amy nods thoughtfully. "Should we let him out?" Amy says, and you call out from the floating dark, *Yes! Let me out!* You can imagine the black sky above you opening like a lid, and the two of them will peer down from the heavens, the light behind their heads, light pouring onto your face. *Help! Let me out!* you call.

But the girl says: "Not yet. It's not time."

And then their voices aren't there anymore. *Amy?* you call. *Xzavious?*

Still dreaming? Still not dreaming? *You don't know, you don't know, you don't know,* you seem to be moving and not moving at the same time, and when you try to lift your bound ankles you don't know whether you did or not. Water and air and your skin, all the same temperature, so that you can't tell if you still have a body or not.

And you think, *They did warn me after all. Three times they warned me.*

"Scoot over, Sweetroll," you hear Rabbit say. "It's so fuckin' cramped in here."

But for some reason you don't feel that scared anymore. You think of this girl that you met once at a party, the two of you sitting in a corner passing a joint back and forth, she was telling you about astral traveling. She was teaching herself how to do it, she said. She'd done it, like, once.

"It's the point-of-view switch," she says. "That's how you know. One minute you're in, like, the first person, looking out through your own eyes, and suddenly then you're seeing yourself in third person, you know? You're above your body, looking down at it while it's sleeping."

"And are you, like, transparent?" you ask her, and you like her hair a lot. Long, brown, with magenta streaks in it, but not like she's trying to make a big statement. "Do you have clothes on?" you say.

"You don't have a body at all!" she says. "You're just like a *presence* that can move around without it. But you still have all your senses— maybe *more* than all of them!"

"Like," you say, "what? You mean telepathy, or, like, you can see through walls? Or . . ."

"You can see through *everything*," she says. "There's no such thing as solid. But it's hard to explain. It would be like trying to tell a deaf person about music."

You get it now. Let's say you're doing it. Astral traveling.   Moving and not moving at the same time. It's like that.

You can float up out of this tank, down the hallway, back out the door into the snowy street; *your mom's car* isn't there anymore. Lift up a little higher and you can see the whole of Lyndhurst from above, just like Google Maps. Like that old screen saver your dad still has on his computer, you're moving backward through outer space, and the stars pull away from you in an endless stream, an eternal tunnel, stars upon stars upon stars.

You can fly like that. Through a tunnel, you move across Rabbit's house, your own house, the graveyard where Rabbit is buried under the undignified name of Bruce. You ride for the first time in a plane with your mom, you get to sit in the window seat, and your mom smiles and says, "Can you see the ground?" And you gape down! "Only clouds," you say. "Only the tops of clouds!"

You can picture Rabbit in this same chamber, the same coffin, passing in and out of dreams just like you, hoping, like you, that someone was going to open that lid and let you out. Did he hope that you were going to find him? Did he, maybe, forgive you in the end? Probably not.

You can picture your brother fucking that skinny, prissy-looking girl you'd seen on his Facebook page, the two of them in his little single bed in his dorm room, and Dennis frowns, flinching as you glide past. You can see the ashes of your mom, still in a clear plastic bag in a cardboard box in your dad's study. He won't ever scatter them like she asked him to. He won't ever let her go like she wanted.

You wonder if Aqil is going to kill your dad. Maybe he has already? But for some reason you don't think so. With your dad it's something else Aqil wants, maybe something even worse. He wants to drag him down to the bottom and then look in his eyes. *A certain kind of energy*, that's what Aqil wants, but you don't know if it's just random, or if somehow Dustin invited it.

And then you wake up and your dad is sitting on the edge of your bed with his hand on your back, rubbing in slow circles like he did when you were little. "Are you asleep?" he whispers. And you whisper back: "No."

But you are. You're pretty sure you're not awake, even though when you open your eyes it's only darkness. The sound of your heart, the sound of your breath. Can't really tell where your skin ends and the water begins, and when you try to squirm you feel like you're turning end over end in outer space, weightless.

Maybe someone will realize, you think, maybe someone will put it together

       maybe

and

"Do you know the funniest thing about dying?" Terri says.   "It's that you have to live through it."

   You can feel her pressing against your back, she says, "Kiss me." She says, "Even if you just have five minutes left, you're still moving into the future, you're still thinking about what you're going to do next, making plans, there's a part of you that's still saying, *everything's going to work out somehow* . . ."

That tattoo on Rusty's neck. REMEMEMBER

Aware of   as particles that are beginning to dissipate

    Are you awake? Are you dreaming?

      Wait—? Are you still alive?

PART ELEVEN

April 2014

In the end it is the mystery that lasts and not the explanation.

—SACHEVERELL SITWELL, *For Want of the Golden City*

"I THINK I have it figured out," Dennis says, but then he looks over and Laura is asleep.

They are driving down the interstate in a rental car, heading from Denver to St. Bonaventure, Nebraska—a little town not far from the Colorado border, according to his phone. The phone speaks to him from the cup holder where he's placed it.   "Continue on. I-76. East. For. One hundred and. Sixty-three! Miles," the automated female voice of his phone proclaims, and he peers out at the un-winding interstate. The yellow sod-grass fields pocked with melting snow. He thought Colorado had mountains? But he can't see any.

His girlfriend, Laura, has her earbuds on, and her eyes are closed, and Dennis can hear the metallic beats of the EDM music she likes emitting ghostly from the shell of her ear. The screen of his phone flickers briefly, as if it were about to say something but then changed its mind.

He is on his way to identify his father's body, and he is trying not to think about it. The body is in a morgue in St. Bonaventure, Nebraska—the corpse found five days ago, floating in an irrigation ditch on the edge of an alfalfa field, and it had been there for a con-siderable amount of time, the coroner said.

Dennis made the mistake of doing an Internet search for *drowned corpse*, so he has a pretty good idea of what his father might look like. The skin is usually taut like a balloon, the body swollen. Often the mouth is a round *O* shape, like the mouth of a blow-up sex doll.   The lips will be thickened, as if with collagen injections; the tongue will be extended, the color of pâté.

But he doesn't think about this. He puts his hands on the steering wheel at ten and two and stares out at the road. Thinks about smok-ing a joint. But it's probably too cold to crack the window open; he doesn't want to disturb Laura's sleep.

It's April—nominally spring. Though this is the kind of landscape that doesn't seem to know what spring is.

His dad has been missing for about ten weeks, and it's been even longer since Dennis actually *saw* him. Not since right after Christmas, not since Dennis had made his excuses and headed back to college early. Just feeling kind of uncomfortable and skeezed out by all the dynamics at home.

Back in Ithaca, he thought he could imagine his way back into the role of normal college student. Sitting in his dorm room and watching bad movies on his laptop, smoking a lot of weed. Spending a lot of time with Laura, and everything else kind of fell away for a while. Laura said he had a certain kind of energy, a certain kind of aura that interested her, and no girl had ever thought he was *interesting* before. He felt like maybe his life would work out after all. Just like Bob Marley said: *Everything little thing gonna be all right!*

That was when the shit suddenly began to pour down on him. Aaron missing. Then his father missing. Police coming to talk to him in his dorm room. Aunt Kate calling, crying, not making any sense.

They said that his father had killed a man in Chicago. He and Laura had sat and watched the news report of it—Russell Tillman, recently acquitted and released after spending thirty years behind bars, killed by his adopted brother. "A bizarre case on the west side," the news anchor said, and then there were video clips. People heard shots fired; they came out into the hallway as Dennis's dad fled from the apartment, carrying a gun. People took photos of him with their cell phones as he ran out; there was video of him—clearly it was him, though Dennis could hardly believe it.

He and Laura sat side by side on the narrow dorm-room bed, the laptop on their thighs, and watched the videos over and over, like it was the Zapruder film.

Here: Dennis's father is outside the building; he comes to the curb.

He stops and stands still. His body language suggests astonishment. His mouth opens. He looks to the left and right, urgently. Seems frozen with confusion, his eyes panicked.

"See?" Dennis said. "He thought a car was going to be waiting for him! There was someone else with him."

"That seems like a stretch," Laura said. "He just looks scared."

And so they rewound and watched again. He comes out and does a double take. His mouth hangs open in surprise. He looks left and right.

Behind him, a small group of apartment residents has gathered. Some of them are taking videos with their phones. "You better run, motherfucker," someone off-camera says. "I just called the police." And there's a kind of resigned, melancholy quality to the off-camera voice. "What are you standing there for?" the voice says, and Dennis's father begins to stumble uncertainly down the block. A bus pulls up at the corner, and we watch as he gets on it, dropping the gun on the sidewalk like he's discarding a gum wrapper. The bus doors fold closed, and someone in the crowd that's watching cries, "He's getting away!" but no one pursues him.

So how did Dustin get from Chicago to an irrigation ditch in Nebraska? No one knew. The last time we saw him, he was getting on a city bus. Surely if he'd changed buses at the station, he'd have been caught, right?

"Oh yeah," Laura said. "*Surely.* Because when an ex-convict bum gets killed at a flophouse, the cops pull out all the stops to find the killer. A massive manhunt ensues."

"Well," Dennis said. Nonplussed. Laura ran her soft fingertips over his arm.

"Does it matter how he got there?" she said. "We'll probably never know. But that's not the most important thing."

And in fact there was so much that wasn't known.   Dennis himself hadn't known that his father had a brother—or an adopted brother, at least.

He had to find it on the Internet—the massacre of his father's parents and aunt and uncle, the asinine trial, the eventual acquittal. He sat with Laura and read through the old news articles and blog posts and everything, and then she shook her head.

"Oh shit," she said. "Your *dad* was the one who actually killed his parents! Don't you think?"

"What?" Dennis said.

"He didn't want Rusty to tell the truth! That's why he murdered him."

"Well," Dennis said.

He looks over at her now. They are on the interstate, moving down along a blue line that his phone is following, and the halogen lights hang over the interstate and illuminate the glow strip between the lanes, and geometric planes of light move across her face.

"I'm starting to feel like I might figure it out," he says.

It would be nice to know what his mom knew, Dennis thought. She used to joke about the way his dad would space out, trying to normalize it. *Astral traveling*, she called it, as if it were some kind of superpower, but in the end she didn't think it was so cute. Just before Dennis left for college, a few months before she died, she'd clutched his hand in the kitchen. Out of nowhere she grabbed his wrist while he was eating cereal. "Someone needs to keep an eye on your father," she said.

And in retrospect he had to ask: *What was she trying to tell me?*

In retrospect, now that he thought about it, there were signs. He thinks back to Christmas Day, the way his dad kept going on and on about those drowned boys. Dennis was in the kitchen with him that morning, watching as he washed the turkey in the sink, feeling more and more uncomfortable as he rubbed the wet naked skin with salt

452

and rosemary. "I'm thinking of writing a book," he said, and gave Dennis a bright, feverish look. *Something really* wrong *with him*, Dennis had thought. Maybe on the verge of a breakdown? Maybe already in the midst of one?

He thinks of the text that he got from Aaron.

> I guess u know Rabbit is dead. I don't know why u havnt called me maybe ur mad? But weird stuff is happening at home and I rly need 2 talk 2 u.

He thinks of the phone conversation he had with the young FBI agent.   His father a "person of interest" in the disappearance of Aaron, in the disappearance of his friend Aqil. Possibly a number of others. "It's beginning to seem like there might be quite a few," the FBI girl said. "Deaths," she said. "Which your father might be . . . associated with."

Despite everything he knows, he doesn't think his father would kill Aaron. And he can't imagine his father overpowering Aqil Ozorowski—who looked more like an Italian mobster than a Polish cop.

"What do you think of this?" Dennis said to Laura. "What if Aqil went to Chicago with my dad? What if Aqil somehow convinced—or even coerced—him? And that it resulted in my dad killing his brother, like . . . accidentally?"

Laura shook her head. He watched as she pushed her fingers through her bright, curly red hair. "Dennis . . ." she said. "That doesn't really—"

"I don't believe my dad killed Aaron. I don't think he killed Aqil, either."

"You think that they're still alive?" she said. "That they both went into hiding or something? That they both just coincidentally disappeared at the same time?"

"No, of course not," Dennis said. "No. That's . . ." He felt something shift in his brain, like a Rubik's Cube you almost could solve. In the video, his dad was looking for someone, wasn't he? There was a car he was expecting to be waiting for him; he looked for it, scoping wildly: Aqil? Aaron? Someone else?

"Maybe your father wasn't the person you thought he was," Laura said. She shrugged, and then began to knead his shoulder. "That's what sociopaths are like."

A sociopath, Dennis thinks.

He thinks of the way his father would stop talking in the middle of a sentence, hesitating mid-word, as if someone invisible had interrupted him.

Every memory he thinks of now is discolored and ugly. The past suddenly has vanished from underneath him, distorted, memories turned into something he doesn't recognize, something malevolent.

Twenty-nine miles now outside of Fort Morgan, Colorado, and cars keep passing him huffily. He's going too slow, the speed limit is 75, and so he presses on the gas pedal. Up ahead, there is a single bare tree off to the left. It's the only one for as far as he can see. Just the one tree and then flat bare sod. No houses. Just the two lanes of I-76 reaching to the horizon in either direction.

He glances over at Laura: still asleep. *You may have to just accept the fact that you grew up as the child of a sociopath*, that's what she'd told him on the plane, and he thinks of this again as a semitruck abruptly storms past him on the left, a wall of hostile force streaming past their car so close he can feel the shudder of it, and it startles him so badly that he lets out a grunt as if he's been slapped.

He remembers one night during Christmas break, waking up and seeing his dad standing in the doorway of his bedroom. A silhouette watching him as he slept. It had seemed kind of wistful and sweet at the time, his dad an empty-nester remembering his son as a child.

But now it comes back to him again and he can't shake that sensation of being watched by someone you don't know. The feeling that a hidden presence is nearby while your eyes are closed, observing, leaning closer, emanating ill will.

The semi is already moving away from them into the distance. *Must be going fucking 90 miles an hour*, he thinks. *It could have killed us*, he thinks. Laura is still asleep.

There was this one night he remembers. Just before his mom got sick, and he was studying in the kitchen when his dad came in and started rummaging through the silverware drawer. "The Tao that we speak of isn't the true Tao," he was mumbling under his breath. "The name that can be named isn't the real name."

"What?" Dennis had said. He lifted his head from his AP U.S. History study guide and watched as his dad began to eat a peanut butter sandwich. Dustin said it was a poem by the Chinese poet Lao-Tzu, he'd read it somewhere online, and he was thinking that it would be a cool mantra to read to his patients. Dustin took a bite of his sandwich and chewed thoughtfully. It was about ten o'clock at night, and they'd found themselves together by accident. Aaron was upstairs in the bedroom, playing something on Xbox, and their mother was asleep or reading, but for some reason Dustin was prowling around in a philosophical frame of mind.

"I just love it so much," he said. "It's so beautiful! *The Non-Existent and Existent are identical in all but name. This identity of apparent opposites I call the profound, the great deep, the open door of bewilderment.* Don't you think that's gorgeous?"

Dennis could feel him gazing earnestly. Ardently. Dennis didn't want to get into it. All Dennis really wanted to do was finish memorizing dates so he could go to bed. He was hoping that Aaron would have a little weed to share.

"Look," Dennis said.   His father was a little white man in a sports coat and jeans, with a goatee, but Dennis didn't want to hurt his feelings. "Dad," he said. "There's some cultural-appropriation stuff that I think you'd need to frame more carefully. I mean, you're not a Taoist. You're not Chinese. So . . ."

"Well," he said.

And okay, yeah, his feelings were hurt. Things went silent.

"Can I make you anything?" he said at last. "Can I make you a sandwich?"

"Yeah, sure," Dennis said.

And then his dad wiggled his fingers like a magician. "Poof!" he said. "You're a sandwich!"

And Dennis had given him a laugh. It was only fair. He was putting in a good effort.

Now he can't help but think of that moment. He thought of it when the police called to talk to him; he thought of it when he saw the news report and the stuff on YouTube. The idea that somehow his dad had made his way back to Nebraska, that he had gone there to kill himself.

The Tao that we speak of isn't the true Tao. Had his father been trying to give him a message?

The Dustin that we speak of is not the true Dustin. The memory that we speak of is not the true memory.

Who knew what he was really thinking as they sat there together in the kitchen that night?

And now, Dennis thought, *I'll never know.*

Laura wakes up when they pull into a travel plaza, stares for a moment at him sleepily as if she doesn't recognize him. "Where are we?" she says, and he shrugs.

"Still in Colorado," he says. "Just stopping for gas." They're pulled up beside a pump but he doesn't open the door. He just sits there with his hands on the steering wheel, as if he's still driving.

"What's wrong?" she says, and he feels himself shudder. Two men are standing against the side of the "travel store," smoking cigarettes, and they seem to be observing Dennis's rental car with interest. One leans over and whispers to the other, smirking.

"I don't know," Dennis says at last. "I don't want to do this, I guess."

"Oh, honey, I know," she says, and puts her hand on his leg. "It'll be over soon," she says. "One last thing, and then you can start to put it behind you. You can get on with your life." She leans over and kisses his ear, he can hear the sound of her lips, and he shudders as she gets out of the car and walks across the lot toward the restrooms.

It'll be over soon, he thinks. Does she believe that?

The last time he'd heard from Aaron was a text. He woke up one morning and found it on his phone. A string of emojis, appearing without context:

It was weird, because this came a few days after his father told him that Aaron was missing, and he typed back:

Fuck you, Aaron! Where R U ?!?

But there was no answer. At the time, Dennis thought it was some kind of joke from Aaron, a confirmation that Aaron wasn't missing at all. Aaron was fine, and his dad was just crazy and hysterical, and Aaron would turn up eventually when he needed money. It was all going to eventually be fine.

But now it appears that it will be the last thing Aaron ever said to him. Is that possible? He gets out his phone from time to time and looks at it again. He texts hopefully:

Aaron? Are you there?

And then he looks at the set of emojis again. Is it a secret message? Some sort of code? Did Aaron send it at all?

The name that can be named is not the real name.

Here on the edge of Nebraska he tries again. He sends another text to Aaron's phone, and the phone makes its wistful bloop as the text floats away into the digisphere.

Aaron?

In the distance, giant wind turbines are churning with stately, solemn unfriendliness, and a plastic bag lifts up above the asphalt and spins delicately in the air, tossed by a gust of wind. He glances over and the smoking men are gone, though there is still a tang of something watching.

He puts his phone in his pocket and slowly opens the door of the car. About a hundred miles to go. About a hundred miles from where his father is waiting to be identified.

ACKNOWLEDGMENTS

I'M GRATEFUL TO the many friends and family members who read the book in progress and gave me great advice—John Martin, Imad Rahman, Dan Riordan, Lynda Montgomery, Alissa Nutting, Tom Barbash, Scrounge Rocheleau, my sons Phil and Paul, my sister Sheri, and particularly my friend Lynda Barry, for the conversations we've had over the past few years while I was working on this novel, and for her inspiring books. Thanks, too, to my brother-in-law, Luke Lieffring, for telling me the story that became the core of this novel.

As always, I owe a debt to the members of the Penguin Random House staff for their faith and generosity—Rachel Kind, Jennifer Garza, Bridget Piekarz, John Hastie, Michael Kindness, Liz Sullivan, Nancy Delia, Simon Sullivan, Julia Maguire, Priyanka Krishnan, Grant Neumann, Daniel Christensen, Emily Hartley, and many others! Thanks, too, to Libby McGuire (my former publisher) and Jennifer Hershey (my current publisher) for sticking with me—and to Gina Centrello for her long-standing support.

And finally thanks to my editor, Susanna Porter, who has been remarkably patient with my wild ideas and whose wise advice was instrumental in showing me the path through multiple revisions.

ABOUT THE AUTHOR

DAN CHAON is the acclaimed author of *Stay Awake*, *Await Your Reply*, *You Remind Me of Me*, *Fitting Ends*, and *Among the Missing*, which was a finalist for the National Book Award. Chaon's short stories have appeared in many journals and anthologies, including *The Best American Short Stories*, *Pushcart Prize*, and *The O. Henry Prize Stories*. He was the recipient of the 2006 Academy Award in Literature from the American Academy of Arts and Letters. Chaon teaches creative writing at Oberlin College.

danchaon.com
@Danchaon
Find Dan Chaon on Facebook

ABOUT THE TYPE

The text of this book was set in Janson, a typeface designed about 1690 by Nicholas Kis (1650–1702), a Hungarian living in Amsterdam, and for many years mistakenly attributed to the Dutch printer Anton Janson. In 1919, the matrices became the property of the Stempel Foundry in Frankfurt. It is an old-style book face of excellent clarity and sharpness. Janson serifs are concave and splayed; the contrast between thick and thin strokes is marked.